He has it all – except her*!*

In Bed With Her Tall, Sexy, Handsome Boss

Three exciting romances from three
fabulous Mills & Boon authors!

In Bed With Her Tall, Sexy, Handsome Boss

NATALIE ANDERSON
ANNE McALLISTER
ANNA CLEARY

All the characters in this book have no existence outside the imagination of
the author, and have no relation whatsoever to anyone bearing the same name
or names. They are not even distantly inspired by any individual known or
unknown to the author, and all the incidents are pure invention.

First published in Great Britain 2011
Harlequin Mills & Boon Limited,
Eton House, 18-24 Paradise Road, Richmond, Surrey TW9 1SR

IN BED WITH HER TALL, SEXY, HANDSOME BOSS
© by Harlequin Enterprises II B.V./S.à.r.l 2011

All Night with the Boss, The Boss's Wife for a Week and *My Tall Dark
Greek Boss* were first published in Great Britain by Harlequin Mills & Boon
Limited in separate, single volumes.

All Night with the Boss © Natalie Anderson 2007
The Boss's Wife for a Week © Barbara Schenck 2007
My Tall Dark Greek Boss © Anna Cleary 2007

ISBN: 978 0 263 88433 3

05-0311

Printed and bound in Spain
by Litografia Rosés S.A., Barcelona

ALL NIGHT WITH
THE BOSS

BY
NATALIE ANDERSON

Possibly the only librarian who got told off herself for talking too much, **Natalie Anderson** decided writing books might be more fun than shelving them—and boy, is it that! Especially writing romance—it's the realisation of a lifetime dream kick-started by many an afternoon spent devouring Grandma's Mills & Boon® novels...

She lives in New Zealand with her husband and four gorgeous-but-exhausting children. Swing by her website anytime—she'd love to hear from you: www.natalie-anderson.com

Look out for a thrilling new book from Natalie,
***The End of Faking It*, coming from**
Mills & Boon® Riva™ in April 2011

For Dave: you said nothing is impossible and,
because I'm lucky enough to have your support,
you're right.

CHAPTER ONE

LISSA had just reached the railing when she heard the footsteps behind her. Quickly turning, she sat on the bench in the shadows, hoping she couldn't be seen, just wanting five minutes' cool-down time.

She watched the approaching figure knowing full well she wasn't invisible and that he was heading right towards her. She didn't recognise him. She'd been at Franklin and Co. for five months now and knew everyone. Long legs wrapped in navy denim casually strode out with a grace that signalled a natural athlete. He was tall with dark hair. With the only light on the balcony being the thin streams escaping from the boardroom windows she couldn't see much more. She sighed, her heart sinking. Gina must have sent her friend Karl out to sit with her. Why was it that people thought set-ups were a good idea?

Unable to take her eyes off him she decided to ignore the tightening in her stomach and her promise to Gina to be 'open to possibilities'. Instead she would just get it over with. Tell it to him plain and then she could have some space again.

'Did Gina tell you I was out here?' She used her most decisive, not-to-be-messed with tone.

'No.' She caught a flash of white teeth as he smiled in the darkness. He sat down next to her with a companionable nod, setting his glass beside him. He'd positioned himself across from her, at right angles. His face was in shadow and he was close, too close. His presence radiated out, his legs near hers and she caught a faint citrus scent. Lemon, fresh and cool.

'Look, I'm sorry,' she began, trying for kind yet firm. 'I don't know what Gina told you, but I'm really not interested.'

'Oh.' He paused. 'Really?' He sounded quite surprised.

She took a deep breath and ploughed on, the words tumbling over each other in their rush to get out. 'It may seem hard to believe, what with everyone else so keen to get it on, but I'm really not looking for a bit of fun. I'm sure you are a great guy and all and you'll have no trouble finding someone else. Especially in there.' She emphasised by waving wildly at the window. 'After all, Gina says you're an amazing flirt.'

His sharp burst of laughter surprised her. Even more surprising was the way it resonated within her. It was deep, warm and dry.

'Does she? How nice of her.' He took a careful sip from his glass. 'But you know I don't think I want anybody else. Especially not "in there",' he mimicked her tone.

Her fingers tightened around the cool glass. She still felt hot and bothered and this interruption wasn't helping.

'Please yourself,' she said in resignation. 'But let's get one thing clear. It's not going to happen so we'll just chill, right?' She winced a little at her crabbiness, not intending to have spoken quite so baldly. She snatched a deep breath, trying to overcome it, but breathing properly seemed more tricky than usual when seated next to this guy.

'Suits me.' He was agreeable. 'Are you always this blunt?'

She frowned, her cheeks heating. 'Mmm. I'm sorry if you thought I was rude. I don't mean to be, but I don't want to have any misunderstandings.'

'OK.' He laughed, a shade too heartily for her liking.

She glanced at him, thinking he was pretty relaxed about being rejected from the outset. She could see a broad smile, an inviting smile. The kind of smile that made you want to smile right back and move closer to its warmth. She looked back to the windows and watched with cynical amusement as two consultants vied for Gina's attention. Lissa flicked a quick look sideways at Karl again, wishing Gina had warned her he was the most physically attractive man on the planet and not just a super flirt.

'Now that we have that settled,' he said easily, 'why not tell me something about yourself?'

'What do you want to know?' Lissa asked. She'd just shot the guy down before he'd had a chance to start his engine, she didn't need to be totally rude.

'I don't know.' He stretched out a leg. It crossed in front of hers, a barrier between her and the door. 'How about where in Australia you come from?'

'The South Island of New Zealand,' she replied coolly, trying not to admire the long leg before her.

'Sorry,' he chuckled. Again the sound reverberated within her, tingling her insides. 'Will you ever forgive me?'

She shrugged off the mistake and the sensations. 'It's OK. I'm not one of those Kiwis who has a fit at being mistaken for an Aussie.' She took a sip of her drink. Despite the chilly air she was no closer to cooling down. She sat for a minute and then leaned towards him with a conspiratorial smile. 'To tell you the truth, I still can't tell the difference between Irish and Scottish accents.'

'How shocking.' He leaned in towards her and for a moment she wondered what he was going to do. What she was going to do. His proximity knocked her breathing. 'Which am I?'

'Um…' She was taken aback. He didn't sound much like either. He sounded pretty BBC to her. 'Scottish?'

He inclined his head and sat back. 'Indeed.'

She was feeling a little unnerved by the effect he was having on her. Unnerved by the fact she was sorry he'd just sat back. It was a dark, cool night and she felt warm and wobbly.

Gina popped into view again and Lissa watched as her face lit up as an unfamiliar man walked towards her.

'Oh, that must be the infamous Rory.'

Karl turned his head sharply and looked back through the window. 'Where?'

'With Gina.' Rory stood absorbed by Gina as she talked, her arms gesticulating wildly with her effervescent enthusiasm.

'Well,' said Lissa practically, 'I don't think she's going to have too much trouble, do you?'

'Trouble with what?' Karl looked back at Lissa.

'Rory,' she replied impatiently. 'She must have told you about him. He's just landed after a stint at the New York office. Come back as the youngest consultant ever to be promoted to partner. He's due to start tomorrow but there was a chance he might look in tonight. She's wearing the blue top specially.' She watched the couple for a while longer.

'I can't believe she thought she didn't stand a chance. I thought she hardly knew him. But he's obviously interested, don't you think? And so he should—she's amazing.'

'If you like that sort,' came the noncommittal response.

Lissa turned to him startled. 'She's a petite, natural blonde with amazing blue eyes and is totally vivacious.' She paused before adding with perverse pleasure, 'The only sort that doesn't like that doesn't like girls.'

'Ha!' he laughed softly. 'You think? I think many men might prefer tall, willowy types with big brown eyes and hair like golden honey.' Before she could stop him he reached out and touched a strand of her hair.

She stared, unable to move. Felt him gather a lock and tug gently. Crazily she wanted him to run his hand the length of it. What he'd said finally registered and she bit back a smile. She tried to ignore the tantalising quality in his voice. He'd just, very flatteringly, described her.

'Willowy?' she asked, amused.

'Uh-huh. Very graceful.' His fingers twirled the strands of hair.

She took a deep breath. She was feeling no more comfortable. The whole purpose of her stroll onto the balcony was being sabotaged. He sure knew how to trot out a line. She pulled her hair free and decided to reiterate the position. 'I told you. You needn't bother.'

'It's no bother.'

He was watching her intently. She crossed her legs away from him and wiggled her foot. 'You know, he doesn't look anything like I imagined.'

'Who—Rory?'

'Hmm, I thought he'd be taller and more noticeable.' Her attention was wandering back to the presence beside her. He was definitely noticeable. She became acutely aware of his knee pressing against her leg. He must have moved nearer. It was warm and hard. She fidgeted and recrossed her legs.

'Why? How did she describe him to you?'

'Apparently, he's like God's gift.' Grateful for the diversion, she laughed and ticked the items off on her fingers. 'Tall, dark, handsome, great body, a tough boss, but one that they all admire.' She made a face. 'Sounds too good to be true doesn't he? This is the Gina version, of course. But the clincher is, and I'm quoting here, "when he looks at you, it's like you're the only person in the world. Amazing eyes."'

Her attention snapped to Karl beside her. She couldn't see his eyes at all clearly. The colour was impossible to tell in the shadow. Gina hadn't described them, she'd been more concerned with impressing on her that he'd be a lot of fun. Lissa had the feeling he'd be more than fun and that was dangerous.

She switched back to her description of Rory. 'Apparently he's Mr Hard-To-Get. According to office legend, he has never had even the teeniest brush with any of the crew.'

'And that makes him hard to get?'

'Well, you know what this place is like, they're all over each other.' The flirty nature of the management consultancy where she was temping was legendary. It was staffed by about forty-five bright young things who were all athletic, artistic, intelligent and gorgeous—fun after hours was standard.

'It's not that bad, is it?'

'No, probably not.' She giggled. 'It just seems like it. They're all such shocking flirts. Office affairs never end well. Too complicated.' Complicated being an understatement—it was something she well knew, thanks to Grant. 'Then with Gina trying to set me up with you...' Her voice drifted.

'And what did she say about that?' He sounded very amused now.

She glanced at him and opted for the truth. 'That you were a gorgeous player who knows how to give a girl a good time.' Lissa felt a needle of guilt for so blithely repeating Gina's description but, sod it, Gina had meant it as a compliment and, frankly, the way things were going, she was absolutely right.

'And you're a girl who needs a good time?'

'Gina obviously thinks so,' she answered giving a

rueful laugh. 'But actually no. When I want one, I'll find one myself, thanks all the same. She was concerned about you because you haven't been dating the last couple of months. She thought we'd be great for each other.'

'What, you haven't been dating either?'

She'd been thinking about it—trouble was the only people she met were co-workers and after Grant that was such a no-go. Precisely why Gina wanted to set her up with Karl for a farewell fling before she left the country. But Lissa was adamant the last thing she needed was to go out with a well-experienced flirt. Playing with fire and being the novice she was, it would only end in carnage. Slow and steady when someone safe appeared, that was the answer.

This guy wasn't safe. His knee was pressing against hers again and she could feel the warmth of him. She had the sudden desire to sit even closer to him, feel the length of his leg press against hers, not just his knee. That would be warm, she thought. Who was she kidding? It would be hot. He seemed to read her mind.

'Are you getting cold? We've been out here a while.'

She shook her head and answered quickly, 'I'm fine. Don't let me keep you, though, if you want to go back in,' she said sweetly, half hoping to get rid of him and half hoping he'd stay. He was amusing, and she had to admit she was quite enjoying the light flirtation. Nothing wrong with a little practice was there?

'No, I'm enjoying being out here. It's very refreshing. What is it you're drinking anyway?' He was looking at the contents of the glass dubiously.

'I'm not quite sure.' She studied the colour in the light. 'I think it might be an apple flavoured one.'

'An alcopop?'

She could hear the yeuch in his tone. 'It's nice. Sweet.'

'And it's also lethal if you drink it too fast. How many have you had?'

She sat straighter. 'It's my second.'

'And have you had dinner?'

She bristled. She turned to face him full on. Both her knees knocked against his. She ignored the thrill shooting up her thighs and the naughty urge to part them. She tipped her head back instead and challenged him. 'Are you leading up to an invitation or are you implying that I'm tipsy? Either way, the answer is no.'

He turned and leaned forward, looking right back at her, their faces inches apart. She sucked in her breath sharply; the light from the window was full on his face and for the first time she could see him properly. Peripherally she took in a strong jaw and straight nose, but it was his eyes that captured her attention. They were the most amazing emerald green. She stared—had never seen eyes so vivid. It was some time before she remembered to blink. They were the kind of eyes you could drown in, wanted to drown in. Brilliantly coloured, glittering and warm.

'Is that so?' he drawled, a smirk lifting the corner of his gorgeous mouth.

Fascinated, she watched as his lips curved upwards. They were full and inviting. She became aware that she had leaned towards him further and abruptly pulled herself up. She swung back to face the window. Hell, maybe she was a bit tipsy, she certainly was feeling a bit dizzy. Impossible. She hadn't had much to drink, so it must be lack of food.

'Yes it is,' she said with asperity. 'Don't think you can bully me into a date because of anything Gina said.'

He leaned forward on the seat, put his head in his hands and laughed helplessly.

'Oh, stop,' she said witheringly, watching him half in disgust, half in amusement. 'It wasn't that funny. You're trying too hard and, I've told you, there's no point.'

His laughter didn't stop and she began to wonder if there was something in the joke she was missing. He was finding her just a little too amusing. Enough. She was finally starting to feel quite cold and experiencing urges she needed to control. Urges to get closer to a guy she knew to be a player. Summoning her dignity, she stood.

'Are you going to go back in now and party?' He smiled, rising as well.

She realised then just how tall he was. She was no midget—in these heels she was almost six feet—yet he was a good couple of inches taller again. She had to look up to try to see into those fabulous eyes. Catching them looking at her so warmly, she immediately felt it best to look away, fast.

'Actually I think I'm going to go home.'

'Good idea,' he replied blandly.

She glanced back up at him. There was no conde-scension apparent in his face, but her hackles rose regardless. She needed to get away from here. Correction, right away from him. Had she underestimated Gina's ability to matchmake or what? This guy made her pulse beat.

'It was nice to meet you at last, Karl. Have a good night.' She nodded at him politely and, without thinking, held her hand out to shake his. As soon as he took it she realised her mistake. The physical contact sent a bolt of electricity surging up her arm straight to her heart, causing it to contract. His grip was firm. His skin warm and dry. Another tremor ran through her. His grasp tightened and they stood linked, staring at each other. Her pulse picked up and she felt the flicker of excitement in her belly. She saw the recognition in his face. She jerked her hand out of his instantly, muttered a barely intelligible 'goodbye', and headed for the door.

He watched her step away from him. Should he have told her? Probably, but the temptation had proved too hard to resist, was still too hard to resist. He glanced down the now empty corridor and slipped inside, not turning towards the party as he ought, but heading for the stairs as quickly as possible. An attack of the lusts. Hadn't had one this severe in…well, ever, he didn't think. Five minutes back on home soil and he was utterly tempted by a foreign Venus. He hit the ground floor unable to stop the smile as he stepped into the foyer.

Lissa breathed a sigh of relief. She couldn't do 'a little fun', as Gina had urged. Now was definitely a good time to escape. Deep in thought, she marched out of the lift and straight into the figure standing before it. Firm hands grasped her upper arms and her nose was sore from bumping against the hardness underneath the wool jumper, which was all she could see ahead of her.

'Oh, I'm so—' She stopped short as she looked up at whom she'd just cannoned into. Mr Green Eyes himself. She frowned deeply as she watched his smile widen with quite obvious amusement. 'What?' she asked, unable to stop the rude bite. He nettled her, put her off balance.

'I'm going to drive you home.' The easy note of authority irked her more.

'I don't think so.'

'Yes, I am.'

She frowned at him again. 'You can't drive; you've been drinking.'

'I've had one drink the whole evening and had food earlier. I'm fine to drive.'

Her frown morphed into a glower. 'My mother taught me not to get into cars with strangers.'

'I'm not a stranger. We've just spent the past half-hour getting to know each other.'

She thought about it for a moment, knowing she was weakening. Gina knew this guy well, and quite frankly, the idea of a ride home in a car was appealing. It would beat a crowded tube and ten minute walk at the other end. The strappy shoes weren't great long distance, not even medium distance.

Even more tempting was the idea of spending another ten minutes in his company. Just a little more practice? Sharpen the flirt claws?

'Besides,' he continued to persuade—she knew he could sense success, 'you've made your lack of interest very clear. So you've nothing to fear.'

Have I? she thought. Damn. Seeing all of him properly for the first time in the lit foyer, she realised her instincts had been right. He was one sexy animal. She stood staring up at him, her mind refusing to compute as quickly as usual. All she could seem to focus on were those fabulous green eyes. She saw the amusement in them. Why it didn't bother her, she couldn't say. Rather she simply felt the urge to lean in and share the joke. He stepped closer and held her arms tighter. The contact broke through her clouded mind.

'Well, if you insist.' She attempted a laconic drawl.

'I do.'

She raised her eyebrows slightly and allowed herself to be guided back into the lift. She looked at him in query.

'There's a car park in the basement.'

Leaning back against the lift wall she avoided his gaze and speculated on his choice of car. It would definitely be fast and flashy. Hell, probably a convertible with heated leather seats.

He took her arm again as they exited the lift and steered her through the line-up of closely parked cars. She tried to ignore the sensations that his thumb and every one of those fingers were causing. They were needles of electricity, points of awareness pressing into her. She pulled her lips into her mouth and pressed on them hard.

She wasn't at all prepared for the slightly dented, giant maroon people carrier that he stopped beside. The seven-seater was obviously used to being full. There was the unmistakable smell of infants. An assortment of papers and candy wrappers was scattered on the floor and two of the rear seats were fitted with child restraints.

'Are we expecting anyone else?' she asked blandly.

'No,' came the equally bland response. She sat down and made to fasten her seat belt. Suddenly she stopped. Reaching underneath her, she pulled out a half-eaten pack of now very squashed raisins. Wordlessly she passed them to him.

'Oh, good,' he said, taking them with a pleased smile. 'I was wondering where they went. Supper.'

She couldn't help but glance at his left hand resting on the steering wheel. No ring, no obvious tan mark. Beautiful long fingers, neatly trimmed nails, a broad palm. She shivered and looked away. This was Karl wasn't it? The incorrigible flirt? Confirmed bachelor and man about town? This definitely didn't go with the image.

'It's my sister's car.' He finally offered an explanation. 'Mine wasn't available and so I borrowed hers. She has three kids. Messy ones.'

'Oh, nice for you.' She clicked her seat belt into place. 'So what kind of car do you usually drive, then?'

'What do you think?'

'Oh, I dunno. Some sporty thing. Fast, flash, something to wow the ladies.'

'I don't need to rely on a car to wow the ladies,' he said suavely.

'Oh, really?' She couldn't help laughing.

He shook his head at her, laughter lighting his eyes so they glowed, burning into her.

'So what?' she asked with tart humour. 'You just rely on your dashing good looks, amazing physique, rapier-like wit and charm?'

'D, all of the above.' He nodded seriously.

She bet he did. He had all of those attributes in abundance.

'Now, where are we going?'

She looked at him in confusion before realising they'd been sitting there a couple of minutes and he hadn't started the engine yet.

'Oh, St Katharine's Dock, Tower Hill.'

He looked at her with raised brows, turning the key in the ignition. 'I thought it would have been Earl's Court or Shepherds Bush. Isn't that where all you Kiwis and Aussies hang out?'

'Maybe.' She shrugged. 'I'm not into that scene.'

'Avoiding your country folk?' He edged the car out of the garage and into the line of traffic.

'No, but if I wanted to spend all my time going to antipodean pubs and hanging out with other New Zealanders I wouldn't have bothered leaving New Zealand in the first place.'

'Running away from something?'

'Running to something,' she corrected. 'Don't get me wrong, it's not that I don't like New Zealand, I love it, but I wanted to travel and experience London. It's such a great city.' She sighed happily.

'So you chose St Katharine's Dock?' They were driving along Embankment, and she couldn't help but enjoy the famous buildings as they slid past.

'Yeah.' She smiled. 'Not in one of those amazing waterside warehouse conversions though. There's an old estate just at the back of them. I have a teeny flat there. It's fantastic. You know, I walk past the Tower of London every day on my way to work and every time it just hits me: I'm in London! It's awesome.'

'It's really such a dream for you?'

'Oh, yeah. It's all those years of having to watch *Coronation Street*, I guess.'

'*Coronation Street*?' he echoed blankly. 'But that's Manchester!'

She giggled. 'Oh, *Eastenders*, then, whatever. All those royal variety shows; we get them all, you know.' She turned to look at him, wanting him to understand. 'It's so great here. Anything you want to do you can do in London, everything is here for the taking.' She gestured widely with her hands.

He looked at her and smiled straight back into her eyes, and her breath caught, he had the most magnificent smile. Her heartbeat accelerated alarmingly. She looked away, hurriedly dampening the attraction raging in her.

'You sound like such a tourist, all that fresh-eyed enthusiasm,' he teased.

'What's wrong with that? It's good to have some passion.' Flirt alert—she willed serenity to return to her mind and body.

'I agree. Are you as enthusiastic and passionate in other areas of life?'

She threw him a mock-evil look knowing she'd asked for that one. He grinned wickedly back at her.

She took a breath and played safe. 'I love walking

past the Tower each day, laughing at those other tourists getting ripped off by the most expensive ice-cream man in the world!'

'Really?' He laughed.

She nodded. 'He has his van there by Dead Man's Hole. The most shocking prices.'

'Hmm. But I bet he's not as expensive as the gelato man by Ponte Vecchio in Florence.'

'Really? In Florence?' She sighed longingly. 'I didn't make it there. I'd love to go.'

'It's beautiful. I'll take you.'

She raised a brow at him, hoping her façade was as cool as her insides were hot. 'Will you, now?'

He nodded. 'You have to see Botticelli's Venus. You're a dead ringer.'

There was a silence as she absorbed the compliment. Botticelli's masterpiece hung in the Uffizi gallery. His depiction of Venus was one of the world's most famous works of art. Generation after generation admired the beauty of her. Lissa was amused, 'incorrigible flirt' was definitely the way to describe this guy. The trouble was, she couldn't help but enjoy it.

'Oh, you are good,' she cooed.

He smiled back winningly. 'And is it working?'

Yes, she thought, most definitely. 'That's for me to know…' she began.

'And for me to find out,' he finished. 'Good.'

What did 'good' mean? Had she just issued the man a challenge?

They entered St Katharine's Dock and she directed him to her building. Part of her wanted to escape the car as quickly as possible, but a good half of her wanted to stay and explore 'possibilities' with Karl as Gina had suggested. Then again, he might not really be interested. He might just have been working on his 'rapierlike wit and charm'. She glanced at him and realised he was watching her, an amused smile flitting around the corners of his mouth.

She stiffened. Had her internal debate been written all over her face? Probably. She strove for dignity. 'Thanks very much for the ride home. It was very kind of you.'

'No problem. It was a pleasure.' He replied equally formally.

She undid the seat belt and opened the door, sliding out. Surprised, she saw he was mirroring her actions. He walked round to stand beside her.

'I thought I'd see you to your door,' he explained. 'I wasn't sure you could manage the stairs.'

She looked up at him, amazed. 'Of course I can. What do you think I am? Blind drunk?' Far from it, but she had to admit she did feel wobbly. Food, she reasoned. It was lack of food, not the proximity of the male in front of her.

'No, but maybe a little tired.' He laughed. It had the effect she was getting used to, making her meltingly vibrant. 'Aren't you?'

He was standing too close. She stood looking up at him, mesmerised as he came even closer.

'If you're quite sure you can manage, I'll leave you,' he said softly, still coming nearer.

'Uh-huh,' she replied, rooted to the spot. He was gorgeous. Tall, sexy, fun. She knew she should be marching straight up those stairs pronto, but she just

couldn't seem to get her legs to work. She stared up at
him spellbound.

He reached out and stroked her hair gently. 'Bye,
beautiful,' he whispered. Then he slid his hand down to
the back of her neck in a loose caress, bent his head and
kissed her.

It was the merest touch, light as a feather. Soft, warm,
sweet, his lips just grazed hers. Then he broke the
contact. She drew a sharp breath, her senses kick started
and just when she knew she wanted more he returned,
stealing the initiative, with full pressure. Firm, insistent,
delightful. His hand cradled the back of her neck, his
thumb stroking gently. Small sweeps upwards that had
her softening, leaning closer, wanting yet more. She felt
the weight and warmth of his other hand as it came to
rest on her lower back. She wanted to touch him. She
couldn't help but kiss him back. Her mind wouldn't
focus on the fact that this was a really bad idea. It was
only interested in the sensations he was stirring.

The hands she had raised in a defensive gesture
didn't push him away. Instead they slid up his chest,
feeling the soft wool jumper and the hard muscle it
sheathed, and reached around his neck. It was warm and
smooth. He stepped closer so their bodies touched,
length to length. The impact was so pleasurable she
gasped. Opening her mouth to his she tasted him. Their
tongues met and entwined and her mind blanked out
completely. Her body reacted instinctively, her breasts
tightening, tensing, her mouth softening, ripening,
wanting him in. Eyes closed, she breathed in the faint

lemony scent that was so heady and delicious. Her fingers curled into his hair and she held him to her. Her toes curled in her sandals and tension swelled. The magnetism, their hold, was unbreakable. The simple goodnight kiss became something much, much more.

His hands stroked down her back, pressing her against him. She loved the feel of his hard body against hers, all of it. She melted, her curves fitting to him. She worked her fingers through his hair and pressed herself against him as much as he did against her. Breathless, she trembled and gloried as he tightened his grip in answer. She felt his hands slide down over her skirt, holding her hips to his. Her bones liquefied and an almost intolerable heat washed through her. His hands stroked lower down the length of her skirt, slid under and back up her legs. His fingers encountered the top of her lace stockings and traced over and onto bare flesh. Skin on skin, incandescent. She heard him groan against her mouth as she moved her hips restlessly.

It was the alarm bell she needed. God, what was she doing? She tore her mouth from his and stepped back. Shocked and embarrassed about the ferocity of the kiss, she was unable to meet his eyes. Instead she looked across at the block of flats, begging her body to calm. She feared that if she looked at him again she would throw herself back into his arms.

He had let her pull back and said nothing, but she was aware of his deepened breathing. Her body clamoured for more of that kind of action. That had not been some chaste farewell kiss, it had been the ignition to a passion that would have led to an explosive encounter with only one conclusion. She was not about to have a one-night stand with her best mate's friend. Especially when she knew him to be a flirt, a good-time guy. No wonder he was such a phenomenal kisser. He had plenty of experience. Attraction turned to anger, more with herself than at him. He was just doing what came natural; her response hadn't been. No way could the depth of feeling from that one kiss be natural.

'Goodnight,' she muttered. She walked away from him, fossicking in her bag for her key as she climbed the stairs. It was not until she was up on the little balcony on her floor that she dared look down at him. He was leaning against the car, one leg resting over the other, his arms crossed, staring up at her. Although it was hard to tell in the gloomy light from the streetlamp nearby, she was sure he was grinning. He waved up at her casually. Agitated, she turned and miraculously got the key in the lock first time. She opened the door and slammed it behind her, not chancing another look back.

Five minutes later she tilted her head to let the hot water beat down on her neck as she showered. She couldn't help but smile as his teasing lilt rang in her ears, couldn't help the inner glow as she remembered his smile, couldn't suppress the shiver as she relived that kiss.

Oh, boy.

Big mistake.

Temptation whispered in her ear. It was Karl. Gina's friend. She didn't work with him—it wouldn't be an office affair. What harm could come from a fling? It had been so long. Basic, carnal lust, of lethal magnitude.

Touch an element that hot and you were bound to get burns. Third degree.

And she was leaving in two months' time. It would be madness to embark on something she sensed could be so strong when who knew how out of control things could get? No fling—not with him. Slow and steady with someone safe, remember? That was what she wanted.

CHAPTER TWO

GRUMPY from lack of sleep she popped a fizzy vitamin tab into a glass of water and knocked it back. She'd have a more substantial breakfast later.

'What happened to you last night?' Gina was sitting at her desk munching through a bowl of cereal, her computer switched on and already running through a complicated-looking search request.

Lissa looked at her in surprise. She was almost certain Gina would have spoken to Karl already. She decided to play for time. 'I wasn't really up to it. I sat outside for a while and then went home early. What about you?'

Gina eyed her speculatively. 'I'm sure there's more to it, you have a guilty look.'

Lissa felt her face flush but dampened down the feelings of embarrassment and focussed on Gina's own exploits. 'Well what about you? You must be feeling pretty happy this morning!'

'Why? Complete opposite, actually.'

'Why? It looked like things were going great! You guys looked totally hot for each other!'

Gina looked at her, perplexed. 'What are you talking about?'

'You and Rory,' Lissa said impatiently. 'He couldn't take his eyes off you.'

'Rory? He wasn't even there!'

Lissa's head snapped back. 'Yes, he was. I saw him talking to you; tall, dark, wearing a black leather coat.'

'Oh!' Gina started to laugh. 'That wasn't Rory, that was Karl.'

The earth tilted under Lissa's feet. 'Karl? The guy you were talking to? That was Karl?'

'Of course!'

'Oh, God,' Lissa breathed, her heart pounding. 'Then who was—' She broke off.

Gina watched her curiously. 'Who was…?'

Voices came louder along the corridor and Gina hurriedly put her bowl of cereal behind a stack of books on the corner of her desk. Lissa reached behind her to put another magazine on the pile to hide it effectively. They stood side by side as a group of consultants came in with Hugo, the head researcher.

'Gina, Lissa,' he began with an evil smile, 'we have some fresh blood for you. Gina, you must remember Rory—he's back from the New York office.'

Lissa saw Gina's sharp glance at Hugo. Hugo was by no means deaf and was fully aware of the numerous times Gina had discussed The Return with Lissa. There wasn't much Hugo didn't know. Oh, the joys of working in an open-plan environment.

Then she looked at the tall man stepping out from behind Hugo. Oh. My. God. Tall, devastatingly handsome in a suit and smiling straight at her was 'Karl' of the previous evening. He was Rory? Those fabulously unforgettable green eyes were now honed in on her with wicked laughter lurking in their glowing depths. She stared, unable to think anything but that he was even more handsome first thing in the morning freshly shaved and suited.

Hugo was going on to introduce the other men but Lissa didn't catch any of their names. Her legs were as wobbly as a newborn lamb's. Finally she dragged her gaze away from him and tried to start breathing again. She smiled in automaton fashion at the others and simply wanted the ground to open up and swallow her. Snatches of conversation came back to her: *'God's gift', 'when he looks at you…'* Oh, my God, what had she said?

She became aware that they were moving off to inspect the database terminals in the main library area. Lissa stood right where she was, looking down at Gina's swivel chair.

'I should have told you.'

She looked up, horrified to see that Rory had not moved away with the others, but instead had moved closer to her, too close. He was still smiling and she watched as he looked over her with a glint of appreciation. A trace of anger flicked through her, raising her temperature even higher. She eyeballed him, refusing to acknowledge the flicker of attraction that also sky-rocketed unbidden.

'Yes, you should have,' she whispered.

Annoyingly his smile widened further. Charming, cajoling, overwhelmingly attractive. 'I'm sorry; it was irresistible.'

'It was unforgivable. You must have known I'd mistaken you for someone else.'

'Mmm.' He looked back at the group of consultants before asking with seemingly genuine concern, 'Have you got a headache this morning?'

'Certainly not.' Irritation caused her to raise her voice louder than she had intended. She looked across to the others and saw Gina was watching, round-eyed.

'You'd better go and join the others.' Her body chose that exact moment to reminisce on how well his frame had melded to hers. She felt the fire in her cheeks and swallowed hard. She began to realise the full implication of his true identity. The situation had taken a total dive. He worked here. She couldn't avoid him and she really needed to. She couldn't be into this guy, not if he worked here, not at all.

'I've only been away six months,' he replied. 'I think I can still find my way round the library OK.'

'Well, I have work to be getting on with.' Too mortified to be able to see even the smallest funny side.

'Please don't let me stop you.'

Miraculously she gained the use of her legs and marched over to her desk and sat down, hating the fact that he was there to see that she hadn't even turned her computer on yet.

He leaned nearer. She felt his closeness with every cell. It was almost a pain. Her body yearned for him to reach out and touch her.

'Bye, beautiful,' he whispered.

Flushed with anger, embarrassment and desire, she

stared at her computer screen as she felt him rise and walk away. She could just picture his grin.

Rory only just managed to stop himself running his fingers through her hair by jamming his hands into his pockets and striding back to where Gina and the new consultants stood. He couldn't help the grin on his face, though, and knew it was wholly because of wicked thoughts, not excitement about new computer systems.

First day as partner and all he'd been able to think about was getting to the information centre as soon as possible to see if she really was there; if she was real.

Well, now he knew. Definitely real. Definitely gorgeous and definitely ought to be off limits. He yanked his mind back from its determined wanderings into extremely dangerous territory and thanked God she'd been wearing trousers. He rolled a pen between his fingers, trying to stop the memory of the sensation when he'd crossed from stockings onto bare skin.

He was on the fast track, just made a partner and had worked damn hard to get there. The last thing he needed was distracting by a lust-on-legs temp.

Then again, just because he had career ambitions didn't mean he had to live like a monk. It wasn't as if he were thinking anything serious here. Marriage and kids were in the long-term plan, but short-term? Hey, he was a man, after all.

Office affairs did get complicated, though. He'd seen it a million times. Never got involved himself as a result—part of his unwritten code. Work was for work, play came after.

But she was a temp—and a New Zealander at that. She'd be onto another temp job or another country in no time. Perfect match for a full-throttle, fast-burning fling.

A partner and a temp, though? Dodgy waters.

He smiled his thanks at Gina—absolutely none the wiser about any of the new databases she'd just run through for him.

'Tell. All. Now.'

One look at Gina's face and Lissa knew she couldn't fudge it. 'I thought he was Karl.'

'What?'

'Rory. I thought he was Karl. At the party.'

'At the party?' Gina echoed. 'Rory was there?'

'On the balcony.'

'You didn't come in?'

'I went home early. He gave me a lift.'

'O-K…' Gina stood, positively agog. 'So what happened?'

Lissa felt the heat in her cheeks again. She fussed with her mouse. 'I, er, told him I wasn't interested.'

'What?'

'I thought he was Karl and that you'd set him up to come flirt with me, so I told him I wasn't interested.'

Gina started to laugh. 'And a fat lot of notice he took of that! I knew it would happen like that. Man, that's why I wanted Karl to keep you out of the way so I could have just one chance with Rory before he saw you.'

'What?' Now it was Lissa who couldn't keep up.

Gina sighed. 'Look, babe, I've known Rory for ages

and he's never shown a flicker of interest in me or any other girl here. We all drool over him and he's just Mr Charming to everyone. I was hoping that maybe when he got back he'd see me in a new light. I wanted Karl to eliminate you from the scene.'

'Eliminate me?'

Gina rolled her eyes. 'Look at you. Tall, legs that go for ever, curves in the right places. Long, beautiful hair. Frank and funny. You're a bloke magnet. Look how many of the guys have tried to chat you up and yet you won't go out with any of them. You're the female equivalent of Rory. Gorgeous and unattainable. It was obvious you two would hit it off.'

'Unattainable?'

'Yes, and even if you aren't that's the vibe you give off.' Gina looked at her slyly. 'But I just saw the way he was looking at you and, let me tell you, I've never seen him look that way at anyone before. And I've never seen you look flustered before. And you definitely look flustered.'

Lissa put her elbows on the desk in front of her and rubbed her temples.

Unattainable? She hadn't exactly been unattainable last night. She'd been easy, almost. Until now her desire to be unavailable in the office had succeeded. But Rory had shown that shield to be worthless. He'd shattered the illusion just by looking at her. This couldn't be happening.

He wasn't Karl the flirt. She needed to snap out of it and fast. He was a partner—one of the bosses. Been there, done that, and complicated wasn't the word.

She'd had one of the best graduate jobs on the market and had ruined it by having an affair with her boss that had turned really nasty.

She forced herself to concentrate, and like the others worked through lunch. Come two o'clock everyone was beginning to flag.

'Coffee?' Lissa asked. 'I'll go.' She was eager to stretch her legs.

Both Hugo and Gina looked up; Lissa grinned at the desperation on their faces. 'I'll be back in ten.'

She braced against the chilly wind and got there in record time. Glancing around as she entered, she froze on the spot as she saw Rory with two consultants sitting on the far side deep in conversation and coffee. As she looked across his head lifted and their eyes met. His were glittering green and she felt lanced by them, feeling the impact all the way through to her marrow. She told herself the heat in her cheeks was from the cold air not that hot look.

Placing the order quickly, she stood determinedly watching the barista do his stuff, trying not to listen to any sounds from the seated area behind her. Once she had the coffees she couldn't help a swift glance to the corner where he'd been sitting with the others. To her immense relief, the chairs now stood empty. Breathing out for the first time since she had entered the shop, she left it.

He was waiting by the door. She hadn't seen him and nearly dropped the coffee when he said straight into her ear, 'Let me carry those.' He had the tray from her before she'd computed what he'd said. She had no choice other than to turn and fall into step with him.

'Have you forgiven me?' He was watching her with those dancing eyes.

She said nothing.

'Are you going to talk to me?'

She stopped and growled at him. 'No and no.'

He smiled back at her. She looked away crossly and continued walking. Damn him for having such a gorgeous smile. It made it hard to stick to her resolve— impossible, in fact. 'You should have told me who you were.'

'Probably,' he admitted. 'But it was so much fun not to. It was very enlightening.'

'Gina will never forgive me. I hadn't told her everything.' The last part came out as a mumble and she was annoyed to feel the tell-tale heat rise in her cheeks.

'And I won't either,' he said easily. 'She never needs to know. Have dinner with me.'

The change in tack was a surprise. 'No.'

'Lunch?'

'No.'

'Coffee?'

'No.'

'Why not?'

'I don't do office affairs.'

'Neither do I.'

'Then why are you asking me out?'

'I'm willing to make an exception in your case. Anyway, who said anything about an affair?'

She bit back her smile. She'd walked into that one. She didn't blame him. Different time, different place, she might have been saying yes. But not in this universe. He was a workmate, more than that, he was one of the bosses. But she didn't want to drag up old issues and decided to deflect him with a different excuse. 'I don't like office gossip.'

He laughed aloud. 'What? You told me a fair bit last night.'

That one hurt because she knew it was true. She battled to bolster what she knew was a weak argument. 'I thought we were discussing a mutual colleague. I said nothing malicious.'

He stared at her thoughtfully. She bore the scrutiny as long as she could before glancing around, unable to take the heat and promise that glowed in his eyes. 'No one has to know,' he said softly.

For a moment she was tempted. Then reality slammed back. No, the best thing was to stay as far away from this man as possible. His gaze didn't leave her face.

'That would be impossible.'

'What others think is really that important?'

'Of course.' She frowned, knowing damn well it wasn't. Her mother had taught her to live life by her own rules, with dignity, without hurting others, and then no one had the right to judge. Of course, never date a workmate was one of the rules.

'That was no ordinary kiss, Lissa.'

She was glad she wasn't holding the coffee. She would certainly have dropped it then. He'd spoken so softly for a moment she wondered if she'd dreamt it. She didn't reply, couldn't. Damn, it would have been easier if he had been Karl, the flirt who she should definitely steer clear of. But he wasn't, he was Rory, an altogether different proposition, an altogether different danger and no less inappropriate.

They reached the building and she looked at him expectantly, wanting to take the tray from him. He shook his head and, clenching her teeth, she opened the door. Her heeled shoes clipped on the floor as she strode ahead to viciously press the button to summon the lift.

'You're very quiet today,' he commented. 'Funny, when you seemed to have so much to say last night.'

Oh, she had plenty to say all right, but she sincerely doubted her ability to say it without resorting to a number of four-letter words. But she'd been tactless enough last night. He was a partner, a boss.

They rode the lift in silence. Lissa tried to ignore his nearness and failed miserably. She stole a glance at him and was flustered when she encountered him looking straight at her. She looked away again instantly and watched the floor numbers light up. Unable to stop herself seconds later, she glanced back. He was still watching her. He looked amused and a hint of satisfaction crossed his face. She seethed.

The doors opened on their floor and she burst out of the lift like a jack-in-the-box, desperate to get away from him.

'Don't forget your coffee!' His call brought her up sharp. Damn. She wheeled around. He was standing just in the foyer holding the tray out. Conscious of the receptionist not five feet away, she stalked back. She stopped a foot away from him and reached for the tray. He took a step nearer and placed it in her hands. His eyes not breaking from hers, he carefully put one hand on hers, then the other hand. Her skin sizzled and her fingers moved unsteadily. He curled his own fingers around hers, ensuring she held the tray securely. Thus they stood for a fraction too long. His hands on hers felt wonderful and she knew his full embrace would be equally dynamic. She pressed her lips together—how could this be? He was a man, like any other.

'Thank you.' Oh, was that eager whisper really hers?

'Bye, beautiful.' He gave her hands a little squeeze. Her heart and stomach contracted. He flashed her a heart-stopping smile before letting go and exiting through the staff door to the back offices.

Lissa stood immobile. He'd just taken her breath with him. She could still feel the pressure of his fingers on hers and his blazing smile was all she could see.

'Got a minute?' Hugo strode back into the information centre from a planning meeting. Gina and Lissa spun on their chairs to face him.

'We're reassigning researchers for the teams because of a new project.' Hugo was straight to the point. 'Its very sensitive with major client confidentiality issues. Initially it's just a two-week job and they want a dedicated researcher. Lissa, you're it, starting Monday.'

Lissa stared at him.

'You can't work on other stuff at the same time because you're going to be locked away in a meeting room. It's all very top secret; the IT guys are setting it up now. It's a small team—one partner, two consultants and you. You'll be expected to prepare the final presentation and proposal. Typing and overtime. You OK with that?'

Lissa nodded, fighting the bitter disappointment. She'd spent most of the time working on a project for a company based in Portugal. It was due to wrap shortly and as a reward the team were going to be flown to Bilbao for a weekend and a party at the Guggenheim. She'd been told she would be included if still there at the end of the project. She'd been looking forward to it so much. She hadn't had a chance to go on her own travels there and now had run out of time. Her return ticket to New Zealand was already booked.

'Go straight to Meeting Room Two on Monday,' Hugo continued. 'You can do the searches no problem and your computer skills are excellent. The partner thought you'd be a great asset.'

She smiled, partly soothed by the compliment. 'Really?'

Hugo nodded. 'He hand-picked you. You'll be working directly for Rory.'

After a predictably atrocious night's sleep she arrived fifteen minutes early on Monday morning embarrassed to discover she was the last to arrive.

'It's OK you're not late, Lissa.' Rory stood and walked around the table towards her. 'We started earlier to generate some work for you.'

She nodded, glancing at him. Their eyes met and held. She could see nothing in his other than professional politeness, but that didn't stop her pulse from accelerating as she registered how brilliantly green his irises were. As their gaze held his pupils dilated. Heat emanated and a rush of feeling rose from her belly to her breast. She snatched a breath and quickly resumed her contemplation of the computer set-up. 'I just want to check I have access to all the databases.' She tried to overcome her breathy tone and inject some professional assertiveness.

He nodded and gestured to the lone computer on the far side of the table. He followed her to her seat. 'We'll have breakfast and a debrief in fifteen, OK?'

She looked up at him, her insides flip-flopping all over the show. This time there was a knowing smile in his eyes. This was going to be much harder than she'd imagined. She stiffened and began checking the systems. She was acutely aware of him moving behind her to the other end of the table.

Sheesh. How was she going to cope with two weeks of him right by her side when she was so aware of his every move? When her whole body answered with such responsiveness to a simple look?

Ten minutes later she was satisfied IT had done a good job. Rory called for her to join them. She smiled warmly at Marnie, and then nodded coolly at James. He'd asked her out on a date months ago and had professed his devastation when she had refused. She'd soon learned that he made it his business to ask every temp worker out.

James filled the mugs from the coffee-pot while Rory outlined the project to Lissa. 'Our client wants to find a takeover or merger target asap in top secret.'

Almost immediately her thoughts went AWOL. It must have been the idea of merger. She watched him as he spoke, hoping her outward appearance reflected her concentration. Sure, she was focussed, but not on what was being said. His shoulders looked so darn broad. Fantastic for holding onto. She watched his hand as he tapped a pen on the notepad in front of him. Large and strong. She bet he didn't battle with the lids on jam jars the way she did. But she knew just how gentle they could be. Could imagine only too well how deliciously tormenting they might be on other parts of her body. She shuffled in her seat, a warm flush invading her nether regions.

James handed her a coffee. She took a deep sip, hoping the caffeine hit would clear her befuddled brain.

It worked. Momentarily.

'We'll be working round the clock for the next two weeks, but I'm sure that's not a problem for anybody?' Rory glanced at them.

Lissa was split. More hours with Rory, but her overtime rate was superb. Pots of money for a situation in which she had to fight the most powerful attraction she'd ever known.

He gestured towards the paper on the windows blocking the view to the corridor. 'The secret-squirrel stuff is for real. Save your social lives for lunch breaks, please.'

'What lunch breaks?' interjected James.

Rory grinned. 'I know, but it's only a fortnight and this is worth it. We do a good job and we could win a huge contract for the company. There's a lot riding on this and it could be good for all of us.'

Lissa wasn't at all sure how this could be good for her—locked away in a tiny room for hours on end with Rory? An intense, artificial atmosphere, the perfect

breeding ground for an intense but artificial relationship. She had to be strong.

'So,' Rory continued. 'Lissa, we need you to
research these companies and type up meeting notes,
compile reports and the final presentation.'

'All that typing OK with you, Lissa?' Marnie asked.

Lissa smiled. 'It's fine. I'm just the temp,' she reassured.

'You're not "just" anything.' Rory interrupted.
Lissa's mouth fell open. On the surface she felt embarrassed, but underneath the reaction was volcanic, the
heat bubbling, desire swirling upwards. She looked
down at the papers before her, willing someone to fill
the pregnant silence. After a moment Rory quite calmly
began outlining further details of the project.

She found it fascinating to watch him in action. The
master of charm and attention, he seemed to enchant the
others, made them want to do their best to please him.
Slightly distanced, Lissa watched him weave this magic,
witnessing their seduction. It totally irritated her.

When it came to giving Lissa instruction there was
a flash of unholy enjoyment in his eyes that she couldn't
miss. And a slight chink in her professionalism where
she couldn't help but feel as if she wanted to do the
exact opposite of what he requested.

Late on Tuesday afternoon only the two of them
worked in the room. The silence sat heavy. Lissa tapped
the keyboard and frowned at the screen, determined to
pretend he wasn't there. As if.

Suddenly he stood. Well, she had to look then, didn't

she? He stretched a little, the gesture emphasising his length. She knew she should look away, but it was impossible. He smiled at her—and the need to look away became imperative. Instead she couldn't help the small smile back.

'Come on, team-building.'

Her surprise must have been evident.

'Team-building,' he repeated, the dizzying smile widening. 'Some corporate R'n'R.'

She didn't trust him; that smile had turned a little wicked. 'Half the team isn't here.' She felt nervous about alone time with him outside the office. Memories of that hot embrace flooded her. Excitement trammelled through her, but she bolted it back down in her emotional cellar labelled 'do not enter'.

'They're coming once the meeting is over. Shouldn't be more than fifteen minutes. We'll only have time to get there and order the first round.'

It sounded harmless enough. They were meeting the others there. Besides, he was the boss. She didn't really have much choice. She nodded acquiescence and logged off her computer while he did the same. She got her jacket from the stand in the corner. She pulled it around her and secured the belt firmly, looking up in time to catch him watching her. A definitely sinful smile played on his lips.

Provoked, she deliberately pulled the ends of the belt a little tighter, pinching her waist, emphasising her curves, defiantly holding his gaze. Desire washed over his face, his eyes burning, the skin across his high cheekbones reddening, and she knew her own face mirrored his reaction. Her head tipped back a fraction, she felt the pulse in her lips, felt the longing for him to touch her bared neck. Sharply he turned to exit the room.

They walked to the lift in a silence that hummed with awareness. Mentally she berated herself for the flaunting gesture. Only the tiniest spark could cause an inflammation. Her lower belly and her breasts felt tight from the moment of blatant sexual encouragement. For an instant she'd let her control lapse and now she was paying for it. With every step she felt conscious of his nearness, knowing she wanted to be closer. Much closer. Bad, bad, bad.

Out on the street he surprised her by heading away from the usual company haunt. She tried to recover her equilibrium.

'We're not going to Jackson's?'

'Well, it wouldn't be much of a team-building exercise if we went to the local and had the whole company join us. This is just for us, Lissa.'

Just for us? Her pulse raced, beating off kilter again.

He kept walking, and talking. 'We're going to be working in close quarters for long hours. We need to be a tight unit. There isn't room for any issues or…' he paused '…distractions.'

Despite her flirt moment minutes ago, she had no intention of being a distraction. Nor was she going to be distracted. Uh-uh, no way.

'Marnie and James are competitive with each other. For the most part this is good, but I want the quality of our work to be the primary goal, not one-upmanship or point-scoring or—' he cleared his throat '…scoring at all, for that matter.'

'Scoring?' She stopped and stared at him.

His face was slightly reddened, but he met her look squarely with a gleaming one of his own. 'Lissa, I'll be honest with you. I'm attracted to you. Have been since the minute I laid eyes on you. That attraction only seems to grow the more I'm around you. But I cannot afford to screw up this project by spending my time chasing you when I should be working. Believe me, it's damn tempting. So I'm telling you now. I'm interested in you. If you feel the same, then let me know.'

Vaguely she sensed the movement of people passing them on the footpath, of buses and taxis slowly advancing along the street, but it was as if the world had subsided into fuzzy focus leaving only Rory before her, impacting on her with brilliant clarity.

Time held suspended as she saw him watching her as her brain ran through every ugly reason why she couldn't be honest with him or herself. She couldn't let anything happen, even though minutes ago she'd practically asked for it. He was her boss. Power plays couldn't help but enter the equation and she knew nothing about him. She couldn't risk it.

Finally she spoke, the raw sound embarrassing her. 'Rory, I can't. I just can't.'

He stepped an inch closer. 'Is that can't or won't, Lissa? I know you're single. I know you enjoyed kissing me.'

Denial was futile, her flush confirmed everything, and so silently she waited him out.

He blew out a deep breath. 'I'm taking it as a won't,

Lissa. That's fine. So for now we concentrate on work. But once this project is wrapped then I think we revisit this conversation.'

The blood pounded through her body, her cheeks were still hot, her lips felt full. But she couldn't be a slave to her desire like this. She'd screwed up one good job already. She wasn't going to do that again.

He took her arm and gave her the benefit of a full-wattage Rory Baxter smile. 'Don't look so worried. It'll all work out just fine.'

He ushered her into the bar.

'You choose the table. I'll get the drinks—apple or cherry?'

She frowned at him.

'Alcopop? Which flavour?'

'Oh.' She felt the heat in her cheeks increase and the small smile popped out without her permission. 'Actually, I'll just have a lemonade, please.'

'Going straight tonight?'

Yes. Straight home. Alone. She nodded. She watched his authoritative stride to the bar. The barmaid leapt to attention, flicking her hair and offering a flirtatious smile.

Turning away before she acknowledged the sudden burst of irritation, Lissa chose the table under the brightest light in the middle of the room. No tiny dark corner to be secluded in, no hint of romance, of intimacy or intensity. She should have known it wouldn't work. Her brain had slipped a gear out of professional mode and into seduction. Her seduction. His approach on the street had surprised her, his unashamed acknowledgement of his attraction to her. But he had made it clear;

work came first. This was good. What had he called it? A 'distraction'. That was all it would be. She needed to remember that. Men who had office affairs weren't thinking marriage and kids. More a bit of fun to liven up long hours at the office and more often than not they'd say anything to get it.

He came across to her, a drink in each hand, and selected the chair directly opposite her. No escape from his handsome face and penetrative eyes.

'You like working at Franklin?'

She had until recently. But her thoughts were interrupted by the harsh beep of Rory's cell phone. With an apologetic look he answered, yes-ing and no-ing for a few minutes. Flipping it shut, he looked at her with a twinkle in his eye that she was unable to interpret.

'That was James. They're held up in the meeting and want to rearrange.'

'Oh, OK.' Lissa knew more time alone with Rory couldn't be allowed. 'I should get on home.'

He gestured to her three-quarters-full glass and his own barely touched wine.

'Can't go wasting company money, Lissa. At least stay and finish your drink.'

It would be churlish not to, but danger signals beat strongly within her. She picked up the glass and had a long swig.

He chuckled. 'Do I make you that nervous?'

'Of course not.' She was more nervous of herself and her own silly weakness. She couldn't let herself be such a fool a second time, but the attraction to him threatened to overwhelm her.

'The indecision in your eyes just about kills me, Lissa.'

She looked down immediately. His soft-spoken bluntness slipped under her defences again. She bolted them down. He was direct at work as well. But was he honest? Or was it all just a line practised time and time again to perfection? Flash the green eyes, flatter the lady and raise curiosity to breaking-point. It would be so easy.

'I really should get home.'

'Should you?'

'Yes.' Definitely.

'Why don't we get something to eat before you do that?'

She couldn't stop the sly smile. 'Nice try, Rory.'

'What?' He put up his hands, all mock innocence. Smiling, he lowered his voice. 'We will reschedule, Lissa.' The serious note struck a chord within her and she knew he wasn't referring to team-building.

Declining his offer of a ride home, she escaped the bar and his breathtaking presence. Never one to miss the opportunity of seeing a few landmarks on the way, she took a bus. She only had weeks left to enjoy the sights. But as she sat in the window seat her eyes were unfocussed, and she was so intent on her own thoughts she missed her stop.

She had thought Grant was honest. Older, only by ten years, but infinitely more experienced. He'd known exactly how to pursue her in a way that didn't scare her off. He'd given her the works; attention, flowers, the romance she'd never experienced, never seen her mother enjoy, only knew of from the movies. That should have told her it had all been an act. She'd thought she loved him, that he'd loved her. That she was going to get the happy-ever-after her mother had missed out on.

Then she'd found out about Melissa. His fiancée. The sordid truth had become humiliatingly obvious. He'd never taken her to his apartment, had encouraged her to keep quiet about their relationship with other workers because he hadn't wanted any hint of favouritism, they'd never gone out—he'd come over to her place instead, cooking for her, flattering her and all the while just using her.

Immediately she'd ended it. Or tried to. Only he'd turned nasty. He'd made her work a living hell—denigrating her in front of colleagues, giving her all the dogsbody jobs instead of the work she was trained for and, occasionally, he had still tried to touch her.

She could have taken a harassment case against him, but she'd felt too bruised already, ashamed by the knowing looks of her co-workers, the mortification of being the 'other woman'—albeit innocently. What a fool.

So she'd packed her bags.

Now she'd met Rory. She knew nothing about him either except, in a matter of only hours and days, he'd breached her defences. She wanted him, plain and simple. Wanted to run her hands over his body, wanted to feel him hard against her, entwined with her. But she couldn't risk ruining another job on her CV. The only way she could think to prevent it was to freeze him out. Retreat behind a frosty veneer, not look at him, not talk to him, only when necessary for work.

CHAPTER THREE

BY WEDNESDAY afternoon Lissa knew her plan was flawed. Rory's constant physical presence got on her nerves. For hours she held her body taut with awareness of his only a couple of feet away. When she looked up and away from her computer screen to rest her eyes, she couldn't help but glance at him. Invariably, she would find him watching her or he would look up as she watched him. She would look quickly away, biting on her lip. When that happened for about the fortieth time that day she was so mad with her weakness she rose to make an escape to the bathroom for two minutes. Just to get away from him, to stare in the mirror and remind herself exactly why she shouldn't be letting her lust for this guy affect her work. No distractions.

Walking back down the corridor on her way back, she was startled as her arm was wrenched and she was practically hauled into a meeting room two down from theirs. The door shut after her. She whirled round staring at Rory who now stood in front of the door, blocking her exit, his arms folded across his chest.

'What are you doing?' she whispered, struggling to regain her equilibrium. His nearness made it difficult for her to breathe, let alone concentrate on work. The tension between them crackled. The stance accentuated the breadth of his shoulders and she felt herself soften in response to his forceful masculinity. Her breathing became shallow and she tried desperately to stay focussed on the job. Think computer passwords, think phone numbers, think of anything but how sexy he looks. Suddenly his lips twisted and he laughed a little. It made it worse.

'Lissa, look, so we can't be lovers, I get that and I'm sorry if I embarrassed you, but can't we at least be friends?'

She looked at him with a sceptical frown. 'Do you really think that's possible?' When there was this much sexual chemistry simmering away barely below the surface, it felt as if it would take nothing for it to envelop and swamp them.

He looked across at her, his sensuous lips pressed together in a teasing half-smile. 'Oh, I think it's possible. I'm not going to have you on the desk at the first opportunity. I think I can keep my baser urges under control.' He lowered his voice and challenged, 'Why—can't you?'

She stared back at him in silence, her mind wanting to answer but her body having fixated on the idea of having him on the desk, the idea of having him full stop. She could picture him above her, easing her onto the hard wood, papers swishing to the floor. She caught her lip with her teeth and bit down, wanting the pressure to ease the pulsing. What she really wanted was another kiss.

His eyes narrowed as he regarded her. He stepped closer. Frustrated, she tore her eyes from his and looked down. He stepped still closer and took her chin with his fingers and tilted her face back up to his. 'Can't you?' he asked again, his voice rough. His fingers slid along the side of her jaw and down to her neck; his thumb gently rubbed over her lips, forcing her to free the lower one from her teeth. He rubbed his thumb back over, soothing it. It did nothing to stop the throbbing.

Their gazes locked again. She fought the urge to open her mouth and suck his thumb in. Appalled with herself, she jerked away from his touch, backing away from him so the table was between them.

'Don't worry, I'm not into sexual harassment.' He glared at her, his hands on his hips. 'I promise I won't touch you again unless you ask.' He stuffed his hands in his pockets as if to emphasise it. 'If you keep freezing me out like you are today, then the rumour mill will swing into overdrive. And I know how desperate you are to avoid any sort of gossip.' Dripping with sarcasm.

She pressed on her lips again, deciding on her reply. 'Well, if you keep making comments like that one the other day, the tongues will already be wagging furiously.'

He raised his brows and looked mystified.

'The one about not being "just" a temp,' she explained crossly.

The brows shot down and a lazy smile stretched across his lips. 'Well, you're not "just" anything. You're just amazing.'

She looked away, attempting to diffuse the power that smile had over her. 'That's not helpful, Rory.'

'No, but at least it's honest.'

'Meaning?'

'Why not try being honest about why you're really refusing to go out with me?'

Too astute. There was more to it. She knew it and he knew it. She opted for denial.

'I have been honest. I don't like being talked about.'

He shook his head. 'No, I think there's more to it than that.'

'Like what?' Her heart banged even harder.

'I think you're scared.'

'Of what—you?' She tried for sarcastic but knew she'd failed. She sucked in a deep breath. He did frighten her, but she frightened herself more.

'No. Maybe. Yes.' His eyes bored into her. 'Scared of this pull between us. It's damned strong, and don't pretend you don't know what I mean. I see it, Lissa, I see it in your eyes.'

Hell. She wondered if it would be OK to wear sunglasses in the office. She shrugged, deciding not to try to deny something that was so obvious to both of them. She knew he was right, about everything. This was Rory. Everyone got on with him, considered him an all-round good guy. The partner everyone wanted to work for. Her attempt at a reserved professional approach was too pointed, too icy to be unemotional. It would be misconstrued or, more likely, construed correctly. She needed to smarten up.

'It's new to me too,' he said softly.

She closed her eyes. She sensed he spoke honestly but it terrified her. She couldn't let her guard slip. She felt like a tiny metal pin attempting to resist a giant magnet. The laws of physics would deny her. But she knew she had to try. To jump into a fire this hot with her boss, when she had only weeks in the country? No. Not unless she wanted more heartbreak in her life. Which she didn't.

'I'm sorry. We'll try to be friends.' She looked around the room, wishing for another exit. 'Are we done?'

He looked at her sardonically. 'Not by a long shot.' But he stood aside and opened the door for her. She made her escape knowing he was only two steps behind.

Lissa rubbed at the pain in her temples. Last night she and Gina had spent a reasonably quiet couple of hours over a bottle of wine, and a plate of pasta in the corner of their favourite bar alternately discussing men—Gina's favourite topic—and travel opportunities—Lissa's. She'd needed to escape the office and her own thoughts and had hoped that a night out with Gina would help her achieve just that. She frowned as her computer clunked through processing her latest request. It hadn't worked. She utterly distracted; the cause of her headache was over six-feet in height and a force looming beside her, captivating her thoughts to the exclusion of all others. It was so frustrating. She sighed. Marnie noticed and guessed about her head.

'You've had your hair scraped back so tightly all week it's no wonder you have a headache.' Without further ado she came and stood beside Lissa, undid her clip and loosened her hair so it tumbled around her shoulders.

'Marnie!' Lissa protested.

'It's for your own good. Now…' Marnie sank her fingers into her hair and pressed on her scalp. Lissa had to admit it felt fantastic.

'I did a massage course to learn to relax.' Marnie explained. 'Is that OK?' she asked Lissa as her hands kneaded her skull right where the bands of pressure had been building.

'Oh, it feels great.' Lissa closed her eyes, the pain receding. 'That's amazing.'

'Don't I get one too?' James asked with a randy light in his eye impossible for anyone to ignore.

'No.' Marnie was basically rude.

'I can just watch,' he said, unabashed. 'I'm happy to watch.'

I bet you are. Lissa glanced at Rory to see what he was making of this bizarre situation. He was resting his jaw in his hand and watching too. A small smile flickered round his mouth.

Marnie finished. 'There you go. All better.'

'Can I have my clip back?'

'No, I'm confiscating it. You should wear your hair down. It looks nice.'

She didn't want it to look nice.

Rory looked thoughtful. 'Anyone got special plans for lunch?'

No one answered in the affirmative. Lissa assumed he wanted them to work through, again.

'Right, we're going out, then. Our missed team-building date.'

Lissa suppressed a sigh. Marnie and James were already grabbing their jackets and heading out the door, eager to escape the dungeon. Lissa sat fiddling with her mouse. Rory looked at her in inquiry.

'Do you need me?' she asked. 'I mean,' she continued hesitantly as she watched the dark look grow in his face 'you guys are the consultants. I'm just here to research and type.'

'I've told you already, Lissa—' his eyes glinted as he walked towards her '—you're not *just* anything. You're as much a part of this team as I am.' He stood right next to her and bent so they were eyeball to eyeball. 'You're coming even if I have to make you.'

He would make her come, all right. Of that she was certain. She sat stunned at her thoughts. Cursed that her mind should interpret his words in such a James-like fashion. She simply couldn't stop the wry twist to her lips. He saw it and his attention dropped to her mouth. Her lips softened and parted under the heat of his gaze. She heard his indrawn breath. She badly wanted to lick them they felt so dry and needy. Even more badly she wanted to taste his. Every fibre in her sprang to life as he inched tantalisingly closer.

Marnie popped her head back around the door. 'Coming?'

Rory's head lifted sharply. Their eyes met again and Lissa saw her own amusement reflected. He spun round. 'Just as soon as we can.'

Marnie glanced at Lissa. Lissa smothered her appreciative chuckle, met her gaze as coolly as she could and walked out the door after her.

They went to a small Italian restaurant not far from the office. James sat next to Lissa while Marnie and Rory were across from them. It was not a large table and as they sat Lissa felt Rory's knee press against hers. Hurriedly she moved back a little, studiously perusing the menu and avoiding the smile she knew would be on his face.

They ordered and ate and Lissa sat quietly letting the leisurely work chat wash over her. The food was delicious and she was starving. The main course passed by in a flash. She smiled at the waiter hovering near, nodding for him to hand her the dessert menu. She licked her lips as she mentally debated between the white chocolate and raspberry torte and the lemon syrup cake with raspberries. She adored raspberries. She perked up the instant the waiter reappeared, welcoming him with a beaming smile. With his eyes on her he asked if they wanted dessert or coffee.

Forgetting about the others, she ordered immediately. 'Can I have the lemon syrup cake with raspberries and boozy cream please? And—' with a conspiratorial smile she looked up at him '—can I have a little extra cream?'

The waiter smiled back. 'Of course.'

Lissa looked around the others expectantly and was disconcerted to find them all staring at her with slightly shocked expressions. She felt like a bug under a microscope.

'What?' she asked in confusion. 'Is that OK? I'm

sorry. Don't we have time for dessert? Do we have to get back to the office?'

'No, it's fine,' Rory answered. He picked up the menu and glanced at it swiftly. 'I'll have the white chocolate and raspberry torte.'

'Just an espresso for me,' Marnie chimed in.

'Ditto,' added James.

'You're not having dessert?' Lissa asked Marnie incredulously after the waiter had left. 'I *never* miss dessert,' she declared emphatically.

Marnie laughed. 'Well, now we know how to keep you happy. You've been quiet as a mouse all lunch and now dessert's on its way you've sprung to life.' She gave her a critical look. 'How do you stay so slim if you always eat dessert?'

Lissa shook her head with a smile. 'I'm not slim. I'm tall—more room to hide it.'

'No, you're slim,' Marnie disagreed. 'Do you work out?'

'No, I'm not a gym fan. I just walk the streets looking at things.'

She stole a quick glance at Rory and saw him smiling at her. 'Playing the tourist?'

'Absolutely,' she replied, tilting her chin.

James looked from Rory to her and back again. 'What do you do to keep fit, then, Rory? You're in good shape and still knock back dessert.'

'Rugby,' came the reply as Rory sat back for the waiter to present the dish.

'Rugby? You'll appreciate that, Lissa, coming from the land of the All Blacks,' James said, smiling at her with a touch of malice. 'Don't all Kiwi girls play rugby now too?'

'Actually, I think of it as Thugby,' Lissa said, concentrating on slicing her cake with a fork. 'All that macho male aggression, jumping on each other, mucking around in mud.' She rolled her eyes.

'Aren't you comfortable with macho men?' Rory challenged. 'Rugby is a good sport for us Neanderthal types. It provides a safe environment for us work off our energy and frustration.'

Her skin prickled. Frustration, huh? She couldn't stop raising her brows slightly. She glanced up at him and caught his fiery gaze on her.

'I can think of better ways to do that,' James said with his all too familiar lecherous tone.

Lissa ignored him, fascinated instead by the expression on Rory's face. Amused, heated, knowing. They could all think of a better way to ease frustration, but, while it was James who would express it, it was Rory and Lissa who wanted to do it. She knew it and he knew it. But she couldn't let that happen.

Marnie filled the sudden silence. 'Are you looking forward to going home, Lissa?'

Rory looked back to his plate.

'Yes, I haven't been back since I left. It'll be nice to catch up with friends. There are still a million places I want to go to, but I can travel again some time.'

'You don't want to stay in London?'

She shrugged. 'Even if I wanted to I couldn't. My working visa expires in two months and then I'll have to leave.'

'You could always find yourself a British husband, Lissa. Then you could work anywhere in Europe for as long as you like.' James waggled his eyebrows. 'If you need someone for the job, just let me know.'

The expression of distaste Rory flicked at James was comical. Lissa gave them both a saccharine smile. 'Why, thank you anyway, James, but as I only intend to do it the once, if and when I marry it will be for love.'

She looked back at her plate, deciding to get what pleasure she could out of the wonderfully syrupy cake. The citrus scent reminded her of being in Rory's embrace and she indulged in the headiness of it. She ate each mouthful with relish until she was left with just a few berries and a pile of cream. Throwing all good manners aside, she put her fork down and picked up a single raspberry, swirling it in the cream, covering it completely. Happily she put it in her mouth and licked the remaining cream off her fingers. It was delicious. Just the right amount of liqueur had been added to the cream to give a sweet, warm tingle in the mouth. The tartness of the raspberry a perfect foil. Ignoring the others completely, she repeated the procedure until the last of the berries was gone. Then she dabbed her finger in the cream and licked it off, glancing up and meeting Rory's eyes as she did so. The burning intensity of his gaze shocked her and she lowered her hand nervously. Desperately she tuned back into the conversation. Marnie and James seemed to be talking tennis.

Lissa couldn't help but look over to where Rory was dawdling his way through his dessert. 'What's the torte like?'

'Magnificent.' He looked at her with a sly smile. 'Want to try some?'

'Oh, no,' she said immediately, shaking her head vehemently. 'No. No, thanks.'

He picked up his fork and speared a piece with it. Then he held it across the table towards her. 'Go on. You know you want to.' His voice was as soft and tempting as the cake. His eyes held the dare.

Staring across at him, she felt the dampened flick of desire flame again. Damn, she shouldn't have been so greedy. With his arm stretched across the table, in front of Marnie and James, it was impossible for her to refuse. Carefully avoiding contact with his fingers, she took the fork he held and lifted it to her mouth. He was right, it was magnificent, but it did nothing to assuage the hunger that clawed at her lower belly.

He was watching her intently. She handed the fork back, uncomfortably aware of the intimacy of sharing it.

'Care for some more?' His voice was low and she couldn't look away from him as she silently shook her head. She sucked her lips in and pressed down on them, desperate not to lick them and show the sexual tension she was feeling. But she knew the action showed it anyway; his eyes flickered as answering heat rose.

Marnie and James had fallen silent, and Lissa remembered their presence with a start. 'Uh, you guys want to try some?' she asked with pseudo-brightness trying to shake off the intense atmosphere that had descended over the table. Both declined. Lissa looked away, embarrassed.

James left to make a call while Marnie rose at the

same time for a trip to the bathroom. Good manners required Lissa remain and keep Rory company as he slowly ate the rest of his torte.

He looked at her, his eyes focussed on her mouth. 'You have a little cream.' He raised his hand to his chin.

'Oh.' She lifted a hand and wiped at her own.

He smiled. 'No, you missed it. Here.' He reached across the table and ran his finger just under her lower lip.

She breathed in sharply and his finger stopped, still pressed against her. She wanted to taste him with her tongue. She parted her mouth to do just that, desperate to lick her lips, to be ready for him. There was a silence. Then he moved his finger again, upwards this time to stroke over her lip and back again. She sat frozen to the spot, melting.

'Tell me you don't want me to touch you,' he dared her softly.

Lissa had several talents, but lying wasn't one of them. Her eyes flickered and she was silent. He traced her lips again, the lightness of his touch a teasing torment. She wanted more. She wanted his lips on hers. She leaned closer, her eyes trained on his mouth.

'Lissa?' he breathed. 'Do you feel this? Do you?'

The rawness in his voice jerked at her.

'It's just sex.' She pulled back, desperate to retrieve the situation. She thought about blaming the boozy cream, but knew that had more aroma than impact.

He looked across at her, heat and amusement mingling in his gaze. 'If it's just sex, why don't we do something about it?'

She recoiled. Just have a fling? A one-night stand?

Go for it like rabbits and get it out of their systems? Again, she was tempted. Damn tempted. She was leaving the country soon—why not have an affair? Gina had suggested she do just that with Karl. Her heart thundered—too dangerous.

She looked at the table. He reached across to her again and tilted her chin up. She met his eyes, now glowing with heat and something else that she couldn't define—warmth? Gentleness? 'Because it's not just sex?' he said softly.

Her heart drowned in the knowledge that he was right. This attraction seemed to be more than just physical. Even more reason to say no. 'It can't happen, Rory.'

His hand dropped. 'Not until you say.'

When they returned to the office and resumed work things had changed. There was a lightening of the atmosphere between them. She had admitted to the attraction that he had so openly referred to earlier. And despite her intention to do nothing about it, it was a secret they shared, a bond between them. Their eyes met with silent laughter when James made one of his outrageous comments. Fingers brushed when they passed paperwork. She knew he watched her as surreptitiously and as often as she watched him. It was a dangerous game but she thought that she could just, just keep a lid on it. Keep things as they were. They had acknowledged the temptation, but that was as far as it would go. For sure.

Before home time she asked him to check some figures she'd inputted into one of the databases.

Standing behind her, he leant over her shoulder, pointing at the screen. She had to forcibly stop herself leaning even closer. She could feel the heat of his body behind her. It would take nothing to lean back against him, to feel him hard against her just as she'd been dreaming, night after night.

He seemed to sense she'd lost her concentration on the work. 'What shampoo do you use? Your hair smells delicious.'

'It's called Esprit de Fleur. You can buy it in the supermarket for five ninety-nine.' She couldn't stop the tart reply, a gut defence against his nearness, a way of trying to push him away because if she didn't she was in grave danger of pulling him closer—literally, physically, now.

She felt his withdrawal and knew he was about to walk away and suddenly that prospect was worse.

'I don't suggest you do, though.' She quickly turned to him.

'Why not?' He came tantalisingly close again, his attention trained on her.

She looked back at her screen. 'Whatever you currently use suits you.'

'It does?'

'Mmm,' she answered as matter of factly as she could, despite her thumping heart and the audible catch in her voice. 'Lemony. It's nice. Fresh.'

'You noticed?'

I notice everything about you. To say that would be to go too far. She was playing with fire already and she knew it. Trouble was, it was irresistible. He was irresistible.

He lingered, perhaps waiting for another move,

another sign from her. So with superhuman strength she kept her focus on the computer, wishing the others hadn't left already, until finally, after what seemed like eons of sweet torture, he lifted away and went to sit back at his own screen.

She breathed out. Close, too close and yet not nearly close enough. Mentally she begged for the fortnight to pass fast; every day was killing her. Why was it you always wanted what you couldn't have?

Rory decided to take the stairs back up to the office after the breakfast meeting with the client. Anything to burn off the excess energy and frustration welling in him. Damn it. The situation was eating him up and he was struggling to concentrate on the project. So much for forgetting about her until it had wrapped. Who the hell was he kidding?

He wasn't the most arrogant guy, but he knew when someone was interested, and she wanted him. He'd seen the way she watched him, the way she flushed when he stood near her, had felt her tremble as his hand brushed hers when working at her computer together.

She'd even admitted it—tried to fob it off as just sexual attraction. But it was more than that. He'd yet to figure out quite how much more, but definitely more. Not just attraction but undeniable need, he had to get closer to her. His body screamed for it. The frustration that she wouldn't give in to it was almost greater than the frustration that he felt from not being with her. It was like being tortured on the rack, slow and painful.

Hell, he should never have commandeered her for

his team, but he hadn't been able to stop himself, the temptation to have her near too great. But he hadn't banked on how totally it affected his concentration. Then again, if she weren't under his nose he'd be spending his days wondering about her.

He'd never been bewitched before. It was humiliating and he needed to do something about it. He knew exactly what he *wanted* to do, but he had to understand her resistance to conquer it.

It wasn't as if she was totally off men. Hell, she even had Gina trying to matchmake her with her mate. He ran up the first flight of stairs swiftly, deep in thought.

All this rubbish about office gossip was a smokescreen. She was a temp, for goodness' sake; she'd be heading home to New Zealand in no time. Why care what a bunch of people here thought when soon she'd be out of the place?

They could have a lot of fun together before she did take off. She should be taking in all the experiences London had to offer. He was determined to be one of those experiences.

So if not fear of gossip, then fear of what? He could do scared; hell he was a little scared himself. He'd never felt a pull like this. He could give her time if that was what she needed. Some time anyway. OK, maybe not much more time.

He mulled over that first night they'd met. She'd been so funny. So damn sexy. Her hair loose, her tongue loose. He smirked—very loose. He couldn't believe she was the same woman so buttoned up in the office the next day. Hair swept back, a frosty manner. That wasn't really her. No, the hints of the tantalising, enthusiastic siren underneath were all too clear. Her cynical amusement at the competitive interplay between James and Marnie, the enthusiastic way she ate her dessert, her passion for the city, the lust in her eyes when they touched. She wore stockings and suspenders, for heaven's sake. The woman was a sensualist hiding behind ice.

Bounding up the fourth flight of stairs, he decided he must remember to keep raspberries and cream in the fridge. Watching her eat that dessert with her fingers had given him the biggest hard-on he'd had in years. He'd had to take ages over his own cake to give himself time to regain control before they stood up at the table. Control. Was that what she was afraid of losing? What he could do to her to make her lose control. He ached to do it, every wild fantasy spinning in his head.

She needed a shake-up. He wanted to strip away that frost, strip away that fear and then strip her, literally. He laughed at his crassness.

Running up the next flight, he looked up and his heart seized in his chest. Suddenly he was as breathless as if he'd been running a marathon. There she was, standing at the landing at the top, staring at him, her hand clenched on the banister. He stopped and eyeballed her. Perfect. Time for a little conversation. Without breaking eye contact he slowly climbed the remaining five steps to stand on the step just below her. It almost brought them to eye level. Her mouth only an inch or two below his. Perfect positioning.

He breathed deeply a couple of times and studied

her. She was breathing as hard as him and she'd only come down six stairs. It pleased him. He got to her, just as she did him. She sucked her beautiful pouty lips into her mouth again, pressing on them as if she was holding back the words. He wanted to free them with his finger, to feel the soft fullness. He wanted her to say whatever it was on her mind.

He decided to cut right to the chase. Her hand still gripped the banister. He covered it with one of his own. It trembled.

'I think it's time we faced up to this, don't you?'

Her eyes darkened.

So did his mood. 'Tell me why not.'

'You're my boss.'

Bingo. An honest reason and one he felt compelled to overcome. 'That's just a situation.'

'It's unethical.'

'No, it's not. It happens all the time.'

'That doesn't make it right. There's an imbalance of…power.'

'I wouldn't abuse that and, even if I tried, you wouldn't let me.'

A shadow crossed her face. His heart pounded. They could get over this. They had to.

The direction of her gaze transfixed him. Slowly it lifted from his mouth to his eyes and he could see the golden flickers of light burning in the depths of the warm brown.

He was desperate to touch her. Desperate to wrap his arms around her, kiss her. He forced himself to go slowly. Move gently. He couldn't afford to scare her off him any more than she was already. He cursed the circumstances in which they'd met. It wasn't great for him either.

'OK,' he said softly. He climbed the final step, taking her hand off the banister with his and walking towards her. She stepped backwards. He kept walking. Forcing her across the little landing until her back was against the wall. He took another step nearer so only a fraction of air hung between them. He kept hold of her hand, his thumb stroking her wrist. He could feel her pulse hammering. He stared down at her, searching her eyes. The spark of defiance was there, but so was the heat and suddenly it was all heat. Satisfaction settled into him.

'We're both adults. We're on equal footing,' he said in a low voice.

She opened her mouth to argue and he stopped her the best way he knew. She melted into him immediately, her yielding sigh spilling in his embrace. His already hard body tightened further in response. Her mouth was so soft, so sweet as it opened for him. He fought for the strength to be gentle, not to ravish as his inner caveman wanted him to. But he couldn't stop the escalation. Couldn't control his desire to touch her everywhere, especially *there*. He'd been dreaming about it for nights, remembering the sensation as his fingers had skimmed from soft silk to even softer skin.

He reached down, sliding his hands under her skirt and slowly up her thighs. He had to know. Yes, there it was. His fingers reached the top of her stockings and flowed onto bare skin. The jolt of desire toppled his self-control and he groaned against her. She rotated her hips against him and he knew she wanted more. The floodgates had been opened and she was kissing him as hard and as hungrily as he kissed her. Her fingers pulled in his hair, holding him to her. He loved it. He ground his hips into hers and his senses sky-rocketed when she rocked viciously back against him.

His fingers traced up alongside the suspender strap. She parted her legs to give him greater access. He slid sideways until he reached the lacy edge of her panties.

He was certain she felt it as badly as he did. Wanted it as badly. He wanted to talk to her, to say it, to hear her say it, but he couldn't bear to tear his lips from her silky skin and that reddened mouth. He teased her, running his fingers along the elastic of her underwear, and felt her try to spread her legs further against the tightness of her skirt.

He let her pull back from his kiss to gasp for air, pressing his mouth along the length of her throat as her head fell back to rest against the wall. Still his fingers teased even though her gasps and wriggling hips told him of her growing impatience. He smiled against the skin exposed at the top of her shirt, breathing in her flowery freshness. And then he felt her hands on the back of his thighs, felt the heat from them through his trousers as they swooped upwards, felt the pressure as they squeezed his butt, and he knew he was in trouble. Inner caveman began to assert dominance. Enough teasing. He cupped her mound with the flat of his palm, while stroking his fingers lower, deeper between her legs; he felt the dampness through the silk and lace and almost shook with need. He very nearly ripped the fabric away so he could taste her there with his mouth.

Then he heard it. The slamming of the stairwell door above. He pulled away from her, staring into her eyes. She stared back at him in confusion, the dazed look almost killing him. He wanted to keep going so bad. But not now, not here. He jerked his head in the direction that footsteps were approaching. He saw her eyes widen in shock as she registered their downward descent.

'Damn,' he muttered, wanting to swear far harder and louder. She pulled at her skirt in panic and deftly he took her by the arm and led her down. They seemed to fly. Excitement drove him. She couldn't deny it now. She was as hot for him as he was for her. Lovers. He could hardly wait.

He swiped his pass and opened the door to the basement, pulling her inside, desperate to get that close to her again. Not wanting the brief moments apart to have given her a chance to build walls again

Too late. She'd already skated out of his grasp and was facing him square with the icy barriers back in place.

'I thought you said you weren't going to touch me again unless I asked you to.' She'd whispered, but it echoed anyway in the dimly lit concrete car park. *Touch me, touch me.* It was all he heard, all he wanted to hear.

'You asked.' It came out low and rough. He knew he was in dangerous waters with this whole boss/temp thing. Knew her discomfort about it was partly justified. Damn, but he'd been told she was right for the project and he'd wanted the chance to get to know her. And for that he needed time. Contact time. The sooner the job wrapped, the better; he'd make sure they weren't assigned to the same one again.

She glared at him, her eyebrows raised, but the fire in her eyes wasn't all anger.

'You asked.' He repeated with more confidence than he felt. He wished he could just pull her into his arms again and show her, but the moment had passed.

She made to refute but he held his hands up to silence her. Then he pointed to her face. 'You asked with your eyes.'

Her gaze dropped instantly, her pale eyelids hiding the gold-flecked brown orbs that told him so much. He saw her struggling, saw how much this thing between them affected her. Well, she wasn't the only one thrown for a loop. He shoved the inner caveman back behind his rock and aimed to lighten the moment.

'Don't worry,' he said with a laugh that sounded as forced as it was. 'Next time I'll wait to hear the request.'

She looked up then and he almost gasped at the torture in her expression. She looked so torn. He wished she'd talk to him. Wanted her to open her heart and mind to him as much as he wanted her to open her body. He wanted the whole damn lot from her. Everything.

Hell, that was a first.

For a moment it looked as if she was going to say something, but then she bit on her lips, the action almost driving him to break his word. He said nothing as she walked past him and re-entered the stairwell. He stood, trying to catch breath, trying to the control the Eiffel Tower in his pants enough to be able to walk up the damn stairs again, let alone return to his desk and concentrate to some degree on work.

God help him if she never did ask.

CHAPTER FOUR

OUT of the corner of her eye Lissa watched Rory. He looked deep in thought, frowning at his laptop. She had avoided him as far as possible since the incident in the stairwell. She'd spent the weekend sightseeing in Bath with a girlfriend and had almost succeeded in forgetting about Rory for a three-hour period. The rest of the time he'd been foremost in her thoughts.

Back at the office on Monday the work had cranked up. Now the presentation to the client was only two days away and they were working round the clock. She'd been able to slip home ahead of him. Marnie and James were constant fixtures at their desks so they were never alone. Besides, she had the distinct impression he was waiting for her to make the next move. Fine. All she had to do was ensure she didn't make it even if that was the toughest thing she'd ever had to do. Far tougher than walking out on her life nearly two years ago.

She'd told him the reason she couldn't be with him. But she hadn't realised the extent of her own vulnerability to him. Within two seconds of his touch she'd been his. Uncaring about how little she knew about him, uncaring of the fact that they had been in a public area and could have been caught at any moment. Almost had been, in fact. If he hadn't acted they would have been. He'd been far more grounded than her and that terrified her.

He'd said she'd asked him to touch her and she knew he was right. In her mind she'd been begging and he'd read it. What a mistake. They'd discovered her weakness together. That he just had to touch her and all her resistance melted. She was not going to risk ruining her career a second time. She wanted to end this contract on a high, not a messy low. But even more scary was the depth of her reaction to him. It didn't seem normal. This wasn't your average case of the hots. She knew that if she gave into it she would be on the road for major heartache. A distraction for him seemed to be something more for her and she was too afraid to analyse exactly what.

So she reverted to ice-princess mode again, unable to meet his eyes for fear of what she might see there or, worse, what she might give away. Marnie and James were too busy to notice. And, perhaps, so was Rory.

Suppressing a sigh, she went to find Gina for five minutes' light relief. She stole a look as she passed him on the way out and caught him staring at her with an expression of such want that she felt herself blush all over. Her eyes darted back to the door ahead. Not too busy.

Gina, happy to hang for a moment, gave her a concerned look. 'Hey, come on, they're having drinks down the pub tonight. One of the other projects has wrapped. Come and have a few and relax.'

Lissa opened her mouth to refuse and suddenly thought better of it. 'Good idea.' These last few days she'd been working so hard she had been feeling almost reclusive. She was supposed to be making the most of her last few weeks—she should be out and about every night instead of lying awake for hours at a stretch dreaming about a guy she shouldn't and couldn't have.

A night out with Gina and the gang would be a great way of relaxing. Rory and the others should be working late again, so no fear of having to see even more of him.

'Good, you're looking too pale and miserable. You need a good night out.'

Lissa attempted a grin back, forcing levity into her voice. 'You know, you're absolutely right.'

A few drinks, get the whole Rory thing into perspective.

Rory knew the minute the door opened that she was back. He could tell her soft step on the carpet, could smell the freshness that was uniquely her. Clenching his jaw, he welded himself to the spot, refusing to turn around and take in the view as he really wanted.

He looked across at James, who was openly appraising Lissa. Irritation flared again. He didn't like the way James looked at Lissa, uncomfortably aware that it was exactly how he looked at her himself—with lust. But James, he knew, was only about lust, whereas increasingly he wanted to understand the whole package.

Something about her got to him, and made him want her more than he'd wanted any woman.

Next thing he knew she was approaching him waving a piece of paper.

'Rory, I need you to sign my timesheet for last week. I need to fax it in to the agency this afternoon to be sure I get paid. I forgot to get you to do it on Friday and I've only just remembered.'

Well, he knew exactly why that was. Friday. The stairs. He looked up into her face. She was staring at the paper she'd laid on the desk next to him. Not giving anything away. She hadn't since those stolen moments in the stairwell, moments that he'd been replaying twenty-four seven ever since. He cursed the interruption, desperately dreaming up ways in which he could try it again. The desire to touch her so overwhelmed him, it threatened his work and he hated that. A large part of him hated the effect she had on him.

No way was he seriously drawn to her, was he? Not someone who, frankly, could be more than a little stroppy. Well, yes. Besides, he had a feeling the stroppiness was related to the battle to keep him at a distance. Once they were over that, he was more than aware of the ways she would be able to make up for it. She was fun. He saw the amusement, the humour, all too often in her expression. Why couldn't they have a couple of months' excitement?

Realising he'd been staring at her for far too long and that as a result her face now glowed rosily, he jerked his attention from her to the page before him. He gave it a perfunctory scan before adding his signature to the bottom line. Then something caught his eye.

'Your full name is Lisette?' He didn't exactly know hundreds, but he'd never come across a New Zealander with a French-sounding name before.

'My father was French Canadian.'

He digested that for a moment. 'Was?'

She nodded and he saw the brightness in her face dim.

'Did you learn French?'

'No. Actually he died before I was born.' The shadows in her eyes grew darker. The golden flecks faded in brilliance.

'That must have been hard on your mother.'

'It was. But she was a survivor.'

'Was?' His heart thumped a little harder. He didn't mean to pry, but he knew he was getting information that was vital. Clues that might help him understand the faint sense of mystery about her. Some fact that might help him figure out why she was so reluctant to follow what he knew she wanted. What his heart and body wanted so much.

'Was.' She snatched the paper up and walked away from him. He quietly watched her as she sat back down in her chair, avoiding looking anywhere in particular, especially at him.

An orphan. Fatherless from birth and motherless since—when? The questions nearly burst forth, but her shuttered expression told him he'd got as far as he was going to—for today anyway.

He went back to the figures on the screen in front of him and for the first time in his career wished his work away. Wanted the project to be over so he could have the time to focus on her. Disgusted, he jabbed at the keyboard. What on earth had come over him? He'd said quite clearly he didn't want distractions. But meeting Lissa was more than a distraction. It felt like a life-changing event, one beyond his control and one he wasn't sure he could handle.

Lissa escaped earlier than she'd thought she'd be able to, leaving the others up to their elbows in charts. She raced along the footpath to Jackson's, the bar where Gina and the others were already on their second round. Gina waved her over excitedly and Lissa was soon ensconced with fresh pineapple juice in hand, slightly distanced persona in place talking with some of the junior consultants.

Suddenly she felt an elbow in her ribs. 'Come and meet Karl.' Gina had such an expectant look on her face as she dragged Lissa near the door that Lissa had to stifle a giggle. She recognised him from the party at the office where she had mistaken him for Rory. She cringed afresh at her blunder. While Karl had a great physique and a fabulously cheeky grin, he was no Rory. They were poles apart in terms of dynamism and sheer animal magnetism.

Karl took her hand and gave her the benefit of the cheeky charmer grin. 'Great to meet you at last. I've heard so much about you.'

'As I have you.' Lissa smiled at him. She was surprised as she caught the vestige of a wink. Not a suggestive wink, but more one aimed at a co-conspirator. That was funny. Unless she was reading things wrong this guy wasn't interested in meeting someone new in the least. She sipped from her glass, appreciating her decision to go with the refreshing juice, watching the interplay between him and Gina.

Gina was her usual bubbly self, but Lissa noticed the serious glint in Karl's eye as he watched her. It took about fifteen seconds of observing this for her to make the connection. Gina disappeared, called away by another friend, and Lissa lost no time in calling him to account.

'You've fallen for Gina, haven't you?' She looked at him full on.

He stared back, his eyes widening a fraction before looking away to where Gina stood chatting safely out of earshot. 'Guilty as charged.'

She saw the flicker of insecurity flash before he hid it behind a self-deprecating smile.

'Waste of time, though, when she's only interested in types like him.'

She glanced around to where he was looking and drew a painful breath. Rory had arrived and was standing next to Gina and staring at them with a thunderous expression. She felt floored by the ferocity of his gaze. She turned back quickly, looking down at her drink, feeling the heat in her cheeks. What was he doing here? She'd thought she was in the clear for just a few hours. Her Rory-Proximity Indicator, aka her pulse, started its crazy zigzag. She found her attraction to him so hard to control and she knew it would only take a moment alone with him for it to snap. She had to prevent that from happening.

'Hmm.' Karl grunted.

Lissa could just about hear the cogs creaking as they turned in his brain.

'Who is he?' he asked.

'Rory. One of the bosses.' She said it to remind herself more than to inform him. 'Look, great to meet you, Karl, but I need to head home.'

With a wave she left him and started to move towards Gina to say goodnight.

Rory stepped in front of her, blocking her slow trail across the room, his chest a more effective barrier than the Great Wall of China. 'So Gina was right, then?' He asked, his voice rasping harshly.

'About what?' she asked cautiously. She'd never seen him look so grim.

'That he'd be the perfect good-time guy for you.' He jerked his head in Karl's direction. Anger oozed from every pore.

If she weren't so strung out she'd have laughed. Instead she sighed. Their situation was fractious enough without having unwarranted jealousy compounding it.

'Actually, no, she wasn't right about that.'

The hardness in his eyes remained.

'But she was right about one thing,' she continued, the need to set him at ease overruling her plan to keep him at a distance.

'What's that?'

'You do have the most amazing eyes.' She looked at him and let her attraction shine out clearly. Time stopped and, fascinated, she watched as his expression softened from anger to amusement and then to desire. The unspoken communication held them in thrall. She felt heat mount in her cheeks and a thrilling tingle rippled through her as she saw an answering flush rise in his. The desire she had been trying so desperately to hold in check this last week was spiralling upwards—again.

She finally recognised that it was never going to go away of its own accord. The feelings she thought she could control were not lessening with each day. Instead the attraction mounted. With every day came new knowledge, more familiarity, more fun. And the need to be one with him grew. It felt inevitable. Uncontrollable.

She didn't want him thinking she was even remotely interested in Karl. The idea was laughable. Right now she felt as if she'd never want anyone the way she wanted Rory. The thought scared her half to death.

Finally she spoke, a whisper. 'I'm going home.'

'Let me come with you.' An equally quiet whisper.

A wry smile lifted the corners of her mouth. 'No one's coming tonight.'

A rueful look crossed his face. She knew he'd caught her *double entendre*. 'More's the pity.' Regret swirled between them.

'What's happened? Don't tell me the computers have crashed and we've lost the reports?' James broke in on them, his hilarity jarring her back to her surroundings. He stood with a drink in each hand, brows raised, flicking his glance from one to the other in query. She glanced back at Rory. He'd retreated and was looking coldly at James who was still talking. 'You need a drink, Lissa?'

She shook her head. 'I'm just leaving. See you tomorrow.' She walked away before either of them could say anything more.

She waved goodbye to Gina, who came to meet her at the door.

'People are asking if you and Rory are having an affair,' Gina said without preamble.

Lissa's head jerked back.

'Don't get mad,' Gina added hurriedly. 'I've said not as far as I knew. I just thought you'd like to know.'

Lissa forced herself to shrug. It was hardly surprising. Even Karl had immediately spotted the attraction between them. Coupled with the few incidents in front of Marnie and James and the soul-searching looks they'd just swapped in the middle of the crowded bar, of course people were going to wonder. Despite what she'd said to Rory, she didn't really care. People would think what they liked with little regard for the truth. She'd learnt that one a long time ago as the only child of a single teenage mother. Besides, it wouldn't be the only office affair to be speculated on and nor would it be the last. There'd be another shortly, she bet, knowing the antics of some of the junior consultants.

'Are you OK?' Gina touched her arm, bringing her back to the here and now. 'Look, Lissa, if you don't want to tell me, fine. But I know there's something going on. You guys put all the "izzle" in sizzle.'

Lissa smiled, aiming for nonchalance, unwilling to unload the sorry saga onto Gina. 'I'm fine. Just tired, that's all. I'm going to call it a night.'

* * *

Thursday passed in a flash. Despite another night of minimal sleep, she sped through the final version of the reports. By mid afternoon they'd been checked and she was printing and binding copies to be distributed at the presentation.

Then she set about perfecting the online slide show and ensuring that the equipment Rory and the others needed to take with them on Friday had been checked by IT and was ready to go. The others had been in conference at the other end of the table for most of the afternoon. Lissa glanced down at them, taking a breather from the figures in front of her. They all seemed hyped on an adrenaline rush. Rory's energy levels were phenomenal. He paced the end of the room, eyes gleaming as he grilled Marnie over and over on her part of the presentation. He seemed to thrive on the excitement of the challenge. Looked so competent, so assured, so focussed.

Lissa grimaced and looked back at her computer. She felt anything but—her suit crumpled rather than crisp, her body hot and sticky. Her throat was sore and her head felt heavy and seemed to have the army band drumming in it. Even her eyeballs ached. She put her hands to her cheeks; they were burning up and her cold fingers soothed them a little.

She was tired. Tired of staring at computer screen and graphs and figures for hours, tired of being cooped up in this tiny room, but most of all she was tired of being so close to Rory and yet not being with him. She wanted him. Badly. The thought consumed her and so did the resulting anger. She was allowing her physical attraction to him to overshadow her work. Such a thing had never happened before. The thought of him fevered her mind. It clouded her judgment and, she worried, affected her performance. She resented his ability to be able to switch it off. How could he be so focussed on work if he felt the same overwhelming passion?

Suddenly it was well after six and the office had all but emptied leaving just their small team. Marnie and James went to get pizza, insisting on going out to get it rather than order delivery. Marnie said she was desperate for fresh air. James took the orders. Distractedly Lissa said she'd be happy with anything but seafood. Damn, she needed to get this finished so she could get away. Her nerves were shot to pieces. It was all she could do to sit there and keep some semblance of concentration on the screen.

She battled to finish the remaining few pages. Part of her wanted to get out of the room and head for home as fast as possible and the other part wanted nothing more than to leap onto Rory and ravish him. Her reservations about an office fling were fading fast under the weight of the desire she felt for him. They would only have a few weeks together. But then that was a whole problem in itself. As the days progressed and her attraction steadily grew she knew she had to be stronger than ever because she could end up heartbroken. Total no-win situation.

She wanted him so badly but she couldn't have him.

A heavy silence filled the room. She sat fuming at the apparent ease with which he could continue working. He had such focus despite her proximity whereas she was practically having a meltdown. She couldn't resist jibing at him.

'People are saying we're having an affair.' Her tone was as bitter as burnt coffee grinds.

'Really?' Rory didn't look up from his screen. 'I'm surprised. They know I don't usually fool around in the office.'

'And why don't you *usually*?' Lissa demanded, anger sparking within her.

'Work's work and play's play,' he replied easily, his eyes still fixed on the computer before him.

'And never the twain shall meet?' she asked tartly. She wasn't sure why, but she felt the need to goad him. To prove he wasn't as immune as he appeared.

'It's easier that way. Otherwise how do you concentrate on work?' Suddenly he jerked his head up and glared at her. She shrank at the blaze in his eyes. He continued, his volume rising with every word. 'How do you cope if the woman you've fallen for is sitting across from you, only inches away, and yet you can't reach out and touch her the way you want to? How the *hell* do you get any work done?' He swore viciously and pushed the keyboard away.

Satisfaction slammed into her. But still she continued prodding brazenly. 'So you'd rather out of sight, out of mind?'

'No,' he replied with a mirthless laugh. 'Never out of mind. But it makes it damn hard to concentrate on bloody numbers when you're wearing a slightly see-through blouse and all I want to do is rip it off to see what's underneath it properly.'

Heat consumed her. Heart thudding, she stood and reached for her suit jacket. Just as quickly he rose and came around the table. He reached out a hand and grasped her wrist. His grip was hard. Her jacket fell to the floor. They stood staring at each other. She was certain he could feel the frantic tempo of her pulse. She watched as he lowered his gaze to her lips, then down to her chest. With a deep breath she realised her breasts had tightened and swollen. He stared at them and they tightened still further. With her arm outstretched pulling the fabric of her shirt taut across her body, she knew there was no way he could fail to see their aroused outline. He looked back up at her face. His pupils were so large there was only the smallest ring of dazzling emerald around them.

'Feeling cold?' he mocked.

Desire and anger merged and grew. She was so close to the edge. She sucked her lips in and bit down on them, trying to suppress the throbbing desire, wishing the pressure on them could be his lips rather than her own teeth. Then she took a breath. 'Practically hypothermic.'

The hint of a smile softened his blazing stare. The pressure of his hand on her wrist grew and he pulled her towards him. His other hand came up and cradled her jaw, his thumb sweeping down from her cheek to her chin in soft strokes.

'Why do you care so much what they think? You don't do what you *want* because you think people might say something behind your back. Why should you even care?'

She stared up at him. He was wrong. It wasn't about

other people. She didn't do what she wanted because she knew from past experience that it would be the worst thing for her. An office affair was a fantasy that invariably ended as a nightmare. The environment was false; you worked as a close unit for a short time, living in each other's pockets. Adrenaline and excitement gave an unnatural high. It wasn't the real world and who knew what secrets were in Rory's life outside the office? What would happen when he was locked away in another project room with another temp he might find attractive?

His thumb continued its gentle stroking. The response in her bones was not so gentle. Despite what her brain was telling her, she wanted him badly.

'Let's really give them something to talk about,' he said softly, his focus on her mouth. His thumb stroked her lips. They parted a fraction. He stroked his thumb across again, pushing it in slightly so she felt it brush against her tongue. Her desire to taste him intimately flared.

'If they're all thinking it, it seems a shame not to make the most of it.' He looked down at her, hesitating.

'What do you want from me?' She stared at him, feeling tortured.

He looked at her with such solemn intensity that she knew she was about to get a painfully honest answer.

'Everything. I want to touch you, taste you. I want to see you writhe in pleasure. I want to see you lose control.'

'Why?' She barely recognised the croaky whisper as her own.

He gave a wry smile. 'It would make me feel good.'

'What—to have control over me?'

'No.' His eyes darkened in frustration. 'Not like that. I want to know that I can touch you in ways that drive you crazy, that I can satisfy you.'

Her eyes widened in surprise. She didn't try to hide it. Her head ached and she was using all her energy to stay on her feet. She couldn't possibly hide anything from him right now. She answered huskily. 'You should know that already.'

His eyes blazed, boring into hers. 'Are you going to let me?'

'I don't think I have much choice.'

He growled. 'Of course you do. You decide.'

'I'm sick of fighting it.'

'Fighting me?'

'No, fighting me.'

His thumb continued rubbing her jaw gently and his gaze dropped to her mouth again.

She knew he wanted to kiss her but he held firm, watching, waiting for her to acquiesce. He seemed to be holding heaven out to her and all she had to do was lean forward and take it from him. The long days and even longer nights of loneliness and want and need overwhelmed her. She blanked the future, no longer caring, no longer able to think. All that mattered right now was this.

Her control snapped. 'I want you to touch me,' she whispered fiercely. 'I want you.'

She didn't just agree, she became the aggressor. It was what she had been wanting for so long. With a speed and strength that surprised both of them she reached up and ran both hands through his hair, pulling his head down to meet her hungry mouth. She licked and tasted him. Vaguely she heard him groan and then she moaned in delight as he pulled her hard up against him. They met length to length. She let him take her weight. He held her easily. The pressure of his hard chest against her sensitive breasts was dynamite. She squirmed her hips against his, her delight at feeling his arousal rendering her unable to control her writhing action. They were the perfect height for each other. Her long legs ensured that they met in the middle, just where they were supposed to. He put his hands on her hips and gripped hard, holding her while he slowly rocked against her, simulating the closer connection that she craved. And all the while their lips, teeth and tongues swirled and danced in a kiss so passionate she never wanted it to end, never wanted any of it to end.

But it wasn't enough. She was desperate to feel his bare skin against hers. Desperate to have him touch her intimately, taste her, suck her, fill her. She tugged at his shirt and moaned in frustration when it wouldn't give. He pulled back from her slightly.

'Lissa,' he said raggedly. 'Lissa, we can't.'

It was not what she wanted to hear. A feral growl escaped her and she reached up for him again. He held his head back firmly. 'They might come back any minute.'

Who? she wondered, half crazed. Right now she didn't give a damn.

He swore softly. 'Hell, beautiful, why did you have to pick tonight of all nights?' He stared into her eyes, and her need must have been clearly evident. 'I'll give you what you want, honey,' he whispered softly as he stood back from her a fraction. And then his warm, strong hand slid down the waistband of her skirt and straight into her panties. She gasped in surprise. His palm pressed hard against her and his fingers delved lower, stroking those lips. Her legs buckled and he caught her with his other arm. He backed her up so she was pressing against the table. Her legs spread wide of their own volition and she found herself leaning back on her hands before she knew it. He kept his hand where it was and his fingers started stroking rhythmically. He bent over her and claimed her mouth once more. His other hand lifted and caressed her breast, teasing the already hard nipple—swirling around it, rubbing, gently squeezing. Her whole body shook with delight, her aching mind relieved of thought, only capable of absorbing the sensations he incited.

After a few heavenly minutes she wrenched her mouth free of his, gasping for air. His lips trailed across her jaw and down her neck. Big, open-mouthed kisses that alternately sucked and soothed. She was on fire, in ecstasy and hurtling towards oblivion. Her breathless gasps accelerated to audible moans as his fingers continued their erotic torment and his thumb rotated around her sensitive nub. It made her want more, much more. She wanted everything. She stirred against him, and murmuring against her, he upped the pressure and pace.

The tempo and volume of her soft moans increased accordingly and she threw her head back, her hips bucking as her body tensed, on the edge of release. The cry of pleasure already building in her chest.

Then he was gone. Without warning he'd pulled back and with a muttered oath whipped his hand free.

'No!' she moaned, frantic. Just a few seconds more, just one second more!

'What is it with us and timing?' He grasped her shoulders and stood her upright, then quickly turned and pulled her chair out for her. She practically fell into it, breathless and stunned and so, so frustrated. She had been so close to what would have been the most powerful orgasm of her life. She sat dazed, wondering what the hell had just happened. Then she heard them. Voices, along the corridor. Rory must have heard the elevator bell.

'Come home with me tonight,' he said urgently in a low voice as he dug his hand into his pocket and pulled out a handkerchief before sliding into his own seat. He looked across at her, his eyes stormy and brilliant.

She stared at him, barely able to breathe let alone think or reply. Suddenly her headache came pounding back, blindingly vicious. The euphoria of the previous moment vanished and the void was rapidly filled with an icy cold. What was she doing? The emptiness was unbearable. She stared at him as horror sank in. Her uncontrollable desire for him appalled her. She was far on the road of no return and she needed to fight it. Fight hard. She curled her shaking hands into fists on her lap. She opened her mouth, bracing herself for her reply. She needed to shoot this down *now*.

The door opened and in walked James and Marnie

bearing large pizza boxes. The smell hit Lissa like a wall of slime. Disgusting.

She didn't stop working as they ate, knowing she was on borrowed time for getting the last of the work done before this headache rendered her utterly useless. She nodded as James set a piece of pizza beside her, but ignored it completely as she desperately focussed on ensuring there were no errors whatsoever in the final version.

Finally she sighed and clicked the save icon for what she hoped would be the last time. 'Can someone check this? I think I'm done here.'

Marnie came straight over waving another slice of pizza at her. Lissa shook her head and winced as pain knifed through her temple.

'Are you OK?' Marnie asked.

'Fine,' she replied softly, aware that Rory's head had jerked up at the question. She could sense his scrutiny.

Marnie watched over her shoulder as she scrolled through the pages. 'Looks great to me. Awesome. You are done!' she said at the conclusion.

Lissa let out a breath in relief and began to tidy away her things. Her hands shook slightly as she tried to work methodically through the pile.

Marnie's voice seemed to come from a distance. 'Hey, you're really flushed. Are you sure you're OK?'

She looked up and summoned the strength from who knew where to reply. 'It's just a headache.' She waved a vague hand at the computers. 'All that staring at the screen.'

Marnie smiled and nodded. 'Go home and SLEEP.

You're so lucky this is all finished for you tonight. We've still got the big exam in the morning.'

She smiled weakly. Yes, for her it was over. Tomorrow she'd be back at her usual desk in the information centre. HQ would be a plain old meeting room again. The paper removed from the windows. Rory would be working on the floor below. The soreness in her throat sharpened.

'Is there anything else you'd like me to do?' her voice rasped. She avoided looking at Rory by fussing with her bag.

'No,' she heard him say quietly. 'You've done more than enough for tonight. We can take it from here.' He paused. 'Thank you.'

Did she imagine that tender stress in the way he said thank you? She couldn't bear it. As she reached the door she turned and addressed the room in general. 'Good luck for tomorrow.'

By the time she got home she was shaking head to toe. Alternately hot then cold, it was all she could do to get a glass of water, strip off her suit, pull an old tee shirt on and collapse into bed. Restful sleep eluded her. Flashes of moments with Rory span chaotically in her mind. She relived snatches of their meetings, the flare between them. She tossed and turned, her body either aching or on fire. It was close to dawn and the birds had started chirping when she finally descended into a dreamless sleep.

CHAPTER FIVE

RORY ran up the stairs back at the office with more energy than a nuclear reactor. The blood in his veins sang. He felt vitally alive and his excitement was palpable. James and Marnie had fed off it too. The meeting had been fantastic. The client had bought it hook, line and sinker and awarded a massive project to Franklin. He'd proved his right to win that promotion well and truly.

And now he was going to win what he'd really been racing for. Lissa. No holding back. Last night, she'd blown him away. So passionate. So damn hot. Utterly on fire for him. He'd nearly lost all reason and had her on the table then and there. How good that would have looked when James and Marnie walked back in with that pizza.

He laughed aloud exultantly. He'd hardly slept but he wouldn't have with the meeting today anyway. He didn't mind that it had scuppered the chance of being with her last night. It made the prospect of tonight even more exciting. It felt as if he'd wanted her for ever. It had been good to have the presentation to concentrate on in the end; reciting facts and figures had been a way to finally get to sleep rather than twisting and turning all night with the most enormous erection of his life. Of course, he'd been dreaming of her when he woke. The ache in his body had been growing since the night he first met her. She was so alive. So refreshingly blunt. Her laughter. So sexy with those long legs and caramel hair. But her reluctance in the office nearly killed him. It was all he could do to stop himself from teasing her, tormenting her into betraying herself. Making her reveal the sparkle and enthusiasm he knew bubbled under that cool façade.

His body tightened at the thought of the night to come. Unbuttoned and tousled. Oh, yes, it was all going to happen. After her response last night he knew she wouldn't say no to him.

He wasn't sure what she'd wanted to do just as the others got back. He'd seen the fear in her eyes and guessed she wanted to try to push him away again. But she couldn't. She'd opened up to him and going back now was impossible. He *knew*. He knew her passion for him was as blazing as his for her. And she knew he knew.

He strode into the library wanting to establish a date even before going to debrief George, the managing partner, on how the meeting had gone. He came to an abrupt halt by her empty chair. Damn. He looked around, encountering Gina's bland look.

'She's not here,' she said.

Disappointment hit him in the chest and a bad feeling rose with it.

'She's at home. Sick.'

He flinched, the bad feeling bang on. 'What's wrong?'

'Flu, I think. She sounded terrible.' Gina and Hugo were both watching him closely. Did they know something of what was going on with him and Lissa? Frankly he didn't care what they thought, but he knew Lissa did.

'Right,' he said. 'I just wanted to let her know how we got on today.'

Hugo nodded and went back to his work. Rory glanced at Gina. Her sceptical 'yeah, right' expression let him know he hadn't fooled her one iota. He winked and left.

An hour and a bit later, after meeting George with James and Marnie and wangling the afternoon off as time in lieu, he was bounding up another flight of stairs. Thank God he'd driven her home that night otherwise he'd have had to con her address out of Gina or HR. That would have definitely raised eyebrows.

He reached the door of her flat and pounded on it. If she was sick, he'd take care of her.

Hell.

He'd do anything for this woman.

He stopped banging as he absorbed that idea. Anything?

No, he'd do the same for anybody who was unwell. Compassion, a normal human reaction. He wasn't driven by any greater urgency just because it was Lissa, was he?

He hadn't had a serious girlfriend in a while, didn't

want one. Had dated, sure, but nothing much more. He'd been too preoccupied with his career. Damn it, he was still preoccupied with his career. Only now something else demanded his attention.

Lissa.

After waiting a while he rapped again, harder this time, unable to stop the drive that insisted he see her. Finally, he heard some movement on the other side of the door. It opened a fraction and when he saw her big tawny eyes staring at him in surprise, he pushed it right open.

She was wearing an old white tee shirt over panties and nothing else. At least he hoped she wore panties; the shirt hung down to mid-thigh and he couldn't quite tell. All the blood in his body headed south—fast. He forced his eyes back up.

A sheen of sweat bathed her face and her eyes looked huge in her pale face. Huge and slightly glazed. She'd twisted her hair back into a loose, low pony-tail but large sections were escaping. He thought she looked beautiful, but while his gut twisted with desire he could see she was in no way up to a marathon session of love-making. She looked about ready to collapse on the spot. The protective male bit in him reared its head.

'What?' She looked stunned to see him.

'I wanted to make sure you were OK.' Well, he wanted that and a few other things, but they'd have to wait right now.

'I'm fine.' She leant back against the wall for support.

'No, you're not,' he said softly, stepping into the tiny hall and closing the door behind him.

She pulled upright with visible effort and walked through into the main room. Rory followed, looking about him with growing concern. The place was tiny. A studio apartment and freezing to boot. His concern leapt into worry and then manifested as irritation. He couldn't help but notice the big bed in the corner with the sheets in disarray. He looked away hurriedly. She obviously wasn't sleeping too good, judging by the way the covers were tossed about. Either that or she never made her bed.

'Have you eaten?' He tried to focus back to the basics.

She shook her head weakly.

'Drunk anything?'

Again she shook her head.

His voice rose in irritation. 'Taken any medication?'

She put up a hand. 'Don't start lecturing me. I'm fine; it's just a wee bug.'

He stood back watching as she tottered back to the bed, obviously trying to control the shivering. 'Like hell it's a wee bug. You look half dead.' He swung around the room. 'Where's the kitchen in this place?'

She gestured to the bi-folding cupboard doors in the far corner. He wrenched them open and stared in disbelief. The kitchen, or kitchenette he supposed it would be called, consisted of a bar fridge, a shelf for groceries, about three plates and assorted mismatched cutlery, a microwave, twin hotplate and sink. He looked at the few packets on the shelf. Cereal, cereal and more cereal. All quarter to half full. He opened the fridge, already knowing what he'd find.

Just as he'd thought; skimmed milk and a couple of tubs of yoghurt. The bottle of chocolate sauce standing alone on the middle shelf diverted him momentarily. Wrenching his mind away from the extremely exciting vision of licking chocolate off her breasts, he slammed the door shut with force. 'This is ridiculous. What do you eat?'

'There's a supermarket just around the corner,' she replied defensively. 'I haven't been for a couple of days.'

'Obviously. No wonder you're so trim. You're half starved.'

'I eat at the office,' she said resentfully.

'You eat cereal at the office. Don't you eat anything else?'

'I really like soup,' she replied, tilting her chin up, daring him to criticise her.

Resisting the urge to plant a kiss on those upturned lips as he wanted, he rolled his eyes instead. 'When did you last have a decent home-cooked meal?'

'This is my home. I do cook. And it's none of your business.' She flung herself down on the bed and ruined the defiant effect completely by doubling over and coughing. He moved across to her and rubbed her back in gentle wide circles as she hacked away. He could feel her warmth through the thin tee shirt and he tried not to notice that there was no bra strap under it.

A few minutes later she looked up at him with watery eyes and mumbled, 'Rory, I feel awful.'

He sat down next to her and put his arms around her in the age-old gesture of comfort. He felt no resistance as she leaned into his embrace and he continued to rub gently up and down her back. 'I know, beautiful.' He gently pushed her back onto the bed so she was lying down and hastily pulled a rug up to cover her long legs. Her eyes closed and she shivered spasmodically. He watched her closely. She really looked sick. He could feel the frequent bouts of shivering, and her skin was burning up. The cough was nasty. He guessed she had the flu with a chest infection on top of it. Looking around him, he felt frustrated. She couldn't stay here alone like this. In this condition she wasn't capable of looking after herself and she sure as hell wasn't going to be making any trips to the supermarket for supplies in a hurry. He stroked her arms gently. She appeared to have gone to sleep.

Quietly he stood and surveyed the scene critically. She hadn't a lot of possessions, hadn't bothered to make much of a personal mark on the place. Clean and clutter-free, it looked as if what she had could be thrown together reasonably quickly. An assortment of candles sat arranged on a shelf; he could smell their vanilla fragrance even unlit. Next to them leaned a framed photo of a woman who looked as if she could be Lissa's sister. There were no other photos. New Zealand, eh? Beautiful mountains there, good for snowboarding. He smiled.

A huge pile of books stood stacked in two towers by the bed and he glanced at a few titles with interest. Novels, biographies and a few travel guides. A map of London was taped to the wall. A toiletries bag stood neatly on the chest of drawers. The suit she'd worn yesterday lay in a crumpled heap on the floor by the wall, which surprised him. That didn't seem to fit with the way she wore it so creaselessly. He'd thought she'd be fastidious about hanging her clothes up. She must have been feeling terrible when she got in. Frowning, he picked up the skirt and jacket, shook them out a bit and draped them over the back of a chair. He didn't poke into the wardrobe, feeling as if he was intruding enough.

He spun about quickly; he needed to do something about her. She couldn't stay here alone. He didn't know if she had other friends to call on and in any case she was in no condition to get to them. Besides, if he knew her at all, she wouldn't even if she could. Miss Cool Independence. He did know one thing for sure; she hated admitting a weakness. Well, undoubtedly she'd hate him for what he was about to do, but tough. Sometimes, he figured, you've just got to lie back and let others help you. He grabbed the keys lying on the table and, flipping open his cell phone, strode out of the flat.

She never wanted to wake up. The dream seemed so real and lovely. She floated in a state of bliss. Soft, comfortable, secure. But it hadn't started that way. Someone had been shining a light in her eyes and from a distance she'd heard an unfamiliar voice asking questions, annoying questions that tried to rouse her, made her feel as if she'd been taken hostage by the Spanish Inquisition and she just wanted whoever it was to go away. Then she'd been hot, so hot and dreadfully thirsty.

Her mouth had been too dry to be able to swallow and her lips were cracking. Then he'd appeared. He'd cradled her and helped her drink something cool and refreshing. Then he'd moved away and she'd felt so bereft and so alone. She'd called to him. Asked him not to go.

'Not going anywhere, beautiful.'

She'd rested back against him, smiling, her irritated skin feeling soothed against something smooth and soft. At last she'd slept, cocooned in arms that were tender and strong.

She opened her eyes and blinked at the wall lazily. At least her eyeballs didn't hurt quite as much as they had last time she'd used them. When was that? It felt like hours ago. She came to with a rush. Rory. Rory had turned up on her doorstep. She lifted her head off the pillow and looked around her. Where was he now? Wait a second—where was *she*? She stared at the totally unfamiliar room. There was a snowboard leaning up against the wall and a couple of boxes stacked beside it. The curtains were pulled but she could see a chink of pale light through the gap. What time was it?

Then she became aware of regular breathing near her and she turned her head, rolling over onto her back to look properly. Rory, clad in jeans and a tee shirt, was lying on his side beside her, sound asleep. Her heart stopped in her mouth as surprise came and went in a flash. Fascination took hold. She had never seen him so vulnerable. Until now she'd only seen him in suits or corporate casual wear and even though he had that easy charm he always exuded self-assurance, a commanding style. Now, just in jeans and tee, he looked younger, a little less like the boss and more like a sporty hunk. She studied his mouth, the fuller lower lip that curved into such a devastating smile when he was awake. She took in the long dark lashes resting on his cheek, a hint of a shadow on his jaw. Her fingers itched to rub against it. He looked relaxed. It was incredibly appealing.

She really hoped she hadn't got some form of selective amnesia and was unable to remember what should have been the most awesome sex of her life. She wriggled a little experimentally. While her body ached, it wasn't the kind of ache you got after a night of passionate lovemaking. And he was lying on top of the bed fully clothed. No, somehow she'd got to his place and he'd looked after her. She remembered her dream, and knew him helping her drink had been real. Guilty pleasure swamped her. She shouldn't be here, this shouldn't have happened, and yet she was so pleased it had. She glanced around the room again with more interest now she knew it was his. There wasn't a lot to make it personal—just the snowboard hinting at athletic pastimes and boxes signalling the recent return from his time overseas. The walls were painted a warm creamy colour and she wondered what the rest of the place was like.

Then she looked under the bedclothes and made a shocking discovery.

'*What* am I wearing?' she screeched.

Rory jerked awake. 'What?'

She watched as alertness sprang into his features and repeated the question.

He frowned as her words sank in. 'Oh,' he mumbled. Then as she watched, amazed, an embarrassed flush mounted in his cheeks. 'You were h-h-hot and sweating.' He was actually stammering. He cleared his throat. 'You said the cotton was too rough on your skin. You were aching. You were complaining about the sheets too.'

'I *what*?' Oh, dear God. She was mortified. She remembered feeling hot and uncomfortable. She must have been feverish. What else had she been muttering while in that delirium? She masked her embarrassment with aggression. 'So what—you just happen to have a selection of silk negligees for whoever comes to stay? I assume this is your, your…'

'Spare bedroom. Yes.' He looked directly at her. The flush had receded. 'And, no, I went and bought it especially for you. In fact—' his eyes gleamed '—I bought two.'

Her mouth hung open for a second before she remembered herself and snapped it shut. She said nothing, absorbing the fact that she was wearing nothing, *nothing*, other than a simple, long silk negligee. No lace, no knickers. 'Did I get changed myself?'

He started to colour again and looked away.

'I didn't think so,' she muttered darkly. Then a coughing fit took over.

'Hey, you're OK here.' His low comment did nothing to soothe her.

She sat up sharply, knowing damn well she wasn't, and the room spun horribly. She wasn't OK and it wasn't the flu bugging her.

'Take it easy,' he said, pushing her back down with a gentle but firm hand on her shoulder. 'You've been very sick and you haven't eaten in days.' His hand lingered. His warm fingers on her bare skin were heavenly. She realised she was hungry. And not just for food.

'What time is it?' she asked abruptly.

He checked his watch. 'Seven p.m. Saturday.'

'You mean Friday.'

'No, I mean Saturday. You've been out of it for over twenty-four hours. You've had me damn worried. But I think half of it was just exhaustion. Once the fever broke, you slept like a child.'

Saturday.

'You want to use the phone at all? Will anyone be wondering where you are?'

She ignored the question in his eyes and simply shook her head. No, if friends called they'd probably think she was out with someone else.

He seemed to have forgotten his hand still rested on her shoulder, his thumb smoothing over her skin. The touch did crazy things to her insides. She shivered and this time it wasn't the fever causing it.

He frowned. 'You lie still and just relax. I'm going to get some food.'

He slid off the bed and she felt sorry as the warmth and weight of him disappeared. She cringed at the hazy memory of begging him to stay with her. What else had she let slip? But she couldn't stop watching him leave the room, his butt shown off beautifully in the low-slung jeans.

She bit her lip and looked up at the ceiling. She was in trouble here. Big trouble. The question was, did she get up and try to go home now, or did she just give in and let the inevitable happen? She tried sitting up again and slumped back in a hurry. The inevitable. No contest.

He reappeared twenty minutes later bearing a tray that, she had to admit, smelt heavenly.

This time, she discovered, she was able to sit up no problem at all. She propped the pillow up behind her. He carefully placed the tray across her knees and smiled. Her heart thumped slowly and she tried to ignore the tenderness in his actions.

'This is great.' She gazed in pleasure on the laden tray before her. In the centre was a bowl of rich red soup accompanied by a plate of fingers of buttered toast. A smaller bowl of freshly cut fruit was also on the tray; it included, of all things, raspberries. She was in heaven. She picked up the glass of juice on the side and tasted. Pineapple. How did this guy know all her favourites? The question must have been written all over her face.

'You were begging for it last night.' He grinned. 'I had to go to the twenty-four-hour shop to get it.'

'Thank you.' She put the glass down, having drained half of it. She felt bad for having reacted so ungratefully before. 'I've put you to a lot of trouble.'

'No trouble,' he said easily. 'Eat your soup—roasted red pepper.'

She didn't need to be told twice. But while she was hungry, she wasn't hungry for a huge amount of anything much and this platter was exactly what she would have chosen herself. 'What about you?' she asked between mouthfuls.

'I ate earlier,' he replied, settling down on the end of the bed.

She couldn't manage to eat it all, but when she finally sat back she felt a million times better. He smiled at her. She wished he wouldn't; every time he did her resolve disappeared another inch—make that mile.

'Now you need these.' He shook a pill bottle at her. She frowned.

'Antibiotics,' he explained. 'You have a chest infection as well as the flu. The doctor prescribed these to clear it. So far you've been good about taking them.'

'Doctor? What doctor?'

He grinned at her. 'One of my mates is a GP. He came round after work yesterday and gave you the once-over.'

That explained the man from the Spanish Inquisition.

'You were that worried about me?' She took the dose and washed it down with the remainder of the pineapple juice.

'I was.' He smiled, the warmth lightening the atmosphere. 'Want to stretch your legs?'

She did. She definitely did—stretch them all the way home, or so she ought.

'Do you have something that I can put over the top of…um…' Her voice trailed away and she gestured towards her breast with her hand. She saw the flare in his eyes as he followed the movement of her hands and hurriedly put her arms in front of her breasts to try to hide the all too pleasurable reaction there.

'There was a matching robe.' He stood and went to the chest of drawers, pulling a long cream-coloured silk robe off the top. 'I'll see you in the lounge. You can't get lost.' And he swiftly exited the room.

Bit late for modesty now, she thought ruefully as she swung her legs out of the bed. Still, who was she to be concerned about modesty? If she remembered right she was the one who had been on the desk, begging him to screw her in the middle of the office when people had been due back any minute. Had she no shame? Nope, she realised. Not when it came to Rory.

She sat on the bed for a few seconds, making sure she had her strength together before standing. She was still weak and, underneath it all, still tired. But she didn't want to be lying in bed with Rory lounging on the end of it. That was just too much in the way of temptation.

She pulled the robe around her and glanced in the mirror hanging on the far wall. Her pallor surprised her. And her hair was a mess. She grimaced. What she really needed was a shower. Leaving the room, she discovered Rory was right; she couldn't get lost. Following the sounds of activity, she passed another door—open, showing the bathroom—and another closed; she guessed it must be his bedroom. She quelled the desire to open it and take a peek.

He was in the kitchen, holding two large towels in his hand. The guy really was a mind-reader. 'Want to have a shower? You'll feel better.'

She stopped in front of him and stared. He really did

look incredible in those close-fitting jeans and tee shirt. His chest just about took up all her vision, it was so broad. Two towels—one each? Where had her self-control gone?

'Thank you.' Her voice was husky. Her body was starting to feel all sensitive again and this time it wasn't because of the fever.

Slowly he held them out to her, his eyes fixed on hers. Her heart thudded faster. She reached out and took them and looked away from him in a hurry. She had to get out of here or there would be no stopping things. 'I should go home after. Could you give me a lift?'

'You're not going home tonight.'

She'd known he was going to say that. She was also aware she wasn't going to fight him. Much. 'Why not?'

'It's getting late. You're still weak. That flat of yours is freezing.' He'd obviously been storing up a few reasons.

'I forgot to switch on the radiator,' she broke in.

'You're staying here.' They stared at each other. His mouth curved into a wry smile and his eyes twinkled. 'Don't worry. You'll be quite safe.'

Yeah, right. It wasn't him she was worried about. It was her own weak, needy self.

'I'll get that other negligee for you,' he said quietly. 'I'll leave it in your room. I grabbed your toiletries bag from your flat; hopefully it has everything you need in it. It's in the bathroom. I didn't want to pry so I got a toothbrush and comb from the shop just in case.'

'Gee, you've thought of everything,' she said sarcastically, still fidgeting with the belt on the robe. 'Do you do this often?'

He laughed, that open, warm sound that had had her melting on the night she'd first met him. 'No. Pretty much everything with you is a first.'

She wondered what he meant by that.

She headed for the bathroom pronto.

Just as he'd said, her toiletries bag sat on the vanity. She peered inside it. She always had it pretty well packed—just in case she was hit by a sudden urge to take a weekend mini-break. Just beneath her body spray rested her pill packet. She picked it up. She didn't take them for contraceptive purposes, having not been involved with anyone since Grant. The little plastic bubble marked Saturday was full. It was still Saturday. She popped it from the foil and quickly swallowed it. A girl could never be too careful.

Stepping into the shower she turned the taps on hot. The pressure was marvellous and she couldn't resist standing there for long moments letting the water pound on her head and body. It felt so good to get rid of the sweat. She tried not to think about him. Tried to ignore the desire swirling in her belly. It was like trying to stop a tidal wave with a flannel. They were alone. The outside world had disappeared at the door. Just her and Rory. Out of the office and in his home. And she knew and she wanted it to be just so, just for now. She reached for the shower gel—the packaging advertised its thera peutic powers—'invigorate'. She flipped the lid and caught a whiff of the lemony citrus flavour that she as-sociated with him. The gel lacked the underlying masculine tang that was pure Rory but it was close enough. She closed her eyes as she washed indulging in the feeling she was being enveloped by his presence.

He knocked softly on the door as she towelled dry. 'Lissa, are you OK?'

'Fine, I'll be out in a tick.'

Clad in the second negligee—the same as the first only in a pretty pastel blue—and the robe, she padded back out to the lounge. The flat was marvellously warm. Even her feet, which were usually like blocks of ice, were cosy despite being bare.

He knelt, fiddling with the gas fire. 'Sorry,' he said, obviously hearing her arrival. 'You were a while and I was worried maybe you'd collapsed in the shower or something.'

'No.' She grinned. 'It's a girl thing. We take our time in the shower. You guys are all the same. Turn it on, jump in, jump out, get dressed without drying properly and it's all over.'

'Really?' He raised his brows. 'And how do you know so much about it?'

'Flatmates arguing over the power bill.' She smiled teasingly and pulled the robe tighter. She had to admit she loved the silky feel against her skin. Smooth and sensual. Its simple design clung to her; she liked the soft rustle as she moved. She knew it had probably been out-rageously expensive. It made her feel sexy. She couldn't help but have sex on her mind. She realised she'd been staring at his jeans-clad thighs. The denim showed off their strong, muscular outline better than his suit trousers. She looked up with a start. She was so aware of him.

'Could I get that comb? I didn't have one in my bag.' Her voice wobbled a bit.

'Sure. I'll go get it.'

She expelled the pent-up air from her lungs as he left the room briefly. But her blood started zinging again the instant he returned, comb in hand. Her fingers brushed his as she took it from him. The sensation from that slightest of touches was enough to send a tremble through her. In the hour and a half since she'd woken up her body's awareness of him had been growing stronger and stronger. Now just the sight of him and the tiniest touch had her craving more. Her breathing shallowed. It was madness to have agreed to stay. But it was a madness she couldn't stop.

She sat on the sofa and tried to comb her hair. After just a few seconds she felt exhausted from holding her arms up. It was pathetic. He seemed to know. She wondered if he knew everything, if he knew how turned on she was feeling, that his nearness drove her crazy. That he was so damn sexy that she just wanted to reach out and plant her mouth on his. Hard.

'Here, let me,' he said in a low tone. He took the comb from her nerveless hand. She turned away from him so she sat sideways on the sofa. He tucked the towel around her shoulders and carefully lifted her hair over it. With long, sure strokes he worked the comb through. The regular rhythm was soothing. Detangling and smoothing.

He stopped and she heard the click as he set the comb on the table. She felt him press the towel on her hair, sponging up the damp. Then he slid the towel away. She sat still, half holding her breath. He seemed to have paused too. And then, just when she knew it would happen, she felt his warm lips on her neck.

CHAPTER SIX

SHE could have stopped what was happening so easily. A look, a word, was all it would have taken. But she said nothing. Her eyes closed, she tilted her head, inviting Rory's kisses to continue. They did. Slow, gentle, incredibly erotic, his lips inched down her neck. At the junction where neck met shoulder his teeth bit down gently.

A soft moan escaped her and his arms slid round to embrace her. One arm encircled her waist firmly, the other seeking her breast. He caressed her, his thumb stroking around her tight nipple. She leaned back into him. This was what she wanted, more than anything. All her concerns started slipping from her mind. Besides, she reasoned dreamily, they weren't in the office, were they? It was perfect.

His arms tightened around her and he lifted her up, settling her across his knee as he sat back against the sofa.

She looked up at him as he held her loosely. She could feel his erection pressing against her side. She knew he was waiting for her reaction, giving her the chance to pull away. Slowly and deliberately she licked her lips. 'Kiss me,' she whispered, her voice wobbling with the force of the need she felt.

Just as slowly and deliberately he lowered his head. She held hers up, in perfect position. The gentle graze of his lips against hers set her nerve ends trembling. She immediately opened her mouth for more and just as quickly he came back with it. Kisses between them could never be small and gentle for long. Their banked-up passion was too strong to be contained.

She felt as if she could keep on kissing him for hours. Long deep kisses in which she finally had the freedom to explore his beautiful mouth, feel him enter hers and make his claim. But slowly, inexorably, the feeling that it wasn't enough soared. She wanted more. She moved restlessly. His hands began a deeper exploration of her body. He loosened her robe and pushed it off her shoulders. The thin straps of the negligee followed. She lifted her arms free of them and the soft material slid to her middle, revealing her breasts. With a groan he quickly lowered his head and fastened onto the nearest nipple. Alternately licking and sucking, he created the most exquisite sensations. She watched him through half-closed eyes, turned on even more by the look of intense pleasure on his face.

His fingers trailed up and down her leg, going higher with each sweep, sliding the silk away so her thighs were exposed. Such delicious torment that she squirmed and her legs parted. Finally his hand hit the top of her thigh and slid against her warm, wet groove.

She groaned in delight. That was what she wanted, more, more, more.

He lifted his head and smiled at her. 'You like that?'

Like wasn't the word. She rocked against his hand. He obeyed her silent order and started a slow, rhythmic stroke. She smiled back at him and pulled his head to hers, wanting to taste him again, feel him with every inch of her body. He trailed kisses over her face, down her throat and over her breasts again before passionately returning upwards to her lips and then beginning again until her face and torso were on fire, and she panted helplessly, unable to move, unable to do anything but revel in the sheer, blissful torture of his touch. His fingers gently circled and stroked until she was slick with moisture and rotating her pelvis against his teasing hand. He muttered softly between kisses. 'I want to see you come. I want to feel it, taste it. I want to hear you. Come alive for me, beautiful. Come for me.'

It didn't take long. His words, his lips, his hands, his fingers drove her wild.

'Rory,' she gasped. 'Rory, I want…' she gasped again, unable to get the words out. Not sure what they were any more. Relentlessly his mouth and fingers drove on, not giving her any respite. Her feet arched and her toes curled as the first shudder ripped through her. Still he worked, sucking, stroking, squeezing. Her body arched uncontrollably again and again as sensation zinged through every cell. He pulled the cry of ecstasy from her with ease.

She stilled. Shocked. Her mind refusing to function.

Having felt only ache for the last few days, her body wallowed in the weightless warmth now spreading through. She couldn't have opened her eyes if she'd tried. She was vaguely aware of his hand gently stroking her arm, her legs, of being held closely to him. A small part of her whispered for more, that there was more to come, but she wasn't able to focus. Her consciousness floated away.

It was dark when she woke but the room was partially lit with light coming from the hallway through the open door. She blinked, her eyes adjusting to the dimness, her brain reliving what had happened when she'd last been awake. Oh, boy. Aroused again in seconds, she hungered for the main course. He lay next to her, his arm resting on her hip. He breathed evenly but she knew he was awake. She could feel the vitality emanating from him.

She smiled into the darkness. 'Where am I?'

'Where you belong.' His low growl was immediate.

Her stomach swooped. Her pulse stepped up a gear. 'And where's that?' Knowing the answer but wanting to hear it. Wanting to hear the passion in his voice.

'In my bed.'

A rush of satisfaction pooled in her belly. It merged with desire and she pulled his head to hers, fixing her mouth to his, and passionately tongued him. Nothing else mattered. Nothing but being with him in this moment.

She pressed her body length to length against his and elation filled her as she discovered he was gloriously naked. Hot, hard, huge and finally hers.

She pulled her head back and challenged him. 'Where's my negligee?'

She saw the flash of white as he smiled. 'It slipped off.'

'You got a thing about stripping me while I'm asleep?'

She felt his hot breath on her as he chuckled. She explored his chest with her fingers, tracing through the hair. She revelled in the feeling of his hard thighs pressing against her. She longed to run her hands over those too and burrowed a little in the bed so she could.

'I'm sorry I went to sleep on you.' Her voice was slightly muffled. Her hands crossed over his taut abs and down. She found his nipple with her tongue and worked around it, swirling and tasting.

'I'm not. It was beautiful. You're beautiful.' He smoothed a hand down her back.

'I'm awake now,' she said as she reached the top of his thighs with both palms.

'No kidding.' He seemed to struggle to get the words out.

Pleased and emboldened by the night, she took him in her hand. She'd only stroked him a couple of times, appreciating his length and girth, when he stopped her, his hand gripping her wrist like a vice.

'Inside you,' he muttered hoarsely. 'I want to come inside you.' He pulled her back up the bed and kissed her long and hard and deep and when he finally lifted his head she knew she was lost.

'Then what are you waiting for?'

He growled with laughter and she melted more.

'I've been waiting too long for this to have it over in two minutes.'

Oh. Excitement trammelled through her, an almost nervous anticipation. She didn't know if she could handle much more. She wanted him now. It seemed as if she'd wanted him for ever. But he was relentless. His hands, his mouth, slowly, reverently, traced her body, igniting tiny fires all over that built and merged and threatened to overwhelm her reason. He tossed the bed-covers back, the heat between them keeping them more than warm enough. She learnt his body as he learnt hers. She gave free rein to all her desires, to touch him, to kiss him as she'd dreamed of night after night. But he soon pulled free of her, groaning as he reclaimed control. Then she could only lie back and let him caress her in ways she'd blushed about when fantasising.

He nipped gently at the smooth skin of her inner thighs with his teeth, then soothed the skin with lush kisses.

'Rory,' she whispered brokenly, 'I can't take any more.'

'Yes, you can, beautiful.' And then he kissed her right *there*. His tongue hungrily tasted her sweetness, lashing her with its length, his mouth fastened onto her, regularly sucking until her hips arched and her hands fisted into his hair. His fingers came to tease inside her while his other hand tormented a rock-hard nipple.

Her head thrashed and her body shook as she proved her point—her mind and body imploded as the sensations he stirred catapulted her into ecstasy.

He pressed slow kisses up her belly. 'Are you still with me?'

The power and intensity of that orgasm had far from satisfied her. It had only worsened the unbearable ache in her womb. She needed him there.

'Make love to me, Rory. Please.'

He stared down at her intently, rigid with desire, and then he kissed her, pressing her head down into the mattress with the force of it. The weight of his body settled onto hers and her excitement level sky-rocketed again. She felt the dampness on his skin and knew he was only just keeping himself in check.

He reached across to the bedside table.

'It's OK,' she said. 'I'm on the pill.'

'OK.' He gulped in a deep breath. 'You're sure? You're sure you're ready for this?'

She was more than sure and she wanted nothing between them. He moved closer and she could concentrate on nothing else but him. Her ears were finely attuned to his roughened breathing and her own shallow pants. She pulled at him to hurry, but he held back, braced above her, fixing her in place with his beautiful burning eyes. Then, as smoothly as a hot knife sliding through butter, he filled her. Oh, boy, did he fill her.

Finally.

It felt so damn good that for a moment her mind blanked completely as the sensation short-circuited her whole system. She realised the moan of bliss had been hers. She opened her eyes and looked up at him with a slow, rapturous smile. His unwavering gaze beat down on her. She saw the wonder and delight she felt mirrored in his face. She flexed her hips up to him a fraction.

His breath hissed between clenched teeth. 'Not yet—' his voice tight '—or it won't be two seconds, let alone two minutes.'

She watched as he fought for control, thrilled that he, like she, had almost been obliterated the instant they had joined together. That he felt the passion for her as strongly as she did him.

Slowly he brought up his hand and stroked her hair, then down to frame her face with fingers that shook slightly. Not taking her eyes from his, she turned a little to press a tiny erotic kiss into his palm. She gave him a saucy grin and saw his serious look lighten in return.

At last he moved. Slowly releasing, then pressing close again. Slow, sure strokes that seemed to break through every barrier she'd thought she'd installed permanently. With every movement he filled her, came further into her, breaking into her heart, becoming part of her. And the thing was, it felt wonderful.

She arched to meet him, length to length, stroke to stroke. She ran her hands down his taut muscles, delighting in the ripple of hardness that greeted her.

Slowly, teasingly, he danced with her, sometimes kissing her, sometimes holding her gaze. She kissed his neck; he kissed her breast. But inevitably the pace increased. So too did the intensity and sheer physicality until at last they were pounding hard together. Over and over they met as one until her mind blanked again as he sent her over the edge. Shuddering, she was just conscious enough to feel his big body spasm as he fiercely gathered her closer, his fingers gripping her to him, roaring as finally he too lost his fight for control.

* * *

Sweat-slicked and sated, she slept. Silent in the tight embrace that he'd locked her into once he'd shifted the bulk of his weight off her. Somewhere in the back of her mind the thought niggled that she should be going home. That she should be running, far and fast. But she was tired. So tired. And so content. She would wake, see him, want him, have him and then crash again. She couldn't remember whether that had happened three, four or five times through the night. All she knew was that it still wasn't enough. He was a sex god. She'd never experienced such pleasure. Now that she had, she wanted it again, over and over. Just this night, she told herself, just let me have this one night.

In the morning the magic sanctuary of the darkness remained. It was as if a bubble had descended, enclosing them in a world where only they existed. Where doubts and pasts and futures lay forgotten, forbidden. She sat on one of the bar stools at the kitchen bench in her silk negligee, loving the sight of him pottering in the kitchen wearing nothing but a pair of tent-shaped boxers. There was something so decadent about the scene. He cooked her soft, creamy eggs that slipped down her throat. She beamed at him, ignoring the fact that the strap of her negligee had slipped from her shoulder and she was dangerously close to flashing him. When had anyone cooked for her last? When had anyone made her feel so cared for? So cosseted? So *loved?*

Her smile died as she stared at him, her breakfast abandoned. This couldn't be love. This was just attraction. That was all it could be. He held her gaze as he tossed the pan aside and came to her, his eyes lancing, exposing her doubt. Then he bent his head and with only a few gentle touches made her forget. Forget her concern, forget her rules, forget the egg. She went up in flames. Hard and fast with her perched on the edge of the bench, him standing before her. Her negligee rucked up, his boxers halfway down his muscular thighs. Then he suddenly scooped her off the edge and took her weight himself, deeper, harder, joyous. It was as if he wanted to support all of her himself, be the foundation from which she could fly.

She leaned against him in recovery, breathing hard like him, still overwhelmed by the tornado-like climax they'd shared. He cradled her for long moments, the after-play of his hands soothing her, keeping the devils at bay.

He picked her up again and carried her to the bathroom. Stood with her under the hot shower, soaping her back, massaging her shoulders. Invigorating was definitely the word for his showers. He aroused her again, slower this time, but no less passionately.

She slipped into the robe knowing she ought to be pulling clothes on instead. But the tiredness controlled her and she pushed the thoughts away, tried to turn the mute button on the doubts whispering at her. *What are you doing? You shouldn't be here. You're making a fool of yourself—he'll make a fool of you…* She pressed the mute button again. It worked that time. He bundled her up in a soft mohair blanket on the sofa, put a selection of books on the floor beside her and a jug of water. His ministrations were so tender and caring she was afraid to read the motive that lay behind them. No one had cared for her like this, not since her mother had died. Weakly she closed her eyes, blocking out the significance. Seconds later she fell asleep.

'Lissa we need to talk.' The sofa had sunk under his weight as soon as her eyes had opened.

'No, we don't, Rory.'

'I think we do.'

'No.' She looked at him firmly. She didn't want this, not now. She just wanted to feel. Just wanted to prolong the magic a little longer before she had to end it for her own protection.

His eyes were full of the unspoken. She allowed herself to indulge for a moment. But those doubts came rushing in. Was this going to be the talk where he made promises? Promises of the kind that Grant had made? As her mother's boss had made to her? Insincere? Meaningless? She couldn't trust him. After all, she barely knew him. The weak part of her rebelled—she did know him. She'd witnessed his integrity at work, his drive, his charm. She was in his apartment, for goodness' sake, something that had never happened with Grant. There certainly was no sign of another woman's presence in his life.

No. She had to believe this was just a brief moment. A fling. Once she went home, it would be over. She could never have a relationship like this in the office.

She knew he watched her intently as she thought. 'Lissa…'

Unwilling to listen to what she thought would be lies

and too afraid to take the chance they weren't, she moved quickly to silence him, literally swallowing his words.

Later he went back to the kitchen, bringing her more soup. They ate leisurely and had each other for dessert.

At one point she woke, her body aching but sated. Her head rested on his thigh as he sat at one end of the sofa and she lay along it. Music softly played as he read. A great wave of tenderness bathed her. He was gorgeous. Such a generous lover. She wanted to do something just for him. She smiled a small secret smile. Who was she kidding? She wanted to do it for herself, while she could. She rolled over so she was facing into his body, his crotch in front of her. Before he could stop her she undid his jeans and freed him. He was rock-hard in seconds. She took him in a firm grip, squeezing slightly.

'Lissa?'

She loved the husky note in his voice. She shushed him. 'Just let me.' She leaned forward and began her oral exploration. She heard his book thud on the floor. Then she was caught in her own pleasure of discovering him. She traced the ridge of him with her tongue, closed her eyes and breathed in his maleness. Nuzzling, stroking, she loved the pulsing she felt in response. Her awareness of her surroundings faded completely as she lost herself in the taste, feel and smell of him. With both hands she worked him, keeping him in place as she caressed and kissed and sucked, hot and hard.

'Stop, stop, stop!'

She finally heard his cries. She glanced up at him.

'I'm going to come,' he panted.

She chuckled, her hands continuing to stroke. 'That's the whole point,' and then lowered her lips again and sucked as she would her favourite lollipop. He pulsed and jerked and she revelled in the sound of his harsh groan as he gave her all he had. She loved the power of reducing him to merely a body capable of nothing but enjoying mindless pleasure, the power he had over her. A weekend of physical pleasure, that was all it was, all it could be—right?

Licking her lips, she looked up at him with a satisfied smile. 'I'm sure it's good for me.'

'I *know* it's good for me.' His face was flushed and he breathed hard. 'You're going to give me a heart attack if you do that again.'

She pouted.

'Just warn me next time so I can be ready,' he explained.

'You're always ready.' She slapped at his chest playfully. 'That's what I like about you.'

She yawned and stretched her toes. Turned again and resettled her head comfortably on his lap. Her eyes drifted shut. Warm and snug by the fire, cocooned in his arms, she'd never felt so content.

His amused voice seemed to come from miles away. 'I thought I was supposed to be the one who rolled over and went to sleep.'

CHAPTER SEVEN

SHE kept the mute button on those damn alarm bells that kept trying to ring off in her head. As the day dragged into evening neither of them raised the subject of her going home, or work, or what was happening between them. After she'd stopped his attempt earlier it was as if they had an unspoken agreement to ignore it completely and just enjoy the now.

She knew she should leave, that staying meant it was only going to be harder tomorrow, but she was still so damn tired and it wasn't just her body fighting fatigue, but her will as well. She just couldn't deny it any more. Her desire for him was overwhelming. And now she had known the fulfilment of it she couldn't seem to give it up. She just wanted to give into it over and over. One more night, she promised herself as he pulled her to him, just one more night. But the mute button was failing so she tried mental earmuffs. Ten seconds into his kiss she was in the clear, her mind latched onto one thing only.

* * *

The loud beeping of his alarm startled her.

'Damn,' he groaned. 'I have to go.' But he made no move to leave the bed; rather he proceeded to awaken her fully with his own playful style.

He wandered off to shower and, appalled, she felt the lethargy return. As she lay recovering she broached the subject she'd been ignoring for the last thirty-six hours.

'I should go home and go to work.' She said it as soon as he walked back into the room.

'No. You're still sick.'

She half drowned his reply as she hacked through another coughing fit. Holding his shirt, he looked at her with the most outrageous 'I told you so' smirk.

She sighed, her eyes watering. 'I should at least be recovering at home. The fever has gone.'

'No.' The finality in his tone was unmistakable. No doubt about it. He was used to getting what he wanted. Getting used to having her. Trouble. Ignoring the fact that what he wanted from her was exactly what she wanted from him, she forced irritation to the fore.

'Rory,' she began crossly, 'I can't stay here.'

He leaned over her, his arms imprisoning her in the bed. He kissed her slowly. 'You can't go. You've got no money, no clothes, and I've got your keys.' The devilish glint in his eye softened. 'Just get some sleep, beautiful. We'll talk tonight, OK?'

Incredibly she did spend most of the morning asleep. The cough still racked and her body felt as if it had been hit by a bus. Not surprising given the workout it had had in the last two days. She smiled. Rory had amazing stamina.

She scavenged in the kitchen for brunch and realised she was looking forward to him walking through the door. Counting the hours, in fact. Uh-oh. The phone rang and she stared at it, holding the fridge door open although it wasn't that causing the chill on her skin. It clicked to the answering machine.

'It's me. Pick up.'

Rory. She picked it up immediately, instinct overriding better judgment. It was a brief call; he seemingly had nothing of great importance to say. She was certain he'd only called because he'd wanted to make sure she was still there.

'I'll be home as soon as I can.' He rang off.

Home.

She slowly put the phone back on its cradle and stood staring at it for long moments. Where was home? She had been travelling for almost two years loving every moment. But her time was up. Her ticket already booked. She had friends she hadn't seen in all that time already planning lunch dates. She was looking forward to it, damn it. The old saying popped into her head, mocking her. 'Home is where the heart is.' Tears sprang at her eyes. She knew just where her heart was—in trouble.

She leaned against the bench for support as she began to realise the full consequences of what she had done. She'd tried to stay away from him because she knew how dangerous office affairs could be. But she'd succumbed to the attraction in the privacy of his home. And in doing so she'd opened herself up to a far greater hurt. Even if she did think for a moment, just for a moment, that he was as crazy about her as she was for him, it still wasn't going to work because her flight was booked. She was going to have to say goodbye to him. And as hard as that would be it would only get worse the more time she spent with him now. Saying goodbye sooner would be better than later.

Her mother had suffered years of loneliness and heart-ache after the death of her lover, Lissa's father. He'd died when Lissa was only a tiny life growing inside her and her mother had been little more than a child herself at the time. To lose a lover, your true love, be it through death or geographical circumstance, was devastating.

The force of her emotion terrified her and she knew in her bones it was only going to deepen further. She'd really fallen in love with him. He had his career here, his family, his life. Even if he wanted to she wouldn't let him give that up. Besides, this was just an affair for him. Who was to say it was anything more than a weekend's 'distraction'?

Doubts raced at her, scurrying through her mind, making her feel fear, making her want to run. She tried to fight it.

She went back through to the lounge and stared half-heartedly at the bookcase. She needed something to read for a while. Daytime TV depressed her and if she went back to bed now she wouldn't get a wink of sleep tonight. Then again, maybe that wasn't such a bad idea—a night of insomnia with Rory for company? Bad idea. She shook herself; she had to get this under control.

She stared at the spines of the books, uninspired. And then she saw the album on the bottom shelf. Guiltily, knowing she shouldn't but unable to stop, she pulled it towards her and opened it. Rory the gorgeous as a baby, aged two, and onwards till it ended with him looking about sixteen. She turned the pages, entranced at the images of him. Amazed that the features she adored had been so noticeable from such a young age. Those vivid green eyes, and thick dark hair. She traced the development of his strong male physique. No boy should have shoulders so broad. She half laughed at the awful clothing he'd worn as a young teenager, knowing she'd been as guilty of the same crime. She studied the pictures of him with his parents and sister. They looked a close family. A happy family. It was obvious they still were—devoted Uncle Rory. She sighed and looked across at the fire, gloomily pushing away the spark of envy. They were poles apart. How could they ever have a future together when their pasts were so different? She'd had only her mother, her father dying before she was born, her grandparents had rejected both her mother and her. After her mother had been killed in an accident she'd been alone and naïve and fallen for Grant. She seemed destined to make this kind of mistake.

Game over. She paced, ready for him. She'd been wearing a groove in the rug half the afternoon, going stir crazy. Getting incredibly anxious about the mess she'd got herself into with her uninhibited indulgence. She needed to get outside. Most of all, she needed to get away from him. She'd woken from the dream and those alarm bells were ringing non-stop. Nothing she could do would silence them now. It was only a matter of time before he hurt her, intentionally or not. Sure, she'd just had a weekend of the best sex of her life and she loved the way he could make her laugh, but it wasn't going to last and she needed to get out now before she ended up totally wrecked. She had to say thanks, goodbye and move on. Back to work, back to platonic. For a moment she dreaded his reaction—would he turn on her as Grant had? Surely not. But she had a goodbye planned, one she was determined to enjoy.

The key sounded in the lock and she marched over to meet him. She watched as he entered and with bitter-sweet pleasure saw the desire already evident in his face. It grew as he looked her over. She had dressed in a pair of his boxers and a shirt, unbuttoned to the waist. She saw the gleam of anticipation in his eyes.

'Come and sit on the sofa,' she invited softly. 'You must be tired from a hard day.'

'Tired is the last thing I'm feeling,' he replied, but complied anyway, taking a seat in the middle of the sofa.

She looked down at him, a soft smile curving her lips. She watched as an answering smile spread across his features. His eyes twinkled. She loved that lusty, ex-pectant look he got. She loved it that he was hot for her the minute she looked at him. His hand went to loosen his tie.

'Uh-uh,' she said, shaking her head, determined to keep it light, keep it fun.

He stilled and his grin turned wicked.

'OK,' he said. 'You're the boss, huh?'

'Damn straight,' she replied. He certainly was a quick learner, but then she knew that already.

With a fluid movement she peeled off the boxers she was wearing. She moved forward and straddled him on the sofa, her knees comfortable in the soft cushions on either side of him. He rested his head back and watched her as she undid his belt and trousers, pulling them aside just enough to free him.

'You're every fantasy I've ever had, you know that?' he muttered.

She smiled.

'Only more,' he added reverently. 'Much more.'

She touched her mouth to his, protecting herself from those powerful eyes and tempting words.

He was ready and she'd been ready for hours. There didn't seem much point in mucking around. She bent forward and feathered kisses along his jaw.

'I'm going home tonight,' she whispered as her hands slid down, holding him where she wanted him.

His head jerked up. She stopped him replying by placing a finger on his lips and squirming her hips down on him hard. She felt him gasp as she took him into her all the way. Then she leant forward and kissed him ruthlessly. She couldn't block the emotion: desperation and sorrow and all her desire. She held nothing back. Then passion increased and it flooded out the heartache. She longed to give everything to him but she couldn't. All the while her hips moved sinuously against him with a slow and crazy rhythm. When she freed him from the kiss he was panting, his hands hard on her hips trying to control the tempo and pull her even closer.

She tossed her head back. 'I'll stop right now if you don't agree.'

Who was she kidding? She couldn't stop now if she tried, her hips seemed to have taken on a life of their own and she desperately rode him harder. He knew. He bucked upwards and she sucked in her breath, unable to stop the answering rotation of her hips. A lazy grin appeared on his face, but the red tinge in his cheeks gave him away.

'Oh, so you're playing hardball,' he mocked.

'You'll be the one with hard balls if I don't get what I want.' She could do this; she could. It was to be their last time together and it was going to be dynamite.

'I've got what you want and it's right here, beautiful.'

True, but only for a limited time. Doubt gnawed at her. Part of her would love to believe in him, in this. She pushed the thoughts aside and strove for nonchalance; she was not going to ruin this final coupling.

She raised her brows, moving slowly against him. 'Cocky.'

'Very.' He nuzzled against her breast. 'I bet I can make you come before I do.'

She pulled back and looked at him. A smile tugged her lips. 'Well, now, that is a challenge. And the prize?'

'Where you spend tonight.' His hot mouth covered one of her hard nipples and sucked on it hard. The desire to ravish him increased threefold.

'Fine.' She threw her head back as she savoured the tugging sensation at her breast. God, he was good. But she could be too. She flexed her most feminine muscles, hard, several times.

He whistled slightly as he sucked in a sharp breath. His fingers bit into her hips a second before he shifted slightly beneath her. Then he looked up at her and grinned slyly. 'You forget—I'm getting to know you, Lissa. I know what you like.'

She pressed her lips together. That was certainly true. She opened her mouth to breathe out heavily. She needed to regroup, but his attentions were proving hard to ignore. She closed her eyes. What was his thumb doing? Pushing all the right buttons. She moved and tightened again, retaking control. She felt him tense and smiled a little. This was one bet she couldn't afford to lose…

In the finish they tied. It hadn't been a long race either, the pleasure of giving doubling the pleasure of receiving. They lay sprawled on the sofa, him still half dressed, clothes askew, her completely naked and wanton.

Coldness stole into her. She sat up and pulled on his shirt, wrapping it tightly around her. It was finished. It had to be.

'I'm going home tonight, Rory. Even if I have to walk there barefoot and break the window to get in. I'm going home.'

He stared at her moodily.

'You can't have everything your own way,' she continued, looking away from the disappointment she glimpsed in his eyes.

'I want you to stay.'

She jerked her head back. It had sounded suspiciously like a command.

His green irises darkened, drawing her in. 'We have to talk about this.'

She rose from the sofa, turning her back on him, ignoring his frustrated growl. She needed to keep this light. Not enter into a heavy conversation in which declarations might be made. False promises, the rashness of passion. Better to chalk it down to a fun weekend— one to be walked away from. 'What would you have me do—stay here for ever as your sexual playmate?' She glanced over her shoulder at him.

A wolfish grin leapt across his features. 'Not a bad idea.'

She ignored him and started on her arguments. 'I'm going back to work tomorrow. I need to get home and sort my stuff out.'

'I don't think you should. You're still pale, you look exhausted.'

'And who's to blame for that? You think I'm going to get much sleep here?'

'What if I promise not to touch you?'

She threw him a sceptical look. 'Look what happened the last time you promised that. Forty-eight hours later you were ravaging me in the stairwell. I need to get back to work. They'll be getting a temp in to cover for the temp. I want to go, Rory.'

He studied her and she met his gaze squarely. He looked sombre and she knew she had won.

'OK, I'll run you home after dinner.'

'No, I should go now.'

'After dinner.' He spoke abruptly. He looked at her and softened a little. 'I've seen what's in your fridge, remember?'

She decided to quit while ahead.

They barely spoke through the meal. She tried to eat something but her appetite had vanished. She caught him looking at her several times with knowledge in his eyes and, coward-like, she looked away, trying to buy a few minutes' more time before she had it out with him. Despite the frenzied love-making they had just shared her body was starting to ache with want again and she knew she needed to get away from him fast.

They drove across London in silence. His car wasn't too flashy, not a convertible, but big, German and fast with plenty of leg-room. Many women would be wowed. She wasn't. She didn't like thinking of him wowing the ladies as she'd joked that first night. She stared out the window, her mind absently ticking off the sights, her heart, for once, not in it. It was occupied by something else. The big, tall hunk of a man next to her she was determined to reject.

He pulled up in front of the estate. He turned the engine off. She made no effort to move. They sat in silence. Her brain whirred.

Finally he looked at her and sighed. 'Go on, then, say it.'

'Say what?'

'Whatever it is that's been on your mind all evening.'

She stared at him and then focussed ahead on the motorbike parked outside one of the ground-floor units. He was right, time to say it.

'I wanted to say thank you for being so good to me while I was sick.'

'And?' he prompted. He wasn't making things any easier.

'And I really appreciate it, I do. And I wanted to thank you for...' she faltered as she searched for the words '...for giving me such a great weekend.' She could feel the heat from her blush on her cheeks. This was ridiculous; she sounded like a schoolgirl thanking her best friend's parents for a nice trip to the movies.

'But?' he prompted again.

She grimaced at his ability to pick her mood so easily. 'But I don't think we can continue this any further.'

'What?' he asked.

She turned and looked at him. 'We go back to being work colleagues tomorrow,' she said firmly. 'Nothing more.' The fatal words were uttered and she felt her heart shatter into a million pieces.

CHAPTER EIGHT

INCREDIBLY Rory laughed. He threw his head back and laughed, really hard. 'You're kidding, right?'

Lissa stared at him, shocked.

He sobered and stared back. 'You're serious.' The wonder in his tone did nothing for her confidence. A smile twitched at the corner of his mouth. 'Lissa, don't you get it? It's too late. The volcano's erupted, the dam's burst, the horse has bolted. The genie is out of the bottle—'

'Enough with the clichés.' she interrupted sarcastically.

He carried on, ignoring her. 'There's no going back. We're on a runaway train, darling. There's nothing you can do but hang on for the ride.'

And wait for it to crash? No, thank you. She inhaled deeply and spoke sharply. 'Stop it. Next you'll be talking in management speak. All about low-hanging fruit and synergy.'

'Well, we do have the most amazing synergy.' He sighed. 'Lissa, you can't be serious. We've just had the most incredible weekend together. I know you haven't wanted to talk about it, but you can't deny it. This isn't just anything. This is special. Why can't we enjoy it while it lasts?'

For once it was panic rather than lust speeding up her pulse. 'Rory, it was just great sex.' She stared at the motorcycle. How could she ever have thought this was going to be easy? This was Rory, champion charmer and people manager.

'That's bull and you know it.' He seemed to be going for the less charm, more honest approach. 'We made love, Lissa. Your words. Remember?'

She gulped and tried to ignore the direct hit. She couldn't let it work. 'No, Rory, it finishes. You know you're the same. You never blur the line between your private life and your professionalism.'

'Professionalism?' He swore sharply. 'This is crazy. You're wanting to throw this away on some temp job?'

She clenched her teeth together. The panic receded and anger ran icily through her veins. He thought it was just some temp job, did he?

'Yes, I am,' she said coldly. 'Because that temp job is important to me.'

She saw anger flash in his eyes. 'Don't you think it's just a little too late for this?'

'It's never too late. These things can be contained. It was a fling, Rory, that's all.'

'Really?' His eyes glittered and she realised she'd just made him very, very angry.

Before she could move he'd leaned across and pressed his lips to hers. Not hard and fierce, but gentle and tender. Taken by surprise, she let her guard slip. Her mouth softened and, oh, so skilfully he parted her lips with his tongue, slowly deepening the kiss. It was beautiful. Absurdly she wanted to cling to him. Why did he have to make this so hard? He lifted his head, his eyes still flashing fire.

She looked back at him, willing the silly tears in her own eyes to disappear. The awful tiredness had returned and she just wanted to crawl off into bed. With him, but that was something she could barely admit to herself.

'Why do you want to stop this?' he asked softly, and she closed her eyes against the desire she saw in his and summoned the anger and hurt she'd felt in the past.

'Just because you're my boss at work doesn't mean you can boss me about here. You don't call the shots.'

She heard his sharply indrawn breath. 'Now, hang on, Lissa. It really bothers you, doesn't it? The fact that I'm your boss.'

She clenched her teeth. The whole thing bothered her. How had she let this happen? She beat her head back on the headrest of the car seat.

'Look, if it makes you feel any better I can arrange it so we're not assigned to the same team again. I won't be your direct manager.'

It was like Grant all over again. She couldn't stop the barrage.

'You think that makes it OK? That it's fine that you can rearrange my career for me? That who I get to work with, or what project I'm on, is down to you. That my work options are limited because of an affair that we're having?' She'd had one boss who had unfairly controlled her employment options. She refused to have another.

'Well, what would you have me do, Lissa?'

'The situation is impossible. It will never work. We stop this thing now.' The anger was all to the fore now; she could ignore the icy pain in her chest.

'So you're telling me that for as long as we're working together we can't *be* together.'

'That's right.'

He stared down at her thoughtfully. 'OK, beautiful, have it your way.' His face had hardened and remoteness replaced the tenderness in his eyes.

She opened the door and stepped out into the chilly night only just catching his low murmur, 'For now.'

She trudged up to her door feeling as if she'd just ripped out her heart, stuck it in a Ziploc bag and shoved it in the bottom of the freezer.

Rory strode down the corridor unable to stand it any longer. He hadn't seen her for two days and it was killing him. He'd purposely avoided the information centre. She obviously needed time to cool off and think about things. Maybe the weekend had been too overwhelming. It sure had blown him away. Maybe they should have talked about things earlier instead of leaving it till that car ride home. But he'd known she hadn't wanted to talk much and, to be honest, nor had he. He'd just wanted to go with the moment and had hoped that every time they'd made love she had sunk deeper into his web as he had hers. Magic—no other word for it. But doubt gnawed at him. For the first time in his life he felt uncertainty. He couldn't see where this was going. Wasn't sure he wanted to. All he knew was that he wasn't ready for it to end. Not yet.

His gut tightened. But what about her? Could she switch off just like that? Maybe it had just been a weekend of wild sex and nothing more. Maybe it *was* all over as far as she was concerned. She pushed him away at every corner.

He thought back to that parting kiss. She'd wanted more then. No, he couldn't believe it was finished, but he needed to know for sure she still wanted him. He stopped off at the Gents on the way to calm down and get a grip. He couldn't exactly just march in, grab her and kiss her senseless even if that was all he wanted to do. He stared at his reflection in the mirror. Something was bugging her. She'd said she didn't like being talked about. That was why her behaviour was usually so circumspect in public. He grinned; she wasn't quite so circumspect when she was dealing with him. In public or private. She couldn't seem to stop herself from reacting to him—teasing him as much as he loved to tease her. He got to her and he needed to play on that for all he was worth.

She hated that they worked together. Hated that he was her boss. He frowned. She hadn't been impressed when he'd suggested he arrange it so they were no longer on the same team. Too late to change things now, but he was sure she'd be pleased when she learnt what had been done. And at least it removed that particular obstacle.

The fact was he wanted to spend more time with Lissa. And not just time in bed. She was beautiful, smart, funny and he loved the way she teased him. He loved the way she laughed at his lame jokes. He found her zest for life intoxicating. She was fun to be around.

And then there was the sex. Spectacular. He'd known she was passionate but, flu or not, she was amazing. Every waking moment of that weekend she'd been at him. It made him want to throw his head back and roar like a lion. It made him want to stake his claim big time. He wanted to go exploring with her. He wanted to tag along on her tourist outings. Laugh with her about being ripped off by ice-cream vendors in Italy. He couldn't believe she hadn't been to Florence. He wanted to take her there. Stand with her when she saw Botticelli's Venus for the first time, wink with her in front of Michelangelo's David. Drink wine, eat lots and make love morning, noon and night. It was as if he'd come home to a holiday romance.

His heart beat faster with every step nearer her desk. She was looking magnificent in a red suit, the jacket buttoned up. She'd swept her hair back into a severe style, the golden tresses locked away. He grinned. She looked the *über*-professional ice queen. She would. She didn't look up as he approached. Only when Gina said, 'Hi, Rory,' did her head fly up. He watched her intently. No mistaking the flash of fire in her eyes. She quickly dampened it but he took perverse satisfaction in watching a slow tide of colour rise in her cheeks. An uncomfortable silence prevailed.

'How can we help you?' Gina finally broke it.

He thought about his reply a second, wishing he'd had the nous to actually think up an information request before charging up here.

Lissa suddenly stood. 'I'm going to sort out those CDs,' she muttered.

Rory wasn't sure to whom. She marched down to the other end of the room behind the book stacks to where the search computers were. So she wanted to get away from him did she? Tough. He couldn't help but watch her as she moved. Her red skirt ended just above her knee. He mentally slid a hand under the skirt, imagining the stockings and suspenders he knew he'd find underneath. He drew in a sharp breath and studied the painting on the wall nearest him. Geometric blocks of colour sploshed haphazardly over a white canvas. Thank God. A nude or even a still life with ripe, round fruit would have been a problem. He needed to think neutral thoughts or he'd be in big trouble.

Equilibrium restored, he turned to follow Lissa. He found her viciously shoving CD cases back into their respective shelves.

'You know—' he forced himself to speak lazily '—for someone who wants to avoid attracting gossip, you're going the wrong way about it.'

She didn't look up. 'If you're wanting some information, Gina can help.' Her hands continued sorting the CD-Roms.

'I don't want information.'

She hesitated. 'Then—'

'I want you,' he interrupted. He watched happily as she stood breathing shortly in front of him. Puffed from handling a few CD cases? No, that was him; this thing between them. Electric. How it had always been. He stepped closer, she didn't move away.

'I missed you.' He spoke honestly. He didn't know

what else to do. He saw indecision on her face and offered a smile.

'Rory, please.'

She didn't smile back; if anything she looked more distressed. Then he recognised it—fear.

After a couple of false starts he managed to say the words he hoped would reassure her. The words he meant with all his heart. 'I'm not going to hurt you.'

Her lashes swooped down, hiding her response.

He didn't know if it had been a dumb thing to say. He waited another second, watching the tide of colour in her cheeks flow and then slowly ebb.

She opened her mouth and suddenly he knew he didn't want to hear what she was going to say. He put his fingers on her lips and before he could stop himself he swooped and stole a quick kiss. It blossomed immediately. His heart thundered. He felt her soften and he swore he heard a soft moan escape her. His hand lifted to hold her head to his and he felt her tremble. Hurriedly he pulled back. They would go from naught to two hundred in a nanosecond, but not here.

She stared up at him. He watched as emotions warred within her. He decided to relent for now. He'd found out what he needed to. The rest could wait. She'd come to it soon enough. There was no reason they couldn't be together until she left. They needed to have a big talk, preferably one that ended up in bed, but now was not the time.

He smiled at her. 'That was a freebie. Next time you ask. See you 'round, beautiful.'

He turned and walked away, only just winning the

battle not to swing back and take another look at her.
It might only be lust, but she couldn't deny that she had
feelings for him and those feelings would win out. Rory
one, Lissa nil.

Having the most orgasms in her life in a three-day period
had the most unfortunate after-effects for Lissa. It was as
if now she'd been switched on she couldn't be switched
off, walking around in a permanent state of semi-arousal.
It took only the slightest friction or most fleeting thought
of Rory to result in a flood of heat and the mad desire to
go find him, press against him and take him in. She could
only be thankful that their two-week period confined in
a room was over. There was no way she could hold fast
to her resolve if he were in such close proximity. She tried
to concentrate on the information request before her, but
every time someone entered the information centre she
looked up—the original rubberneck.

She tried to blame her struggle for concentration on
the after-effects of the flu, but her heart knew better. She
kept replaying that morning's all too brief kiss with
Rory at the other end of the library. He'd completely
ignored her call to end it. He wasn't giving up on her.
The knowledge made her giddy. He'd sought her out
and proved to her that he could move her. What the hell
was she going to do? The fact that they could have
been seen by anyone wandering in the library hadn't
occurred to him. Maybe the thought of people knowing
they were an item didn't bother him. Grant would never
have taken such a risk. In a perverse way this pleased
her. Here was Rory, the one and only, the guy who

never fooled around in the office, messing with her, Lissa, the temp from New Zealand.

He'd said he wouldn't hurt her and maybe he genuinely meant it. But he would hurt her, whether he meant to or not. She was already hurting and the only thing she could do now was lessen the severity.

Gina and Lissa logged off simultaneously and called into the bathroom to fix their hair and make-up. Lissa refused to spend these last few weeks moping. She was going to go out tonight, drown her sorrows and resurrect her party spirit. She was going to plan some mini-breaks for her last few weekends and see some of the sights and she was determined to enjoy it. She would not let her flingette with Rory ruin her last weeks of tourism.

Gina turned to face her and shook her hair. 'Am I OK?'

Lissa appraised her. She was wearing a baby-blue pencil skirt teamed with a white roll-neck cashmere sweater that hugged her curves in all the right places. She'd applied a soft pink gloss to her lips and brushed her curly blonde bob so it shone. Her blue eyes sparkled and silver earrings hung from her ears. She shone from the inside out. A petite firecracker. 'You're a doll.'

'Yes, but am I a sexy doll?'

Lissa laughed aloud. 'Absolutely. What about me?' She adopted a mock-model pose for inspection, smoothing her hands down the black silk shirt she'd just changed into and down her slim red skirt. She tossed her freshly loosened hair with a feeble laugh.

Gina rolled her eyes. 'Lissa, you exude sex. You've got legs to your armpits, boobs to match, long golden hair and this haughty 'look but don't touch' façade. Now with this flu thing you're all pale and fragile-looking too. It's a killer combo. You're irresistible.'

'Ha!' Lissa snorted. She knew Gina was over-egging it, but her ego needed the boost and she was happy to receive it.

They quickly walked through the cold rain, sharing Lissa's umbrella, and climbed the steps leading into the pub. A nauseous feeling rose as the combined smell of beer, wine and perfume met them at the door and Lissa knew the idea of drowning her sorrows was a dumb one. But nor did she go for pineapple juice. Too many memories there. She opted for cranberry, alone and on the rocks.

Lissa was chatting to a young consultant about bungee jumping in New Zealand when Karl made an appearance. He wandered over to Lissa and surprised her completely by snagging her hand and tugging on it. She looked up at him in query. 'What?' she asked.

'Come here, I've got something to show you.' He pulled her over to a quiet corner and turned her so she stood facing the room and he stood with his back to it.

'Jeez, Karl,' Lissa began. 'What's going on?'

His eyes were dancing, but she noted a steely deter-mination shining underneath. He stood with his hands on his hips, and she could feel the pent-up energy within him.

'You're going to do something about Gina?' Lissa asked.

'Uh-huh.' He nodded decisively.

'What?'

'In my book, actions speak louder than words. I'm going to show her how I feel.'

She watched in amused surprise as he undid the top few buttons on his shirt, opening it just enough to reveal the tight tee he wore underneath. Emblazoned across his chest in bold type were the words 'satisfaction guaranteed'. Subtlety wasn't something that Karl did. She looked back up at him and the giggles burst out of her. 'Perfect.' It was as outrageous as he was, as Gina was. The two beautiful flirts were definitely a dream match.

He grinned wickedly back at her, doing the buttons back up. 'I thought so too. Time to make a move.'

'Go get her.' She laughed. 'But, Karl!' He stopped and looked at her. 'Don't forget we chicks need the words too.'

He grinned and saluted and wandered in the direction of the bar. Lissa looked about, trying to spot Gina. She caught sight of her, cornered by a couple of consultants as usual. Lissa watched with satisfaction as Karl approached her. She glanced away and found herself looking at James, who had somehow appeared right in front of her without her noticing.

'What are you doing standing in this dark corner all alone?'

'Oh.' She didn't know what to say and took a quick sip.

'Waiting for someone?' James asked.

'No, I was just talking to someone, but…' She let her voice trail away. James didn't seem overly interested in her reply. He stared at her. She coloured a little, not sure what he wanted. She held her glass in front of her with both hands, hugging it against her body in an unconsciously protective gesture.

'Seems funny to be back at the usual desk, doesn't it? I miss our little team. It was very illuminating.' He paused and looked her over.

Lissa shifted on her feet uncomfortably. She definitely didn't like the way this was heading.

'There's a whole lot more to you than meets the eye. I miss you, Lissa. I liked sitting near you. You're a pleasure to be around, you know that? A pleasure to look at, a pleasure to talk to, and I bet you'd be a pleasure to kiss.'

Whoa, this was too much. The last thing she needed tonight was a charm offensive from James. Hadn't he got the message the last time he'd asked her out? Obviously not. Maybe he thought the two weeks in close quarters with him had made her radically change her assessment of him? She nearly laughed aloud. She'd barely noticed him. She'd felt nothing but awareness of Rory.

Lissa glanced around, half hoping for a saviour. There didn't seem to be anyone near enough to draw into the conversation; most of the crew were over by the bar. She took another sip of her drink. She'd just have to straighten him out. Trouble was, she knew from past experience he was fairly resilient.

'James, I'm sorry, but—'

'But nothing, Lissa. Come on, give me one date. Come to dinner. Get to know me. You might even be pleasantly surprised.' He gave her a charming, overly confident smile that did nothing for her.

Yes, he was persistent, she'd give him that.

She looked over to where Gina had been and saw that Karl had managed to despatch the two consultants who had been loitering earlier. He had Gina alone and both looked serious.

She looked back at James, trying to get him to listen to what she was saying. 'James, I already know you and you're a nice guy, but I'm not interested.'

He frowned. 'You're not interested.' He said it as if there were something wrong with her. 'How come you don't date anyone? Got a murky past?' He moved closer to her, invading her space.

She tensed. How dared he start prying into her personal life? His arrogance astounded her and she felt it time she made herself understood clearly. She was unable to manage polite rebuff, her emotions too on edge. She opened her mouth to give him a piece of her mind when suddenly an arm snaked around her waist and firmly pulled her back against an extremely taut body. Her own body flared and fitted against it perfectly. Rory. She hadn't even seen him approach. His arm reached right around her and his hand spread wide and firm on her lower abdomen. His other hand reached to her shoulder, holding her back against him length to length. A ripple of awareness shivered through her entire body. He couldn't have adopted a more possessive stance if he'd tried. The shock temporarily robbed her of speech.

'She's seeing me, James,' his voice rasped. Lissa felt his anger and her insides melted. He was jealous.

James stood back and looked them over. 'So I see. I wondered about that, but I thought maybe not.' He took a swig of his drink. 'Still, can't blame a man for trying.'

Rory said nothing and Lissa couldn't think of a thing to say either. The uncomfortable silence hung over them, but James didn't take the hint and move off. Rather he looked at them for a few moments. Malice glittered in his eyes.

'Well, Rory, no wonder you had Lissa ditched from the team.' He spoke with a confident swagger. 'Shame for you, Lissa, missing out on the biggest deal Franklin has seen in years, especially when you helped win the contract. Still, now Rory's free to concentrate on the mega project and have you as recreation on the side, while you're stuck doing the filing or something boring back in the library.'

Lissa felt her jaw go slack. What had he just said? She replayed his words. Their meaning sank in. Rory had ditched her from the project? Back to boring library work? So he could have her on the side?

A wave of shock flooded through her. No, no, no. He wouldn't have done that, would he? It was Grant all over again, controlling her career, manipulating her life for his own purposes.

She needed to get away from him. Away from them both. From the whole damn lot of them. She tensed and made to pull away, but Rory's arm was like a steel band pinning her to him. She turned her head to look up at his face, but he held her so close and tight against him all she could see was the clench in his jaw.

She felt the animosity ignite between the two men.

They were like two lions, circling around the kill. She certainly felt as if she'd been mauled. Why would Rory treat her like that? Just so he could keep sleeping with her? Horrified, she felt tears prickle the backs of her eyes and angrily she summoned control. Icy, icy control. She would not be humiliated like this. Not here, not now.

'Things are never quite that simple, James,' Rory said curtly.

James shrugged. 'If you say so.' He gave Lissa a penetrating look, and with a nasty smile he departed.

Rory's arm didn't loosen one iota.

'Let me go.' Her voice dripped with venom.

'We need to talk.' His jaw still clenched tight, ditto his grip.

'I don't think we do. I don't think there's anything to be said.' She clawed at his hand, digging her nails in, not caring at his wince. No way could that scratch hurt him as much as he had just hurt her. He loosened his arm a fraction and she turned in it to face him. Her body still pressed close against his and she was furious with herself for feeling that rush of desire for him when he'd been such a rat. She breathed heavily and with each inhalation her breasts pressed closer against his chest. She was painfully aware of him, of his heat. His magnetism was such a force that even now she was drawn to him. But her heart was breaking and her head filled with a cold furious pain that drove her to repel him.

His rock hard body matched his expression. 'What—you're just going to believe what that jerk said without even hearing what I have to say?'

'Am I off the team?'

'Yes.'

'So we're not working together. You arranged it so you could keep sleeping with me.'

He paused and his eyes flickered.

He had. Used his position as her boss. Exactly what she'd been afraid of. She pushed both hands against his chest with all her might and broke free. Stepping back, she stared at him, her eyes flashing fire.

He moved after her, lifting a hand to touch her.

She stepped out of reach.

His hand fell. 'Lissa, it's not that simple.'

'I trusted you,' she said lowly.

He frowned. 'This isn't about us, Lissa.'

'There is no us.'

God, would she never learn? Why did she always fall for guys who let her down? Who were all about what they wanted, not caring about her at all. Well, never again. Never, ever again would she let a guy get to her like this. He'd just screwed her over. She turned and headed for the door.

It was impossible to get up much speed through the bar now full of merry patrons. She gave a hurried look over to where Gina and Karl had been but she couldn't see them. She didn't give them a second thought, all she wanted to do was get out of there and lick her wounds.

Maxine from Reception stepped before her, blocking her path. 'What's going on with you and Rory?'

Lissa stopped and stared. She'd forgotten that half the staff had probably been watching their little encounter in the corner and drawing goodness knew what conclusions. 'You really want to know?' she asked shrilly. She wasn't sure quite how it happened, but the noise of the bar had receded completely. There seemed to be nothing but her and Maxine and a constant hum in her own head. Vaguely she saw others turning her way. She couldn't care less. Anger and hurt made her reckless and voluble.

'We had an affair, but it's over now.' Her voice rang clear as a bell. Maxine's eyes widened.

'Wrong, Lissa,' Rory boomed behind her. She spun around furiously to face him. He stood broadly, inches away, legs apart, anger apparent in every muscle. He looked her up and down, raking her body with the heat in his angry glare—a move that only served to enrage her further. Her entire body tensed. It seemed everyone in the room held breath.

'You know damn well it's not over,' his voice drawled through the bar.

For a split second there was total silence. Then there was a collective gasp and a lone wolf whistle.

'Go get her, Rory,' someone yelled.

Lissa stared at him in fury, seeing his pale anger and force of will. And despite it all a trickle of desire was pooling in her belly. She still wanted him. He'd betrayed her and yet her body still wanted to feel his hardness against her.

Disgusted with herself, she turned and ran for it. Pent-up energy gave her speed. Opening the door and flinging down the entrance stairs, she got a good start. The fight-or-flight instinct had kicked in. She was going for both. Her heels tapped as she clattered down the stairs at breakneck speed. She glanced back up. Rory was following three at a time.

'I don't want to talk to you,' she called to him as she started along the footpath. The cold wind bit into her.

'Well, it's about time you bloody did. I want to talk to you.' He advanced closer.

'And it's all about what you want?' she flung back at him. She'd left her umbrella inside and rain was falling in large splats. She increased her pace so she was practically running.

'Lissa, slow down. You'll fall and break an ankle.'

Indignation burned. 'I can run a marathon in these heels.'

'Fine, but not tonight.'

He caught up to her, grabbed her arm and pulled her to a stop. She jerked her arm out of his hand. He stared at her, his jaw clenched. People moved to avoid where they stood in the middle of the footpath.

'Still care about what other people think, Lissa?'

'You know what, Rory?' she yelled in his face, ignoring the interested stares of the passers-by. 'I couldn't care less. What I care about is being used.'

'Finally some honesty,' he yelled back. 'So let's forget about the audience and sort this mess out.'

She hardly heard him as she berated herself, her hands fisting at her chest. 'God, I promised myself I wouldn't do this again. How could I be so trusting and *stupid*?'

He stared at her in silence, waiting for her to continue.

'I should have known you would let me down. It was just a matter of how.' She stood before him, getting wetter as the rain fell, watching as the defence leapt in his eyes and he took breath.

'Lissa, listen to me.' Calm, coaxing.

She closed her eyes and forced her blood to freeze. She would not be manipulated by him.

'What James said wasn't even close to the truth.'

'You wouldn't know what the truth is, Rory. Let alone be able to tell it.'

He flinched, his hands fisted, not quite so calm now. 'Lissa, you're tired and overwrought and being completely irrational.'

'I am not irrational.' No way was she going to let him play the 'you're an irrational female' card. One sign of tears and they thought a woman was all out of control. Typical.

'Yes, you are. You won't even listen to me.'

'It wasn't your place to take advantage of your position. To take advantage of me,' she overrode him furiously.

'I did not take advantage of you and you know it,' he flung back, his voice betraying that he was as angry as she.

She stared back at him. No, he hadn't. She'd been as willing as he had. What a fool she'd been. She'd given in to temptation and lost her heart in the process and now she was paying the price.

'You don't get it, do you? You just organise things the way you want them. I told you we couldn't be together while you were my boss and so you just rearrange my job without any regard to how it might impact on me. Maybe I would have liked the extra hours, maybe the money would have come in handy when I go home. All that matters to you is maintaining your source of hot sex!'

'Lissa, you are so far off base.' The words flew out, demanding her attention. 'The decision was made well before you said that to me, Lissa. George decided last week after the meeting with the client.'

'Last week? George?' She wasn't buying it. He wasn't going to charm his way out of this with his brilliant eyes.

'Lissa, I knew you were gutted about being taken off the Portuguese project; Hugo told me. When debriefing with George the other day it was agreed that, as this project is long-term and the Portuguese is about to wrap, it would be better for Gina to take on the new one and send you back to the other. That way there is better continuity. It was George who suggested it, and George who decided. I just agreed. I think he wanted you to get the Bilbao trip. And I wanted you to have it. I know how much you'll love that gallery.'

She stared at him. Hearing the words. Blinking as they sank in. 'Bilbao?'

'Yes, the weekend bonus, remember?' He glared at her.

Hell, she'd forgotten about it. All disappointment of missing out had been obliterated in the heat and storm of her affair with Rory. Three weeks ago she'd have been moon-walking with delight over the prospect, now it felt hollow.

A raw energy poured off Rory as he continued to enlighten her. 'I think you're just spoiling for a fight and I'm fairly sure I know why. You want to push me away? Fine, but be honest about it. Don't use this as an excuse.' His words whipped, his frustration unmistakable as he stood like a warrior charged and ready for action.

Her shoulders slumped as the fight drained out of her. He was right. She'd been wrong. He hadn't abused his position. In fact he'd been on her side. But it made no difference to their relationship. She was too scared, too hurt and hopeless. Humble pie time. 'I'm sorry for blowing up at you before giving you a chance to explain.'

She stared at him, committing his features to memory; despite the blur of the rain she saw him more sharply in focus than ever before. His height, the dark springy hair and the brilliant eyes that right now were glittering with a fire that had several sources of fuel.

It had to be over. She was leaving. The heartbreak now would be nothing to what it could be. With a final, soft, 'I'm sorry,' she turned and, heedless of the rain or the fact her shoes probably weren't going to make it, started the walk home.

CHAPTER NINE

LISSA had only walked half a block when the black cab pulled alongside her, its engine low as it slowed to keep pace with her. Then it paused just ahead and the door flung open.

'Get in. You want pneumonia or something?'

She stared at Rory as he sat forward, like a jungle cat ready to leap and pounce. His peremptory command was an audible expression of his grim tension. He was still angry. He was still gorgeous.

Her heart thundered, the heat in her body rose, despite the cool, wet air. She hated that she wanted him so much, it just didn't make things any easier. 'Just a ride home.' Utterly unable to resist the order in his eyes, unable to resist her need to spend time with him—even five more minutes.

He shrugged and sat back as she bent to step into the cab.

She perched on the edge of the seat feeling more than a little humiliated. She winced as she recalled the words they had traded in front of the entire bar. 'I'm sorry if I embarrassed you in front of everyone tonight.'

'You didn't embarrass me. I'm happy for the world to know; half the population will be dead jealous. But I admit to being surprised—for someone who once said she wanted private, you picked a hell of a way to go public.'

His gaze slid over the damp blouse clinging to her. She was grateful for her jacket—although unbuttoned, at least it covered her hard and aching nipples. She felt anger at her unrelenting desire for him. His attention then dropped to the edge of her skirt. She pressed her knees together, wanting to stop the excitement. He still looked ferocious, but in a wickedly wanting way. She turned her head to stare out the window, unwilling to look at him. Not wanting to be tempted all over again. *Focus.* 'I don't care what they think, Rory. That wasn't why I said no to you at the start.'

'No.' There was a tiny pause. 'So why did you?'

'I didn't want to get involved with you because we work together, more than that you're my boss, and one thing I learnt the hard way was not to get romantically involved with someone you work with.'

'How learnt the hard way?'

'My mother had an affair with her boss when I was sixteen. She thought she was getting love, marriage, the works. But he was just using her. I last spoke to her as she was driving home after he ended it with her and she lectured me, told me not to make the same mistake. She had the accident five minutes later. Of course, when I was older, I made the same mistake.'

'Fell for your boss?'

She nodded, looking back at him. 'Pathetic, isn't it?

My graduate job. He pursued me, flattered me. Told me to keep it a secret from the others because he didn't want me getting flak from them about favouritism. We never went out in public. I didn't really notice or question why—I was just enjoying thinking I had someone. Someone who loved me, who would care for me. I'd been alone for so long. I was so naïve.'

'He was married?'

'About to be. When I finally found out I was horrified. I tried to end it but he got nasty. He started giving me all the donkey work, the boring assignments, harassing me when no one else was around. In the end the easiest thing to do was leave. I'd made the exact mistake my mother had and I vowed not to do it again. Then I met you.'

He looked serious. 'I'm not either of those guys, Lissa. I've always been honest with you and I always will be. There's no one else. You know that. Just you and me.'

The cab had been idling outside her flat for at least five minutes now. She had barely noticed. The air crackled between them. The flames in his eyes still burned. *Just you and me.* She felt the softening deep inside, the want, every cell screaming to get closer to him. The anger and pain of moments before transmuted again into the heat of desire. She tried to force it back.

'It doesn't matter, Rory. It can't continue anyway. I'm leaving the country in less than six weeks. I'm sorry for mucking you around.'

'So you still think it's over?'

'It has to be. It's better to end it now.' Knowing that was the last thing she wanted to do, but how else did she stand a chance of saving what was left of her heart?

'Six weeks is ages.'

Yes. Long enough to cause permanent heart damage.

'It would be a mistake.'

'So that's it, then?' A darkness grew in his expression, one she couldn't read.

'I think that would be best.' She couldn't stop the heat coursing through her body. Here she was arguing with the man, trying to end it with him, and yet her body wasn't listening. It was her body wanting to get closer. Aching for his touch.

She broke the invisible bonds trying to draw her to him, turning quickly away and stepping out of the cab. She heard the door slam shut behind her and, without looking back, she raced up the stairs, desperate to get inside and lock the door behind her for fear she'd change her mind and go after him willing to take any last crumbs in these remaining few weeks like the hopeless case she was.

'Know what I think of that idea?'

She whipped around. Only three paces away Rory strode after her. Glancing over the balcony, she saw the cab driving round the corner, passengerless.

He stopped an inch from her. 'I think it's rubbish.'

Her breath came shorter. 'What do you suggest, then?' She stood beside her front door, unable to get the key into the lock, unable to move, transfixed by the passion in his eyes and the heat in her belly.

'I still want you and I'm pretty sure you still want me.'

The way she couldn't tear her focus from his mouth must have been the give-away.

'One night.' Unable to resist, unable to fight the fire

in her body, she capitulated instantly, leaning towards him as she spoke. 'Just one more night.'

'Now.'

'Yes.'

A whisper as the inch of space between them became nothing. No holding back. His kiss was ferocious. She tasted the frustration, anger and want in him. The same frustration, anger and want that she had felt all week.

While still able to, she turned in his arms, forcing the key into the lock and turning it while his arms came around her to rake down her body, pulling her back against him so she felt his tension and rigidity. He stripped her jacket from her shoulders, leaving her damp blouse clinging to her. Waving her arm free of the jacket sleeve, she pushed forward and opened the door. He lifted her from behind and thrust her through the doorway. He stepped after her and had slammed the door behind them before she could take breath. Wheeling in front of her, he pressed her back against the closed door with the full length of his body. She lifted her face and welcomed the hard demands of his mouth, ravishing him with a fierce passion the way he was doing to her. She nipped at his lips with her teeth drawing a vicious thrust from his hips; she panted with pleasure and immediately wanted more. She knew there was going to be nothing slow or leisurely about this merging and nor did she want it that way. She pulled off his tie and fought with his shirt buttons, freeing them and then dragging both shirt and jacket down together so he stood bare-chested against her. He wasn't

having the same ease with her blouse and she heard the
tear of fabric as in frustration he simply ripped it apart.

With fingers made nimble by sheer will she worked
his belt open and his trousers and boxers down, sliding
her hands round to hold his butt and urge him closer to
her.

He yanked up her skirt so it bunched around her
middle and pulled aside the silky strip of her panties with
his strong fingers, his erection pressing against her
wetness.

He lifted his mouth from hers and for a half-second
paused.

'Yes,' she cried. 'Now!'

There were no other preliminaries. With a single,
hard thrust he was there and she arched her neck back
in abandon. 'Yes!'

She curled her leg around his waist and he immediately hoisted her up so she could wind her other leg
around him too. The door and his thighs bore her
weight.

His breathing was harsh and ragged as he continued
to plunder her lips, her neck, her breasts still confined
in their lace scraps. His mouth hot, hungry and unbelievably delightful. He ground into her, deeper, longer.
She knew he was as out of control as she'd ever seen
him and she wanted it even more.

'Harder,' she incited him, 'harder.'

He pounded against her, inside her, with her and she
used her hands, her mouth and teeth to wantonly recip-
rocate as best she could—alternately nipping, sucking,
rocking, driving him to go more powerfully, faster. She

raked her hands across his shoulders, down his back, pulling him closer, ever closer. The door rattled on its hinges as she moaned further entreaties for him to show no mercy, loving the wildness of it, until the ferocious and primitive mating resulted in a climax, the noisiest and sweatiest she'd ever experienced.

Utterly lax and sated, she rested against the door, still supported by him. His heart thundered beneath her palm and she used her thumb to brush aside a trickle of sweat from his hair-dappled chest. He'd buried his face in the side of her neck and she felt his hot, laboured breath blowing against her.

'Are you OK? Did I hurt you?' He lifted his head to look at her.

'No. I'm more than OK.' She opened her eyes and smiled at him through lips that were swollen with passion. 'That. Was. Fantastic.' She closed her eyes again, feeling thoroughly replete. For now the devils were well and truly chased away, the stress of the last week physically worked out of her. 'Feel better?'

She heard his sigh. 'Hell, yes. Will be even better when we're curled in bed together.'

'I might need you to carry me there. I don't think I have the energy to move.' Or the will. It was so nice being held by him, still part of him, locked in his arms.

'OK, beautiful. But I need to rest you here for a second. I've still got my shoes on and my trousers round my ankles. If I try to walk we'll both end in a heap on the floor.'

With a half-laugh she unhooked her legs from his waist and he eased her down a little so she could stand.

Leaning back, she watched as he quickly kicked off his shoes and stepped from his trousers, leaving them in a dark puddle on the floor together with the rest of the clothes they had managed to remove. Then with a mischievous grin he leant forward and caught her round her middle, swinging her up over his shoulder so she hung upside down over his back.

'Hey, what am I? Your snowboard?'

He laughed. 'Hell, no, you're a lot more fun to ride.'

Her mouth fell open at his cheek and then she realised she was in a perfect position to assess the quality of his other cheeks, and reaching down, she gave him a playful pinch. 'Huh!'

His chuckles didn't abate. After five paces he laid her on her bed and with gentle hands undid her skirt and freed her from the rest of her clothes.

'Now that we've addressed the raging inferno, let's get back to the slow burn shall we?' He traced his hand slowly, softly down her body and unbelievably she felt the flicker all over again.

'Just for tonight.' She turned into the curve of his warm body and he lifted her to lie on top of him, his fingers gently tracing patterns down her back. She blankcted her body over his and slowly, lazily stroked him, soothing the marks she'd left on him in the passion of moments before.

Holding her head away for a moment, he smiled at her. 'Let's take it one day at a time.' Then with a simple kiss he obliterated all argument from her mind.

She woke early. Alone. She tried to block the immediate stab of pain in her heart. He'd understood then—

one last night only. She doubted her ability to see out the last few weeks at Franklin's. He was far too much of a temptation and she knew he meant a whole lot more to her than just a fling. He had been right last night when he'd accused her of wanting to push him away. Of course she did because she wanted more than an affair. She wanted for ever. And that wasn't going to happen. It had never been on the cards. He'd said six weeks was ages. Ages for their affair to burn itself out? For him maybe, but she had the sinking feeling it would take a lifetime or more for her. At least by ending it now she could start the long, slow road to recovery. Maybe she should investigate a final trip to Europe for these last few weeks. She sank deeper into the bed, for the first time ever finding the idea totally unappealing.

The key turned in the lock. She sat up, the sheet clutched to her as, round-eyed, she watched Rory stride in with several overloaded supermarket bags.

'I know what's in your pantry and, unlike you I cannot live on cereal alone.' He calmly set about stocking her tiny kitchenette with fresh coffee and a brand new stove-top caffetiere. Croissants followed, together with cheese and ham to fill them as well as raspberry jam. A couple of litres of fruit juice—one being pineapple, she noted. He was good, she had to admit it.

He tossed the Saturday paper on the bed. 'Rest up, you need it. You still look off colour.'

'How long are you planning to stay?' She finally found her voice still worked.

'At least 'til you've had something decent for breakfast. Got your energy back.' He winked outrageously.

Her cheeks burned. Her mushed-up heart started its crazy pulse again. She knew she just wasn't going to be able to help herself.

Later he dressed again, ready to leave, telling her to stay the afternoon in bed. 'I need to get home and get changed. Have dinner with me tonight. I'll cook. I'll pick you up at six. Don't forget to pack an overnight bag and bring some good walking shoes. I've got a great sightseeing trip planned for you tomorrow.'

She gaped at him. 'Last night was our one last night, Rory.'

'No. One day at a time, remember?'

Awfully, it wasn't that she couldn't say no to him; she couldn't say no to herself. Even worse was the fact that she couldn't chalk it all down to lust either. It wasn't only the sex. She liked walking with him, talking with him and, most of all, the laughing. When he smiled at her, the warmth it brought to her heart was like the most addictive drug—his company something she couldn't get enough of. Oh, yes, she'd fallen for him big style.

She thought of her mother and for once didn't think of that final heartache of what had happened with her boss. Instead she thought of her mother's love for her father. And how she'd explained it to Lissa, how she had got through the months of grief after he'd died. How she had repeated to her the old saying—'better to have loved and lost than never to have loved at all'. And she knew she couldn't give Rory up. Not even for her own well-being. Not until she was forced to.

* * *

Sunday night, after a day together that Lissa wanted to burn into her memory, he said he wanted to spend the night at her flat. She felt unsure about turning up to work together the next day.

'Well, everyone knows, Lissa—what difference is it going to make?'

None. He was right, of course. Theirs wasn't the only affair going on in the office and certainly wouldn't be the last. And he'd said himself it was one day at a time, no looking to the future. There was no future. In a few short weeks she would be flying out of the country for good.

No one batted an eyelid when they walked out of the lift together at the start of the day. And when he stopped by her desk at the end of the afternoon wanting to know what time she'd be free to go home, Gina answered for her.

And she just couldn't say no.

By Thursday they were well into a routine—a night at hers, a night at his—and Lissa felt stirrings of panic. She was merely digging a deeper hole to bury herself in at the end of this affair. Anxiety began to gnaw at her, her stomach flipping and churning, and an overwhelming tiredness started to pull her down.

'You not getting enough sleep, Lissa?' Gina asked with a coy smile as they munched on their cereal together while waiting for the computers to log on.

Lissa frowned, pushing away her cereal, her appetite lost. She knew the faint blue shadows under her eyes were darkening with each day. Frankly she felt awful, but put it down to the increasing stress she was under. Stress both caused and relieved by Rory. The best parts of her life at the moment were those spent with him. Where, without realising it, he made her forget the impending end, using either his charm and humour, or his physical skills. 'I think it's just the flu is taking longer to get over than I thought it would.'

She couldn't shake the tiredness. During the day she wanted nothing more than to curl up and snooze—she even dreamed of doing so under her desk. But at night things were different. She couldn't get enough of Rory. From the moment they walked in the door to the moment they left again the next day for work they were together, in every sense of the word.

Rory put some coffee on first thing Friday morning— he liked a hit before walking out the door. Lately he'd been having two. Lissa usually had one too, but not today. The smell was abhorrent. Nauseating. Bile rose. She left for the bathroom in a hurry, only just making it. Wiping her face down with a cold flannel after to try to stop the shaky feeling. She grimaced away the horrible taste and brushed with extra amounts of toothpaste.

'Lissa, are you OK?' He knocked on the door. No space, no let-up.

'I'm fine.' Her legs trembled. She took some deep breaths to restore calm. She stared at her pale reflection in the mirror and tried to remember what she'd eaten the day before. Could it have been the coronation chicken sandwich at lunch yesterday? That would be it.

She left the bathroom to face his intense scrutiny. He pulled upright from the wall he'd been leaning against and took her chin in his hand, tilting her face, his all-seeing eyes inspecting every aspect of her expression.

'I'm really OK.' She laughed it off, blaming the hapless sandwich.

'You shouldn't go to work.'

'I'm fine to go to work. It's all gone now, believe me!'

After another thoughtful look he relented and drove her there, her hand held in his the entire journey.

Once at work the nausea returned and unable to concentrate, she muddled about all day, barely able to cover it up. Fortunately Rory was in meetings all day. Come home time, however, he took one look at her pallor and the circles under her eyes and drove straight to his flat, abandoning the plan for drinks at the pub with the company.

Once back at his flat he bundled her into his warm, welcoming bed. She fell into it gratefully, pulling at him to join her.

He held back for a moment. 'You're still unwell.'

'I'm tired, that's all. And never too tired for this.' She ran her fingers across his jaw, feathered them down his neck and fell asleep in his arms half an hour later.

She had felt exhausted, yet at four a.m. she woke, her mind clearer and sharper than it had been for days. She remembered she'd left her toilet bag at her flat. Not too much of a problem as she now had a spare tooth-brush and other items in Rory's bathroom cupboard.

But that wasn't what had jolted her awake. It meant she didn't have her pill with her.

Her stomach started churning again as she lay in the darkness, listening to Rory's even breathing, feeling the weight of the arm he'd snaked around her to hold her close. It rested on her belly. And a female certainty settled in her as she listened to what her body told her. Trouble of the lifelong kind.

CHAPTER TEN

SATURDAY morning Lissa pleaded exhaustion, which was no lie, having not slept another moment since waking in the wee small hours. Reluctantly Rory agreed to them spending the night apart.

'You call me if you need me.'

She slipped to the pharmacy and within five minutes of getting in the door again she had her fears confirmed.

The blue lines appeared immediately. Not just the control line, but the line giving visual proof of what she already knew. One of the new tests so sensitive it could give a positive result even before your period was due.

She slumped on her bed. How in the hell was it possible? It wasn't possible. She hadn't missed a pill. She checked the packet to be sure—all were missing where they should be. This just couldn't be right.

His words came back to her—'one day at a time'. This was a fling with the temp who was leaving the country shortly. No strings, no commitment. Merely a wild fling for the fun of it. A 'distraction'—for him anyway. There'd probably be another temp to fill her place in a few weeks.

It wasn't serious. It never had been. It has never been meant to be anything long-term. Lissa knew this. Her mother had spelt it out clearly. Grant had proved it. Why on earth had she set herself up for this again?

Rory had said he wasn't like those guys—that there was no one else in his life. And while that was true it didn't mean he was any more serious than they had been.

What would he do? Would he walk away? Would he accuse her of trying to trap him? She told him she was on the pill and she was. It had been no lie.

She did the second test.

The nausea returned and she raced to the bathroom. She smacked her forehead with the palm of her hand in anger, raking her fingers through her hair and pulling hard on it. How could she have made this mistake? Sure, she'd been thinking about a farewell fling—but her boss? She'd known it was a dumb move but she hadn't been able to resist the lust. And now look where it had got her. In a few weeks she would be homeless and jobless. Returning to a country in which she had no family to speak of. And to cap it all off she was pregnant.

She inhaled deeply. Her mother had survived an accidental pregnancy and done a great job of bringing her up—and that was as a teenager. At least Lissa had a few more years on her side. Shame she didn't have any more sense. Now she had gone and done the one thing her mother had warned her of. Not once but twice. The first time it had only been her job she'd lost. This time, the price was far higher.

Her thoughts returned to Rory. Terrified of his reaction, she debated when to tell him. Whether to tell him.

She blanched.

No, she had to tell him. But not yet. She couldn't face it just yet. Besides, it was so early. She should leave it a few days and retest. Maybe it was wrong. Could you get false positives?

Emotionally drained, she dragged herself back to her bedroom and collapsed in a heap. Every old fear and doubt crowded in on her, rushing back, stronger than ever. Exhausted, she lay awake all night, lonely and at a loss.

It felt as if the next few days were a year in the passing. Each hour seemed to take for ever. She frequently went to the toilet, hoping she was wrong. Trying to hide how bad she felt from him, but unwilling to spend time apart because everything felt right again when she was in his arms. It was her sole source of comfort; weak as she was, she couldn't help herself. Despite her fears of how he would react when he found out, despite knowing their affair was going nowhere, she couldn't stay away from him. And she hated herself for it. But she couldn't fight the need, couldn't fight the fact that she just wanted to be with him for as long as she could.

And she couldn't help but recall the photos she'd seen in his album that first weekend they'd had together. The images of the emerald-eyed boy who had had such a gorgeous smile and broad shoulders even then. And she dreamed of what their own child would look like— would it be a junior Rory? Would it have those beautiful eyes? And she couldn't help but hope for yes.

But Rory was no fool. He saw how tired she was, how much of a battle it was to eat.

Finally he challenged her. 'I think you should see a doctor.'

'No!' The vehement refusal rang out.

He gave her a sharp look.

'It's just a tummy bug or something.' She winced at the pleading note in her voice.

'If it's a bug you should be over it by now. It's been more than a few days.' He was right. He knew it and she knew it.

It was impossible to mask how terrible she was feeling. Another week had passed. She'd retested. Same result.

She worried more. For the future and frantically about how she should tell Rory. She knew she had to, but she just couldn't bring herself to do it. Terrified of his reaction. Unable to bear the anger and scorn she'd certainly face. But, most of all, terrified of where this news would take them. She finally found the strength to pull away from him. She'd better get used to it after all.

She spent two nights home alone, telling him she just needed some rest and would be better in no time. She walked along her favourite riverside walks, looking at the buildings she loved, trying to recapture the excitement of being a foreigner in London and the love of life before Rory. She went to the Tate to escape into art, but only had the energy to sit and watch the people go by. And she watched them, the couples, the families, the friends, and the fear simply wouldn't go away.

The third day, after a gruelling few hours at work she left early. Back at her flat she'd just flushed away another bout of sickness when she heard the knock at the door. Only one person knocked like that. She quickly brushed her teeth and scrubbed at her face. The second she opened the door he brushed past her into the main room looking less than pleased.

'You've just been sick again, haven't you?'

She stared at him. How could he be so acute? He'd only just walked in the door.

'You look pale and your eyes are all watery.'

Definitely watery; they had been for a few days now.

'Here.' He handed her a paper bag.

'What is it?'

Sighing, he took it from her and pulled out a blue rectangular box.

Her eyes widened. A home pregnancy test.

'I think you should do it, Lissa.' He spoke softly, his expression serious.

'No.'

'Come on. I've seen my sister go through three pregnancies; I know the signs.'

Her blood turned to ice. He wasn't looking at all happy. In fact, he wasn't looking at her at all. He stared at the box he held, drumming his fingers on the top of it. All her fear came rushing to her. Every reaction she'd imagined came to her—all of them bad. Did he think she'd done it on purpose? That she'd lied to him about being on the pill? Would he hate her? Would he walk away?

'No.' She couldn't do it.

'Lissa, it'll probably be negative; you said you were on the pill. Why not take the test, just to eliminate it?'

'I don't want to.' She turned away from him, unwilling to watch the scorn she knew would flash in his face. Her hands twisted together and she tried to grow courage.

'Why not?'

She bent her head. 'I don't need to. I already know.'

His sharp inhalation spiked her adrenaline higher. 'Know what?'

She turned back to him, like the condemned refusing the blindfold, unable to resist witnessing her own execution. Her words dropped heavily between them. 'I'm pregnant.'

He stood stock-still, staring at her. She could hardly meet his gaze but was determined to, bracing herself for the explosion.

'How long have you known?' Soft, so soft it hurt more than if he'd yelled. A whisper of disbelief.

'A few days.'

'How many?' Not quite so soft now.

She coughed. 'I'm not sure; a few.'

He stared at her and she knew he saw through her, knew she'd known for a while. 'And when—' he stopped and cleared his throat '—when were you going to tell me?'

She couldn't answer that one. She didn't know.

'*Were* you going to tell me?'

'Y-yes.' Even to her own ears it sounded hesitant.

'Or not! What were you going to do—just skip the country and have my child thousands of miles away without ever telling me?' She watched as his anger grew. Knowing he was wrong but not knowing how to fix it. He stepped closer and his voice dropped. 'That's assuming you were planning to have it.'

'What? Yes, of course!' Tears, never far away, flashed in her eyes and out of defence her own anger was stoked. 'Of course I am having this baby.'

'So are you going to start taking care of yourself, then?' He swore loud and long and paced the tiny room. 'Are you going to let me in on this? Are you going to let me help you?'

He turned on his heel and dug his cell phone out of his pocket. Flicking it open, he pressed a couple of buttons. She watched him, unnerved, and wondering what on earth he was up to. His body spoke volumes. He was livid. She knotted her fingers together and waited.

'Doc? It's Rory. Sorry to bother you again… yeah…fine. Look, who's the best obstetrician you know?… OK… No chance you've got the number?… Great, got it.'

He pressed a button and, open-mouthed, Lissa, watched as he immediately punched in another number. A minute later and it appeared he'd made an appointment for her with some obstetrician for ten the next morning. His high-handedness galled her. He swung back to face her and, heedless of the storm in his eyes, she struck out at him.

'You have no right to do that. You have no right to tell me what to do.'

She had never imagined this.

He stepped up to her, speaking quickly. 'And you have no right to keep the news of my child from me. I don't think you're in much of a position to say no right now, Lissa.'

Silently she took that one on the chin. Fair enough, and secretly she acknowledged a feeling of relief. She did want to see a doctor, talk to one. She had been feeling so awful and she wasn't sure if it was normal morning sickness or not and, after all, it wasn't as if she could ask her mother. She couldn't believe she hadn't thought of arranging it herself. She hadn't been thinking straight. She hadn't really been thinking at all.

He seemed to read her mind and his stance softened. 'You're not alone, Lissa. We're in this together.'

But that she knew to be wrong. She turned away from him. 'I'll go to the appointment.'

She sensed him also turn away to stand against the window bracing his arms against the frame, staring out across the basketball court below. 'We'll get married as soon as it can be arranged.'

'What?' She jerked her head to look at him full on.

'It shouldn't take too much to organise. Less than a couple of weeks, I think. We'll go as fast as we can.' He still stared out the window.

'What?' Her breathing came short and shallow and dizziness threatened to overcome her. She couldn't be hearing this right.

'I'm sorry it's going to be such a rush. We can always have the big party later, but we need to get legal as soon as possible.'

'Rory, I'm not going to marry you. We can't get married!' This wasn't happening. Her brain wouldn't compute. She had never expected this. Never expected him to suddenly take control of her life.

'Well, what did you think would happen? We need to get onto it; we haven't got much time.'

'Rory, we don't have to get married. I would never stop you from seeing your child.' The last thing she wanted was a marriage forced upon him. It could only lead to unhappiness for everybody.

He whirled to face her, his face taut. 'Your visa is close to expiring. We need to make sure you can stay in the country. I want this baby born in the UK.'

Oh, God.

Of course he would. Why hadn't she thought about this? Of course he would never react as she imagined Grant would have. Rory was a different breed entirely. But that didn't make things right. He hadn't asked how it had happened. Hadn't challenged her on whether she really was on the pill. Had he guessed her feelings for him? Did he think she'd set out to trap him?

'No.' She shook her head and backed away. She hadn't done that. She would never be so manipulative. Never use an innocent child like that. She wouldn't use him like that. 'No.'

'Look, Lissa. I'll admit this is a hell of a shock, but the hows and whys don't matter now. What matters is how we deal with it and this is the only way. No child of mine is growing up away from me.'

She felt faint. She wished she knew what he was thinking. Wished he would blow up and reveal himself rather than treating her as if she'd become his latest project to manage.

He stared at her grimly.

She needed space, time to think. For the first time, she truly wanted him gone. She couldn't cope with his presence. 'Tell me where the obstetrician is and I'll meet you there.'

'No, I'm staying here tonight.'

She didn't want him to.

And then he did reveal his thoughts. 'The fact is, I'm not sure I can trust you, Lissa. If I hadn't forced you to admit it, I'm not sure I would ever have known about our baby. That's not a nice feeling.'

Sadness pulled at her. She could understand his view. He didn't trust her and she hadn't felt able to trust him. Their blazing affair was just that, an affair, and she didn't think there was enough depth for them to be able to handle the consequences.

Rory paced across Tower Bridge on the pretext of getting a curry for dinner. He'd left Lissa, knowing she wasn't up to food. To be honest he didn't fancy it himself, but he'd needed to escape for a little bit. Part of him wanted to escape a lot, for good.

He'd just asked a woman to marry him. Hell, he hadn't exactly asked, he'd just told her it was happening. Marriage. Kids.

It had just come out of his mouth with his brain disengaged. It was what he was meant to do, the honourable thing. The only thing a decent bloke could do. Get a girl pregnant, you had to deal with it responsibly. But did he want to? Could he really live with this?

It was supposed to have been an affair. A mind-blowing affair, but an affair nonetheless. He'd always known she wasn't going to be around for long, and when she'd told him six weeks that had seemed just fine. Long enough for it to burn out. So blazing it had to be just lust.

Now the whole thing had been turned upside down completely.

It wasn't the child's fault. But he knew how damn hard work they could be. The nights of sleeplessness, the crying, the nappies. He'd seen the strain his sister had been under. Witnessed the occasional tenseness between her and her husband as they'd negotiated their way through this new development in their relationship. And they were happily married, had been university sweethearts. A love match. This was a lust match.

He walked back across the bridge again. The Tower of London was lit up and mocking him. The former prison now a tourist haven. His own heavenly tourist, Lissa, had just imprisoned him. His well-considered life plan had been beheaded. He hadn't planned for the whole serious settle-down thing to happen for a few years yet.

How the hell was it going to work? Could it work? He clenched his teeth. He'd never failed at anything he'd set his mind to. But setting his mind to this? He wasn't sure he was able to.

Lissa felt the evening pass slow and awkward. He'd come back—after an hour or so in which time she'd agonised over whether indeed he would actually return. Then she'd felt guilty all over again for doubting him when he'd walked back through the door. He'd flicked on her little telly and stared at the screen, apparently uncaring of whatever was showing and effectively ending all conversation. She crept into the bathroom to change into her pyjamas—the only time she'd worn anything in bed with Rory. After a time he switched the television off and slipped out of his clothes, silently sliding into bed but turning away from her.

For the first time they shared a bed but not each other and Lissa had never felt so alone.

CHAPTER ELEVEN

SHE woke early feeling warm and secure. Blinking, she realised Rory had curved around her in the night, his arm around her, holding her. She closed her eyes again quickly, wanting to remain in the quiet half-asleep, half-awake dreamland where the bad things could be forgotten and the blissful things could come true.

He must have been awake because he moved away from her immediately. 'Don't move. I'll get you something.'

He left the bed and soon returned with some plain toast and a glass of water. She nibbled on it. The strained silence grew.

Rory rang work for both of them explaining they'd be late. Rapidly getting used to his managerial ways, she didn't care. That was one she could let him away with.

The silence remained unbroken as he drove them to the doctor's rooms. He parked and turned to look at her as he switched off the engine.

'We'll work this out, Lissa.'

'It doesn't have to be marriage, Rory.' It couldn't be. She would be responsible for ruining his life. She could take care of herself and would manage their child. Her mother had done it, and so could she. She didn't want to be married to a man who wasn't in love with her.

Nervously she sat next to him in the waiting room. She felt appalling—had already been sick twice despite the fingers of dry toast. The doctor appeared and called for her. She stood, mortified as Rory rose as well.

He read her like a book. 'Lissa, I have touched and tasted every inch of your body. I am coming in with you.'

They walked into the consultation room together.

The doctor wasted no time getting her to do another test. She returned with it and he questioned her as they waited for the result. 'So how far along do you think you are?'

'Not very. Maybe a few weeks?'

She sat watching the test, keenly aware Rory's attention was fixed on it too. The confirming line appeared instantly.

'That's a strong positive. There's no doubt you are pregnant.'

'You can't get false positives?' She couldn't help the last vestige of hope.

He smiled and shook his head. 'Not unless you've been on fertility treatment. And you've had severe symptoms already?'

Rory answered that one, detailing her all-day sickness, the fatigue.

'I think we should do a scan. See what we can find there.'

Lissa looked up.

The doctor smiled benignly. 'Just routine. It won't take a minute—be nice to see your baby, won't it?'

She stepped behind the curtain and readied herself on the bed with the modesty blanket provided, quelling the nausea, fighting the anxiety.

The doctor pulled the curtain back and Rory came to stand by her head. Not looking away from her face, he took her hand firmly in his. A reassurance that somehow he knew she needed.

She stared up at him as fear skated through every cell. She wanted this baby to be all right regardless of what happened between her and Rory. This baby would be loved. Unplanned maybe, but certainly not unwanted.

He met her gaze squarely, somberly, his jaw tense, and again she wished she had the ability to read minds. In the past he'd been easy to read, his brilliant eyes telling her of his desire, his frustration, his humour. But now they were clouded, and she couldn't fathom his thoughts at all, let alone his feelings.

'Ah,' the doctor murmured. 'There's the problem.'

Problem. She tensed and felt Rory's hand tighten on hers. She saw the flash in his eyes, but before either could speak the doctor continued.

'Take a look at the monitor.' The doctor didn't sound concerned, he sounded kind of smug. 'There you see a heartbeat.' Lissa stared at the little blob. Kind of like a jellybean with a pulse. Fascinated, she felt her heart pull. A tiny life growing.

She hardly heard as the doctor spoke again. 'And

there—' the doctor pointed across a little way on the screen '—is another.'

For a split-second Lissa stopped breathing, unwilling to understand what he meant.

'Twins.' Rory said it aloud.

'Congratulations.' The doctor beamed.

Not one, but two. Denial burst out of her.

'But I can't be pregnant; I'm on the pill!'

'It can be easy to forget one.' The doctor printed out a picture and then switched the equipment off.

'But I haven't. I didn't!'

He handed the picture to Rory, then looked at her.

'Been on any other medication recently—antibiotics?'

Her head thumped back on the pillow. Antibiotics. For her chest infection. Of course.

'You have.' The doctor smiled at her kindly as he moved to take his seat at his desk again. 'You need to use another form of protection while taking the antibiotics because they can reduce the effectiveness of the pill.'

Lissa nodded dumbly. How could she have been so dense?

Dazedly she righted her clothing before stepping out from the curtain to join the two men. As soon as she sat Rory reached out and took her hand in his. Hers shook while his was firm.

'Are there twins in the family?' The doctor tapped notes into his computer.

'Not that I'm aware of.' Not in her mother's, but she had no idea about her father's.

'Twins are increasingly common. There is some research to suggest that your chances of conceiving twins are higher if you conceive while taking the pill, and also the frequency of intercourse can be a factor.'

She couldn't look at Rory. High-frequency sex, huh? She supposed she should be grateful they weren't having triplets.

She zoned out as the doctor started talking about care for the next few months. Twins. Two babies. Double the work, double the money, *double the fun*—an imp whispered to her. It was Rory who took the information sheets he offered and Rory who asked the questions. She sat in shock. The thought of going through this alone terrified her. She thought she might just handle one; it would be hard, but if her mother had done it, then so could she. But two? At the same time? And she realised her ability to choose her future had been taken away from her. There was no choice.

She sensed the appointment was concluding when she heard Rory quietly ask another question.

'Can we still...uh...?' His voice trailed away. 'I don't want to hurt her, or them.'

The specialist obviously understood the silent bit in the middle. 'Intimate relations won't do anybody any harm, but you might need to get creative a few months down the track because she's going to be very round with this pregnancy.'

He still wanted to have sex with her? He was still interested? Despite the shock and stress a flicker of pleasure surged. She still wanted him too, but the situation had just taken an even more dramatic turn and there was more to a relationship than sex. Even the most amazing sex didn't make a marriage work.

She paid no attention as the next appointment was booked and was quite unaware of how they ended up walking along the footpath back to the car.

Rory breathed in deeply, needing an extra dose of oxygen to help clear his head. Twins. He couldn't believe it. He hadn't wanted to believe she was pregnant at all, not logically—he didn't see how it was possible. But he'd had a feeling in his bones. Was there such a thing as male intuition?

The antibiotics. It felt good to have that explained. He hadn't doubted Lissa, had believed her when she'd said she was on the pill. Figured maybe she'd forgotten it once. Hell, he hadn't really thought about it at all. He was still trying to get his head around the whole idea.

And now there were two.

Double the amount of nappies and noise and half the amount of sleep as one baby. It didn't bear thinking about.

He glanced at her. She was staring down at the footpath, her hand lax in his, not holding him, but not pulling away either.

'Talk to me,' he said.

'I can't believe you asked that.'

'What?' He couldn't stop the wry grin. 'About whether we can still sleep together?'

She nodded.

'Lissa, I fully intend to have sex with my wife. Lots of sex.' My wife. The words seemed to gum up his mouth and he froze. He let go of her hand to run his fingers through his hair and hoped his doubt was masked from her. He'd once told her he wouldn't hurt her and he didn't want to, but he couldn't be sure he loved her. He couldn't be sure he could cope with any of this.

'I've an idea,' she said softly. 'I don't think we should make any big decisions yet. Why don't we just take it one day at a time?'

He blew out a huff of air in relief. He looked at her, wondering if she was as doubt-plagued as him. Of course she was. They needed space to think, to see if there was another solution. One day at a time. Trouble was, there weren't that many days left.

It should have been one of the most exciting weekends of her life. On a plane with a gang of friends from work, off to enjoy an all-expenses-paid weekend in a beautiful city with one of the most incredible buildings in the world to admire—and it housed great works of art. Bliss, right?

The nausea on the plane was only just manageable. She told the others she often suffered from air sickness and it enabled her to sneak to her hotel room early and not go clubbing with the rest of them. Despite the exhaustion she couldn't sleep. The dilemma and doubts raced in her mind. And she missed Rory. Missed the warmth of him, the comfort in his arms despite the chasm that lay between them during the day.

She decided to forgo the shopping trip and head straight to the Guggenheim. Wanting to see it in the bright morning light as well as lit up at the function scheduled for that night.

She walked around marvelling at the curves, the genius melding of glass, stone and titanium. Her digital camera hung uselessly from her wrist; pointless even trying to capture the magnificence and complexity in thirty-five millimetres. As she stared up at the skyline her vision began to wobble. She blinked rapidly to clear it but the dizziness only increased, and then the pain came, knifing into her, and as the blackness swallowed her sight she could only call for one thing. Rory.

It was the longest five hours of his life. He wished he could break into the pilots' cabin and demand they put their foot down, or make the wind blow them there faster or something, anything.

He'd never forget that phone call. The terror, the difficulty in getting air to his lungs. The shock at the realisation that he'd been on the verge of losing the most precious thing in his life.

They'd told him he didn't need to fly over, that they'd get her home OK. But that wasn't OK for him. He needed to see her, needed to be with her, needed *her* full stop. Nothing else mattered.

In the end the woman next to him insisted he take the aisle seat—she obviously couldn't cope with his fidgeting. He went and stood by the emergency exit, pacing in two square feet for the rest of the flight.

He'd so nearly stuffed up. He'd been umming and ahhing when he should have been moving heaven and earth to ensure he got what he wanted.

Lissa. Whole, healthy, his.

How could he have been so uncertain? He couldn't believe it had taken this to make him understand what he wanted. He'd been increasingly anxious; the panic over her looming departure and their situation had rendered him unable to think, unable to see his way through. Now it all came with brilliant clarity. He had been such an idiot. He'd just had the biggest fright of his life and he wasn't chancing it happening again.

She lay on the hotel bed, pale but calm. He fought to maintain an equally calm exterior, but his insides churned.

'It's OK Rory. I'm OK.'

He'd obviously failed to hide his alarm. 'You don't look OK.'

'Just tired, that's all. The doctor said I have to take it easy.'

He knew this. He'd spoken to the doctor just before entering her room. She was exhausted, her body firing a warning shot. Telling her she needed to take things easy. Minimum stress, maximum TLC and she and the babies would be just fine. He nearly maxed out with guilt. The sense of responsibility was huge, and his need to protect her primal.

There was only one way he could ensure it. His gut had spoken for him when he'd first found out she was pregnant. The solution simple. But his brain had interfered and pulled him back, letting doubt in instead of going with the base emotion. Love.

Now he needed to convince her it was the only thing

to do. Marriage, a.s.a.p. And the way to get her to agree was by using the babies and her looming departure as the bargaining chips. He'd make her see the sense of it. He needed to make it OK. It was a huge step, but it was the only one they had. The only one he finally realised he wanted to take.

She looked away from him, out the tiny plane window from which nothing could be seen but the dark night sky. Her pale face was reflected and, despite her physical weakness, he read the determination there.

'I'm sorry I didn't tell you sooner about the pregnancy, but I promise I was going to. I just didn't know when or how. I was scared.'

'Scared of what?' He studied her. Her cheeks were rosier now and she still wouldn't meet his eye. 'What did you think I'd do?'

His heart sank. 'You thought I'd walk away, didn't you? That I'd abandon you.'

She looked around at that and made to speak, but he waved her silent. He could read the look in her eyes and knew she had doubted him. 'When have I ever given you reason not to trust me?'

'It wasn't you. It was the whole…whole situation.'

Sure, the situation was difficult, but the fact was she didn't trust him. He was nothing like her ex-boyfriend, but that didn't matter. She still didn't believe in him. He hadn't got anywhere with her. It hurt more than he cared to consider. Without trust, how could there be love?

He knew things had happened faster for him than

they had for her. He'd fallen for her. He kicked himself for not recognising it sooner. Couldn't believe it had been the thought of nearly losing her completely that had jerked the fact into his consciousness. Events had overtaken him.

But he didn't know if she loved him. Yes, she wanted him; yes, they were compatible on many levels other than the obvious, but did she actually love him or was this merely a hot affair? He had to try regardless.

'Lissa, I want to marry you. We can make this work. It's the only way forward. I can take care of you and the babies. You have to let me.' It was the nearest he could come right now to a declaration. He knew she wasn't ready for him to swear undying love. She wouldn't believe him. Another difficult situation, more bad timing. And frankly he wasn't ready to put himself on the line like that. Not when he really hadn't any idea where her heart lay.

'OK.'

His breath hissed out. His gums were sore from clenching his teeth together so tightly. He'd been so un-certain of her answer. Been so ready to present his case, working through the arguments the entire journey to get her.

But she'd agreed, just like that. Not that she looked that happy about it. He kept himself in check, not reaching for her and loving her as he wanted.

Well, if she didn't love him yet, she would. He would do everything in his power to make it happen. He loved her. She was his and carrying his two children. But he didn't want to scare her off with flowery vows. It was early, early days. No, the way forward was to get the ring on her finger first, and then show her. Once they were married he'd prove to her it was the only thing their hearts would let them do.

Until finding out about the twins she'd refused to contemplate a wedding. He remembered what she'd said at lunch with James and Marnie. She'd said she would only ever marry for love. And that was the problem. She didn't love him. Only now she was backed into a corner. He felt desperately sorry for her. Wanted to scoop her up, protect her, tell her it would all be all right, tell her how much he loved her. But he forced it all to stay inside. He couldn't tell her. Not yet.

She finished at Franklin. He worried about her, alone and isolated in his flat. She'd chatted briefly on the phone to Gina but had told her nothing. He wouldn't have minded if she had—they were all going to find out soon enough and he figured she might need her friend right now. But instead she'd spent the time soothing Gina over some falling-out with her friend Karl.

In only a few days he watched, helpless, as she withdrew. She allowed him to make the decisions with seemingly little interest in what he was deciding, signed the visa application forms without even reading them. Her fatigue worried him, the difficulty she had in finding something to tempt her to eat. Sure, the pregnancy was knocking her around, but he knew it was more than that. He didn't know how to combat her unhappiness.

But in the night when he slid into bed with her, she

turned to him, time and time again. In the darkness, or the semi-light of dawn, she wrapped her legs around him as they came together, the difficulties forgotten in the moments of physical closeness and relief. In those moments he felt she was loving him and he wanted that more than anything.

He looked down at her and saw her eyes were closed. He hated that. Usually she gazed right at him. Made him feel that she was drinking him in with her eyes as well as her body. Letting him see into her warm, generous soul. But now he felt shut out.

He pulled almost right out of her. 'Open your eyes.'

They flicked open, and slowly he re-entered her, gradually plunging as deeply as he could. Holding her gaze, he pulled out again. Intently he watched her as he continued the slow, exquisite torture of being almost all the way out and then all the way in. Emphasising the purpose of them joining, making her see it was him there with her, inside her, longing to be part of her. That they were right *together*, that they were meant to be.

Her eyes widened further, her reddened mouth parted and her hips rose to meet him, to hurry him. He wasn't having it, not yet.

Bending his head, he kissed her with all the intensity and love he felt. He tasted her cry of ecstasy and held her as she trembled, only then willing to release himself.

When he lifted his head to look at her he saw her eyes were closed again. And he couldn't help the feeling that, somehow, he'd lost her.

CHAPTER TWELVE

EXHAUSTED Lissa sat on top of her old pack and tried for what felt like the fiftieth time to pull the zip closed. She'd boxed the books and clothes she no longer wanted and left a sign on them to be taken to the charity store. All she had left was the travel backpack she'd left New Zealand with, a suit bag and her small daypack. She'd come to the flat the instant Rory had left for work and nearly killed herself with the effort of getting it shipshape. They were supposed to be moving her gear from the flat and she would be living with Rory permanently. Things had happened so fast and she couldn't keep up the pretence any more.

This weekend she would be meeting Rory's family for the first time. What a way to be introduced. Here's the girl I got pregnant and now we're having a shotgun wedding. She couldn't bear it.

She had tried to argue they needn't marry in a hurry, but he insisted. Rory the honourable, trapped into a wedding, a lifelong sentence. She had been so wrong to doubt him earlier. He was nothing like Grant. He had integrity, always one to 'do the right thing'.

Oh, sure, he wanted her. The sexual attraction between them was dynamite, but it wasn't enough. It couldn't last, especially under the strain of having not one, but two newborn babies to look after.

At least he hadn't pretended to her. He hadn't used those three little words. He wouldn't. Lying for Rory was impossible. He'd told her once he was an honest person and so he was. Painfully so, Lissa now acknowledged. She would have believed him if he'd said them, simply because she longed for it so much. But they were unsaid. Unsaid because they were unfelt.

I love you.

Rory. And she did. Wholly. And it wasn't the hormones from her pregnancy driving her towards security; she'd known she was sunk since that first weekend they'd had together. For her it wasn't just the fire of passion, it was the warmth of humour, the sunny pleasure of common interests, the glow she felt by spending time with him.

She loved him and hated the idea of him stuck in a one-sided marriage. Couldn't cope with the thought of him unhappy, saddled with a wife he hadn't wanted, unable to be free to find a woman he would love in the intense, all-consuming way she loved him.

One day at a time. Their affair had been on the count-down to its end and not once had he brought up any suggestion of a future. He hadn't planned on there being one. It should have been over and she couldn't bear knowing their marriage was because it had to be, not because he wanted it. That was why she had to do it. She had to leave.

With superhuman effort she lugged her bags downstairs and to the street where she stood waiting for a cab to go past.

Heathrow Terminal Three was as busy as ever with people arriving and departing everywhere. She held tightly to the little bag in which she kept her passport and the ticket she'd booked months ago. One way to Auckland, New Zealand. She handed over the millions to the cabbie who had driven her the long drive there. He must have sensed her exhaustion and despair because he was out of the cab and loading her bags onto a trolley for her before she had the chance to ask him.

She headed slowly towards the Air New Zealand counters, already hearing the familiar accent from the people in the queue. She pushed the heavy trolley into place at the back of the queue and dug out the ticket to check her flight number.

'Daddy!'

The little boy careered through the snaking line of people, narrowly missing her trolley, and threw himself at the legs of the man who must be his father. The man in question bent down and, with a grin as wide as the little boy's arms had been, scooped him up and swung him around. The child's chortles were the sweetest sound. His father hugged him close and both were beaming as they embraced.

Daddy.

Her hand crept to her belly. And her brain started working again with clarity. How could she deprive her children of knowing their father? A father who might not be in love with their mother, but who certainly wanted them. A father who would love and protect them. She had no right to do that. Especially when she knew how it felt to want a dad so much. She'd dreamed of meeting him, spent years wondering what he must have been like, what his family were like, wishing like crazy fate hadn't been so cruel as to take him from both her and her mother.

She'd felt bitter envy of her classmates on sports days and festivals when both parents had turned up to take pride in their achievements. A father to scoop a wee girl up and swing her around. How she would have loved that.

Her children would never forgive her if they'd had that opportunity and she'd denied them it. Aside from herself and her own love for them, she had nothing else to offer them—no aunts or uncles, no grandparents, not even the basics: a job, or a house for herself. Rory could give them all that. How could she be so negligent? How could she be so selfish? She bowed her head. There was a way around this, she just had to be strong.

Blinking back tears, she took the ticket in both hands and, before she could think further, she tore it in two. She looked around for a rubbish bin—damn, they never had them. With a piece of the ticket in each hand she pulled the trolley around and headed back towards the exit and the rank of cabs. And there stood Rory.

Just inside the door, watching her from a distance. Tall, pale and grim and angrier than she'd ever imagined he could be.

She didn't take her eyes off him as she moved towards him, saw him take a deep breath as he strode towards her. 'What the hell do you think you're doing?' His voice carried across the terminal. 'You're not going. Not going anywhere.'

'I know. I'm not. I'm not going.' She spoke quickly. To prove it she held out her hands, offering him the torn ticket. He took the pieces, one in each hand, looking down as he held them together, reading the destination. The hardness in his jaw failed to ease even a smidgeon. His hands curled into fists, screwing up the ticket halves as he thrust them into his pockets and glared at her.

'How did you know I was here?' She wished he hadn't caught her. She didn't want him to know about her cowardice.

'I tried calling you at home. Got concerned when you didn't answer. Then I remembered this was the day you were originally scheduled to fly.' The fury poured off him and she could sense hurt in his expression as well.

Utterly remorseful, she made to head for the exit. With a growl he motioned her aside so he could push the trolley. She hurried alongside him as they went to the cab at the head of the queue, slid into the seat as he stowed her bag, and braced herself. As soon as he'd given instructions to the cabbie she turned to him, the words spouting forth, wanting to make things as right as they could be.

'I'm sorry I put you through this. You've been nothing but wonderful to me, Rory, and you didn't deserve this.'

His tense position didn't alter; if anything he grew even more rigid. She forced herself to continue.

'I will marry you, Rory, if you still think it's best. But you have to promise me something.'

His eyes sparked and she sensed he was only just reining himself in.

She looked away, twisting her hands together. 'We've been having an affair and, now, things have become complicated. But I don't want your life ruined because of one simple mistake. If you meet someone, fall in love with someone, then I'll just bow out; we can have a quiet divorce. I'm sure…' her voice caught '…sure we can arrange something for the children. They need you and your family. I don't want to trap you in a loveless marriage.'

She chanced a look back at him.

He was even paler than when she'd first seen him at the airport. 'Loveless marriage?'

'I know you don't love me, Rory. And that's OK, really it is. I don't expect you to. It's not possible.'

'Not possible?'

She felt her flush mount, her skin felt clammy. 'Everything has been so sudden.'

There was a pause.

'You don't think it's possible to fall in love with someone quickly?'

She looked at him, fear stabbing—had he guessed? How humiliating.

'Isn't it possible to fall in love almost the moment you meet?' He paused and took an audible breath.

Tears welled and she looked away from him. 'It's

possible,' she mumbled. Of course it was; she knew first hand.

'It's possible all right. Especially if she's a tall, willowy type with big brown eyes and hair like golden honey.' The words came out angrily, as if they were being forced out.

She turned to look at him as she registered the repetition of how he'd described her that first night. She hadn't forgotten and now she knew he hadn't either. He was still pale, still tense; his eyes flashed a message she was terrified of believing.

'It's possible.' The heat in her cheeks became unbearable. Her heart thumped so hard she thought it might burst from her body. But she took her courage in both hands and jumped. 'Especially if he had wickedly gleaming green eyes and a smile high-wattage enough to melt the Antarctic.'

The tension broke to a tentative dawn. He leaned a little closer, the vestige of one of those smiles playing at the corners of his full mouth. 'Are you going to lay your cards on the table, Lissa?'

'I thought I'd let you go first,' she whispered, unable to stop leaning towards him too, unable to stop the hope burgeoning in her heart, breathing deeply for the first time in days.

He spoke quickly, intently. 'I can't go falling in love with someone else, Lissa, because I only have one heart and it's already been taken.' He reached out and took her chin in his hand, the touch light and yet it kicked her desire level sky-high.

'I fell in love with you the minute I saw you stepping

out onto the balcony that night. I couldn't stop myself following you, wanting to meet you, find out about you. At first I put it down to sheer lust, but I was deluding myself. It's always been more.' He inched closer. 'I love you.'

He drew her closer still, so their lips were almost touching.

'I love you too, Rory.' The admission whispered out just as he moved to close the gap entirely.

He pulled back instantly. 'Say that again.'

'I love you.'

He gripped her upper arms, squeezing as if checking she really was there. 'Thank God.' And then he kissed her. Tiny kisses over and over, all over until she begged him to kiss her properly. And when he did she felt sure she'd died and gone to heaven.

'We have a lot of talking to do,' he muttered before claiming her mouth again.

None of it got done in the cab. The rest of the ride back to his flat was spent indulging in lush kisses that soothed and inflamed at the same time.

He made her wait while he quickly lugged her bags inside. She could hardly contain her excitement, didn't want him disappearing from view for even those few seconds. Returning to her, he took her hand as she stepped out and then swung her into his arms.

'No more snowboard-style?' she teased.

'Hell, no!' He laughed. 'At least, not for about eight months or so. Besides, I'm practising.'

'What for?'

'The whole over-the-threshold thing.'

He carried her indoors, marching straight to his bedroom.

'I thought you might need a lie-down.'

'Oh, absolutely.'

He stood her on her feet, but still cradled her to him, his hand sweeping down her back in long strokes. She flared, wanting to be with him, wanting to make love.

Then his stomach rumbled.

She giggled.

'I didn't have lunch.' He grinned back ruefully.

'So what do you fancy, then?' she asked.

His smile was immediate and broad. 'Well,' he said, musing slowly, 'I thought I'd have this for starters.' He traced his finger around her lips, pulling the lower one down a little and brushing the inside. A ripple of excitement went through her. He lifted his finger from her lips and she licked them in anticipation.

'Then,' he continued softly, not taking his eyes from hers, 'I thought I'd have these for main.' He took one breast in each hand and with his thumbs stroked slightly. She was sure he was able to feel the taut nipples through her sweatshirt. She smiled, liking the idea so far.

'And then—' he was smiling with a devilish glint now '—I thought I'd have this for dessert.' He slid a hand down and brazenly rubbed across her belly and curved into her pelvis.

She sucked in a deep breath and wantonly squeezed her thighs together, effectively trapping his hand.

'Thing is,' he said with a small helpless gesture and an innocent look, 'sometimes I just have to have dessert first.'

She reflected desire back at him. Suddenly all patience was lost. They kissed and kissed again, her passion and happiness effervescent, sparking. She twisted against him, wanting to drive him as crazy as he did her.

'There's only one thing in the world I want more than you in my arms right now,' he said, his voice sounding rough.

'What's that?' she asked breathlessly.

'You *naked* in my arms right now.'

'I think that can be arranged.'

'I was hoping you might say that.'

Action was instantaneous. She pulled her sweatshirt and tee shirt over her head at the same time and stood just in bra and jeans. He yanked his tie off before taking over immediately, reaching for her, ravishing her. She fought with the buttons on his shirt, undoing them and slipping it off together with his jacket. He was gorgeous. Their lips remained locked while they hastily undid belt buckles and buttons and tried to kick off jeans and trousers.

He laughed hungrily. 'Shoes, darling. Shoes.' He bent and slipped off hers before hurriedly attending to his own. He couldn't move fast enough for her. She needed to hold him close. Finally freed from their clothing, they literally fell onto her bed in a tangle of limbs. He held her firmly, using his mouth to explore every inch of her. She fought his grip as she tried to do the same to him. It was frantic and passionate, both desperate for fulfilment.

'I can't get enough of you,' she confessed feverishly

as she pressed kisses across his chest. He was driving her wild. She wanted everything, all of it right now, but at the same time she wanted to savour it, cherish every moment. The dilemma was driving her crazy.

'It's OK, beautiful.' He shushed her with a deep kiss. 'We have for ever.' The kiss sealed them and their rhythms matched. He was right. He was her lifelong mate and this was the first dance of many more to come. They teased each other until, unable to wait any longer, he settled his weight over her and she sighed with contentment as he pushed inside. She would never have enough of this.

She lifted a hand to frame his face as they both stilled to savour the moment. 'I love you.'

His mouth moved over hers—a tender torment as his body began a slow and welcome rhythm. 'You're everything to me.'

He gathered her closer and together they moved slowly at first, and then with increasing ferocity until they were both past the point of tolerance and with joyous cries they tumbled together from the heights.

Lying twisted, still connected, panting, she had to ask. 'I can't believe you love me. Are you sure? It's not just because of the babies?'

He gathered a section of her hair and pulled on it teasingly. 'Silly. I'm excited about the babies, of course I am. But it's you I love, Lissa. I can't even imagine them yet. It's you I want. You I don't want to live without.'

'But why didn't you tell me?'

'How could I? I really wasn't sure where I stood with

you, Lissa. I didn't want to freak you out and send you running by declaring undying love for you when you were still learning you could trust me. I didn't want to overwhelm you.'

Her eyes smarted. She had been such an idiot. Letting her fears and insecurities from her past colour her judgment of him. She'd almost walked away from the best thing ever to happen in her life. Rory. OK, so it hadn't exactly been slow and steady as she'd once thought she wanted. It had been fast and furious and much, much better.

'Don't cry, beautiful, please don't cry.' He tilted her head back so he could see into her eyes.

'Happy tears.'

'Oh. Well. That's OK, then.'

They lay close again. She felt complete and relaxed until another thought needled into her mind.

'Rory, what are your family going to say?' Terrified about meeting them, she waited anxiously for his answer.

His smile turned wicked. 'They can't wait to meet you. My sister's been hounding me for ages.'

'Ages? She's known about me for ages?' She sat up and looked down at his amused expression.

He nodded. 'I had to return her car to her that first night, remember? She took one look at my face and knew something was up. Immediately guessed it was a woman, and has been crowing to my mother since that she knew first.'

'What about the babies? Will they mind about that?'

He really laughed that time. 'Hell, no, they'll be

thrilled. Mum has been nagging me for some time about settling down, having a family, not wasting all my energy on my career. I'm pushing thirty, you know.' He said it in such a way she knew he was mimicking his mother and she laughed.

He ran his hand over her belly, his eyes softening. 'They won't be too much younger than their cousins; heaven help they won't be influenced too badly by those toads.'

Lissa's smile broadened, the doting uncle all too apparent.

'They'll love you, Lissa, don't worry about that.'

Suddenly he sat up. 'There's something I need to do. Something I need to rectify.'

She waited while he reached down the side of the bed and scrabbled for his trousers. Her heart thudded as he pulled out a small black velvet box from the pocket.

He looked up with an intent expression.

Emotion threatened to overwhelm her. 'You don't need to do this Rory.'

'I do.' He smiled at her. 'I do.'

Her eyes filled again. Damn hormones.

'What am I going to say when our kids ask about our marriage? That I just said to you, "Right, that's it, we're getting married." You deserve a proposal, Lissa. You deserve to be asked properly.' He paused, a humorous light in his eye. 'Just make sure you give the right answer.'

She smiled away the tears. 'And what am I going to say to the kids when they ask where this beautiful proposal took place? Not some fancy restaurant, or some scenic mountaintop. But in bed with your father, both naked in the middle of the afternoon?'

He shrugged. 'Beautiful things happen in bed with you, Lissa.'

He knelt in front of her, his light-hearted look replaced with a sincerity she felt in her soul. 'Lissa, I love you and will to my dying day. Will you marry me?'

'Yes, I will, Rory, because I love you too.'

He opened the box and held it out to her. 'I know lots of people go to choose a ring together, but I saw this and knew it was right.'

Not right, perfect. The ring was beautiful. A large brilliant cut diamond flanked on either side by two golden topaz. All three stones glittered.

'They remind me of your eyes, the golden lights in them and your hair. There are two, one for each baby. But the diamond is you, Lissa. You're the prize for me.'

The tears flowed again as he lifted it from the box and slid it down her finger, home.

'You really thought about this.'

His smile was one of the sort that really knocked her sideways. 'Like I said, it was right.'

'It is. When did you get it?'

'I picked it up this morning, I knew it couldn't wait any longer; I needed to tell you how I was feeling. I knew you were unhappy and it was my last shot.'

'And then you came and found me headed to the airport.' She felt terrible.

His smile vanished. 'Yeah, that was a real low point.'

'I'm sorry. I could never have done it, you know. I

thought I could, but I just couldn't.' She took his face in her hands, smoothing away the grim recollection.

He bent his head, kissing her with such loving tenderness the tears in her eyes spilled over. He kissed them away gently. Her heart felt complete. He lifted her onto his lap and she pushed closer to him, onto him, and together they increased the rhythm, creating the most exquisite friction. Passion overrode the tender tranquillity and they clung to each other with quickened breathing. At last she knew the joy of loving and being loved. Wholly. Elation soared through her.

Some time later he spoke again. 'There is one other thing I have to tell you.'

She raised her brows; he sounded guilty.

'I've booked the honeymoon.'

'You have?'

He nodded decisively. 'Florence. I promised you I'd take you—remember?'

How could she forget the magic night she'd met him? 'Ponte Vecchio.'

'And gelato for my beautiful Venus.' He lifted his head off the pillow. 'Can you have gelato when pregnant?'

'I can't think why not.'

'What flavour are you going to have?'

'Lemon.'

'Really? I thought it would have been raspberry.'

She shook her head. 'Definitely lemon. I love the smell of lemon. But maybe—' she twinkled '—maybe I'll have a scoop of each.'

'Two, huh?'
'Double the pleasure.'
'Always.'
And it would be, always with him.

THE BOSS'S WIFE
FOR A WEEK

BY
ANNE McALLISTER

Award-winning author **Anne McAllister** was once given a blueprint for happiness that included a nice, literate husband, a ramshackle Victorian house, a horde of mischievous children, a bunch of big friendly dogs, and a life spent writing stories about tall, dark and handsome heroes. "Where do I sign up?" she asked, and promptly did. Lots of years later, she's happy to report the blueprint was a success. She's always happy to share the latest news with readers at her website: www. annemcallister.com, and welcomes their letters there or at PO Box 3904, Bozeman, Montana 59772, USA (SAE appreciated).

For Haine, in friendship forever,
and for Chuck who taught Ted everything he knew.
So it's the wrong book. We know life isn't fair,
but thanks for making mine so much better.

CHAPTER ONE

It was paperwork that kept Sadie Morrissey tied to Spencer Tyack. He was hopeless at it.

If paperwork were left to Spence it would never get done. And that was no way to run a business. Tyack Enterprises was an enormously successful property development business because Spence had a good eye, great insight and a prodigious work ethic—and because he had Sadie to take care of the details.

She'd been doing it for years, ever since she'd been in high school and he'd been barely twenty-one, a boy from the wrong side of the tracks with grit and goals and not much else. Now, twelve years later, he owned a multinational business and had his finger in property developments on five continents.

He'd have taken over the world by now, Sadie sometimes thought, except she couldn't keep up with the paperwork.

"You need to file faster," Spence always told her, flashing that megawatt drop-dead gorgeous grin of his as he breezed through the office on his way to London or Paris or Athens or New York.

"Not on your life," Sadie always replied, wadding up a piece of paper and throwing it at him. The grin flashed again and he winked at her.

Sadie resisted the grin, resisted the wink. Resisted Spence— something else she always did.

"I'm busy enough, thank you very much," she told him tartly. "And it's not only filing."

Of course he knew that. He knew it was Sadie who kept things organized, who could lay her hand on any piece of paper at any given moment, who could set up a meeting between people on four continents at the drop of a hat, whose address book was even more stuffed full of information than his own.

He only said it to annoy her. Then he'd grin again, rattle off half a dozen more things she needed to do, and then he'd vanish, off to catch another plane while Sadie got back to work.

Not that she cared.

Until last year she'd had a reason to stay in Butte. She'd been determined to care for her elderly grandmother, to make sure Gran would be able to stay in her own home as long as possible.

Now that Gran had been gone six months, her parents were urging her to come to Oregon where they lived, and her brother, Danny, had promised her job interviews galore if she came to Seattle.

But Sadie hadn't gone. She liked Butte with its wild and woolly history. Loved Montana. Delighted in the change of seasons, in the wide-open spaces. It was still, as far as she was concerned, the best place on earth.

And she liked her life—what there was of it. Mostly there was her job. But that was all right. She and Spence had always worked well together, and the job was exciting and demanding, even though she was always going like mad, working insane hours as she did her best to keep the ducks in a row and the details aligned so that Spence could get on with buying up the world piece by piece.

Some days—like today—Sadie thought she ought to have been born an octopus. But even eight arms would not have been enough to deal with all the Tyack Enterprises projects she was juggling this afternoon.

The phone had been ringing when she'd opened the office door at eight-thirty this morning. By lunchtime she had talked four times to an Italian determined to encourage Spence's interest in some condominiums in Naples even though she'd assured him that Spence wasn't there, he was in New York. She'd listened to an imperious Greek tycoon named Achilles who wouldn't take no for an answer, either. And in between those and all the other calls, she'd worked on finalizing Spence's meeting in Fiji next week.

Arranging the logistics for him and his co-investors to spend a week on one of Fiji's smaller islands at a resort for stressed-out and overworked businessmen and women was, to put it bluntly, a challenge. Movers and shakers like Spence and his partners did not have schedules that permitted them to laze around for a week in paradise.

"We don't want to laze around," Spence had told her last time he was in Butte. "We just want to go, see the place, crunch the numbers and, if it works out, buy in."

"That's what *you* want," Sadie had agreed. "But Mr. Isogawa wants you to experience the peace you're going to be investing in."

That had been clear during the first conversation she'd had with Japanese businessman Tadahiro Isogawa. Mr. Isogawa wanted partners, yes. But not just any partners. He wanted partners who believed in the resort's concept—and who would experience it firsthand.

"The piece we're investing in?" Spence had frowned. "We don't want a piece. We want partnership in the whole place."

"*P-e-a-c-e,*" Sadie had spelled patiently. "He expects you to all turn up and spend a week getting to know the place—and each other—and reconnecting with your families."

"I don't have a family."

"So tell that to Mr. Isogawa. He's very big on marriage and family. It's why he works, he told me. But he believes sometimes people who work so hard get their priorities mixed up. Hence the need for Nanumi. It's Fijian for 'remember,'" she'd informed Spence. Mr. Isogawa had told her that when he'd explained his reasons for the resort development.

It hadn't impressed Spence. He had given her that sceptical brows-raised look Sadie knew all too well. She'd just shrugged. "Up to you. But he says if you want in, he wants all of you— and your spouses—there for a week to experience it."

Spence had rolled his eyes. But his desire for the resort won out and finally he'd shrugged. "Fine. Whatever he wants. Set it up."

And so she had.

Besides all the rest of her work, it had taken her days to make sure everyone had a clear schedule for the week to come and then to make all the necessary travel arrangements from the far corners of the world to the island resort. In the process she'd answered thousands of questions from astonished spouses who had rung to be sure the proposed week's holiday in Fiji was actually on the level.

"We never get holidays," Marion Ten Eyck had told her. "John is always working."

Steve Walker's wife, Cathy, had said much the same thing. And Richard Carstairs' wife, Leonie, had rung her every day, saying, "Are you sure? Quite sure? Does Richard know?"

And Sadie had assured her over and over that indeed Richard did. She was beginning to think Mr. Isogawa knew what he was talking about.

And just when she finally got everything sorted and began to go over a contract Spence had faxed her for a development in Georgia he was involved in, the phone rang again.

Sadie closed her eyes and prayed for patience. It actually wasn't eight hands she needed, she thought wearily as she reached for the phone. But eight ears certainly wouldn't hurt.

"Tyack Enterprises," she said and was rewarded by the crackle of a transoceanic connection and a voice whose first language was clearly not English. On the plus side, it wasn't Italian or Greek, either.

"Ah, *Isogawa-san, konnichi wa*. How lovely to hear from you!"

And it really was. Mr. Isogawa was the one person she hadn't talked to. "Everyone arrives on Sunday. I have all the details right here."

She happily relayed the information and smiled at his cheerful approval.

Mr. Isogawa, she had discovered, had had little experience with westerners beyond the ones he saw in films. Since Sadie was more given to hard work than car chases and shooting people to get things done, he thought she was a miracle worker. He took all the information as she relayed it, then said, "You must come, too."

"Thank you. I'd love to," Sadie replied with a smile. Who wouldn't want to spend a week in a South Pacific paradise? "But I have work to do here."

"Even so," Mr. Isogawa said. "You work very hard. You should have a holiday, too. A life."

How did he know she didn't have a life?

"You talk to Spencer," he said. "He will arrange it."

Spence didn't take vacations himself. She knew he wouldn't see any reason for anyone else to, either. Officially she had two weeks a year. She couldn't remember ever taking them.

"Maybe someday," she said to Mr. Isogawa. When hell froze over.

Still, after Mr. Isogawa hung up, she thought about what he said.

Not about going to Fiji. There was no chance of that. But maybe she ought to consider getting away. Moving away. For years she'd assured herself that she thrived on the variety and busyness of her life.

But was it really a life?

Rob McConnell, the man she'd been dating for the past few months, was sure it wasn't. "You never have time for anything but your damn job," he complained over and over. "You're not getting any younger, Sadie."

Usually Rob wasn't quite that blunt, but she knew he was getting irritated at her refusal to want more than a casual relationship. She didn't blame him. He was a genuinely nice man. He wanted to marry and have a family. He'd said as much. And he was right, she wasn't getting any younger. She was twenty-eight. If she was going to get serious, she needed to start.

Sadie wanted to get serious. Truly. But not with Rob.

And that was the problem.

Maybe she should move on. She'd been thinking about it ever since her brother, Danny, had come home from Seattle to visit last week, bringing his wife and their one-year-old twins with him. That had been a shock. Danny had always been as footloose as Spence. Seeing her brother as a devoted family man had jolted her.

It seemed to have given Danny pause for thought, too.

"Who'd have thought I'd settle down before you," he'd said the night before he'd left. He'd been sitting in her living room with a twin in each arm, looking exhausted but content. And then he'd considered her slowly, making her squirm under his gaze as he'd said, "But then, you are settled, aren't you, Sadie?"

"What do you mean?"

His mouth twisted. "You're settled in as Spence's drudge."

"I am not!" Sadie had tossed down the copy of Spence's itinerary she'd been going over, making some last-minute adjustments, and jumped up to prowl around the room. "Don't be absurd."

"It isn't me who's being absurd, Sade. It's all work and no play with you. Always has been as been as long as I can remember."

"I play," Sadie had protested.

"When you work seventeen hours instead of eighteen? Hell, you're as driven as Spence."

"We have goals!" she informed him loftily.

"Spence does," Danny had corrected with an elder brother's ruthlessness. "You're just hanging on."

Sadie had whirled around to glare at him. "What's that supposed to mean?"

Danny met her glare head on. "You know damn well what it means"

"I have a great job!"

"But do you have a life? Come on, Sadie. You're the one who always used to name your kids when we were growing up. You're damn near thirty and you barely even date!"

"I'm twenty-eight, not *damn near thirty!* And Rob—"

"You're not serious about Rob McConnell. If you were you'd have invited him over while Kel and I were here. You didn't. So find someone you are serious about. Get married. Have that family you always wanted." He threw the words at her like a gauntlet, and Sadie couldn't pick it up.

"I'm fine," she'd said stiffly.

"Yeah. Sure you are. You could get a job anywhere. Come out to Seattle. Kel will find you a hundred dates. Believe me, you're wasted on Spence."

"I'm not dating Spence."

"And thank God for that," Danny said. "He's my friend, but he's not exactly marriage material, is he?"

He wasn't telling her anything she didn't know. But she shook her head. "I work for him, that's all," she said.

"So quit."

"I can't."

"Why not? Does Spence own your soul?"

"Oh, for heaven's sake. Of course not!" But her face had burned and Sadie had hoped Danny wouldn't notice.

Fortunately he'd just shaken his head. "Well, it makes a guy wonder. You've been working for him for years! Since high school."

"Because he needed the help. You know Spence. He's great at wheeling and dealing. Great at finding properties and renovating them. Great at potential. He can see the big picture. But he's not great at paperwork. Not at details."

And Sadie had always been marvelous at both. She could organize anything.

"Anyway," she'd reminded her brother. "I didn't stay. I left, remember? I went away to college. Four years at UCLA."

"And then you came back, you idiot. To him."

"To the job," Sadie insisted. "He pays me a mint. And I get a percentage of the business, for heaven's sake. And where else could I possibly go and manage a global property-development business at my age? And still live in Butte?"

"Oh, yeah, that's a real plus. Butte! The hub of the western cultural world."

Of course it was anything but. But the old mining city was making a comeback. Long depressed, Butte was making a slow climb back toward prosperity, thanks in large part to Spence and a few other guys like him who were determined to turn things around.

"Don't be sarcastic. And don't knock Butte." Sadie's voice had been frosty at his dismissal of their hometown. "It's home. Spence doesn't knock it, and he has more right than you do."

She and Danny had had a good childhood with stable, loving parents. Spence had not. For all that he was now a real-estate tycoon of international scope, Spencer Tyack hadn't been born with a silver spoon in his mouth.

"Not even a copper one," he'd once said with a wry grin, a reference to Butte's copper-mining past. "But I survived."

No thanks to his own parents, that was for sure. Sadie remembered Spence's grandfather as kind and caring, but the old man had died when Spence was ten. From then on his life had been hell. His alcoholic father hadn't been able to keep a job and rarely turned up at home except to fight with his mother or take a swing at Spence. And his mother's bitterness toward her husband found its most convenient target in their only son.

Sadie, whom Spence had never permitted to set foot in his house while she was growing up, had still got close enough on occasion to hear her shrieking at him, "You're just like your father!"

He wasn't. Not even close.

Unlike his father, Spence had always been driven. Even when he'd been something of a juvenile delinquent in high school, he'd been determined to be the best delinquent of the bunch.

A probation officer who had insisted they meet not in his office but in the cemetery by Spence's grandfather's grave had put an end to the delinquency. After that Spence had been determined to do the old man proud. To succeed. To achieve. To become the best man he possibly could.

He'd gone to work wherever he could. He'd saved and scrimped and had bought his first house the week he turned twenty-one. To call it a "fixer-upper" would be kind. It had been little more than a hovel with a leaky roof.

As soon as he could, he'd gone to work in the mine, making better money driving those behemoth trucks all day. Then he'd come back and work on the house all night. Several months later he sold that house at a profit, bought another, then did the same. He did it again and again.

By the time he was twenty-two he'd been able to apply for his first commercial-property loan. And that's when he'd hired

Sadie to create order out of the paperwork chaos—in his truck. He hadn't had an office.

"I can't waste money on an office," he'd told her.

So for the first year she'd worked out of the back of his truck camper, using a shop light run by a battery, and a filing system that she carried around in a cardboard box. It was primitive. But it worked.

And so had Spence. Constantly. Within the year he'd had a building. Then two. During her senior year in high school, Sadie finally got an office to call her own. Spence had even bought her a silly plaque that said, "Sadie's office."

And he'd been furious when she'd told him she was leaving to go to college in California.

"I got you an office," he'd protested. "I thought you were going to work for me!"

"Not forever," Sadie had replied.

Because she couldn't. It was more than her sanity was worth, the thought of working for Spence forever—because she was in love with him. Had been for years. As long as she could remember, in fact.

Not that he knew it. God forbid. He'd have been appalled, because he certainly wasn't in love with her.

Sadie knew that. She didn't like it, but she accepted it. She'd tried a little flirting with him, and he'd completely ignored it. So she'd gone to UCLA to get away.

She'd hoped she would learn a lot, get wonderful job offers and meet a man who could make her forget Spence. That had been the plan at least.

And if she'd come home every summer to help Spence out, it was only because he refused to hire anyone in her place while she was gone.

"No need. It can wait for you," he'd said. "You'll be home, anyway."

Which was true. She'd come back to spend summers at her parents' house, to see Gran, to visit Butte. But she hadn't intended to come back permanently. Ever.

Everything went the way she'd planned. She'd learned a lot, graduated with honors and had lots of wonderful job offers—including one from Spence.

He'd come to her graduation. "Why not? I feel like I have a vested interest in your business degree," he'd said blandly. And he'd offered her a job that very afternoon.

He'd promised her a remarkable amount of money, a completely refurbished office in one of Butte's historic landmark buildings that he was painstakingly renovating, and a percentage of his business empire.

"A percentage?" Sadie's eyes had widened in surprise.

But Spence had just shrugged. "Why not? You've worked almost as hard to put Tyack's on the map as I have. You deserve a share. So, what do you say?" The characteristic Tyack impatience was all too clear.

Sadie hadn't known what to say. The truth was she still hadn't gotten over him. His killer grin could still make her knees wobble. His hard-muscled body could still make her quiver all over. And when his steely-eyed stare grew softer and gentler, as it did on rare occasions, her heart seemed to simply turn over in her chest.

She was hopeless, she'd thought grimly. What she needed, she'd decided, was shock therapy. She needed full-scale immersion into Spencer Tyack's world. That would undoubtedly cure her of all her starry-eyed fantasies.

So she'd said yes.

She'd been back for almost six years.

A lot had happened in those six years. She'd done her best to get over him. Told herself she *was* over him. She was dating other men. Just because she hadn't found one yet who set her heart to pounding the way Spence had didn't mean she wouldn't.

She knew Spence wasn't for her.

"I like working for him," she'd told Danny. "It's exciting." Spence was a mover and a shaker. He now had properties in seven countries. He owned apartment complexes, office buildings, condominiums. He always had new ideas. And he always talked about them with her. He sought her opinion. They discussed and analyzed—and argued—together.

"You've got a stake in it," he always said.

And that was true. She did. She might not have a life, but she had a stake in an exciting business. Last week Spence had been in Helsinki finalizing a deal for an office building. This week he was in New York looking over some apartments with father-and-daughter investment team Tom and Dena Wilson, who had done deals with him in the past. And next week, with luck, he would be part owner of a South Pacific resort.

And, as first Danny and now Mr. Isogawa had reminded her, she would be in Butte. Sadie sighed.

It was nearly five. She could leave at five. If she left at five, maybe she would get a life—even though she had piles more work to do.

The phone rang again and unhesitatingly she answered. "Tyack Enterprises. This is Sadie."

"*Say-dee, case-me, meu amor.*" The voice was like rough velvet.

Sadie grinned, recognizing it. If there was ever a man—besides Spence—who could send a woman's hormones into overdrive, Mateus Gonsalves was that man. Trouble was, he knew it. "Hi, Mateus. *Obrigada*. But no, I still don't want to marry you. And Spence is in New York."

He sighed. "I don't want to marry Spence." Mateus Gonsalves switched to perfectly clear, though accented, English. "I want to marry you—and take you away from your slave-driving boss."

It was a conversation they'd had a dozen times at least. From the first time Spence had brought his Brazilian friend to Butte, Mateus had been full of Latin charm, flirting like mad with her, always asking her to marry him.

"She won't," Spence had said cheerfully, not even looking up from the file cabinet he was riffling through. "Sadie's a man-hater."

"I am not!" she'd protested, pushing him out of the way and plucking out at once the document he'd been looking for.

Spence had grabbed it. "See, she's a genius. Knows where everything is," he'd told Mateus happily. Then he'd turned to her. "You don't date."

"I do, too," she'd said. "When the mood hits," she qualified, but that was the truth. She certainly didn't hate men.

"She will date me," Mateus had said with complete assurance.

But she never had. "I don't mix business and pleasure," she'd told him.

"You should," Mateus had rejoined irrepressibly. And he hadn't stopped asking her to come to Rio and marry him every time he called.

"Life is a party in Rio," he said now. "We know how to live down here. You should dump that workaholic and come to work for me."

Sadie laughed at that. "You work almost as hard as he does."

"But I hide it better. And I take holidays. What do you say?"

"Maybe someday I'll come to Rio for a visit," Sadie placated him. "Now, what can I do for you?"

Mateus shifted gears as easily as he always did. "I need to talk to Spencer about a building in Sao Paulo."

"I'll tell him."

"Give me his cell phone number."

"He never turns it on." Unless he was expecting a call, Spence kept his cell phone off. But he always expected her to keep hers on so he could reach her. "When he checks in, I'll have him call you."

"*Obrigado,*" he said. "Tell him I've got a proposition for him. And one for you."

"I'm not marrying you, Mateus," she said firmly.

"No marriage," he agreed sadly. "But seriously, Say-dee, you should come work for me. I'm opening an office in Texas. You could run it with one hand tied behind your back."

And have a life besides, Sadie reflected for a brief moment. But then she sighed and shook her head. Battling Mateus off could make life even more difficult than working for Spence who didn't seem to remember that she was a woman. "Thanks. But, no, Mateus."

"Think about it."

"I'll think about it," she agreed because it was easier than arguing with him.

"We will talk later," he promised. "*Adeus, carinha.*"

"*Ciao, Mateus.*" She hung up, then picked up the contracts, determined to take them home and read them. At least that way she could say she'd left the office by ten past five. But her cell phone rang as she did so. She saw who it was and glared.

"It's after five," she said irritably when she picked it up.

"So?" Even when she was annoyed at him, the sound of Spence's rough baritone could cause her pulse to speed up. Damn it.

"I have a life," she snapped.

"Whoa. Who ticked you off?"

You, she wanted to say, even though it was really herself she was annoyed at. "It's been a madhouse here today."

"Well, good. Glad to hear it." Which she supposed he was. "Need you to do something for me," he went on briskly.

Sadie grabbed a pen, ready to write, but he didn't say anything. "Spence?"

"Yeah." He sounded suddenly distracted. His normally quick speech grew even quicker. "No big deal. I just need you to get my birth certificate and the divorce decree and bring them to New York."

Sadie stopped dead. "What?" She felt as if she had been gut-punched. "Do what?"

"You heard me. My birth certificate. The divorce decree. I need them. Tomorrow. In New York."

She'd always thought that breathing was in involuntary reflex. Now she wasn't sure.

"Sadie? Are you there? Did you hear me?" His voice was sharp now.

"I heard you." She managed that much. Couldn't manage any more.

"Great. So just get them and hop on a plane tonight. Or tomorrow. I don't care which. Just so long as you're here by 2:00 p.m."

She didn't speak, just stared mutely at the pencil she'd broken in her hand.

"Sadie!"

"Yes!" she snapped back at him now. "I heard you!"

"Well, good." He paused. "You could congratulate me."

"Because...?" she said, though she knew without asking the reason, even though it stunned her.

"Because I'm getting married." He said the words almost defiantly as if expecting her to argue.

She knew better than to argue. But she couldn't help the sarcasm. "Tomorrow? Isn't that a little precipitous? I mean, considering your track record and all?"

Shut up, she told herself. *Shut up. Shut up. Shut up.*

"It'll be fine this time," he said flatly. "Not like Emily."

"It wasn't Emily I was thinking about," Sadie said, unable to help herself. "You didn't marry Emily."

"I remember who I married." He bit the words out.

Sadie remembered, too. He'd married her!

A wedding on the rebound. When society belle Emily Mollineux had stood him up for their Las Vegas wedding, he'd been gutted. His desperation had reminded Sadie of his boyhood pain when his father walked out and his mother had unleashed her fury on Spence.

So when he'd slammed out of the chapel with a fearsome look in his eyes, Sadie had gone after him, unsure what he might do. She'd never imagined that half a dozen whiskeys later he'd decide the answer was to marry *her!*

But he had. He'd been most insistent. "You'd marry me," he'd said firmly, but there had been just a hint of doubt, the tiniest question in his words, in his gaze. "Wouldn't you?" he'd persisted when she hadn't answered.

And Sadie, because that moment if no other seemed to call for absolute honesty, had to admit she would.

"If you asked me," she'd replied because it was only the truth.

And then, heaven help her, he did.

"Marry me," he'd said. And he'd met her gaze with all the intensity Spencer Tyack was capable of in those midnight eyes.

And so she had married him. Within the hour.

They'd got a license, done the deed. And they'd gone back to the honeymoon suite and made love. Passionately. Desperately. Dazedly. It had been the most amazing night of her life.

And she'd awakened in the honeymoon suite the next morning to find Spence already awake and fully dressed, pacing furiously, raking his hands through his hair and saying, "It was a mistake."

Sadie had barely got her eyes open when he'd come and loomed over her, all harsh expression and anguished bloodshot eyes. "It never should have happened. We never should have— *I* never should have— Hell!" He'd shaken his head as if he didn't believe it. "I'm sorry, Sadie. I never meant— Damn it! I don't know what I was thinking! But it'll be all right. Don't worry. We'll get a divorce."

"A d-divorce?" She'd managed that much. Had simply stared at him slack-jawed.

Spence had nodded vehemently. "Well, we can't get an annulment," he'd said grimly. "But it won't be a problem. I promise. I'll handle it."

He'd been adamant, determined. Just as determined to divorce her as he had been to marry her only twelve hours before. It might be some sort of record, Sadie had remembered thinking. She'd blinked rapidly and tried hard to swallow against the boulder lodged in her throat.

Had it been that awful? That wrong?

Apparently it had.

At least it hadn't seemed like the time to declare her undying love. She'd simply nodded. "Right," she managed, though she'd nearly strangled on the word.

Spence peered at her closely. "Are you okay?"

Oh, yes, terrific. Never better. Having been married and found wanting in the space of half a day was exactly the sort of thing to give a girl a heap of self-confidence!

"I'm fine," she said as steadily as she could. "Why?"

"You don't look fine."

"Thanks very much."

"I didn't mean— I just—" he shuddered visibly "—sorry. I don't know what I was thinking. I'm sorry. Sorry about the marriage. About..." His voice trailed off. His gaze shifted southward, away from her face. Down her sheet-draped body.

Sadie felt immediately self-conscious. So he was sorry they'd consummated the marriage? Sorry he'd made love to her?

He was sorry, apparently, for everything.

"Don't think about it," he said. "I'll handle everything. You don't even have to mention it."

Was he afraid she might? Stand on the rooftops and announce that her husband of twelve hours was dumping her? She stared at him, speechless.

"You're tired. You have to be. Go back to sleep. The room is booked through Wednesday. Stay until then if you want."

As if she would stay on in the honeymoon suite by herself while her husband was divorcing her!

"I won't be here," Spence said quickly, misinterpreting the appalled look on her face. "I called Santiago this morning. I'm just going to head to Barcelona a few days early. But I'll arrange for the divorce before I go. Okay?"

Sadie shrugged. What else could she do?

Seeing the shrug, Spence gave her a strained smile. "It'll be okay. I promise." He paused, then said, "It won't change things, will it? You'll stay on."

"Stay on?"

"Keep working with me. It doesn't have to be awkward. We're friends." He said this last almost insistently and with complete seriousness. And why not? Last night had meant nothing to him—beyond an error in judgment. He wanted her as a friend, not a wife. And he was remedying that as quickly as he could.

She didn't know what to say.

"No" would undoubtedly have been smart. But she had been afraid that saying no would make him think their marriage mattered far more to her than he wanted to believe. And if he thought it did, would he change his mind? Stay married to her because he felt sorry for her?

The very thought made her squirm.

"I'll stay," she said. "For now."

He'd grinned then, that perfect, sexy drop-dead gorgeous

Spencer Tyack grin that Sadie had spent years trying to resist. "That's all right then," he'd said happily. "You're a pal, Sade."

Wasn't she just?

"I knew you'd agree. I'll ring a lawyer from the airport and get him to do it. I'll give you a call tomorrow from Barcelona. But don't worry. Consider it taken care of." And grabbing his suitcase, he'd bolted out the door.

And that, basically, had been that.

Except that when he'd called her from Barcelona the next day, he'd said, "Are you okay?" in a worried tone completely unlike any he'd ever used with her.

"Of course I'm okay. What do you think?" Sadie had retorted. She was damned if she was going to let him think he'd cut her heart out.

She must have been convincing because he'd never asked that question or sounded that worried again. And the first morning he was back in the office, which was a month later, he'd said, "Don't worry. It's sorted. I've got the papers. It's all taken care of."

And so her short, better-forgotten marriage to Spence had been over.

He'd never mentioned it again.

Neither had she. She'd thought of it again, of course. Plenty of times in those first few months. Minute by minute almost. But eventually she'd managed to put it aside. Not to forget, but to consider it with detachment, as if it had happened in some alternative universe. Like a dream. Or a nightmare.

It had faded over the past four years. Until now. Now she said, "I don't know where the papers are."

"In my safe deposit box. You have a key."

"Yes, but—married?"

"It's business, Sadie. Did you think I'd fallen in love?"

She didn't know what to think. "Business?"

"I'm marrying Dena Wilson. Who'd you think I was marrying? Someone I just picked up on the street?"

"I—"

"It's perfect. A great idea. Dena and I joining forces. I don't know why I didn't think of it sooner. Together we've got twice the clout. Twice the expertise."

"Yes, but—tomorrow?"

"So we'll be married before I head to Fiji. Which reminds me, can you book a flight for Dena?"

She was going to kill him.

"You don't have to do it tonight," he said, all magnanimity. "You can do it tomorrow from here. Just bring the papers and show up at the courthouse tomorrow afternoon. Ceremony's at two. I'll book you a room in a fancy hotel for tomorrow night for your trouble, okay? The Plaza? The Four Seasons? You name it. Think of it as a vacation. Right. I've got to run. Tom and Dena just came in the door. See you tomorrow."

There was a click—and a second later, a dial tone.

Sadie stood staring at the phone in her hand and felt as if the bottom had fallen out of her well-ordered world.

Where the hell was she?

Spence checked his watch for the tenth time in five minutes and raked fingers through his already disheveled hair. He'd been pacing the hallway of the courthouse, just outside the judge's chamber for three-quarters of an hour.

He'd got there an hour before that, wanting to be there when Sadie showed up and not certain when she would arrive. Last night he'd kept his phone off, not wanting to get any calls from Sadie telling him he was making a mistake.

He wasn't making a mistake.

The Emily fiasco had been a mistake. No doubt about that. Four years ago when he'd intended to marry Emily Mollineux, he'd been out of his mind—a victim of his own youthful en-thusiasm, infatuation and hormones—not to mention a mis-placed determination to wed a beauty whose family was all about Old Money.

And marrying Sadie for God-knew-what insane reason after Emily hadn't shown up—well, that had been an even bigger mistake.

He should never have imposed on her, never proposed! Never put her on the spot like that.

But at the moment he'd been out of his mind. Insane. Rejected. The word still made him wince. But Emily's defec-tion had seemed to confirm his deepest fears—that, as his mother had always claimed, he was worthless.

And so he'd turned to Sadie—had used her unwavering friendship to restore, however briefly, his shattered self-esteem. It had been easy enough to do, damn it. For all that she would argue with him forever about business propositions, Sadie was putty when it came to people—when it came to him.

And in the morning when he'd awakened to find her in bed beside him, when he remembered how they'd spent the night, he'd been appalled at what he'd done.

Christ, she'd even had a boyfriend! And he hadn't given a damn.

He'd just turned to her and said, "Marry me," and he knew that that night he wouldn't—couldn't—have taken no for an answer. But in the morning's harsh light he knew regret. He knew he'd made a mistake.

And so he'd done his best to make it right.

He wasn't making that mistake again. This marriage was business, pure and simple. He and Dena both wanted exactly the same things. It would be fine.

Provided, he thought, shooting back his cuff and glaring at his watch again, Sadie showed up.

He didn't know where she was or what time her flight had been expected to get in. He might have known, he reminded himself, if he'd turned on his mobile phone last night. But he hadn't. He hadn't wanted to talk to her last night—just in case she tried to talk him out of this marriage.

Sadie was, after all, an idealist, a romantic. As long as he'd known her, she'd been deluded by the notion that someday she would meet "the one." It was one of the reasons he'd known he had to divorce her as quickly as possible—to give her a chance to meet her Perfect Man.

So he hadn't wanted to hear how Dena Wilson wasn't his Perfect Woman. She was all about business—not at all about home and family. She didn't want them any more than he did. And that, to Spence, was about as perfect as she could get.

So he'd shut his phone off and, consequently, he had no idea where the hell Sadie was or when to expect her. He'd tried calling her, but her own phone was shut off.

He knew, of course, that if she was still in the air, she couldn't have it switched on. But good God, she'd better not be in the air now. The ceremony was due to start in less than fifteen minutes.

"Well, Sadie is certainly cutting it a little close," Dena said, appearing at his side. She was smiling her usually imperturbable smile, but there was a hint of strain around her mouth.

"She'll be here."

"Of course. Just give me a heads up. I have some papers to go over," Dena said. "I'll work on them."

She went back into the room, and Spence continued to pace the hallway. He cracked his knuckles. He tried her number again. And again.

Ten minutes later the door to the judge's chambers opened and Dena's father, Tom, appeared. "I'm meeting Sawyer in Savannah at nine. Let's get this show on the road."

"Sadie's not here."

"You're not marrying Sadie."

"She's bringing my papers. Birth certificate. Divorce decree." He hadn't wanted to mention the divorce, but of course he'd had to.

Dena had raised her eyebrows at the news, but then she'd shrugged. "Makes no difference to me."

"Get married now. Worry about the paperwork after." Tom suggested.

"Without Sadie?"

"Why not? No big deal, is it?" Tom said with the air of a man who bent the rules to meet the circumstances. He checked his watch pointedly.

Spence shrugged. "Of course not."

It was sensible. Sane. Logical. It was making the best use of time and resources—just as their marriage would be.

As Mr. and Mrs. Spencer Tyack, they would improve their business standing enormously. Dena's considerable assets alongside his would add to their portfolio and their viability on the property-development front in the long run. And in the short run it would solve a problem with Mr. Isogawa and his "happy family" scenario. One of Spence's partners had a wife with a wandering eye. In Barcelona last month it—and she—had wandered in Spence's direction. Into his bedroom, in fact.

The last thing he needed was her pulling a stunt like that at the resort. Having a wife along, he'd determined, would make sure it didn't happen.

He understood that Tadahiro Isogawa was, as Sadie had said, all about happy families. So was he, even though his personal experience of them was negligible. Marrying Dena, though, could solve his problem and create enormous opportunities for them in the future. He could certainly be happy about that.

And Dena, when he proposed the idea, had understood at once.

"Smart," she'd said after only brief consideration. "We'll do it—for the business. And sex, of course. But no kids. Those are my terms."

"No problem," Spence had agreed promptly. Those were his terms, too.

So here they were now—all of them, except Sadie.

Where the hell was she?

"So, are we ready?" Tom said briskly.

"Sure. Why not?"

Tom smiled. "I'll get Dena."

The clerk went to get the judge. Tom reappeared moments later with Dena, still carrying her briefcase. Spence put his suit coat back on and straightened his tie.

The door opened and the judge swept in. "I'm in recess," he announced. "Not much time." He glanced at Spence and Dena. "You're the couple? Come up here."

Spence took Dena's arm and went to stand in front of the judge, who cleared his throat and began to speak rapidly in a monotone. It was all legalese. Mumbo-jumbo. Not real estate law so Spence didn't understand any of it. It didn't matter. What mattered was saying "I do," at the right moment. And finding Sadie.

Suddenly he heard a door squeaking open behind them. His head whipped around.

Sadie!

But hardly the calm, centered, settled Sadie he'd been expecting. This Sadie's hair was windblown, her eyes bloodshot with dark circles beneath. Her skin was so pale that her normally golden freckles seemed to have been splashed across her cheeks by an impressionist run amok. And the look she gave him was of a deer caught in the headlights of a semi. A deer clutching a red leather portfolio against her chest.

"Don't just stand there, young woman!" the judge barked. "Sit down! I don't have all day."

"I need to—"

"Shut the door and sit!"

Sadie shut the door and sat.

Clearing his throat, the judge began again. More legalese. Something about the power vested in him by the state of New York. Blah, blah, blah. Behind him Spence heard someone— Sadie?—fidget in her chair.

"...must ascertain if there are any legal impediments or reasons why this marriage should not take place. Any objections?" Then without pausing, the judge continued, "No. So we'll move on then and—"

"Yes." It was Sadie.

Spence jerked around to stare at her. So did Dena and Tom.

"You object, young woman?" the judge demanded.

"I, um, yes."

The judge's brows drew down. "On what grounds may I ask?"

What the hell was she playing at? Spence scowled furiously at her.

Sadie shot one quick unreadable glance at him, then turned her gaze back to the judge again. "He's already married. To me."

CHAPTER TWO

"WHAT!" Spence stared at her.

The judge's jaw sagged, Tom Wilson's eyes bugged, Dena's mouth flew open, and Sadie understood perfectly. She'd done all of the above.

Now she wet her lips and made a faint and fairly unsuccessful attempt to smile. "I'm afraid it's true," she said apologetically to the judge and Tom and Dena. But by the time her gaze reached Spence, she hoped there was no apology left in it at all.

"What are you talking about? That was years ago! The divorce papers—"

"We need to talk about that," Sadie said. And she hoped they had reached the point in their years-long relationship where nonverbal communication was a no-brainer.

"Damned right we do," Spence said. He shot a quick glance at Dena—also apologetic, Sadie noted—and one that seemed to say, "you just can't get good help these days," to the judge and Tom. And then he stalked over and took her arm none too gently. "Come on."

"Don't be long. I've got a plane to catch," Tom called after them.

Spence didn't reply. He hustled her out of the room and into the hallway, looked around at the various people in the corridor and opened the door to a room across the way. "In here." He kicked the door shut behind them, then spun her around to face him. "What the hell do you think you're doing?"

"Trying to stop you committing bigamy," she suggested.

"Don't be ridiculous. That was hardly a marriage we had and—"

"It was quite legal in the state of Nevada."

"And I filed for divorce the next day."

"Correction," Sadie said, "you called a divorce lawyer and told him to handle it."

"Which he did! I got the papers!"

"You got an envelope," Sadie corrected him. "You didn't open it." Which was pretty much Spence all over. Delegate and assume it would be done.

Too bad he hadn't delegated arranging their divorce to *her!*

Spence's jaw tightened. "I didn't want to look at them," he growled. "Would you?"

"No." She had to admit she wouldn't have wanted to see their folly in black-and-white, either. It had been far too painful in those days. "But I would have made sure it was done."

He shook his head. "So what was that?" He frowned as she withdrew the envelope from her portfolio. It was a bright-red portfolio, one he had bought her after she'd complained that she couldn't find things in her office if he came in and dumped papers on them.

"Put them in here," he'd said, brandishing the shocking-red leather case. "You won't mislay them, then."

Sadie forbore telling him she never mislaid anything, he just covered things up. Instead she'd thanked him—and made good use of it. Now she took the papers out of the envelope and showed them to him. The first one was the cover letter thanking him for contacting them and telling him they would be happy to handle the case if he would simply fill in the forms enclosed and create a Nevada residence which he needed to maintain for six weeks before filing. Another six weeks after, and if the divorce was uncontested, it would be finalized.

"No problem," the letter had concluded. "We are specialists at correcting such mistakes and we will file your papers as soon as you verify your Nevada address and fill in the necessary forms."

Spence stared at them. He flipped through them. Read them once—and then again. And then he lifted his gaze. He looked furious. "Bloody hell." He slammed the papers down on the desk and spun away, prowling the room. "They could have called! Did they think I'd changed my mind?"

"That is apparently exactly what they thought," Sadie told him. "I rang them this morning."

It had been too late last night by the time she'd gone to the bank and searched for the papers he wanted. She'd found his birth certificate right away. But the divorce papers weren't there. In desperation she'd opened the only thing she thought they could be in—the unopened envelope from a Las Vegas law firm. And when she'd read the letter, she'd stood there stunned, realizing that Spence had never read it, hadn't even bothered to open it.

And then, she, too, had thought that surely he must have had some other contact with them.

"I called the courthouse to check, when I didn't find the papers. They said there was no divorce on file. By then it was too late to call the lawyer. So I did it this morning on my layover." That had been another disaster—a plane with mechanical problems that had landed for an unscheduled maintenance stop in Detroit. But at least she'd been able to confirm her worst suspicion.

"They checked their records. They had nothing beyond a note of your initial phone message. They said it happens more often than you would think," she added, "people changing their minds."

Spence just stared at her.

Sadie shrugged. "So, it appears we are still married."

The notion had had her brain buzzing all night. *Married?*
She was still *married?* To *Spence?*

"Bloody hell," Spence said again, then raked a hand through
his hair so it stood up in dark spikes all over his head.

Good thing she hadn't expected him to be thrilled. "Sorry,"
she said with some asperity. "I realize it upsets your plans."

"Damned right it does." He ground his teeth, then sighed.
"Not your fault," he muttered grudgingly. He slanted her a
glance. "You would have seen it was done."

"Yes," Sadie agreed.

They stared at each other. In his gaze Sadie could see he
knew it was true.

"But I didn't want to put you to the trouble," he muttered.
"It was my screwup. My mistake."

"I'd say we both made a mistake," Sadie replied. She, after
all, had been idiot enough to agree.

There was a light knock on the door. Before either of them
could say, "Come in," it opened and Tom poked his head around
the door. "Sorted?" he asked Spence.

Spence shook his head. "We have a small...hang-up."

"How small?"

"Not very," Spence said grimly.

Tom's eyes widened. He looked at Sadie. "You're still married
to her?" His astonishment—and disapproval—were obvious.

"So it seems. Just go to your meeting, Tom. I'll talk to Dena.
We'll sort things out."

"But the wedding—"

"Is off. For now."

"But what about the island resort project?" asked Tom.
"What about Carstairs? Leonie? What will Isogawa say?"

Sadie frowned at these references to the people she had just lined up to attend the meeting at Nanumi. What did they have to do with his marriage?

"What *about* the island resort project?" she asked. "What about Mr. Isogawa and Richard and Leonie Carstairs?"

"Why? What do you know about Leonie?" Spence demanded, fixing her with a hard look, as if he thought she'd been prying.

"Nothing," Sadie said. "Well, nothing much," she corrected herself. "She just seems a little insecure."

Both men stared at her.

"She keeps ringing me," Sadie said, "very worried that Richard will come to the meeting without her. I assured her he wouldn't, that Mr. Isogawa wants couples, that she'd be very welcome."

Spence's jaw tightened. Tom gave him an arch look that Sadie didn't understand.

"She would be," Sadie said. "Mr. Isogawa said wives were welcome. Encouraged, in fact." Was that why he'd wanted to bring Dena? But she couldn't ask—not in front of Dena's father. Even though Tom Wilson was as much of a businessman as Spence, it didn't seem like the thing to say.

"Right," Spence muttered. "It's just—never mind." He broke off and turned to the other man. "Just go on now, Tom. I'll be in touch."

"What about Dena? What are you going to tell my daughter?"

"I'll explain."

Tom just looked at him doubtfully, then shook his head. "If this blows up—"

"It won't."

Tom looked doubtful. But Sadie knew that Spence didn't do doubt. He stared Tom down until finally the latter pressed his lips together and gave a curt nod. "Fine. Handle it, then." And he was gone.

In his absence there was silence.

"We can get a divorce," Sadie felt compelled to say.

"Not in the next half hour."

"Well, no. But—"

"Forget it. For now," Spence amended. "I need to talk to Dena."

"I'll come with you."

"No, you won't."

"But—"

"No. This is between me and Dena. Our wedding may have been business, but she's my friend. And I owe her the courtesy of telling her what's going on personally. Privately."

"I just thought it might help if—"

"It wouldn't," he said harshly. "And I think you've helped enough for one day, Sadie. Just wait here. I'll be back." And he stalked out the door, banging it shut behind him.

She'd helped? As if this were all her fault?

Well, it wasn't. But some of it was. She needed to make a break. She would see about the divorce this time—and get it done properly. And then she would leave. Find a new job. Sell Spence back his percentage of the company. That would certainly make it permanent. She needed to stop waffling around, trying to make a life for herself while all the while she hovered on the edge of Spence's.

Enough Spence.

There would be a time, as Danny had said, when she would finally need to grow up and take control of her life—to *get* a life.

"And the time," she told herself firmly, "is now."

Dena didn't even look up when he came into the judge's chambers. She was reading some legal documents, completely absorbed. No one looking at her would ever have imagined she'd just had her wedding cut out from under her. As always, she was immaculate and composed. Not a blond hair was out of place. The lipstick she'd put on right before the ceremony still looked fresh, not gnawed.

Spence, on the other hand, felt as if he'd been dragged through the New York subway system backward and shot point-blank with a stun gun.

He was *married?* To *Sadie?* Had been married to her for the past four years?

Dena finished the page she was reading before she looked up at him expectantly and smiled her own cool, self-possessed smile. "Well," she said. "That was interesting."

He knew she didn't mean the papers in her hand. His jaw clenched and he had to make an effort to relax it. "Yes." But he couldn't keep from biting the word off, and apparently that was the only clue she needed.

"So, it's true?"

"Apparently." He explained haltingly. Not about Emily. He just said he and Sadie had been in Vegas. They'd got married. In the morning he'd realized it was a mistake. It was hard not to sound like an idiot. So he tried not to go into too much detail, just hoped that sane matter-of-fact words came out of his mouth until finally there seemed nothing more to say.

"Obviously, I should have read the damn letter. I assumed it was a done deal."

Dena let the silence gather for a few seconds before she said mildly, "That'll teach you," as if it were only a minor folly, not a full-scale disaster.

"It will," Spence said. His jaw locked tight. His head pounded.

"So, okay. As long as we know," Dena said, shifting gears. "I just don't want to see the deal fall through."

He stared at her, surprised that she was taking it so calmly. But then, he reminded himself, it was just business to her. Business deals collapsed all the time. And in any case, it was his problem, not hers.

"It'll be fine," she said. "You just take Sadie instead."

"What?" Spence stared at her.

Dena gave him a completely guileless look. "Well, she's your wife."

"Yes, but—" He couldn't finish. It would never be "just business" with Sadie. It couldn't be.

Sadie was businesslike, but she didn't see the world the same way he did.

"Well, what else are you going to do?" Dena said reasonably. "It won't look very good to Isogawa and his 'happy family' theme if you show up having just filed for divorce."

"No." He was trying to think. He was usually so damn good at it. Solutions were always at his fingertips, always on the tip of his tongue.

"You've worked too long, too hard on this resort. It's a once-in-a-lifetime opportunity," Dena reminded him.

"I know that," Spence said tersely. There were bigger investors in the deal— Richard Carstairs for one—but Spence was the one who had made the initial contact with Mr. Isogawa. He was the one whose reputation was riding on it. Richard and John and Steve, the other three investors, were old hands at this sort of deal. This was Spence's first resort, first foray into business in the Pacific. He had more stake in it than anyone.

"So you have to make it work," Dena said simply. "And if once upon a time you couldn't keep your jeans zipped and Sadie made you make an honest woman of her, so be it. At least you're married. That's what's important."

Spence barely heard the last part. His brain had ground to a screeching halt at the words *You couldn't keep your jeans zipped.*

All of a sudden memories of a naked Sadie Morrissey were alive and well and rising like a phoenix in his brain.

He pressed his palms to the sides of his head, feeling as if it were going to explode.

"What's wrong?" Dena asked. "Headache? I wouldn't be surprised."

"No. Yeah. I need to think."

"Yes. And thank your lucky stars Sadie showed up."

Spence blinked, then goggled at her. "Lucky?"

"Well, it certainly wouldn't have done any good if you'd turned out to be a bigamist, would it?" Dena said impatiently. "With Isogawa being Mr. Propriety. Let's face it, if he'd discovered you were married to two women, the deal would be in the trash faster than you can say 'bigamist.' And Leonie would have been thrilled. She might have steered clear of you seeing one wedding ring on your finger. But I'm pretty sure two would have allowed her to put her scruples aside." She smiled.

Spence didn't. He was usually pretty good at taking whatever life dealt him and making the best of it.

But he couldn't see how he was going to make the best of being married to Sadie Morrissey.

Dena kept smiling. "You'll be fine. You wanted a wife, didn't you?"

"Yes, but—"

"You've got one. And she knows your business. You'll be fine. Just do what you do best."

He looked at her blankly.

She stood up, put the papers away, then closed her briefcase and patted him on the cheek as she turned toward the door. "Improvise."

Sadie could hear Spence bellowing her name up and down the hallway.

It was tempting to stay right where she was—in the ladies' room. But that would be cowardly, and she'd faced the worst already, hadn't she?

Of course she had. Now they just had to sit down and work out how to get divorced for real. She could do that. And Spence would *want* to do it. He had probably already filled out the paperwork.

"So get on with it," she told herself. "Nothing's changed."

Not really. It wasn't like they were a real couple who had loved each other. She had loved him—still did, she supposed. But that had been foolish. She should have tried harder to get over it. She should have left years ago.

Well, better late than never, she thought. That was what Gran always said. She sent a prayer winging heavenward, a little divine help—or a little encouragement from Gran— wouldn't come amiss right now.

Please, she added as she pushed open the door and stepped out.

Spence was standing with his back to her, punching his cell phone furiously. Then he raised it to his ear and waited. Tapped his foot. Ran his fingers through his hair.

Sadie approached quietly, knowing better than to interrupt his call.

He glared at the phone, punched another button furiously, then snarled into it, "Damn it, Sadie. Where the hell are you?"

"Right behind you."

He whipped around. He glared at her, then at the phone. Then he flicked it shut and stuck it in his pocket. "Where have you been?"

"I went to the ladies' room while you were talking to Dena. Is she all right?"

"Who? Dena?"

"Of course. Was she very upset?"

"Not a bit." He shrugged as if it didn't matter, but there was an edge of annoyance in his voice. Had their proposed marriage, perhaps, not been totally business, after all?

Sadie didn't want to think about that. She'd always liked Dena, and among the many reasons she'd hated having to announce their marriage so bluntly today was the worry that, despite Spence's assurances to the contrary, Dena might really be hurt. "I'm so glad. I wouldn't have wanted to hurt her."

"Hurt her? What about me?" Spence said indignantly.

"It was just business for you!"

"My business could be hurt."

"How?" Sadie cocked her head. "Were you counting on maybe a Caribbean island from Daddy for a wedding present?"

"No, I damned well was not!" His indignation was very real now, and Sadie felt small for having made the remark.

In his entire life Spencer Tyack had never got anything the easy way. No one had given him anything. And it had always been a matter of honor for him to earn everything he had.

"Sorry," Sadie said now and meant it. "I'm sure it's...difficult. And for all that it was business," she added quickly, "you must care. We'll get a divorce as quick as we can and then you can marry Dena."

"No," he said flatly. "I can't."

"Why not?"

"Because I'd have to divorce you first."

"Well, yes, but—"

"And Isogawa's not going to like that. He's as old school as they come. He believes in the sanctity and stability of marriage."

"So do I," Sadie muttered. "Appearances to the contrary."

"You shouldn't have said yes, then," Spence snapped. He looked as if he'd like to hit something.

No, she certainly shouldn't have. But it was too late for self-recrimination now. "Fine," she said. "If you don't want to get a divorce right now, we won't. We can wait until you're back. Until your deal is done. Isogawa doesn't have to know. After all, until less than an hour ago, *you* didn't know! Let him go on thinking you're single."

"Can't."

"Oh, for God's sake, stop being cryptic! Why can't you?" Sadie scowled, perplexed by his stubbornness. "I've talked to him. Yes, he's very into marriage and family. But he doesn't think the whole world has to march two by two." She knew enough of Mr. Isogawa's views to be sure of that.

But Spence just shook his head. "No. Look, I—" He started as if he were going to explain further, but then looked around at the people wandering up and down the corridor, some of them giving the two of them speculative looks, and instead abruptly he took her by the arm.

"I don't want to discuss this here," he said. "Let's get a cab."

"A cab? And go where?"

"To my place." And as he spoke he steered her toward the elevator.

His place? Sadie knew, of course, that he had a pied-à-terre on the Upper West Side. In the past two years, he'd spent so much time in New York that he kept a studio apartment here as well as one in the Caribbean, one in Greece and one in Spain. Sadie had seen pictures of them all, but she'd never been to any in person. In fact she could count on the fingers of a single hand the occasions that she had ever been in Spence's house in Butte!

For all that she had grown up with him running in and out of her house with Danny, the reverse had never been true.

When they'd been children, life in Spence's house—with his bitter mother and unreliable father—had been unpredictable at best. She knew he hadn't wanted anyone to witness it.

But even now that he was master of his own destiny and domain, and lived in one of the old Copper King mansions he'd restored himself in uptown Butte, Spence kept his home separate from the rest of his life.

"It's the way he is." Danny had shrugged with complete indifference when Sadie had asked him about it. "Besides," he'd added with patently bossy big-brotherliness, "you don't want to go there."

Which hadn't been true at all.

Being seriously infatuated with him, Sadie had wanted to very much. But in all the years she had known him and worked for him, Spence had remained a good employer—and a good friend—but a man with definite boundaries.

"You're taking me to your place?" she echoed now, surprised.

"Where the hell else," he said gruffly, "since you're my wife."

He could snarl the words "my wife" easily enough. It was less easy to think about the reality of it. In fact, it was damn near impossible.

Spence sat in the backseat of the taxi carrying them to his Upper West Side apartment and studied Sadie out of the corner of his eye.

His "wife" was sitting in the backseat, too, but as far away from him as she could get, as if she were trying to avoid contamination. She wasn't looking his way, either. Instead she was deliberately staring out the window, feigning complete absorption in the traffic as they hurtled, then crawled, up Eighth Avenue.

That wasn't like Sadie. Sadie usually paid no attention at all to where they were. She was normally focused on him, waving papers in his face, pointing at fine print, rattling on a mile a minute.

Now she wasn't saying a word.

Of course, he knew she wasn't happy, either. This situation—this mess!—was no more normal for her than it was for him, though she'd had a few hours longer to get used to it.

What was she thinking? Usually he had no trouble figuring that out. Usually she was telling him without his having to ask. It was what they did—discuss, argue, debate, clarify.

But now she was as still and silent as a stone. He wished he could see inside her head. Then again, all things considered, it was probably better he couldn't.

This was all his fault. No doubt about it.

He accepted that. Spence was never one to deny responsibility. He should have made sure it was taken care of. Should have faced his demons and his momentary foolishness and made sure it didn't come back to haunt them.

But he hadn't. His mistake.

So it was his job to fix it. Properly. Completely. Unflinchingly.

And he would.

But first he had to deal with the resort. They'd worked too long and too hard on it—both he and Sadie—to risk letting the deal fall apart now. He wasn't sure exactly how to handle it, though. His intuition, normally brilliant—if he did say so himself—seemed to have completely deserted him.

Dena's notion—that he take Sadie—was impossible. She would never agree. And he understood completely. But he couldn't think of any other options.

Sadie would. He was sure. That was the joy of having her working with him. They battled things out. He proposed and she contradicted. Usually he was right, or close enough. But sometimes she had a better idea.

She'd better have a better idea today.

He started to say something, then shut his mouth again. He didn't want to start the argument in the taxi. So he would wait. He would get her back to his place and then he would tell her what they needed to do.

And she could argue him around to something else. Yeah. He smiled at the thought, the first smile he'd managed since Sadie had dropped her bombshell an hour ago. Then he shifted against the back of the seat, flexed his rigid shoulders, took a deep breath and felt considerably better.

They finished the cab ride in silence. When they reached his apartment, Spence paid off the driver and gestured her ahead of him up the stairs to the brownstone in which he owned a floor-through apartment.

He unlocked the door and said, "Third floor," and waited until she started up the steps, then fell in behind her.

"You don't have to bring up my case," Sadie said.

Spence didn't bother to reply. He wasn't getting them side-tracked on another argument. Instead he just jerked his head toward the stairs. Sadie scowled at him, but began to climb.

He went up after her—and found himself at eye level with a curvy female backside that sparked a memory. He tried to resist it.

But his eyes were glued to the view—and the word *wife* was suddenly pounding in his brain. Not just *wife* but *my wife*.

He hadn't seen Sadie as a woman in years—hadn't let himself even consider her that way, except obviously for one very intense night. And now, damn it, was not the time to start!

So he stopped where he was and let her get half a dozen steps ahead of him.

Sadie glanced back over her shoulder. "Something wrong? I told you not to lug it up. It's heavy."

Did she think he couldn't carry her damned suitcase? "It's fine," Spence snapped. "I've got…something in my shoe. Go on."

Sadie raised skeptical eyebrows, but shrugged, then turned and kept on going. Spence waited until she had reached the next landing and had disappeared from view. Only then, when he was no longer treated to a vision of her backside, did he continue up after her.

Wordlessly he unlocked the door and pushed it open, then waved her in ahead of him.

"Not going to carry me over the threshold?"

He stared at her. "Do you want me to?"

"No! Of course not." She scurried into the apartment. "I'm

just being—" she grimaced, then gave him a quick self-conscious smile and a little awkward shrug "—inappropriate."

Spence followed her in and kicked the door shut behind him. "Not as inappropriate as you might think," he said, dropping her suitcase on the floor.

Sadie frowned. "What do you mean?"

"I mean that, as apparently we're still married, on Friday you're coming to Nanumi with me—as my wife."

CHAPTER THREE

Go with him to Nanumi? As his wife?

Sadie stared.

"Why not?" Spence persisted. He began pacing around the room. It was a small room, relatively impersonal, exactly the sort of anonymous place she'd expected he would have. "We're married. You said so."

"Yes. I did. But—" She looked at him more closely. Was he suggesting…? Surely he couldn't mean…?

Her heart seemed to kicked over in her chest as her brain entertained a possibility that had never occurred to her—that Spence would want to continue their "marriage", that he saw her as a woman at last.

He stopped dead square in front of her. "For better or worse, Sadie," he said, as if she needed the reminder, "right now you're my wife. And Isogawa is all about family. You said so yourself. He wants couples at the resort. We're a couple. It makes perfect sense. Right?" He was grinning now, looming over her, daring her to contradict him, to argue.

And Sadie suddenly knew it had nothing to do with wanting to stay married to her at all. He wanted to argue.

This was Spence in confrontation mode. Spence looking for a fight. A challenge. It was the way he worked.

Spence's gut-level instinct picked up and proposed things continually. Sometimes, Sadie thought, his brain worked faster than the speed of light.

It was the way he began each deal. He would spot a possibility, then—using some sort of sixth sense, some intuition that she could never quite catch up with—he would analyze whatever he was considering at warp speed, consider the options, calculate the odds, then fling some sort of outrageous idea at her.

Like now.

Usually, of course, he didn't do it with the edgy fierceness she heard in his voice now, despite the grin. But even with the granite-jawed, I-eat-sharks-for-breakfast glitter in his eyes, the look on his face was decidedly familiar.

He was daring her to confront him, to stop him. He didn't expect her to agree. He was, to put it bluntly, looking for a fight.

And, she was quite sure now, hoping she would provide him with half a dozen other options. It was the way they worked. One of Spence's tests of his intuition, Sadie had realized long ago, was to spring a decision on her, then wait for her to argue.

And Sadie always embraced the opportunity. She loved arguing with Spence. It excited her, exhilarated her. It made her feel as if she were a vital part of his decision-making process, a real member of the team, because Spence really did listen to what she said. And he was, if she was convincing enough, quite willing to revise and reconsider as a result of their battles.

Now she just smiled and said, "All right."

The sudden silence in the room was deafening. Spence stared at her, eyes wide. "*All right?* What the hell do you mean, *all right?*"

"I mean, I agree."

His dark brows drew down, and he scowled furiously at her as he rubbed a hand against the back of his neck. "I wasn't asking you," he said sharply. "I was telling you."

"Yes. And I agreed with you."

"You do? I mean, of course you do," he blustered. "It only makes sense."

Sadie nodded. "Yes."

"You think so?" He was eyeing her narrowly.

What made real sense, Sadie thought, was for her to turn tail and run for the hills. She wasn't used to Spence looking at her like that—with that intense gleam in his eye. But she'd backed down, gentled, calmed and gone on far too much in the past. It was time to stop, for her own sake as much as his.

"Yes," she said firmly, "I do."

"Why?"

She shook her head. She wasn't telling him that. She wasn't even sure she had worked out all the reasons yet herself. But she knew what she had to say.

"It's just business."

He blinked. Then nodded. "Yes."

"So, no big deal." Hahaha, her brain chortled at her naiveté, but she ignored it. "I'll go to Fiji with you. And after, I'll resign. I'll come home. We'll get the divorce. A real one this time—with paperwork completed. All i's dotted and t's crossed. Official. Legal. And then I'll get out of your life."

"Don't be ridiculous. I mean, the divorce, yeah. Sure. Fine. But you don't have to get out of my life!"

"Yes, I do."

Dear God, yes, she absolutely did. She certainly did not want go through this again, get *another* divorce from Spencer Tyack and then go back to being his office manager. She'd been foolish enough and self-deluded enough to try it once. And to a degree it had worked. But she hadn't ever got over him. And if she stayed she never would.

She looked up and met his eyes with as steady a gaze as she could manage.

"I'll be your wife for the week. And then I'm gone."

Spence's jaw tightened. He glared at her for a long time, then shrugged. "Suit yourself."

"I am."

It would, she decided, serve her right. She would go to Nanumi with him as his real, honest-to-God wife for a week. And she would let herself act like a wife. She would have a week of the dream that she'd always wanted. And then she would leave. There would undoubtedly be a bit of shock value in it. Maybe it would wake her up sufficiently to force her to get on with her life.

Spence didn't look completely convinced. And she wasn't going to stand there and argue with him about it now.

"I'm filthy," she said. "And I've been up all night. I need a shower. May I take one?"

He looked startled. His scowl deepened. "A shower? Here?"

"You have a bath, I think. Indoor plumbing? I know I've never been to New York before, but surely—"

"Yes, damn it." He jerked his head toward a door beyond the small kitchen area. "Go for it."

"Thank you." She shrugged, glad now to have her suitcase and fresh clothes at hand. "I've been on the road since yesterday evening."

"Then why were you late?"

"Plane trouble. We had a wiring problem. Spent five hours on the ground in Detroit. Just think, if the plane had gone down, you would have been a widower and all would have been well." She smiled up at him brightly from where she knelt and opened her suitcase.

"Don't be an ass!" Spence snapped.

She was trying hard not to be. She pulled out a pair of linen slacks, a scoop-necked T-shirt and some clean underthings, and got a grip on her wayward emotions. Only when she was sure she was in control again, did she stand up to face him.

He was standing in her way, staring at her. "Do you mind?" she pressed when he didn't move. "A shower?" His gaze seemed fixed on the clothes in her arms and she wasn't even sure he'd heard her. "Spence?"

He gave a quick shake of his head. "No, of course I don't mind." And as if he suddenly realized why she wasn't moving—because she couldn't—he moved out of her way.

"Thank you." She slipped past him. "I'll hurry."

"Take your time," he muttered. "I'll get...us some food."

"Sounds good," she lied, certain she couldn't eat a thing. She went into the bathroom, then turned and gave him one last bright determined smile.

He was still staring at her when she closed the door.

Sadie wore silk underwear!

Those were peach-colored silk panties she had in her hands, not to mention a lacy scrap of a bra that looked as if it had come right out of some Hollywood lingerie catalog. Not the sort of underwear she could have bought in Butte!

Spence's mind went straight from the sight of those lacy garments in Sadie's arms to a vision of her wearing them. He sucked air.

The unexpectedness of it had him gasping. Not just the un-expectedness of the peach-colored lace and silk—which was astonishing enough given Sadie's sensible matter-of-fact demeanor—but even more his brain's almost immediate and very vivid notion of what she would look like wearing it.

Somewhere back in Sadie's teenage years, Spence had begun to notice that Danny's kid sister wasn't built like a stick insect anymore. He'd even found himself, more than once, lying in bed thinking about her curvy body and her long long legs and ima-gining what they'd be like bare and wrapped around his waist.

One night he'd actually made a remark about her feminine

attributes in front of Danny—and found himself knocked off the bar stool.

"Don't even think it," Danny had warned, standing over him, breathing hard. "Sadie's the marrying kind. Or she will be when she's old enough. She's a good girl and she's going to stay that way. So you keep your eyes—and hands—off and your zipper welded shut. She's not for the likes of you! Got it?"

Spence had got it.

And even in his hormone-driven lust-filled early twenties he had known that Danny was right. Sadie *was* a great girl. A good girl. And when she grew up, she would deserve a good man. The best.

God knew that wasn't him. With his alcoholic, here-today gone-tomorrow father and his bitter hard mother, not to mention the chip he carried on his shoulder that was the size of all the rock they'd ever taken out of the Berkeley Pit, Spencer Tyack was no man for a girl like Sadie Morrissey.

So he had kept his hands to himself—and his zipper, around Sadie at least, firmly zipped. But he had still known she was gorgeous, just as Danny undoubtedly knew it—though Spence didn't think Sadie herself ever had a clue.

She had certainly never flaunted her assets. And at an age when lots of teenage girls were determined to practice their feminine wiles on susceptible males, Sadie had never done that.

If anything, as she'd grown older and more beautiful, she'd got quieter and less forthcoming. As a kid she had always been easy to talk to as she'd tagged around after him and Danny. But by sixteen or so, that had ended. And far from flirting with him whenever he came around with Danny, she became almost distant and remote.

"What'd you do to her?" Danny demanded, seeing her reticence himself and deciding it was because of something Spence had done.

"Nothing! Not a damn thing!"

He'd have spilled blood—even his own—to prove it to Danny. But his protests apparently were enough.

"See that you don't," Danny had said.

"Count on it," Spence had replied. He just figured she didn't like him anymore. As a kid, she'd tagged after him, but as a young woman, she'd evidently seen him for who he was and decided he wasn't worth bothering with.

Better that way, Spence had thought. Better that he not think about Sadie anymore at all.

But then one winter afternoon when he had been in the Morrissey kitchen talking to Danny and tearing his hair over the state of his office and his paperwork, Sadie had walked though, listened a minute, then said, "That's silly. Just file it."

"I would if I could figure out a system!" It wasn't the easiest thing in the world.

"I could figure out a system," Sadie had said blithely, as if she held the answers to all the mysteries in the world.

Spence had snorted. "I doubt it."

"I'll prove it," Sadie had countered.

And the next day she'd shown up at his truck. "So where do you work?"

He'd jerked his head toward the camper top on the truck. "Here."

She'd blinked, then goggled at him, but then shrugged and said. "Fine. Show me."

"You don't want to mess with it," he'd said because he certainly didn't want her poking her nose in his living quarters.

"Afraid I'll be able to do something you can't?" Sadie had challenged.

And of course then he'd had to let her in. So he'd opened the hatch to show her the heaps of paper—notes and scraps and abstracts and legal documents—all tossed around on top of the sleeping bag and mattress he slept on and thrust under the platform where he kept his gear. "Still think you can file it?" He'd given her a lazy smug grin.

"Out of my way." And Sadie had pushed him aside, then clambered in, making him swallow hard as he'd got a good full look at her pert curvy backside disappearing into the back of his truck.

Then she'd turned and looked back at him. "Are you going to help?"

"If I were I'd do it myself," he told her honestly.

She'd nodded. "Then go away."

He had. He'd gone out for a run, determined to wear himself out—and get all thoughts of Sadie's bottom out of his head.

When he came back, exhausted, that evening, he felt more in control of his hormones. Sadie didn't look any more in control of the mess in the back of his truck than she had before he'd left. The paper was still all over the place—in different piles now, but not better piles.

He'd been relieved. And since the next day he had been going to L.A. to a business seminar, he'd said, "Nice try. See. It isn't as easy as you thought. Just forget it."

But Sadie hadn't. She'd shaken her head and held out her hand. "I'm not finished. Give me the key to your truck."

"You're insane." But he'd handed her the key.

When he came back a week later, the mess was gone, the camper was bare except for the platform, mattress, sleeping bag and four filing boxes. He felt a moment's panic.

"Where—?"

"There." Sadie pointed at the filing boxes. "Everything is sorted and in its very own place. I can show you how it works," Sadie had offered.

But the one thing Spence had learned at the seminar was the

value of delegating. He didn't want to know how it worked. He just wanted Sadie there making it work. He'd hired her on the spot.

As his employee, Sadie had stopped being quiet.

She would come every afternoon after school to his truck and sit in the cab, making him go over papers with her, filing them, discussing them, arguing about them. Sadie, for all that she'd been only sixteen, had definite opinions. She'd asked questions about things he'd never even considered.

It wasn't long before he'd realized she wasn't just a genius at organization, she had a good instinctive mind for business— one that complemented his—and he was damned glad she was working for him.

She was gorgeous. She was fun to have around. And she'd become an incredible asset to his work.

The second two he could deal with easily. The first was a problem. Or it would have been if he hadn't learned long ago how to compartmentalize his life.

Dealing with his parents had taught him that. And just as he'd built a "family box" around his parents to keep their anger and bitterness and failure out of his life in order to survive, so he isolated Sadie.

He built a mental "employee box" around her. And then every time he'd found himself even remotely thinking about the physical Sadie Morrissey, he'd slammed the lid on that box.

Until the night Emily had jilted him and the lid had come off. At his rawest, lowest point, Sadie had been there. She'd been gentle, warm, caring, supportive.

Loving.

A word—an experience, let's face it—that Spence knew damn little about. And he'd given in to it. He'd needed her warmth, her care, her love that night. He'd needed Sadie. And he hadn't been able to resist that need.

And so he'd asked her to marry him. Asked? How about

coerced? That was closer to the truth. He'd resisted temptation for years. Had resisted Sadie for years. But that one brief night he had succumbed.

He'd married her. He'd made love to her. He'd—God help him!—taken her innocence that night. At the time he'd been shocked and, perversely, delighted. And of course, faced with her beautiful sleeping face in the morning, he'd known what he'd done was wrong.

Then he'd done what he thought was right—divorced her. Or tried to. Even that, it seemed, he'd done badly. The only thing he'd done right was to stuff Sadie and all his intimate memories of her back into that box and slam the lid on. In the past four years he had never once let himself contemplate her big green eyes or her lovely golden freckled skin or her long long legs or supremely kissable mouth. He had resisted all thoughts of the night he had made love to Sadie Morrissey.

And he sure as hell wasn't going to get through a week of sharing a *bure* at Nanumi with her if he was fixating already on what sort of underwear she wore!

The trouble was, now that he knew—and knew that he was still married to her, knew that legally at least he had a right to her—he couldn't get the vision out of his mind. And he couldn't get his mind out of the bathroom where it had gone to watch her strip off her clothes and get in the shower!

The lid hadn't simply come off, the whole damn box he'd put Sadie Morrissey in for years and years—minus that one fateful night—had crumbled to smithereens.

And his imagination, unleashed, was a fearful thing.

"Get a grip," he muttered furiously to himself. "It's Sadie, for God's sake. It's business."

But his mind—and even more important, his body—were busy reminding him that Sadie wasn't only business; she was his wife.

"For a week," he reminded himself. "Only a week."

Or until the contracts were signed and the resort was a done deal. A week. He could build another damn box and jam her back in for a week.

His body begged to differ.

"Hell!" He stalked over to the door of the bathroom and pounded on it. "Sadie!"

The water shut off. "What?"

He squeezed his eyes shut as if that would keep him from visualizing her standing naked and wet in his shower. "What do you want for dinner?"

What if she said, "You?"

Of course she didn't. "Surprise me," she called back through the closed door.

Spence tried not to think about surprises.

And Sadie must have had second thoughts because she suddenly called, "Just get something they don't have in Butte." And then the water went back on again full force.

Spence stood there drawing in ragged breaths and trying to drag his wits back from wherever they had scattered. "Right. Focus," he commanded himself. "Something they don't have in Butte." Shouldn't be hard.

And certainly a lot simpler than trying again not to think about Sadie Morrissey naked in his shower.

Sadie came out of the bathroom, showered and dressed in clean clothes, feeling better—and warier at the same time.

While she'd been showering, she'd tried to pull herself together, to come to terms with what he'd asked her to do, to convince herself that she could do it without making a fool of herself. She knew she had to or die trying.

At the same time she wasn't even sure how she was going to get through dinner.

Spence was in the kitchen setting out containers on the table.

"It's Burmese," he said. He didn't even look her way, just unloaded white cardboard containers of piping-hot food that made her mouth water, then turned to get plates out of the cupboard. He was moving with customary quick efficiency and he didn't sound angry any longer. Was that good?

"Smells wonderful." Sadie smiled, still a little uncertain.

Spence laid out silverware, then added chopsticks from one of the bags, then filled glasses with ice water and set them on the table.

"Do you want wine?" There was an unopened bottle on the countertop.

"No, thanks. I'd fall asleep." She was fresher than she had been, but still feeling the effects of the night on the plane and the stress of the past two days. "You go ahead."

He didn't open the bottle, however. He just nodded toward the chair closest to her. "Sit down. Dig in."

Sadie sat. "It *looks* wonderful, too."

"Usually is." He opened a container of rice and handed it to her. "I eat at this place whenever I'm in New York. There's beef satay and chicken curry and something with pork that I never remember the name of. Prawn salad and some kind of fritters. You won't get it in Butte." He was talking quickly and shoveling food onto his plate as he did. He still wasn't looking at her.

She dished up some of everything, then picked up her chopsticks. She took a careful breath, then let it out again. Things felt almost…normal. Like the business lunches she and Spence often shared. Only those were accompanied by sheaves of paper, contracts, diagrams, and nonstop talking.

This meal had no paper, no contracts, no diagrams and, right now, no talking. What it had was a big fat determinedly unacknowledged elephant in the room.

The "marriage" elephant. *Their* marriage elephant.

And how it was going to work. Clearly he saw this as a

business effort. But ordinarily when they worked on a project and had agreed on what needed to be done, they sat down and strategized how to do it. They divided up the tasks. They worked out how to support each other. They each had their jobs, and they knew what to expect.

Sadie needed to know what to expect.

But Spence didn't tell her. He didn't say a word. Kept his mouth full or was busy chewing all the time. The whole meal passed in silence. They ate doggedly, determinedly. Until finally there was nothing else to eat. The cartons were empty. Their plates were clean.

And then, when she hoped he might finally speak, he jumped up and began clearing the table.

Sadie stood, too. "Let me help."

"No. It's all right. I'll do it. Kitchen's pretty small." And it was clear he didn't want her anywhere in it. "Coffee? Tea?" He had his back to her again, rinsing off plates in the sink. Since when had Spence become so determinedly domestic?

"Tea, then, please." The cup would give her something to hang on to when at last they came to grips with things. And coffee, she was afraid, would make her already-frayed nerves even more so.

"Okay. Go sit down. I'll get it."

She would have liked to offer to help with that, too. But Spence was already filling the kettle with water and it didn't take two to make tea. So Sadie crossed the room to where she could look out over the back gardens of the block of brownstones.

It was a clear spring evening, already gone dark. And even with the window closed, because it wasn't warm enough yet to leave them open, she could hear the sounds of the city, although muted a bit now. The trees were just coming into leaf. One neighbor's window box was filled with bobbing heads of something that she expected would, in daylight, turn out to be daffodils.

Her own daffodils growing against the wall behind her house back in Butte weren't blooming yet. It was still too cold in Montana. But Montana in the winter felt warmer than this room.

All right. Enough. If he wouldn't bring it up, she would. She turned to where Spence was pouring out cups of tea. "You said it was business, marrying Dena. But you could have married Dena anytime. Why now? What's going on at Nanumi that you need a wife for?"

"You said it yourself. Isogawa wants couples."

"But he wouldn't expect you to marry just to please him. So what else?"

Spence scowled, and Sadie actually thought he wasn't going to answer. But finally, after a long moment, he said, "Leonie."

Sadie blinked. "Leonie? Carstairs?" She didn't follow. "Richard's wife? I don't understand."

Spence's scowl deepened, and something that might have been a tide of red seemed to creep up to his jaw. But he didn't speak as he carried a mug across the room and handed it to her wordlessly.

"Thanks." Sadie accepted it and took a sip, then asked, because she still didn't get it. "Why on earth would you marry Dena because of Richard Carstairs's wife?"

"Oh, use your head!" Spence snapped. "Because she doesn't put much stock in being Richard's wife!"

"Doesn't…?" Sadie's voice trailed off. "What?" She considered the implications of what Spence was saying. "You mean…but she's so nice on the phone!"

A harsh breath hissed between Spence's teeth. "How the hell many times has she called you?"

"Three or four. She seems very…nervous. Like she's not sure she's welcome. Not wanting to get in the way."

"Yeah, right," Spence muttered. He hunched his shoulders, looking hunted.

"What's that mean?" Sadie asked. Mentally she ran through the conversations she'd had with Leonie Carstairs. The other woman had seemed perhaps a little overly bright and bubbly when they'd talked, but sometimes a little wistful, too. Richard was always so busy, she'd said. She never knew what she should do.

"She seemed very concerned about whether her husband would have time for her."

"Her husband?" Spence's tone was suspicious.

"Who else?"

He didn't answer, but the fierce red along his jawline and up into his face answered the question for her.

"*You?* You think she's after you?" Sadie gaped at Spence.

"I don't think!" he snarled, dark eyes flashing angrily.

Sadie's eyes widened as she considered the implications. "What's going on?" she finally asked, hoping that inviting him to simply spell it out would get the answers she was missing.

"Leonie Carstairs is a desperate, pushy little tart! A guy is single, she hits on him!"

"She hit…on you?"

"She did." The answer was flat.

"But she's married."

"How naive are you?"

"Oh." Sadie felt her cheeks warm. "Um, I see. But…isn't marrying Dena a little drastic just to get her to stop? Couldn't you just say no?"

"No, damn it, I couldn't!" Spence smacked his mug down on the counter with more force than was necessary, slopping tea everywhere. "I tried that," he added grimly.

Sadie tried not to look agog with interest, just matter-of-fact. But she couldn't help saying, "What happened?" with far more curiosity than she'd intended.

Spence scowled and raked a hand through his hair. "It's a

mess. I've been doing business with Richard for years. Knew his first wife."

"Margaret. Yes, I remember her." While she'd never met either Margaret or Richard Carstairs, she'd enjoyed conversations with them during Spence's dealings with them. And she remembered well when Margaret died five years ago.

"They were perfect together. And then three years ago Richard met Leonie." Spence shook his head. "She's young. He's in his fifties. Hell, his kids are her age! But he wouldn't see reason. He wanted her, and he married her. And now—now it's a hell of a mess." Spence prowled the room like a trapped jungle cat, then flung himself into one of the chairs and looked up at her from beneath hooded lids.

Sadie waited, knowing there were times to prompt Spence and times not to. This was one when she needed to wait him out.

"Now that he's got her, he…doesn't pay a lot of attention to her. Frankly I think she scares him. She scares the hell out of me! She…flirts. To get his attention, I think. At least I thought. Now I don't know. After Barcelona…" He scowled and abruptly stopped talking.

Well, there were some things you couldn't just wait out.

"What about Barcelona?" Sadie demanded. She knew Spence had gone there last month for a meeting. She was the one who'd set it up. And she remembered now that Richard had been scheduled to be there, too. "Leonie was there?" She hadn't scheduled that.

"She was," Spence agreed. "Insisted on coming along, Richard said. But he couldn't take her to all his meetings. So one night she was on her own at the hotel. I didn't pay much attention. It wasn't anything to do with me. I was working. And then, that night, I played poker with some of the guys. Later, when I went back to my room—" he grimaced "—she was in my bed."

Sadie stared. *"In your bed?"*

"You heard me!"

"She was in your *room?* But how…?"

Spence shrugged. "Pretended it was hers. Told a maid she got locked out. She was giggling. Bragging about it. 'A few pesetas is all it takes,' she told me. She thought it was great fun. And she was intent on having more fun. She was—" he rubbed a hand against the back of his neck "—not inclined to take no for an answer."

Sadie felt her mouth go dry. Was he saying he'd slept with Leonie Carstairs?

"I packed her right back out, protesting all the way," Spence answered the question she couldn't ask. "But she wasn't happy about it. 'He'll never know,' she said. 'And if he did find out he wouldn't care.'" Spence shook his head grimly. "Not true. Richard would have damned sure cared. He might leave her for a few hours—she might drive him mad—but as far as he's concerned, she belongs to him. It would have killed our working together. It would have ruined that project. But beyond that, I don't sleep with other men's wives."

Sadie swallowed a surge of relief. "Of course not," she said, happier than she had any right to be.

"When the Nanumi deal came up, I could see Barcelona happening all over again."

"You don't think she got the message?"

"No. She doesn't hear what she doesn't want to hear. But I remembered she tried to hit on Dan Fitzsimmons a few months ago, and then he got married and that was the end of it. She apparently doesn't respect her own wedding ring, but she doesn't poach on other women's husbands."

"So you decided to get married?"

"It sounded like a good idea," he said tersely. "I know you think marriage is all about love and romance and flowers and whatnot, but it's not." He bounded out of the chair and began pacing again. "Marriage, throughout history, has more often been an economic alliance than a hearts-and-flowers romance. I understand that. So did Dena. It would have worked." He turned and faced her, his look challenging her to deny it.

"It still seems...pretty drastic."

"Yeah, well, if you were trying to pull off a several-hundred-million-dollar deal that could be scotched by some floozy with boobs for brains, you might do something drastic, too!"

"And now?"

"Now," he said heavily, "there's you."

Right. The marriage elephant. Front and center.

"So, what are we going to do?" she asked.

"Show up and act like a married couple. In front of everyone else," he qualified quickly. "I don't expect anything else. Don't worry."

Yeah, Sadie had pretty much figured that. But then their gazes met and, for one brief instant, she didn't think that at all. Something vivid and intense and extremely personal seemed to flicker in Spencer Tyack's eyes. Something hot. But before she could be sure, he jerked his gaze away again.

"Come on," he said abruptly. "I'll take you to your hotel."

"Hotel?" Sadie said stupidly, still feeling singed by that momentary heat.

"Hotel. Got you a room at the Plaza. Told you I would, remember?" He was already on his knees, stuffing her pile of dirty clothes into her suitcase and zipping it up as if he couldn't wait to be rid of her.

"I—yes. But I thought that was supposed to be a treat for my having brought your birth certificate and our...divorce papers. I didn't," she added, though she supposed she didn't need to remind him of that.

"Doesn't matter. You've got to sleep somewhere. It's paid for. No sense in it going to waste. Come on." He picked up the suitcase, opened the door and stood there, waiting for her to precede him down the stairs.

And Sadie could hardly say, *I want to stay here*. Could she? No. Of course not.

But the scarier question was: Did she? Was she fool enough to want that?

And if she was honest, then yes, a perverse part—an exceedingly stupid part—of her wanted just that.

But clearly Spence didn't.

He didn't want her. He didn't want to be married to her. And whatever he might have said one night four years ago—those hungry, desperate words he'd murmured that had given her hope that night that she meant more to him than he'd ever let on—had obviously been an aberration, not a heartfelt desire.

Now she sucked in a breath, shoved away all romantic notions of happily ever after, and said what she needed to say. "Very well. Thank you. I'm sure I'll enjoy it." Then, chin held high, she went out the door and down the stairs.

She thought she'd be rid of him then. She'd expected he would hail her a cab and she could crawl into it and stop trying to pretend it didn't matter, that she was indifferent, that she didn't care.

But he didn't just see her into a cab. He got in with her. He accompanied her all the way to the Plaza, where she thought he'd leave her at the door.

But, damn it, he came in with her there. He took care of her registration and then walked her to her room.

"You don't need to," she said desperately.

"I do," Spence said. And she wondered if he heard any irony in his words. Probably not, judging from the studied determination on his face.

She wasn't used to a studiedly determined Spence. She was used to a quicksilver man, a brash, outspoken, clever, wild man. Proper and polite had never been Spence's way—not, at least, around her.

But he was proper and polite tonight. He acted like someone had shoved a copy of Emily Post right up his back.

Go away! she begged him silently. *It's settled. We'll do it. But I need some space. I need some time. I need to be alone.*

The last thing she needed was Spence acting all stiff and solicitous, like this was a duty he was performing—which, of course, it was. It was far worse than being treated in the offhand, breezy way he ordinarily treated her.

At least then it had felt as if they were actually friends. Now that they were still married, there was this terrible tension. It felt awful. Neither of them spoke all the way up in the elevator. He didn't look at her. She didn't look at him.

When they reached her room, he took the key and opened the door for her, then held it so she could precede him. Very stiff, very proper. She felt like kicking him.

The room was big and beautifully decorated and it must have cost him a fortune, not that money was an issue to Spence anymore. He barely seemed to notice the room at all. He'd put her suitcase on the luggage rack, then backed toward the door. There he stopped and looked at her intently. "Are you going to be...all right?"

And what would he do if she said no?

Sadie didn't want to find out. "Why shouldn't I be?" she snapped.

He grimaced. "No reason. It's just...I know it's as awkward for you as it is for me. I'm sorry. About everything and—"

"Well, you don't have to keep going on about it!" She had reached the end of her rope. "Just go!"

"I'm going," he said. "I'll be back in the morning to take you to the airport."

"Don't bother. It's entirely unnecessary, and I can certainly get to the airport by myself." Sadie was grateful that her voice sounded cool and composed. She felt like screaming. "I'll want to get an early flight. That way I can be back home by noon. I have work to do."

He looked almost relieved, as if he could hardly wait for her to be out of the city. "I've got to work in the city all week. I won't have time to get back to Butte before we head out to Fiji."

"I know."

"Right. So get yourself a ticket on my flight to Fiji and I'll see you in L.A. The charter from Fiji won't be a problem. I'll let them know you're coming." He started out the door, then stopped in the hallway. "I just thought…can you get someone to cover while we're gone?"

Cover the office, he meant. They were never both gone at the same time. Or they never had been before. Except once. In Vegas four years ago.

Sadie met his gaze. "I can get someone. Don't worry. Thank you for seeing me here. I won't keep you."

"They have to be competent. No air heads," he went on as if she hadn't spoken.

"I know that." Did he think she was an idiot? "I'll take care of it." *Just go, damn it!*

"Good." There was another pause. He shifted awkwardly. "Thanks." Then he cleared his throat. "I meant what I said earlier, Sadie. You don't have to quit."

That's what all this hemming and hawing was about? He was stalling until he found a way to work that into the conversation.

"It can be like before. We can just go back to—"

"Good night, Spence," she said abruptly.

And she shut the door in his face.

CHAPTER FOUR

IN HER FANTASIES Sadie had spent nights at the Plaza. It was what came of being a bookish child, one who spent hours in the library and who read every single book in the children's section over and over.

She'd loved *Eloise*. She'd read the story of the little girl who lived in the Plaza Hotel until the book cover nearly fell off. To Sadie the Plaza had always seemed more distant than the craters of the moon. She could see the craters of the moon from Butte, Montana. She could only imagine the Plaza.

And now here she was. In her very own room—one that Eloise would have enjoyed immensely. She'd have bounced on the bed and hung by her knees from the shower curtain rod. She'd have rung up room service and ordered whatever she wanted.

Sadie could do that. Spence had said so.

"You didn't eat much at dinner," he'd said when he'd been standing at the registration counter with her. "If you get hungry, order room service. Get whatever you want."

Very magnanimous. Thoughtful. Very proper. A good boss.

Not much of a husband. But then he didn't intend to be.

It shouldn't bother her. She should have got over Spencer Tyack years ago. In fact, she rather thought she had. She had dated other men in the past four years, hadn't she? Just because she hadn't found the right one didn't mean she wasn't looking.

But yesterday, the minute she'd discovered she was still married to him, her world had turned upside down—and all those old desperate completely unreciprocated feelings came right back.

And she couldn't help thinking that, while his wedding with Dena might have been no more than taking their "business" relationship to a new level, no doubt he had planned to spend a wedding night with his new bride. He certainly would not have married her, then packed her off to a hotel by herself while he went back to his apartment alone!

But he'd packed Sadie off to a hotel. He'd acted like he could hardly wait to get rid of her!

She shouldn't be surprised, of course. In fact she wasn't. But it would be so much simpler if she didn't love him, if she never had loved him, if she could just smile carelessly and walk away.

But she couldn't walk away for another week. He wouldn't let her. She sat in the middle of her big bed in the Plaza and felt like crying.

At the same time, she emphatically did *not* want to cry!

She had far more important things to do—like figuring how on earth she was going to survive next week knowing that she wasn't pretending—that she was, in fact, Spencer Tyack's wife.

Wedding nights, according to everything Spence had heard, were supposed to be memorable.

Theo Savas, whose wife, Martha, had painted the murals in Spence's office building, hadn't been able to stop grinning when he'd mentioned his. He'd been completely discreet, of course. Theo would be. But you only had to look at the guy to know that he and his wife had had a very satisfactory time, even though Martha had been in the last stages of pregnancy by the time Theo finally got her to wear his ring.

Lucky Theo, Spence thought grimly.

He could have told Theo a thing or two about memorable wedding nights! He'd had more than his share.

It was mortifying. Humiliating. First Emily's defection four years ago. Then his desperate marriage to Sadie.

And now this! He hadn't had a wedding today—but apparently he still had a wife!

He had tried so scrupulously for four years to forget that night—to forget holding Sadie in his arms, to forget making love to her—that to be hit again with the memories was like being gut-punched.

He might have been all right if he hadn't seen those wispy underthings. When the hell had Sadie started wearing sexy underwear like that?

What he remembered had been cotton and serviceable. Nothing that would stir a guy's libido. Of course, she could have been wearing a gunny sack and it wouldn't have mattered. Once he'd got her out of her clothes, it was all about Sadie.

And his libido had taken over completely.

It had been hard work to walk away from that night—to know that forgetting it was the best thing to do, the only thing to do to be fair to Sadie.

And now it was like all his efforts were for naught.

Why in hell had he had to see those flimsy lacy panties when she'd taken them out of her suitcase? Why couldn't he have been left to contemplate having gone to bed with a Sadie with no more "come hither" attraction than a nun?

Trouble was, he knew Sadie was no nun. Now that he couldn't seem to help but think about that night again, he remembered very well how un-nunlike she had been. Shocked him, really.

She'd always seemed sort of buttoned-down and demure in the office. Well, not demure exactly. But he hadn't counted on a woman who could make his blood run thick and hot.

He'd got one. And so he lay there in his wide lonely bed, twisting and turning, hard and aching—remembering his wedding night!

And, worse, thinking about what it would be like to have Sadie here now—a Sadie in silk and lace. And worst of all, thinking about taking the silk and lace off her. Thinking about running his hands up those long, smooth legs and tugging the scrap of silk down and tossing it aside. Thinking about unfastening that wisp of lace she would call a bra, and letting his hands learn the curve of her breasts, letting his mouth feast on rosy peaks and tease nipples with his tongue.

"Damn it!" He shot out of bed and began pacing the room, his body protesting because walking was *not* what it wanted to do right now. What it wanted was release. Inside warm, wet, willing…Sadie.

Damn it, yes, he remembered!

After years of neatly sticking her in her employee box, her announcement that they were still married had blown the lid right off. It boggled his mind.

He didn't think things like this, or hadn't since he was a hormone-fueled teen. He certainly didn't *do* things like this! He was logical. Sensible. He'd been going to marry Dena, hadn't he?

He was passionate about his work. *Not* about women.

He tried to think. To understand. Was this sudden preoccupation with Sadie because he couldn't have Dena tonight?

It seemed likely. He'd been expecting to have sex with her, and now he couldn't. Even though he admittedly wasn't in love with her, he didn't need love to enjoy a night in bed with a willing woman. He would have enjoyed it.

Enjoyed it a hell of a lot more than he was enjoying this!

He prowled the length of the apartment. It wasn't really big enough for much pacing. But Spence frankly doubted if all of Manhattan was big enough for the pacing he needed to do tonight.

He flicked open the blinds and stood glaring out into the darkness. There were a few lights in other windows. A few others were up at 3:00 a.m. New York never slept.

But he bet Sadie was asleep.

She'd practically nodded off during dinner. She'd sat there with her head bent over her plate, not saying a word. Totally not like Sadie. He was used to her talking his arm off. Tonight he'd got nothing. She couldn't even look at him!

He flung himself down on the bed again and sprawled, staring at the ceiling. Then he rolled over and punched his pillow and kicked the duvet into a heap. It didn't help. He was wired. Strung out.

Sex would help. It would ease his frustration. Relax him.

If Dena were here—

But it wasn't Dena he imagined having sex with! It was a lissome dark-haired woman in peach-colored lace he could see writhing beneath him. It was the same woman he could imagine straddling his thighs, running her hands over his chest, settling lower, taking him in.

"Hell." Spence dragged the pillow over his face. He flung it aside and got up again, then stalked into the bathroom and turned on the cold tap in the shower full blast. Then he stripped off his shorts and stood underneath it, let the frigid water course down his overheated body and cool his ardor.

He stood there until his teeth chattered, until there were goose bumps all over his body. Until he couldn't stand it any longer. Then he got out, dried off and went back to his bed.

And the first thing he thought was that Sadie had been damn lucky he'd been gentleman enough to take her over to the Plaza instead of making her spend the night with him. If he had, he could have peeled those tailored black slacks off her, pulled that burgundy sweater over her head and found the peach-colored tease she wore beneath them.

And damn it to hell, the shower had been useless. Here he was back thinking about Sadie's damn underwear again!

There was a bottle of scotch on the fireplace mantel. It promised solace, consolation. Oblivion. He got up and poured himself a glass, then sat down and stared at it. The fumes tempted him, teased him. Promised him forgetfulness. He'd used it before, right after he'd got the divorce. Or thought he had.

He'd needed to forget. And so he had—until one morning when he actually couldn't remember the night before and it had scared him spitless that he was, exactly as his mother had claimed, just like his old man.

Not that John Tyack had wedding nights he couldn't remember. But the old man had sure as hell had spent plenty of other nights in drunken oblivion. Nights that Spence remembered—and hated—all too well.

He'd stopped drinking right then. He only drank after that if he drank in company, and then only a little. Now, tempted as he was, he turned away from the scotch in disgust and flung himself into the armchair and willed himself to calm down, to cool off, get a grip.

He wasn't his old man. He could find another way out of his pain. Surely he could find another way to forget Sadie and the promise of peach-colored silk.

Of course he could. He had plenty of time. He had the whole rest of the night.

"Are you okay?" Martha Savas poked her head into Sadie's Butte office the next afternoon, frowning and giving her a quizzical, slightly worried glance.

"What? Oh, yes, of course I am." Sadie jerked her brain back to the present and tried to paste a cheerful smile on her face. "Why wouldn't I be?"

"You tell me." And instead of waggling her fingers and

heading down the hall to her studio where she was painting gigantic panels to be hung in a recently renovated bank, Martha marched into Sadie's office and settled into Spence's chair. "You look awful."

"Thank you very much." Sadie kept her tone light, even as she shoved a hand through her hair in an effort to make it look better. But she knew she couldn't do much about the circles under her eyes and the lack of color in her cheeks. "I'm just tired."

"When did you get back?"

"Yesterday afternoon. And I leave again tomorrow."

"Leave? Again? Twice in one week?"

Everyone knew that Sadie never went anywhere. She could get away with explaining that Spence wanted her in New York for a meeting one time. But twice in one week was unheard of.

Martha grinned. "Don't tell me you're finally going to take a vacation."

It was tempting to say she was. After all, a trip to Fiji could be called a vacation, couldn't it?

But she didn't want to lie to Martha. Sadie liked all the artists who had studios or showed their work in the gallery downstairs or the co-op on the second floor, but she liked Martha the most.

When she'd first met Martha, a muralist who had come to Butte just last year, Sadie had felt mortifying twinges of jealousy. After all, Martha had only come because she'd met Spence on a plane coming back from Greece and in his cheerful offhand way, he'd said she ought to come paint a mural for him.

Whether he'd actually ever thought she would or not, Sadie didn't know. But he'd been delighted to see Martha when she'd shown up a few weeks later. And he'd told Sadie to help her find a place to live and suggest places she might look for a job.

"Seattle," Sadie had suggested when she and Martha were alone.

Martha had laughed. "Don't worry. I'm not interested in Spence," she'd said, though Sadie had never once implied she had any interest in Spence, either. She remembered saying so vehemently.

"You don't have to say so." Martha had shrugged. "I'm not blind."

Was it obvious, then? The panic must have shown on her face because Martha had smiled sympathetically and shaken her head. "I see it because I feel the same way—about someone else."

About Theo, it turned out—the man who was now Martha's husband.

But it hadn't been all smooth sailing. When Theo Savas had turned up, determined to marry her, Sadie had watched the drama unfold, enchanted by Martha's tough Greek sailor.

But even though Martha loved him, Theo hadn't had an easy time convincing her to marry him.

"He's being responsible." Martha had dismissed Theo's determined pursuit. "He thinks because I'm pregnant, he needs to marry me."

Well, yes. That had been a complication. And Martha hadn't wanted Theo to marry her out of duty. She'd wanted love.

Sadie understood that feeling. Shared it. Had for years wanted Spence's love. And didn't stand a prayer.

"It's not vacation," she said slowly. "It's…I'm going with Spence to Nanumi—you know, that resort in Fiji—for a week."

Martha's eyes lit up. "Well, hallelujah! He's finally seen the light." She was grinning broadly. "And I didn't even have to hit him over the head with a frying pan." She was absolutely gleeful, and Sadie hated to spoil her good cheer.

"It's…business," she said.

"Oh, right. Business? No. If it were business you'd be here. You're the home front and Spence is the traveling circus."

Sadie wouldn't have put it quite that way, but she understood

Martha's view. "Ordinarily, yes," she agreed. "But this time I get to go, too."

"And not because he's finally interested? He's taking you to a private resort—" Martha invested the words with oodles of innuendo "—to make you work?" She shook her head again. "He's in love."

"He's not. He just…needs a wife."

The minute the words were out, she would have called them back. But it was too late. Martha was staring at her, aghast.

"You're not! Have you lost your mind, Sadie? How manipulative can he be? You are not going to let that bloody man pass you off as his wife!"

Sadie swallowed. "He's not."

"Well, then…" Martha frowned, confused.

"It's true." Sadie shrugged. "I am his wife."

Martha looked as if she'd choked on her tongue. Her mouth opened, but nothing came out. Then she snapped it shut, her eyes still wide and unblinking, and profoundly disbelieving, which had the effect of making Sadie feel about two inches high.

And then quite suddenly Martha's whole expression changed. Her outrage softened. Her features gentled. And she reached for Sadie's hand and squeezed it between her fingers. "For how long?"

Sadie swallowed. "Four years."

She expected Martha to yelp in astonishment. But Martha only sighed and squeezed her hand again. "Oh, you poor dear girl."

The other woman's acceptance and sympathy were very nearly Sadie's undoing. She gulped against the lump in her throat. "It's…my own fault."

"Oh, I doubt that," Martha said dryly. "I know Spence. He can manipulate with the best of them."

"He…well, yes, he can," Sadie admitted. "But he didn't. I mean, he didn't intend to. It's just—"

And then Sadie had to explain. Not all of it. The bare

minimum. She knew Spence would hate her dragging up the past and talking about Emily's jilting him. But in order to make sense of what had happened, Sadie roughed out the general sequence of events, ending with, "He said, 'You'd marry me, wouldn't you?' And, I should have said no."

"I'd like to know how," Martha said tartly. "When Spence gets a notion, he doesn't back off. He's like a bulldozer. Besides—" her tone softened "—you loved him."

"But he didn't love me!" Sadie protested. "You wouldn't marry Theo when you thought he didn't love you!"

"That was different," Martha said. "I didn't know Theo. Not really. We hadn't known each other for years like you and Spence. We'd had a fling. And that was my fault, not his."

Sadie stared at her. "Your fault?"

"Long story," Martha said with a wry smile. "Suffice to say I was the one who pushed Theo into the fling. No strings, I said. Just mind-blowing sex—" She reddened. "Stop looking at me like that. I was crazy, all right? Anyway, he agreed. So I knew he only wanted an affair. So when he turned up demanding to marry me after I got pregnant, I certainly didn't think it was because he was in love with me."

"But he was," Sadie said with satisfaction, remembering Theo's determined courtship, his last desperate gesture. "It was so romantic."

"It was insane," Martha said.

"But he convinced you. You knew he loved you then. And so you married him. Not like me. I married Spence because I thought…I hoped…"

But she couldn't even bring herself to voice those desperate hopes. Instead she blinked furiously, hating the tears that welled up in her eyes. "Because I'm an idiot," she muttered.

"He's the idiot," Martha said without hesitation. She crossed one leg over the other knee. "So what happened?"

"He was going to marry Dena Wilson. He wanted me to bring him his birth certificate and the divorce papers. He called, told me, then hung up. And I went looking where he told me to look—and he hadn't got them. He thought he had and tossed the envelope in the file. But it was a preliminary letter, not even close to a decree. And I couldn't reach him because he never turns his phone on. So I had to go to New York…and tell him."

"What? At the wedding?" Martha grinned when Sadie nodded. "Well, that will teach him to keep his phone on!"

Sadie grimaced. "I guess. And we will get a divorce, but we can't yet. He…needs a wife in Fiji this coming week."

"Needs a wife?"

"It's business," Sadie said firmly. "And perfectly legitimate. He's just making the best of a bad situation."

"Did he *say* that?"

"Not precisely."

"Lucky for him. I'd have killed him if he had," Martha said bluntly. She sighed. "This is difficult."

"I know," Sadie agreed. "But I have to do it."

"Why?"

Confronted with the question that bluntly, Sadie couldn't find the words. Finally she mumbled something about owing him.

"You don't owe him a damn thing," Martha said indignantly.

"I agreed to marry him. And I'm still…his wife." Sadie actually managed to get the words out. "I can do this," she said in the face of Martha's doubt. "It will be all right. Then we can divorce. And…and I can walk away."

"Oh, for heaven's sake!" Martha stared at her. "Are you listening to yourself? You *love* him. How can you walk away?"

Sadie knew better than to deny it. "You walked away from Theo."

"Actually, I didn't. Theo left me."

"What?" Sadie stared in astonishment.

"He left Santorini and went to the States. And then I left, too, because it hurt so much to be there without him. And maybe that's when I was really an idiot, because before I was due to go home, he came back."

Sadie's eyes widened further. "Really?" She wanted to hear more. It was far better to hear a story with a happy ending than to contemplate her own miserable one.

But Martha said, "What happened between Theo and me doesn't matter here. What matters is that if you love Spence and have loved him for years—not to mention having spent *four years* married to him!—you can't just walk away. You have to fight for him."

Sadie stared at her.

"You do," Martha said. "Unless you're giving up. And frankly, I never thought you were a quitter." The words dripped challenge.

But Sadie resisted. "And how am I supposed to do that? Arm wrestle him? If I win, he has to stay married to me? No, thanks. Besides—"she sighed "—I wouldn't win."

"So, you're going to give up? Just go for a week in paradise with the man you love, and then turn tail and run?"

"It isn't what I *want* to do!" Sadie protested, realizing the truth even as she said it. "But it's not going to work! I've known him forever, I've worked for him for years, and he's never *ever* even asked me out!"

"But he asked you to marry him," Martha reminded her. "And not for business. Think about that."

Sadie did. She thought about something else, too—the one thing that had kept her hopes up all these years. She thought about what had happened on their wedding night when they'd come back to the honeymoon suite where he'd intended to bring Emily.

Sadie had been wary and worried, waiting for Spence to come to grips with the realization that he had married the wrong woman.

But Spence had been completely intent on her. They'd barely got in the door when he'd kissed her deeply, passionately, with all the fervor of a man in love.

Sadie had been stunned—and delighted. And she'd responded with all the eagerness she'd held in her heart for so long. She'd returned the kiss, had deepened it, had pulled his shirt out of his trousers and run her hands over his heated skin. She'd encouraged him when he'd moved to pull her top over her head. She'd leaned into his hungry embrace, ravenous herself.

And when he'd taken her to bed, she'd gone willingly, eagerly, as desperate for him as he'd been for her—even though she feared he was pretending she was Emily all the while.

Their lovemaking had been fast and frantic and delicious. It had ended with them clinging to each other, shattered and spent.

And then Spence had drawn her tight against him and whispered raggedly, "It always should have been you."

She thought about that now. Had he meant it? Had he even known he'd said it? He'd certainly never said it again, nor anything remotely like it. But still, if he had…

"You're very quiet," Martha said now.

"Just…thinking."

"Finding a reason to fight?" Martha speculated.

Sadie ventured a tentative smile. "Maybe so."

He didn't call Sadie the rest of the week.

Why should he? She'd be in L.A. on Friday. They'd have hours on the plane to catch up on work. He didn't need to talk to her every day, even though it was a rare day he didn't. Or used to be a rare day. Now it wasn't that important. She knew her job. She was clever. She was competent.

She was his wife.

And Spencer Tyack didn't have a clue what to say to a wife. Not a wife who was Sadie, at least.

If he had married Dena, talking would have been no problem at all. They could have discussed work, upcoming projects they might pursue, the logistics of the resort financing.

Of course he'd always talked about business with Sadie, too. Often. But not now. Not when he kept remembering her peach-colored silk. Not when his tongue seemed welded to the roof of his mouth. Not when his memories of the night they'd spent together all crowded back into his brain and wouldn't let him think of anything else.

That Sadie he couldn't talk to at all!

Which didn't matter, of course, because she had never rung him, either. Not once.

She'd never called to say she got home. Had never updated him on any of their current projects—not that there were any in immediate need of his attention—but she might at least have let him know the status of things. She'd never even called to tell him when her flight to L.A. was arriving.

Their only communication all week was when he'd sent her an e-mail or a text message telling her what he needed her to do.

Far more efficient than phone calls, he assured himself. They should have been doing this for years. But that was infuriating, too, because the only response he ever got was the single-word reply, "Done."

He'd sent her five texts today, though, all updating his progress across the country. He never got a reply to those. He'd sent her another as soon as he'd landed in L.A. Again no answer. Of course she might be en route herself.

But he didn't like not knowing.

They were going to have to sort things out as soon as she got here. It damned well wasn't going to work if she ignored him at Nanumi. Mr. Isogawa was sharp. He wasn't going to be convinced that they were a solid stable couple if they snarled at each other or avoided each other the whole week.

And even if Isogawa didn't notice a rift, Leonie undoubtedly would, and there was a good chance she'd try to exploit it.

Spence knew he'd been lucky to get her out of his room in Barcelona without Richard's ever learning that she'd come calling in the first place. And he didn't want the same thing happening again. He liked Richard. He actually even liked Leonie, when she wasn't behaving like a tart. And Richard's millions were an absolute necessity to the resort investment package.

Leonie could destroy that—and her marriage—and that wouldn't be good for anyone.

So no matter whether he and Sadie felt like talking or not, he was going to have to spell out what he expected of his wife. And, God help him, he was going to have to behave like a husband.

"So," a familiar voice said behind him, "I'm here."

Spence spun around at the sound, and yes, she was—right here in front of him: Sadie Morrissey looking exactly the way Sadie Morrissey always did neat, professional, appropriate, in control. Thank God.

And yet, even so, his heart did a weird kick-thump in his chest at the sight of her because his first thought was, what sort of underwear was she wearing?

His eyes screwed shut as his brain tried to get his hormones under control. But did they listen? Not on your life. He steeled himself against his reactions, scowling at how inappropriate they were.

"Obviously you're glad to see me," Sadie said dryly. "Did you change your mind, then?" There was an edge to her voice that said she wasn't any more thrilled than he was.

"What? No, of course not. I'm just relieved you finally got here." He made a point of glancing at his watch. "Cutting a little close, weren't you?"

"Was I? I don't think so. I had things to arrange," she reminded him loftily. "Anyway, I'm here now."

And without another word, she turned, walked straight over to a bank of seats and sat down.

Spence stalked after her, annoyed at what seemed like blatant dismissal, "So you got 'backup'?"

"Of course. I wouldn't be here if I hadn't."

"Who?"

There was a split second's hesitation. Then, "Grace."

"Grace?" He stared at her. "Grace Tredinnick? Have you lost your mind? Grace is eighty if she's a day!"

"Eighty-two, actually," Sadie said, her chin coming up, her gaze steely. "Her birthday was in January. The eleventh. I sent her a card." Subtext: you didn't. "Did you know she graduated from the Butte Business College? She was valedictorian."

"No," Spence said through his teeth. "I damned well didn't know it. And I'll bet you didn't either until yesterday."

"The day before, in fact."

"I don't care if you knew it last month! That doesn't qualify her to run my business. What the hell were you thinking? Tyack's is a multimillion dollar international firm and—"

"—and you insisted that I come with you. And I couldn't answer all the correspondence and deal with the day-to-day stuff from the middle of the Pacific Ocean, so I had to find someone who could. On short notice. I found Grace," she added belligerently.

"Grace can't—"

"Grace certainly can! And in case she wants some help, she won't be doing it alone."

"Oh." He breathed a sigh of relief, still annoyed that she'd just been winding him up to annoy him, but glad she'd got competent help. "Well then—"

"I also found Claire and Jeremy."

"Jeremy!" Now he really was apoplectic. "Claire's all right, I suppose. At least she's not a criminal, though she is about

fifteen. But Jeremy! For God's sake, Sadie! He's a juvenile delinquent!"

"Was. And of course, no one who's ever been a juvenile delinquent could possibly do anything constructive with his life!"

They both knew that Spence had been a far bigger delinquent than Jeremy in his time.

He scowled furiously. "I paid my dues."

"As has Jeremy. He did a fantastic job on the mural and you know it. Besides, Theo and Martha both vouch for him. They think he'll do a terrific job. And you know he won't cross Grace."

"How do I know he won't mug and murder Grace?"

"Because he got sent to juvie for painting graffiti, not for knocking off old ladies! For heaven's sake, Spence! He got an A in bookkeeping last semester. And Claire is in the Future Business Leaders of America."

"Bully for her. Is Grace in the *Past* Business Leaders?"

"I wouldn't know. I do know they'll be fine! And if you don't want them, say so now and I'll turn around and go straight home!"

Her eyes flashed fire, her freckled cheeks were big blotches of red, and she was glaring at him the same way she always did when they were battling it out, and quite suddenly Spence felt a real overwhelming sense of relief. She was still his Sadie after all.

He grinned. And then felt an instant stab of panic as he realized that *his* Sadie might at this very moment be wearing scraps of silk and lace. And was his wife!

His grin vanished. He needed to talk to her about that. But not now. Not when he was beset by a sudden vision of peach-colored underwear. He took a shaky breath. "Well…we'll see, won't we?"

He was talking about Grace, Claire and Jeremy. Really, he was. He was *not* talking about seeing Sadie—his wife!—in her underwear. It didn't even occur to him. Not consciously.

Not then.

* * *

Well, so much for that.

All her hopes and dreams and professed determination to make Spence sit up and take notice and want to stay married to her—the ones that had actually seemed possible when she'd been sitting in Butte, encouraged by Martha—didn't stand a chance.

He was treating her exactly the way he always had. Barking at her, arguing with her. And she was instinctively barking back. Of course she knew that her choice of Grace, Claire and Jeremy would rile him. But she truly hadn't had any choice. Not if she was going to come along. And despite her fretting, the more she thought about it, the more she knew she had to.

As Martha said, she couldn't just walk away without a fight.

But fight over Grace wasn't exactly what she'd had in mind.

"Sorry," she said now as they boarded the plane and settled in spacious business-class seats. "It was the best I could do. And I do think everything will be fine. She does have the number at Nanumi in case there's a problem."

Spence grunted, which she hoped meant he was mollified. She wasn't sure. He had stowed her carry-on in the compartment overhead, but he kept his own briefcase with him and took out a sheaf of papers.

"We need to go over these," he said.

"Now?"

"Of course."

So much for any plans for a heart-to-heart. Obviously in Spence's eyes she had only come along as his wife to play a part.

Sadie ran her tongue over her lips and tried to swallow hard to dislodge the lump of disappointment that seemed to be stuck in her throat. "Fine," she said, with all the equability she could muster. "Let's."

It was back to normal with a vengeance then, as Spence talked nonstop. He seemed to have stored up a week's worth of things to discuss with her, letters he wanted her to write, research he wanted her to do.

While she had spent the last three days gearing herself up for the coming week—trying to imagine how she would deal with life as Spencer Tyack's wife, how she would share a *bure* with him, smile lovingly at him, kiss him—Spence seemed not to have thought about it at all.

"…paying attention, Sadie?"

"What?" Her cheeks reddened as she tried to jerk her mind back to whatever he'd been saying. "I'm sorry. I'm feeling a little cramped. My feet are going to sleep. Maybe if I walked around. I'll be right back."

Spence looked disgruntled, but obligingly folded up the papers and pulled his legs back against his seat so she could slide past his knees to get into the aisle.

At least she had far more room to do so than in coach class. Even so she was acutely conscious of the brush of his knees against the backs of her legs. "Sorry," she murmured. "Back in a minute."

It wasn't a minute. She took her time, walked the aisle, went to the rest room, splashed a little water on her face. When she got back, the flight attendant was just bringing her meal. And after the meal, just as Spence was about to drag out his papers again, the in-flight movie began.

"Oh, good! Hugh Jackman!" Sadie was delighted. And she made more of her delight than was absolutely necessary because, even more than Hugh Jackman, she liked not having to try to deal with Spence for a couple of hours.

"I suppose you want to watch that. Be my guest. I'll get some work done."

And he got out his laptop and began tapping away furiously on it. The film was good. Even so, it took Sadie a while to lose herself in it and not in the mess that was her life. Sometime later, though, she noticed that Spence had stopped typing.

She glanced his way, expecting to see him caught up in the film, too. Instead he was frowning at her.

"Something wrong?" she asked.

He jumped, looking startled, then quickly shook his head. "No." His tone was abrupt, and he immediately went back to his laptop.

Sadie sighed and tried to lose herself in the film again. But all she could do was hear Spence typing furiously next to her. What was that all about?

When the movie ended and the lights came back on again, he stopped typing and looked at her.

"We have to talk." He was looking very dark and grave. Very un-Spencelike.

"All right," Sadie said cautiously.

He didn't, though. Not for a moment. He seemed to be weighing what he was going to say, which was also totally not like Spence. With her, Spence always said the first thing that came into his head and then they argued about it.

"I know why you married me," he said at last.

He knew?

Knew she loved him? Sadie felt her marvelous first-class meal climb into her throat. She clamped her teeth together and prayed it would go right back down again. And she didn't open her mouth until she was sure it had.

Then she said, "Do you?"

She wanted to sink into the earth—a difficult feat at any time but particularly when one was 38,000 feet above it.

He nodded, still dead serious. "And I want you to know I do appreciate it."

Appreciate it? She frowned. What?

She *loved* him and he *appreciated it?*

"I realize now that you were only trying to help," he went on solemnly. "To do what needed to be done, what was best for the company." He leaned toward her earnestly.

She stared at him, stunned. *That* was why he thought she'd married him?

"And I'm very grateful. I know it was hard on you. The marriage. After. And the divorce—well, the nondivorce," he said, his mouth twisting "has only made things worse. But we can make the best of a bad situation. We're adults. Right? Mature, sensible, sane."

Were they? Then why was she feeling like killing him? She didn't say a word, just stared at him.

"We can handle this," he went on. "Can't we?"

He was looking at her expectantly, as if she was supposed to be saying something in response to his comment.

Like what? *I love you, you stupid idiot?* He had no clue.

Spence's expression grew impatient. "Fine. If you don't want to discuss it, we won't. I'm sorry you feel that way. I'm just trying to say I understand. I'm…grateful."

Oh, good, just what she wanted—gratitude!

"I also hope this isn't going to be too difficult for you—what I'm asking you to do," he added stiffly.

"What *are* you asking me to do?" she said, irritated. "Exactly, I mean?"

Might as well get it all spelled out. She was reasonably sure that "loving him forever" wouldn't come up.

At her question, something that might have been a flush climbed into his face. "Nothing compromising," he assured her.

"Compromising? What sort of word is that?" She couldn't stop herself. She'd battled with him too often.

And Spence knew a challenge when he heard it. "You know damn well what sort of word it is! I'm not expecting you to sleep with me!"

Well, she'd asked. *Take that*, Sadie said to herself. "Of course you aren't," she murmured, more to herself than to him.

But he heard her and his gaze narrowed. "I do expect you to act like my wife. My happily married wife."

Deliberately Sadie widened her eyes, goading him. "Which means?"

Spence ground his teeth. "See if you can pretend to like me. Just a little."

"I do like you," Sadie said truthfully. "When you're not acting like an ass."

His brows drew down. "What's that supposed to mean?"

"It means that you trust me to do everything else. Trust me to do this."

He looked momentarily taken aback. Then he nodded jerkily. "Of course. I do. I…just want it clear. So Leonie knows," he added. "And Isogawa."

"They'll know," Sadie promised heavily, suddenly tired.

All her initial determination to make this work was gone. Spence was all about pretending. He didn't want anything real she had to offer.

"Okay, then." Spence let it go for a minute, then added, "You realize we are going to have to share a *bure*, though. One of those thatched cottages. They have a bedroom and a living room. Two beds."

And that was more than Sadie had any desire to discuss right now. Maybe it was because she'd been operating on adrenaline ever since Spence had said he was marrying Dena. Maybe it was because her dreams had suddenly come back to life only to be mocked by Spence's determination to pretend. She didn't know. She just knew she couldn't deal with it—with him!—any longer.

"Right," she said. "Two beds. Fine. Whatever. I will do my best to convince Leonie and Mr. Isogawa and everyone else that

I am a deeply devoted wife. Now, if you're finished explaining my duties, I'd like to go to sleep."

And without giving him a chance to reply, she wrapped herself in the blanket the attendant had given her earlier, reclined the seat as far as it would go, turned her back on him and shut off her light.

CHAPTER FIVE

SADIE slept the whole rest of the flight.

Spence knew that for a fact—because he couldn't.

He tried, God knew. He was used to grabbing forty winks wherever he could—in a bank lobby, on an airplane, standing up in a hallway. A man who'd slept in his truck for two years could sleep anywhere.

Except, apparently, when Sadie Morrissey was sleeping next to him.

He watched her for hours in teeth-grinding frustration, wide-awake, wired and ready to chew glass, while Sadie, having frozen him out when he'd been trying to be understanding, damn it, slept like the proverbial baby.

The trouble was she didn't look like a baby. Babies didn't have tousled dark hair that brushed against their cheekbones. They didn't smile and sigh erotically in their sleep. They didn't twist and turn and flip the blanket away so that bits of bare midriff peeked out.

Spence didn't want to see bits of Sadie's bare midriff. Not if that was all he got to see. He didn't want to feel the temptation to reach over and run his fingers lightly along those few inches of soft, pale skin. Not if he couldn't just hook his fingers right under the edge of her shirt and tug it over her head. Not if he couldn't unzip her slacks and slide them down her endless legs.

"Damn it!" The words hissed through his teeth. He jerked his gaze away and clenched his hands on the armrests of the seat.

"Sir?" The flight attendant appeared at his elbow. "Is everything all right?" She bent down and was peering at him worriedly.

Spence dragged in a harsh breath. "Everything's fine," he said in a low controlled voice. "I just…remembered something."

What it was like to have Sadie naked in his arms!

"Can I get you anything?"

Knockout drops? A stun gun?

"Coffee," he said at last. "Lots of coffee. I need to work."

There was always plenty to be done. And he'd always done it, using work to put his life's circumstances out of his mind. To forget his jerk of a father, to blot out his shrewish mother. He'd used work earlier on the flight, talking about the projects to Sadie because when they talked about work, he had things under control.

The flight attendant brought him coffee. He booted up his laptop again. He opened a file, focused on the specs of the Sao Paulo building Mateus Gonsalves was recommending that they buy.

Tried to focus. It didn't work. He muttered under his breath.

"Mmmm?" Sadie shifted and turned his way.

Swell. Now if he shifted his eyes even slightly he could see her face, feast his gaze on her slightly parted mouth. He had kissed that mouth. Really kissed it. Not just given Sadie the duty peck that he had allowed himself to bestow as a part of their friendship-business relationship.

She had a generous mouth. A kissable mouth. And he was going to have to kiss her again this week. Not just brush his lips over hers but—in the interest of their convincing portrayal of a newly married couple—drown himself in her kiss. And bury himself in—

Stop! Just stop!

Wanting Sadie Morrissey was the last thing he should do.

She didn't want him. She'd married him out of kindness, damn it!

He'd told her he understood why she'd done it—out of care for the company—because the truth was worse. When Emily jilted him, Sadie had felt sorry for him. He'd said gruffly, "You'd marry me. Wouldn't you?" And she had because what the hell else was she supposed to say?

She'd married him out of pity!

The very thought made him cringe. It made him squirm.

He didn't want pity. Never had. He had hated it when the teachers had tsked and murmured about his father, about what a hard life he'd had. Sure, his life might have been easier with different parents, but he'd done fine.

He'd survived, hadn't he? He always would.

He didn't know what the hell she'd got mad about, either. He had only been trying to do her a favor by reassuring her that he didn't intend to jump her bones. He could control himself. He hoped.

Besides they wouldn't be sharing a bed. Only a *bure*. They would be fine.

He glanced her way again, determined to steel himself against the attraction. But there was more midriff showing.

He shut his eyes. Heard her move, then mutter. She flung an arm out and it landed on him. His eyes flew open. Sadie's fingers curved around his forearm, warm and possessive.

They were long and slender fingers with sensible short nails, well-trimmed and neat—just like Sadie. Looking at them a guy would never think they belonged to a woman wearing lacy peach-colored silk. There was nothing particularly sexy or erotic about them—until all of a sudden her thumb began to stroke his sleeve.

At her touch Spence jerked, then looked at her suspiciously. Was she awake? Having him on? Or reading his mind?

But her breathing didn't change. She just smiled. He swallowed and barely breathed, but he didn't move his arm, didn't pull away, because beneath the cotton of his shirt, his skin tingled at her touch.

Once upon a time, four years ago, he remembered burning under Sadie's touch. He shut his eyes and tried not to think about it. He should have had his head examined for insisting she come along.

But it had seemed perfectly sane and sensible at the time, no different than taking Dena.

Ha.

Sadie hadn't expected to sleep. She certainly hadn't expected to be refreshed by it. So she was amazed to wake up to hear the sounds of a breakfast cart rattling nearby and to feel almost human and hopeful again.

She stirred and shifted, keeping her eyes slitted as she turned so she could catch a glimpse of Spence.

He was slouched in his seat, looking stubble-jawed and rumpled, his hair a little spiky, his eyes a little tired as he stared at some papers in his hand. She doubted he had slept at all.

She sighed and stretched and slowly opened her eyes the rest of the way. Spence didn't look up until she sat up and began to fold the blanket. Then he glanced her way.

"Sleep well?" he growled.

"I did, actually," Sadie said. She took a brush out of her purse and ran it through her hair, then fished out a lipstick and a mirror. "Almost human."

Spence grunted and went back to his papers.

When she'd finished to her satisfaction, she straightened and looked over at him. "Did you work the whole flight?"

"I had things to do. Work to catch up on. And I wanted to be prepared." His tone was gruff and he flexed his shoulders as if trying to get a little of the tension out of them.

"You don't think a little sleep might have done more for you?" Sadie said lightly.

"I said I had work to do," he said sharply.

"Sorry," Sadie said lightly. She paused, then decided maybe she'd been a little too abrupt earlier. He couldn't help what he didn't feel.

"I'll do my part," she assured him.

He looked over at her. "What?"

"When we land. I'll do my part. You don't have to worry. I'll…be your wife."

He stared at her a long moment. There was something there in his gaze again when it connected with hers that seemed, to Sadie, almost electric.

Don't, she warned herself. *Do not read anything into this. It's your brain. Your emotions. Your dreams. It's not real.*

And then, "Right," Spence said, and gave her a jerky nod just as the flight attendant appeared with their breakfasts.

They ate. And then after, as the dishes were being removed, the captain announced that they'd begun their descent and they needed to put everything away in preparation for landing.

And suddenly Sadie felt the shiver of nerves all over again. It felt oddly like childhood piano recitals when all of the expectations of her teacher, Sister Catherine Marie, came to rest on her thin shoulders. She trembled briefly.

Spence stood up and put his computer and files away, then rummaged in his carry-on and sat back down again. "Here," he said, almost offhandedly, and a small black velvet box landed in her lap.

Sadie jumped as if it were a grenade.

"It's not going to blow up," Spence said gruffly. "Open it."

But Sadie couldn't. She couldn't even pick it up. Her breath seemed caught in her throat. She regarded the box warily, wordlessly.

"Too awful to contemplate?" Spence growled. "Come on, Sadie. You can't be my bride without rings. What are you waiting for? Me to put them on you?"

His rough tone galvanized her voice at least. "Of course not!" It was just a shock. So…unexpected.

She guessed she shouldn't be surprised. Spence believed in covering all the bases. That's what had made his screw-up of their divorce such a shock. Now she prayed that her fingers wouldn't tremble as she picked up the box and carefully eased open the spring closure.

"It's not booby-trapped, either," Spence said irritably.

"No." She barely breathed the word as the lid opened and she simple stared. Didn't move. Didn't speak.

"You don't like them," Spence said after a moment. His voice was flat. "They aren't exactly…traditional."

No. That was what was so remarkable about them.

Sadie had seen the ring he'd bought Emily—a showy elegant diamond with little rubies all around it. She didn't know what he'd done with it after Emily hadn't shown up. At least, thank God, he hadn't given it to *her.*

She'd glimpsed the engagement ring Dena had worn—a diamond solitaire on a white-gold band. Polished and sophisticated, like the woman who had worn it.

"I suppose I could've just given you Dena's," he said now. "But I didn't think—"

"No," Sadie said, the word torn from the depths of her soul. "No," she said again. "Not those. These." She tipped the box to allow more light in. There were two rings—a thin gold filigree band with an exquisitely cut piece of jade inlaid for an engagement ring. And the wedding ring was pure jade inset into a bead of Celtic knots. Her Morrissey ancestors would have approved. A circle of green and gold fire. Primitive and perfect. Completely her.

"Dena's rings were worth a hell of a lot more, moneywise," he said. "But they didn't…look right. Didn't look like something you'd wear."

Numbly Sadie shook her head. "No. I wouldn't."

If he'd brought Dena's for her to wear, she would have turned the diamond into her palm, clenched her fingers around it and never opened her fist. But it's what she would have expected.

After all, what difference would it have made, if they were only going to be married a week?

These rings, however, were so completely "her" it was spooky. How had Spence known? She shot him a quick probing glance, amazed.

"I didn't buy you one the first time," he reminded her.

"I know. But you gave me that old pipestone ring you used to wear."

He stared at her.

"Don't you remember it? The one that belonged to your granddad."

"My granddad's ring?" He looked stunned. "I thought I'd lost it."

Sadie shook her head. "No. You took it off and gave it to me. Put it on my finger," she told him. "Until you got me something better, you said." She shrugged. He still looked poleaxed by the news. "You really didn't remember?"

He shook his head, looking almost dazed.

"Well, you were gone a month, you know…after. And then I guess I forgot. I should have given it back to you."

The truth was, she hadn't forgotten. And she never would. She'd loved that ring. It was precious to her. And she'd kept it on a chain around her neck for the next month. Only after

Spence had come in and told her the divorce was final had she removed it.

She would have given it to him if he'd asked, but he never had. So she had put it in the drawer of her bedside table. More nights than she liked to remember she opened that drawer right before she went to sleep. She touched the ring and thought about what might have been.

"I still have it." She swallowed, then made herself say words she never wanted to say. "You can have it back if you want."

"I'd...like that." His voice had a ragged edge. "It's the only thing I had that belonged to him. We can trade. If you want," he added quickly. "If you don't like these I can get you something else. I just thought—"

"I *do* like them," Sadie said fervently. "They're...beautiful. Truly. That seems like such an overused word, I know. But they are. They're...perfect." And as she spoke, she reached out a finger and touched them with something almost like reverence. She felt tears well up.

"Good God, you're *not* going to cry!"

That only made her blink even faster. But at least she took a deep quick breath and said, "Of course not. I'm just...I think they're wonderful. Thank you."

"Well, good," he said gruffly. "So, aren't you going to put them on?"

Carefully Sadie took the wedding ring out of the box and slid it onto her finger.

"It might be too big," Spence said.

But it wasn't. It fit perfectly.

"It's the color of your eyes," he said suddenly, surprising her even more. She might have known him for most of her life, but she'd never have imagined he'd know what color her eyes were.

Now she turned them on him and saw that there was a definite flush of red over his cheekbones.

"They're like that forest pool in that kids' book," he told her. And even as he said so, the color got deeper. "The one you made me read you when you were little. That fairy tale." He looked completely embarrassed now.

"I remember that!" When Spence had been in fifth grade she'd talked him into reading her a storybook fairy tale in which there had been a picture of a magical pool like that. Danny wouldn't have been caught dead reading her fairy stories. But Spence had no little sisters pestering him all day, so he'd indulged her. And if he hadn't already, he'd won her heart by telling her that the pool in the forest was the same color as her eyes.

She remembered now that she'd been amazed. "Really? The magic pool? Are my eyes magic?"

"Sure," he'd said then. Now he insisted, "They were that color. It's not like I was making something up."

"No. Of course not!" Sadie grinned. She felt suddenly deliriously happy. She took out the other ring and felt a moment's fleeting temptation to ask Spence to put it on her finger.

But he'd come much further than she'd ever believed he would already. It wouldn't do to push. So she slid it on herself. It, too, fit perfectly.

She lifted her gaze and met his. "Thank you. They're beautiful."

He cleared his throat. "Glad you like 'em. You keep them. After, I mean."

"After?"

"After the week is up," he clarified.

She was still smiling, but it froze on her lips.

"I don't want them back," he went on. "They're for you."

For her? But he was still planning on divorce at the end of the week? She could hear Martha now saying, "I don't *think* so!"

Sadie didn't know what to think.

* * *

The ring thing had shaken him.

Not just the rings he'd bought her, which he was very glad she liked and which suited her—though he couldn't quite make out why she'd blown warm and then very cold right at the end—but even more than Sadie's new rings, what shook him was realizing she had his grandfather's pipestone ring, and that he had given it to her the night they'd wed.

It just proved what a daze he'd been in. He couldn't imagine having given that ring to anyone.

It was big, awkward, homemade. His grandfather's father had carved it out of pipestone he'd found when he'd first come to Montana to mine as a young man. The ring was a heavy dark red inlaid with a piece of mother-of-pearl in the rough shape of a heart.

"He always said he reckoned he'd give the heart to my ma when she got here," his grandfather had told the young Spence. It had taken the young miner three years to save up enough money to bring over the family he'd left behind in Cornwall.

But only the children—a boy and a girl he barely recognized—had got off the train in Butte that summer morning. His wife had died on the voyage.

"So he wore the ring," Grandpa had said. "And the heart."

The red pipestone with its mother-of-pearl heart had stayed on his finger until the day he'd died, though the mother-of-pearl heart had cracked and a chip was missing.

Grandpa had worn it that way, too. "To remember," he'd said.

When he died, it had gone to Spence's dad who had never worn it.

"Don't like rings," he'd always said. He'd never worn a wedding ring either. So the pipestone ring used to sit in the saucer on top of his bureau. Spence would put it on his own finger when no one was around. Then his father left, but the ring stayed, and he tried it on more often. His hands grew bigger. The ring wasn't quite so loose. It didn't feel so heavy.

Then, one day when he was fifteen, the ring, like his father, was gone.

"Got rid of it," his mother said. "Ugly old thing. And with that broken heart." She shook her head. "Bad luck, if you ask me."

"Where'd it go?" Spence had demanded, furious, desperate.

"Took all your father's stuff to the junk shop on Galena," his mother said. "Good riddance."

Spence hadn't cared about anything else, only the ring.

The lady in the junk shop had sold it back to him. "It's not really worth much," she'd said doubtfully when he'd insisted on buying it.

"It is to me," Spence said. It was the only thing he had that connected to a good family memory. The only thing that connected to his grandfather.

And he had given it to Sadie the night she'd married him?

What had he been thinking?

He didn't have time to figure it out, though, because at that moment the plane jolted down onto the runway.

And as it slowed, turned and taxied toward the terminal, Sadie took a deep breath. "All set?"

Spence nodded. He hoped to God he was. He still felt shaken.

Then everyone was getting up and moving out.

"Here," Sadie said as they edged toward the door. And he felt her press something into his palm. "You'll need this."

"Need what?" But he could feel the answer even as he asked.

A wedding ring.

His fingers instinctively closed around it. The edge of it dug into his palm. The rings he'd got for Sadie had been a token of appreciation. He never expected to receive one in return.

"It's called rose gold. It has copper in it," Sadie said when he stopped in the air bridge to stare at it, blocking the way for the other passengers trying to move around them. "It's not a big deal," she added. "But I thought maybe you'd want to—considering Leonie and all."

He hadn't been going to with Dena. But now he nodded. "Good idea."

Leonie would see it and know he was taken. Isogawa would see it and understand that he and Sadie were a pair. It made perfect sense.

He slid it on his finger.

He suddenly felt married.

And not a moment too soon, he thought, once they'd cleared customs and were headed to the charter-plane departure lounge.

Everyone else was already there. He knew both New Zealand couples, Steve Walker and his wife, Cathy, and John and Marion Ten Eyk were getting there the night before. And Richard and Leonie were there, too. The four kiwis were talking among themselves. Richard was, as usual, deeply engrossed in something on his laptop. But as soon as Leonie glanced up from a magazine and saw them coming, she squealed with delight.

"Spence! Darling!" She leaped out of her seat and rushed toward him, arms open wide.

He braced himself for the onslaught, ready to catch her and hold her at arm's length when other fingers suddenly slid into his hand, and Sadie was right there next to him saying smoothly, "Aren't you going to introduce us, dear?"

Dear? Spence opened his mouth and nothing came out.

It didn't matter. Sadie went right on. "Oh, I recognize your voice." She beamed at Leonie, who, apparently seeing Sadie's hand in his, had stopped inches from launching herself into Spence's arms. "You must be Leonie! I'm Sadie."

And she intercepted the hug meant for him and gave Leonie an enthusiastic one of her own.

"S-Sadie?" Leonie sputtered, stepping out of the embrace to look Sadie up and down. "You're *Sadie?* Spence's—"

"Wife," Spence said smoothly. He had his bearings now. "Sadie is my wife," he told Leonie, sliding his arm around Sadie's waist as he did so. "And you can be the first to congratulate us."

Shock, confusion, consternation and a whole host of other expressions skittered across Leonie's face.

"But Sadie…works for you." Leonie's wide blue eyes fastened on Sadie who withstood the scrutiny and didn't give an inch.

"She does. She did."

"It's like out of a romance novel," Sadie told the other woman cheerfully. "You know the ones—years go by and finally the boss wakes up and sees the woman underfoot all day for the woman she really is."

Leonie's eyes went wider still, then just a little doubtful. But at Sadie's determined pleasantness she could hardly do more than smile wistfully.

"Wow. Congratulations." Then she turned a half-sceptical, half-accusing gaze on him. "And you never said a word. Not a single clue. Richard!" She turned to call to her husband, "Guess what Spence has brought with him!"

"Contracts, I hope," Richard said vaguely, not glancing up.

"I'm sure he has, darling," Leonie said impatiently. "But he's also brought a wife!"

Richard's head came up then. "A wife? Tyack's got a wife?" He set the computer aside then and came straight over, his eyes studying Sadie all the way. From the appreciation on his face, Spence thought with annoyance, he apparently liked what he saw.

Richard offered Sadie a hand, kissed her on both cheeks, then beamed at her. "Married the boss, did you? Smart girl. Beautiful, too." He turned to Spence. "Got eyes in your head," he said approvingly. "And you're not stupid, either. This girl's the one who keeps the wheels turning at the home office, isn't she?"

"She does a good job," Spence said stiffly, wondering why Richard was still holding on to Sadie's hand. He scowled.

Sadie smiled and deftly extracted her hand and laid it on Spence's arm. "I try to keep him thinking that," she told the other man.

Richard laughed. "I'm sure you manage." He rubbed his hands together. "Glad we've got a week on the island. Great idea of Isogawa's. It'll give us lots of time to get to know each other better."

Spence stared. Was Carstairs hitting on Sadie?

"I'm sure we'll have plenty of opportunity to visit," Sadie replied easily. Her smile included Leonie, too. "I'm looking forward to it. And to meeting everyone else in person as well," she added as the Ten Eyks and Walkers came over.

Spence made the introductions, but Sadie already seemed to know them all.

"Of course I do," she said. "I made all the reservations. Marion and Cathy and I have spoken on the phone. Cathy's a weaver and Marion paints. She's done some murals like Martha, and next time Theo and Martha go to New Zealand they're going to visit Marion and John."

"They are?" Spence just stood there, somewhere between bemused and stunned, while his wife chatted with everyone as if she'd known them for ages — which apparently she had.

CHAPTER SIX

MR. ISOGAWA was at the dock to meet the seaplane when it landed.

A dapper man in his late sixties with steel-gray hair and a small bristly mustache, he was exactly as Spence had pictured him—a strict, soft-spoken field marshal—a man with Standards and Expectations.

He bowed and shook hands with Spence, but before Spence could introduce everyone, he said, "Come. We will go to the lodge. I will introduce you to my wife. She looks forward to meeting you. It is good you are all here. Nanumi is a place for families."

He made another bow, then he directed a small army of silent, smiling staff members to carry their luggage to various lodgings, then turned and led the way up a plank walkway toward a thatched roof Spence could see in the distance.

He turned and caught Sadie's eye. See?

Sadie smiled slightly and gave an infinitesimal nod in return.

The lodge when they came up on it, was a low-slung, sprawling, native wood, glass and thatch building that over-looked a crescent shaped bay. Spence had seen pictures of it, of course. But in person it was even more impressive than the pictures—not just a beautiful structure, but a harmonious ex-tension of the picture-postcard, Pacific-island paradise in which it was set. Beside him, Sadie seemed to draw in an awed breath.

Dena would barely have noticed it. She'd spent so much time in the Caribbean—her father owned an island there—that tropical beauty held no novelty for her.

But Sadie was clearly dazzled by the island, the resort and the lodge they were entering. It was a spacious high-ceilinged room, one side all glass and open air, facing the bay. A bamboo bar curved around one end, and groupings of chairs and sofas all upholstered in brightly colored Polynesian designs were arranged around low tables.

"Here we will sit," Mr. Isogawa gestured toward them. "And now you will introduce us, Spencer-san?"

Spence did. Mr. Isogawa smiled and bowed and, for good measure apparently, shook hands with each of the men and their wives. It was very cordial, very proper. And then Spence took Sadie by the hand and drew her forward.

"I would like you to meet my wife, Mr. Isogawa. This is Sadie."

"Sadie?" Mr. Isogawa's distant politeness vanished. He stared first at Spence, and then abruptly turned his gaze on Sadie. "This is Sadie? You are marrying *my* Sadie?"

"Your Sadie?" It was Spence's turn to stare as Mr. Isogawa reached out and tapped Sadie on the arm so that she turned to face him squarely.

Sadie was smiling broadly but almost shyly as she nodded. "Yes, he is. Married to me, I mean."

At which Mr. Isogawa clapped his hands together delightedly, then broke into a wide welcoming grin. He bowed now to Sadie—a much deeper bow than anyone else had merited—and then he grasped both Sadie's hands in his and began talking rapidly to her.

In Japanese.

Spence stared. "She doesn't—"

But apparently she did, because Sadie began talking, too. In Japanese.

"Since when," he demanded, "do you speak Japanese?"

Sadie finished whatever she was saying to Mr. Isogawa before she turned to him and shrugged lightly. "Remember Tammy Nakamura, my roommate at UCLA?"

"No." The most he remembered about Sadie at UCLA was how damned inconvenient it had been the four years she was there. Coming home in the summers had never been enough. What he remembered about UCLA was going down for her graduation and hauling her back to Butte!

"Tammy was Japanese-American. But her dad made sure all the kids could speak the language. I made her teach me. When you started doing business with Mr. Isogawa, I tried it out on him." She grinned. "He thinks I'm very clever."

Mr. Isogawa's head bobbed in agreement. "Sadie is very smart. Works very hard. Beautiful, too," he murmured. And he still, Spence noted, hadn't let go of Sadie's hands.

What was it with men and Sadie's hands?

Just then Mr. Isogawa said something else to her in Japanese, and she blushed and held out her left hand for his inspection.

Spence felt a prickling between his shoulder blades as Mr. Isogawa even lifted her finger to scrutinized them in silence. They were only simple jade rings. Folk art. Nothing valuable or even particularly beautiful. And it was obvious that Mr. Isogawa thought Sadie was both.

Spence suddenly wished he'd kept the rock from Tiffany's and had insisted that she wear it. Dena had known what she was doing. He, on the other hand, had let his business sense be blinded by knowing Sadie.

But then Mr. Isogawa smiled. And this was different than his earlier smiles. This one reached his eyes. It seemed to come from the inside out. He held Sadie's hand out for Spence to take.

Slowly Spence took it.

Then Mr. Isogawa looked at Sadie. *"Sono yubiwa, o'suki desuka?"*

"Do I like them?" she translated. "Oh yes!" She nodded vehemently. "I mean, *hai*. I certainly do."

The smile on his lined face deepened as Mr. Isogawa nodded. "I, too." He turned his gaze on Spence, his gaze searching. "I see you chose well."

And Spence didn't think he was talking about the rings at all. His face felt suddenly hot. "I think so. I'm glad you agree."

Still smiling, Mr. Isogawa nodded. Then he turned and beckoned to a woman hovering in shadows on the far side of the lounge. She was about the same age as he was, very petite and beautifully dressed in a silk sarong that seemed to reflect all the colors of the sea.

"My wife," Mr. Isogawa said, "Toshiko."

One by one he introduced her to all of them. And when he got to Sadie, the woman's eyes lit up and Sadie's did, too. They bowed and smiled very properly, and then they were holding hands and talking like old friends.

"I suppose you've met Mrs. Isogawa, too," he muttered.

Sadie laughed. "Sort of. We met on the phone. She's learning English. When Mr. Isogawa told me, I offered to help. We practice together, don't we?" she said slowly in English so the other woman could understand.

"Sadie is a good teacher." Mrs. Isogawa's voice was soft but her pronunciation was clear and precise. "Very smart."

"So I see." Spence was seeing more than he'd ever imagined.

While he'd been putting this deal together, he'd been all over the world, keeping tabs on other deals, as well. He'd sent Sadie the specs and the background and what he hoped to accomplish, and then he'd said she should keep track of things and get in touch with the various people he'd contacted. Then he'd left her to it.

He'd never considered how much contact she'd had, how much work she'd done. He'd just assumed everything had fallen into place because of his intuition and groundwork. Now he saw that Mr. Isogawa's willingness to consider a bunch of western investors was more because Sadie had provided such diligent hands-on care and friendship than because he was a brilliant strategist and had put together a good group.

"We'll practice while I'm here," Sadie was saying now, and Mrs. Isogawa nodded happily.

But then Mr. Isogawa began speaking rapidly to his wife in their own language. Her eyes widened and she looked from Sadie to Spence and then to the rings on Sadie's hand as if seeing them for the first time.

"You are married?"

"Yes, we're married," Sadie agreed.

"Newlyweds," Leonie drawled. "So sweet."

"On their honeymoon," Mr. Isogawa decided happily.

"Well, not really." Sadie shook her head and wrapped her arms across her chest.

But Mr. Isogawa had other ideas. He called to the barman for champagne, then spoke to another man who nodded and disappeared quickly out the door. In a matter of seconds bottles of bubbly appeared, were opened and poured, and everyone was handed a flute.

"And now we will toast your happiness," Mr. Isogawa said. He raised his glass and spoke first in Japanese, then in English. Spence had no idea what he'd said in Japanese, but in English he wished them a long life, great wealth, deep happiness and many children.

"Many many children," he heard Mrs. Isogawa echo, then she smiled at Sadie and giggled.

Sadie blushed.

"Many many many children," Leonie agreed sotto voce. "Wouldn't you love lots of little kiddies, Spence?"

Sadie looked like she wanted to disappear through the floor.

"You're embarrassing the girl," Richard said brusquely. "Let them decide how many they're gonna have in private. But I'll drink to the rest of it. To Spence and Sadie. Congratulations and best wishes."

Fortunately, once the toast had been drunk, attention shifted. Sadie asked about the building, and Mr. Isogawa began to talk about the concept, the furnishings, the native artists whose work was displayed on a rotating basis, the local woods and textiles that were used as much as possible in the upholstery and bedding.

"We try," he said, "to give our guests the very best of this world. We do not let the outside intrude. We make a haven of beauty, as you say?" He looked to Sadie for affirmation that he had the right words.

"Indeed you have," Sadie agreed, running her hand lightly over the back of one of the sofas.

"And your quarters even more, I think. You will see." He glanced up as the young man who had disappeared through the doorway now reappeared. "And as soon as you are ready, Jale will show you to your *bures*." He turned to Spence. "We did not know you were bringing a new wife. This is special."

"Anything is fine," Spence assured him. "Sadie and I don't care."

"I care. Toshiko and I had moved into the honeymoon *bure* because it is small. Intimate. Only for two. Not for families. We did not realize we would have real honeymooners with us. So we'll make a change."

"We don't—" Spence began.

"It's not necessary—" Sadie said quickly.

But Mr. Isogawa raised a hand to silence them both. "It is necessary. *Shinkon-san ni, tekishite imasu.*"

Spence blinked, then looked at Sadie to see if she understood.

"He says it's appropriate," Sadie translated quietly. "He wants us to stay there because it's the appropriate place for newlyweds."

"But we're not on our honeymoon," Spence protested. "We're here on business. We're here to come to terms on the resort."

"But why is the resort at all?" Mr. Isogawa asked simply.

Spence shook his head, confused. "What?"

"We make the resort for couples. For families. To come together," Mr. Isogawa explained. "To remember, yes? Nanumi. To remind ourselves of what is most important. Business, yes, of course we do business. But business is only a part of life," Mr. Isogawa said. "The less important part. You understand?" His dark eyes seemed to bore into the depths of Spence's soul.

"I— Yes."

He understood the concept, at least.

His family had had no idea. The ring he'd given Sadie had been his only experience of that sort of connection. It had been a sign of his great-grandfather's love. A love which had endured loneliness and then death. But his own father had ignored it, had left it sitting in a saucer on the bureau. His mother had, typically, thrown it out.

But Mr. Isogawa was smiling at Sadie—and Sadie was smiling, too, just like she was thrilled, like she was his real wife.

"All right," Spence said. "But we are here for business."

Mr. Isogawa bowed. "Later we will talk business. Now you must share the beginning of your marriage with your beautiful wife."

The honeymoon *bure* was like *Swiss Family Robinson* meets *Modern Bride*.

Sadie stood in the open doorway and looked around in amazement. All of the resort's *bures* or native bungalows had looked beautiful as they'd passed them. But this one, inside and out, was spectacular.

It was a *bure* and not quite a *bure*. A thatched island cottage, yes, but it was built in a tree—like a treehouse. Not cobbled on, either, but exquisitely interwoven so that the *bure* seemed to flow between the branches. The room seemed carved out of the tree, not perched in it.

"Not traditional," Mr. Isogawa had apologized. "But we think, nice."

Nice didn't being to cover it.

The *bure* was nestled a dozen steps up in the spread of a vast tree that Sadie couldn't identify. From the frond-covered front porch with its gently swinging hammock to the interior native hardwood floors and *kiao* mats, from the vast king-size bed— "Almost as big as Kansas," she murmured—to the private open-air waterfall shower and spa hidden from the beach by carefully placed bamboo screens, it was elegant and spacious. With its stunningly printed tapa cloth wall hangings and the airy wicker table and chairs under the window and a pair of sturdy uphol-stered kauri chairs, it was exotic yet homey and welcoming at the same time. With views of a sand-and-sea paradise out of every door and window, it was beyond anything she had ever imagined.

"I hope you will be very happy here." The young man who had brought them along the wooden pathway that threaded through the trees now bowed slightly and left them alone. Together.

In the honeymoon *bure*—with one room. And one bed.

"Well, isn't this nice?" she said brightly when Spence didn't say anything at all.

He hadn't said a word since they'd left the main lodge. He'd followed the man called Jale—which Sadie had figured out was the local version of Charlie—down the path in silence. Ordinarily Spence peppered people with questions. He rarely had a thought he didn't share. But he'd taken in all the *bure's* amenities in complete silence. And even after Jale left he didn't speak.

Now he said abruptly, "We'll have to share the bed. I can't

sleep in the hammock." He jerked his head toward the one swinging lightly on the porch outside the door.

"I know."

"Isogawa would notice. Or the help would. They'd comment. We can't take the chance."

"I know."

He didn't seem to hear. He cracked his knuckles and began to pace. "All the other *bures* have two beds!"

"Don't worry about it," Sadie said. "I'll stay on my own side. I promise I won't molest you."

He stopped dead. "What?"

"I said, I promise not to attack you!"

It was Spence's turn to blink. "That's not what I meant," he said gruffly. "I promised you two beds."

You promised to love, honor and cherish me for the rest of our lives, too, Sadie thought. But she didn't say it.

"I was there the whole time. I could almost see what was going through Mr. Isogawa's head. He was determined to make this special for us."

"You don't mind?"

"I'll live," Sadie assured him. "Will you?"

"Of course! It will be fine."

But even as he spoke, he moved away from the bed, as if determined to put as much space as he could between it and himself for as long as possible.

Sadie tried not to notice. With her thumb she turned the rings on her fingers. The rings proved that on some level at least Spence understood her, cared about her. And the *bure*—well, she was going to take it as a sign that someone, besides the Isogawas, wanted her and Spence to be together.

She kicked off her sandals and flexed her toes against the cool wooden floor. "How about a swim?" she suggested.

Spence glanced at the bed. "A swim sounds fine," he said

quickly. "You go ahead and change. And I'll— Oh, hell, I left my briefcase up at the lodge. I'll go up and get it."

"You'd better be sure not to stay up there and work."

"No." He went out, then stopped on the porch and turned back. "Sade? Thanks."

She cocked her head. "Thanks?"

"I knew everything on this deal was coming together smoothly. I never realized how much of it was thanks to you. Your connections with all of them—the Isogawas, the Walkers, the Ten Eyks, even Richard and Leonie—are what has made this work so far."

"I've enjoyed it all," Sadie said truthfully. "It's been fun. They're interesting people."

"Yeah. They are. But I want you to know I appreciate it." He hesitated, as if he might say something else. Then he just muttered, "Thanks," again, and turned and hurried up the path.

She watched until he disappeared among the palms and then she sank down on the bed and sighed. He'd noticed her relationships with the Isogawas, the Ten Eyks, the Walkers. He *appreciated* them. He *thanked* her for them!

He probably even thought she'd developed them for the good of the company and for no other reason at all.

Sometimes Spencer Tyack was too stupid to live. And before the week was over, she just might kill him.

But—Sadie smiled—since he'd brought her to paradise, she might as well take a swim first.

Sadie swam.

John and Marion joined her. They found the water warm and inviting. Waves were almost nonexistent. It was like a gorgeous peaceful turquoise bath, breathtakingly clear and beautiful.

Spence never came.

"Working," Marion guessed.

"Damn fool," John said.

Was he? Sadie wondered. Or was he just avoiding her? She swam or lazed on the sand for over an hour. He never appeared.

"Richard probably got him," John said. "Trapped him somewhere. Doing ten-year projections. He's even a bigger workaholic than Spence."

Richard? Or had Leonie waylaid him on his way to the lodge?

All of a sudden Sadie thought she'd better go check. "I'll just go have a look," she said.

"You do that. Grab him by the ear and bring him down," Marion suggested.

"Or find something better to do." John grinned and gave her a conspiratorial wink.

Sadie blushed. "Yes, um…maybe I'll do that."

She waggled her fingers in farewell, wrapped the towel around her middle and made her way up the pathway to the treehouse. She could see the door was open when she reached the steps. So no Richard and, presumably, no Leonie.

He was either working or avoiding her.

"Spence? If Mr. Isogawa finds out that you're up here working—" She stopped dead.

He wasn't working. He was fast asleep.

Apparently he had actually intended to come down to the beach because a pair of black swimming trunks lay on the bed beside him. His feet were bare, his shirt unbuttoned. His lips parted slightly. And through them Sadie heart the faintest of snores.

"Spence?" she said, quietly this time, more to be sure that he really was sound asleep than to try to wake him.

He didn't respond. Not even an eyelash flickered.

She shouldn't be surprised, Sadie realized. While she had slept on the flight, he had apparently worked the whole time. And before that flight, she remembered, he'd already flown into

L.A. from New York, a longer journey than hers, over more time zones. No wonder he was exhausted.

And damnably hard to resist, Sadie thought, as she stood looking down at him, drinking in the sight.

He might have been a different man from the one she knew awake. The fierce intensity that so characterized his every waking moment was gone. His mouth was softer. The rest of his face, too, seemed more relaxed. Gentler.

His five-o'clock shadow had gone another twelve hours and was rougher and darker than ever. Sadie remembered the brush of his whiskered jaw against hers when they'd made love the night they'd married. She hadn't touched that stubble since. She felt a compulsion to reach down and brush her hand against his cheek now.

She didn't. Couldn't let herself. This week was roller-coaster ride enough. She didn't need to make it worse. So she tucked her arms across her chest and trapped her hands in case they got the best of her.

Just look, don't touch.

But this Spence was so much more clearly the person she knew was inside the one the world saw that she almost couldn't help herself. In him now she saw hints of the boy she remembered—and of the man she'd married that night four years ago.

When they'd got back to the room, they had made love eagerly, desperately, frantically, barely making it to the bed as they'd torn each other's clothes off as they went. Their love-making had been scorching.

And afterward he had murmured, "It should always have been you." And then, almost instantly, he had fallen asleep in her arms.

And Sadie had watched him sleep.

She had lain awake, astonished at the sudden turn in direction her life had taken, afraid to close her eyes lest when she awoke it would all turn out to be a dream.

And when she finally did go to sleep, she'd awakened a few hours later to find that it had become a nightmare.

Still, she remembered this part as vividly as if it had happened only hours before. Remembered how she'd held him close, relishing the brush of his soft hair against her nose, loving the feel of the rough whiskers on his jaw against the smoothness of her cheek.

She'd feathered kisses there. And Spence had sighed and smiled, had moved his mouth as if to kiss her back, but in the end had slept on.

She saw that man asleep here now, and she could only remember the night—not the morning after. It was all she could do to hug her arms against her chest to stop them reaching out for him.

Go on, Martha whispered inside her head. *What are you waiting for?*

But as much as she would have loved to lie down beside him and wrap her arms around him, Sadie couldn't do it.

He had to want it; he had to want her; and she had to know it.

She started to move away, but couldn't quite do it. Not without, for just a moment, freeing a hand to reach down and let it drift lightly over his ruffled dark hair.

"I love you," she whispered.

It was only the truth—as much as it hurt to think her love might never be returned.

Spence smiled. And he slept.

There was a regular tub in the bathroom that would afford her privacy. But just beyond the sliding glass doors there was a small, screened outdoor patio with a rainforestlike shower that fell into a rock pool.

Sadie had been able to resist sharing the bed with Spence— at least for the moment—but a rainforest shower was too much temptation. He would never know. He was dead to the world. So she fetched a towel from the bathroom and one of the thick terry-cloth robes there, too. Carrying the rose-colored robe and the towel, she padded back quietly through the bedroom to slide open the doors.

Spence had rolled onto his side. But his breathing was still deep and even.

Sadie watched him, assessed the room on the bed and decided that, if he stayed where he was, there would be room for her to slide into the bed when she'd showered. That shouldn't offend his sensibilities too much.

She stepped out onto the decking and eased the door shut behind her. With a quick self-conscious glance back at the sleeping Spence, she wriggled out of her swimsuit. Feeling even more self-conscious and enormously decadent, she stepped into the pool and beneath the shower.

It was heaven. The spray was soft and full, the water lukewarm—absolutely perfect. She tipped her head back and let the spray hit her face, slide down her neck and over the rest of her body.

"Ah, yes." She smiled, turned, let it course down her back. Reaching for one of the tubes lined up along the rock shelf, she squeezed out a dollop of the pineapple-scented shampoo and worked it into her hair, then rinsed it and watched as blobs of lather slid down her arms and over her breasts and plopped into the pool which seemed to be filling with bubbles.

Decadent didn't even begin to describe it. She would never take a shower again in her utilitarian claw-foot tub back in Butte without remembering this one.

Once more she lifted her face into the spray and let it wash over her whole body. A gentle sea breeze stirred the air and the surrounding tree leaves. In the distance she could hear people's voices on the beach. Marion and John seemed to have been joined by Steve and Cathy and Leonie. They were laughing about something. It felt odd to be able to hear them so clearly, be so close—and so naked—and know they couldn't see her.

Or could they?

Sadie craned her neck to look over the top of the screen to make sure. But they weren't looking her way at all. She was completely hidden.

No one saw her.

Except Spence.

CHAPTER SEVEN

SPENCE was dreaming.

They were vibrant vivid dreams in which he was undressing Sadie, then kissing his way up her arms and across her shoulders, along her jawline, all over her cheeks, the tip of her nose and, finally, her luscious beautiful mouth.

And all the while he was kissing her, he was running his hands over her and dispensing with her clothes, her proper tailored blouses and jackets, eager to get to the peach-colored scraps of silk he knew were underneath.

Then, just when he reached the silk and began to unhook her bra, he heard the faint click of the hook.

Click? Of the hook?

He jerked. His eyes opened as Sadie clicked open the sliding glass door to the enclosed shower room. Then the door clicked shut again. And through it Spence beheld a reality more vibrant and vivid than all his dreams and fantasies of Sadie in peach-colored underwear.

As he watched in dazed but dazzled fascination, the real live Sadie Morrissey hung her towel and robe on a hook by the waterfall, then with a quick glance toward the door, turned and peeled down her swimsuit and stepped naked into the water.

His mouth went dry. His eyes didn't blink as he stared at a peach-colored Sadie wearing nothing at all!

He groaned at the sight, at the instant reaction of his body, already primed by his dreams. Sucking in a harsh breath, Spence shut his eyes.

"Damn." He swallowed, then opened his eyes a fraction, hoping against hope that he'd imagined it all, that jet lag and stress and overwork and sexual frustration—not to mention Sadie frustration—had combined to create hallucinations.

Not so.

She was still there. Standing in the shallow rock pool beneath the spray, then doing a little hop-skip, a little dance step, like some water sprite. Her breasts bounced lightly, the water made her skin glisten. He swallowed again.

He couldn't close his eyes now. There was no point. Why bother? He was never going to be able to forget this. He might as well enjoy the show.

She was, after all, his wife.

So he was entitled, right?

He could get up off this bed and strip off his clothes and join her there in the pool under the shower. As her husband, he could run his hands over her soap-slicked body. He could kiss her neck, could kiss his way down across her breasts, could touch his tongue to her navel, kiss lower, touch her—there.

His jaw clenched and he rolled onto his back, his body screaming a protest at not being allowed to do exactly that, at not being allowed to do more.

Why *not* do more?

Was she going to fight him off? She hadn't been as upset about there being only one bed as he had. And he'd been upset because he thought it mattered to her.

Didn't it?

Did she *want* him to make love to her?

She'd married him, hadn't she? his body argued.

But she'd only married him under duress, his brain replied. Because he'd made it impossible for her to refuse. Because she'd cared about him as a friend, because he'd been at the end of his rope and, knowing it, she'd done him a favor. Because she'd *pitied* him!

And why would she want to be married to him, anyway? She knew his family. She knew his background. She knew as well as Danny ever had what poor husband material he was. She was a forever woman—a woman who had always wanted a husband, a home and a family.

She deserved a far better man than him.

So the least he could do was keep his mind on business. He just needed to remember that.

But right now he needed to get out of here.

Spence knew human nature—especially his own—well enough to know that all the rational resolutions in the world could fail in the face of too much temptation.

His father hadn't taught him much. But he'd damn sure taught him that.

He wasn't there!

Sadie had finished her shower, dried off and wrapped herself in the soft rose-colored terry robe. She'd combed her fingers through her hair so she didn't look like a complete scarecrow, and then, taking a deep breath, carefully and quietly as possible, she'd slid open the glass door, hoping Spence had left her a corner of the bed in which to nap.

And he wasn't there! The bed was empty, the coverlet rumpled, but Spence was gone.

Heart slamming against her chest, Sadie ran to the bathroom. He wasn't there. She peered out onto the front deck. No Spence.

She even went out and looked down toward the beach. But everyone had gone. It was empty now, too.

She couldn't see or hear a single soul, only the sound of the sea as it washed against the shore and the rustle of the breeze in the palms.

Where had he gone?

And why?

His swim trunks were missing. The clothes he'd been wearing were hanging in the closet. Had he awakened and grabbed his trunks, thinking she was still down at the beach?

Had he not seen her in the shower?

Naked in the shower!

How could he not? Her face burned as she realized there was simply no way he could not have seen her. While the view from the waterfall into the room was obscured by the sun's reflection on the glass, the view of the shower area was crystal clear.

He couldn't have missed her.

Her whole body was hot now. Burning from humiliation, not the possibility of embarrassment.

He had seen her and looked the other way. *Run* the other way!

She wanted to die. How could she spend a week with Spence in the same room—in the same bed—if he couldn't even bear to look at her?

And she'd hoped to make a real marriage out of this?

What had she been thinking? The very thought seemed laughable now.

And the joke, Sadie knew, was on her.

The sound of drumbeats, deep and hollow, echoed off the wall of the *bure* late that afternoon. Sadie knew what they meant—that the lounge and bar were open, that dinner would soon be served.

And of course she had to be there. It was her job.

For the past two hours she had sat huddled in one of the

wicker chairs in the *bure* crying. It was stupid. Pointless. She told herself that over and over. But it didn't help.

She hadn't any idea where Spence was. Wherever he had gone to, desperate to get away from her nakedness, he had never returned.

He would have to show up at dinner, though. It was a command performance, one of the places Mr. Isogawa was sure to expect to see them together. So Spence would turn up, expecting her to act the part of the loving wife.

"How about the spurned wife?" she muttered, scrubbing at her eyes with a tissue. She wondered if this was how Leonie felt.

Probably. Damn men, anyway.

Still furious, Sadie wiped her eyes, then carefully applied a bit of makeup, hoping it would mask the worst of the blotchiness on her face. Her eyes were still red, but she could always say they were bloodshot from swimming. It wasn't a great excuse, but it was good enough.

Then she went to the closet and took out the red-orange wildly printed sundress Martha had brought over the morning Sadie had been leaving.

"It's seen Greece," Martha had said, thrusting it at her. "I wore it there when Theo and Eddy and I went back a few months ago. Theo thought it was *três* sexy." She'd wiggled her eyebrows and grinned. "Maybe Spence will, too. Anyway, it should see the South Pacific before it retires."

And so it would, Sadie decided. She would do her job, and she would enjoy herself as best she could. The hell with Spence. But she owed it to Martha to give her dress a whirl.

She arrived by herself, and Mr. Isogawa, who with his wife had been visiting with the Ten Eyks, rose quickly and came over to bow and invite her to join them.

"You are enjoying yourself?" he asked.

"Yes, thank you. *Arigato*," she repeated in Japanese, making Mrs. Isogawa smile. "I'm having a wonderful time. The tree-house *bure* is magnificent. And I've been swimming already. The beach is beautiful, the water was so warm. And the water-fall in the spa—I loved it."

She must have been convincing because he smiled. "And Spencer? Did Spencer enjoy? Where is Spencer?"

"Spencer fell asleep," she reported with absolute honesty. "He was so tired after working on the plane all the way down here, he just collapsed. I went swimming without him. And when he woke up, I guess he went out exploring on his own."

And when he showed up, he could damned well tell Mr. Isogawa all about it. What she'd said was the truth—minus her own interpretation of it.

Mr. Isogawa nodded. "I will be interested to hear what he found."

What Spence found, they learned, when he arrived just before dinner was served, was that there was a track up the hill through the bush to a lookout area at the top from which you could see virtually the whole island.

"It has amazing 360-degree views. Blows your mind." He looked bright-eyed and handsome as sin, well rested and com-pletely at ease.

Sadie hated him.

He must have gone back to the treehouse after she'd left, because he had changed clothes and now wore a pair of tropic-weight khaki-colored trousers and a deep blue polo shirt that exactly matched the color of his eyes, though she was sure he had no idea.

"You had a good time, then?" She did her best to sound as cheerful and upbeat as he did, determined that she would do what she'd signed on for.

"Yep." He paused. "Sorry I didn't make it down swimming.

I conked out. I was going to join you, but you weren't swimming anymore when I woke up,"

No, I was naked in the shower. You could have joined me there. But of course she didn't say it. She just pasted a bright smile on her face and hoped she looked sincere.

"I'll take you there tomorrow," he said "You'll love it." And smiling down at her, he slung an arm around her shoulders and drew her hard against him.

The self-preserving part of Sadie wanted to stiffen and resist. The furious part wanted to kick him where it would do the most good. He was such a convincing liar!

But she'd given her word, and to fight now would be disastrous not just for the deal, but it would make everyone uncomfortable. So she leaned into his embrace and smiled. "I'm sure I will."

Then, because she was damned if he was going to be the only one who showed how devoted they were, she turned her face toward his, and kissed him lightly on the jaw

It was Spence who stiffened then, and she saw a flicker of confusion in his gaze, followed by something that looked like determined challenge. And the next thing she knew Spence bent his head and kissed her full on the lips!

It wasn't a passionate kiss, one that should have been saved for the privacy of a honeymoon *bure,* but it lingered long enough to be possessive, and it promised a host of things that left Sadie startled—and shaken—when at last Spence stepped away.

He smiled at her.

She shot him a furious glare, then looked up to see Leonie Carstairs watching.

The meaning of the kiss was suddenly perfectly clear. It was a "keep your distance" kiss, meant for Leonie. He'd intended it to mean nothing to Sadie. Nothing at all.

"Come," Mr. Isogawa said. "It is time for dinner." He took his wife's arm and led her toward the dining room.

Spence, still smiling, held out his arm to her.

And Sadie, after one careful steadying breath, slipped her arm through his and, ignoring her heartache, walked by his side to the dinner table.

"Well, that went well," Spence said briskly as he opened the door to their *bure* after an excellent dinner and an evening of general "getting to know you better" conversation.

"Do you think so?" Sadie said ironically, because, while she'd done her best, she didn't think *well* described it. *Hypocritcal* came closer.

Now she brushed past him into the room, then immediately wished she hadn't.

The bed, which had seemed Kansas-size a few short hours ago, now appeared only slightly larger than a postage stamp. And it was one thing to go to bed with a man you loved if you thought he might find you appealing, and another to go to bed with a man who had turned and run when he'd glimpsed you naked.

And now there was no beach to escape to, no grounds to wander about it. It was all darkness—velvety black with amazing stars and constellations she had enjoyed learning about from John Ten Eyk. But she couldn't stay out there all night.

"Didn't you think so?" Spence sounded surprised. He shut the door and kicked off his shoes. "Everybody was having a good time. The place is in terrific shape, a lot better than I expected. The service seems very good. The food was fantastic."

"Yes."

"Leonie left me alone," Spence said with supreme satisfaction. "And when you get past the starchiness, Isogawa's a nice

guy. So's his wife. And they obviously think you're wonderful. So do I," he said cheerfully.

"Why? Because I scared off Leonie? Because your clever
plan is working? Isn't that just great."

Spence's forehead furrowed as his brows drew down.
"What's the matter with you?"

"Nothing's the matter with me! Nothing at all."

"I can tell. You're so full of sweetness and light tonight."
Spence rolled his eyes.

"You don't know anything about me!"

"So, tell me. Why are you mad?"

His simple question infuriated her even more. "Who said I
was mad?" Sadie spun away, putting the bed between them, as
he came toward her.

"Lucky guess," he drawled. Their gazes met across the bed,
his stony and furious, hers equally mad. He raked a hand through
his hair and scowled deeply. "So, let me venture a guess."

She lifted a shoulder indifferently. "Suit yourself."

"It's about this afternoon. Isn't it?" he prodded, when she
didn't reply at once.

"What do you think?"

"I think I'm doing the best I can, damn it," he snapped. "All
right, fine, I apologize! But I'm not blind, Sadie! If you don't
pull the drapes across the windows, I'm going to get an eyeful.
I can't help it! But I left, didn't I?"

Sadie's jaw dropped. *"What?"*

Still Spence glowered, eyes flashing. "If you didn't want me
to see you naked, why the hell did you leave the drapes open
when you took your shower?"

That was what he thought she was mad about? That he had
seen her naked? Not that he had been so disgusted by the sight
that he'd left the room?

"Well?" he demanded when she didn't reply.

Numbly Sadie shook her head, still trying to fathom that, make sense of it. Finally she could only ask dumbly, "That's why you left?"

"Did you want me to lie there staring at you? Is our Sadie an exhibitionist now?" His tone was mocking.

"Of course not! I needed a shower. I'd come in from swimming in the ocean. It was beautiful, inviting. Not like the bathtub I can use every day. And *you* were *asleep!* I wasn't trying to seduce you!"

"Which is exactly what I figured," he informed her flatly. "And I didn't imagine you would be any less enticing when you came back in the room." Hard blue eyes met hers. "So I left."

But Sadie was stuck a sentence earlier. "Enticing?" She echoed the word as if she had never heard it before. Was he saying. "You thought I was…?" She stared at him in wonderment.

"You're enticing as hell, Sadie Morrissey," he bit out. "And while I would have loved to lie there watching you cavorting under the shower—"

"I was *not* cavorting!" she protested.

"No? Well, dancing then. Hopping around. You hopped." He made it sound like an accusation.

God, how long had he watched? Sadie felt herself go scarlet.

"You enticed," he said again, very firmly. "And I wouldn't have been content with looking. I would have wanted more. And that wasn't part of our bargain. So I left."

Oh.

"So I apologize," he said tersely. "It was all I could think to do at the time."

"All?" Sadie said before she could stop herself.

Their gazes met again, locked this time. Electricity arced between them. Desire. Hunger. Frustration. Need. Sadie certainly felt all of them. She had no idea what Spence felt at his end.

He gritted his teeth. "Don't tempt me, Sadie. Little girls who play with matches are likely to get burned."

It was as if she'd been cut free, her fears banished, her heart hammering. "Is that a promise?"

"Cut it out," he said, his voice sharp. "Get ready for bed. I've already apologized for the bed, and I'm damned if I'll do it again."

"I don't care," Sadie said.

He ignored her. "I'll go out and walk on the beach while you're changing. Flick the light when you're decent and all tucked in." Then, without letting her reply, he opened the door and stalked out into the night.

He stood outside looking up into the night sky, telling himself it would be all right.

He'd survived the evening. He'd played his part well and so had Sadie. Yes, there had been a few tense moments, but he'd handled things well. He'd apologized for this afternoon—not that it had been his fault, damn it—and he'd got out before Sadie could misinterpret anything else.

If he was lucky, she'd just go to bed and fall asleep at once. She hadn't had any rest as far as he knew. Maybe she'd slept this afternoon after her shower, but the bed looked pretty much the way it had when he'd decamped. So she ought, by rights, to be exhausted.

Spence prayed that she'd be exhausted. He certainly was. By design. It was the only way he knew that he could get any sleep in a bed with Sadie Morrissey. He'd left the room this afternoon and he'd walked miles. Literally. He doubted there were many trails on the island that he hadn't explored.

So he could spend the night with her. Of course he could. It wasn't like he was a teenager anymore. He had control.

Then, out of the corner of his eye, he saw the light in their *bure* blink on and off—and all of a sudden his control didn't seem so certain.

Quit, he told himself sharply. *You never get anywhere by anticipating disaster. It will be fine. Give it five minutes. She'll be sound asleep.*

So he waited. He tried very hard not to think about peach-colored underwear and naked Sadie Morrisseys. He directed his mind firmly *away* from whatever Sadie might be wearing, tucked under the covers.

Mind over matter. He could do that. He climbed the steps and opened the door.

She wasn't under the covers at all!

"I told you to get in bed!"

Sadie smiled and stretched languorously. "I don't work for you 24/7. Sorry, but it's after hours."

He glared at her, furious at the enticement she provided sitting there on the bed in some flimsy little short yellow night-gown, all smiling and sweet, as tempting as Eve and her damned apple.

"What are you trying to do?" he demanded.

"To do?" She looked at him guilelessly.

He didn't believe the pose for a minute. "You're flaunting yourself! Trying to tempt me!" He flung words as accusations.

She smiled slightly. "Is it working?"

"What the hell do you think…? Damn it, Sadie! Do you want me to attack you?"

There was a half-second's hesitation. Then she gave him an impish smile. "As a matter of fact, I would."

CHAPTER EIGHT

"SADIE?" HE LOOKED as if he hadn't heard her right. As if he doubted his ears. She couldn't repeat it. So she said nervously, "Unless you'd rather not."

He stared at her. "You're kidding, aren't you?" His voice was ragged. And without another word, he dragged her into his arms, gathered her close, fastened his lips on hers.

He kissed her.

And instinctively Sadie kissed him back.

It was like coming home.

It was an echo of that earlier night—their wedding night— but infinitely better. Those kisses had been hungry and anxious and desperate. Frantic, almost. This kiss was hungry, too. Maybe even a little desperate.

But the similarity ended there. It didn't plunder; it explored. It didn't demand, it sought a response. And even more than that, it offered. It offered her Spence the way she had always dreamed of him. This kiss said he was hers.

Sadie, of course, had been his for as long as she could remember. But until now—until this moment—she'd been afraid that she had given herself wholly and completely to a man who, except for one brief night, would never want more from her than casual friendship and a lot of hard hours at work.

But in his kiss now, in the fine tremor of his hands as he touched her, she knew her fears were baseless. He wanted her every bit as much as she wanted him.

"Sadie." He whispered her name against her lips. She could taste it, taste the mingling of her name and him.

She smiled. "Mmm." She murmured, heady with pleasure as she tugged his shirt up and over his head, then let her hands roam over his arms, his shoulders, the hard muscular breadth of his back. "Yes."

"Yes? Like this?" he asked. His own hands were busy learning her. Touching her. Delighting her.

But he had much more access to her than she did to him. And she reached for the buckle of his belt, but fumbled it. "Lack of experience," she muttered as he undid it for her, then quickly shucked them and the rest of his clothes, and she could see him in all his naked glory.

"Oh yes," she whispered, pulling back to look, then reaching out to touch, to run her fingers lightly over his chest and across his hard abdomen, to brush lightly against his erection.

He tensed. "Sadie!" Her name hissed between his teeth.

"Mmm?" But he didn't answer as she pressed kisses against his jaw, his neck, his shoulders, his chest. His breathing grew faster, shallower. His skin was so hot she wondered if he had a fever. Against her hand she could feel the gallop of his heart. Still no answer, just a strangled sound from deep in his throat. Worriedly Sadie asked, "Are you…all right?"

The sound turned into something between a laugh and a moan. "I'm dying."

The ragged tone of his voice had her pulling back, horri-fied. "Dying?"

"For you, idiot," he muttered. "I've *been* dying for you."

Sadie didn't believe that for a minute. But she didn't mind him saying it. Actually she loved him saying it. "You're sure?"

He pressed her back onto the bed, his body coming full length against hers, settling in, fitting perfectly. "What do you think?"

"Oh." She understood now. She smiled, wriggled against him.

"Stop that." Spence's lips were against her mouth. "You're going to push me over the edge."

"What a shame," Sadie murmured, a delicious smile curving her mouth.

"Tease." Spence's lips moved from her lips over her cheeks. They touched, they pressed, they stroked, they nibbled. They teased and made her burn, too. There was a fine tremor in his fingers as they skimmed up her legs and caught hold of the night-gown, then tugged it up and over her head and tossed it away.

"Spence!"

He raised his head. "What? You wanted to wear it?"

"Yes. No. I don't care, Spence. I—"

He kissed her. "Shh. Lie back and think of Montana."

"No." She was absolutely not going to do that. She was going to participate. Completely. "I get to…to do things, too."

"Oh, really?" His mouth was so close she felt his breath on her cheek.

"Yes, really."

"I thought I was the boss."

"Only in the office. We're not in the office now."

"Now, wait a minute!"

But Sadie was done with waiting. She kissed him to shut him up, then drew her tongue along his lips and dipped it inside. At the same time she ran her hands down his back and over the solid curve of his buttocks, reveling as she did so in the fact that she finally felt free to touch him the way she'd wanted to touch him for years.

"Got a problem with this?" she asked him, wriggling again.

"I think I could get used to it," he muttered, then buried his face in her breasts only to lift his head a moment later and grin at her. And she could hear the awe in his voice when he said, "It really is you, Sadie. It really is you."

"It is." Though after all these years, she could hardly believe it, either.

Then Spence stopped talking once more. He kissed her thoroughly. His hands were everywhere, learning her lines and curves and secrets, making her gasp and squirm. And even though he had her gasping, she was determined to do the same for him.

Four years ago she'd been so overwhelmed by the sudden and bewildering turn of events and their astonishing marriage that she'd done little more than give herself to him. Now she wanted to do more, have more, share more.

And so she touched and stroked. She kissed and nuzzled. And Spence's control was snapped. His breathing quickened. His heart slammed.

"Sadie! Slow—!"

"No! I want you."

"I want…you…too. But I need—" He didn't finish, just pushed away to get off the bed.

"What?" Sadie stared after him, stunned.

But in a moment he'd found what he was looking for in his suitcase. Protection. They didn't need it, Sadie wanted to tell him. She'd be thrilled if she conceived here in this wonderful place.

But Spence had already accomplished the task and was settling between her legs again, finding the center of her, stroking, nudging, probing.

And Sadie took him in.

It had been so long. Sometimes she had despaired of ever having him again, of ever knowing this feeling of completion, of fulfillment. Sometimes, in fact, she thought she'd dreamed it.

But she hadn't. Oh, dear heaven, no, she hadn't! And she knew it now as she drew him into the heart of her being and wrapped him in the wonder of her love.

And then she knew nothing more—only the hot shuddering release of passion and tension and the sensation that at last the two of them had finally become one.

He owed her better than this. More than this. And Spence knew it.

He should have been slower, gentler, more thoughtful. He felt boneless, weightless, though he was sure he must be pressing Sadie into the mattress. Flattening her. But even though he willed it, he couldn't seem to move.

Sadie wasn't moving, either, though he felt her heart beat against his chest.

"That…" Sadie said breathlessly from beneath him, "was amazing."

Spence didn't move. "Yeah?" In what way amazing? Amazingly awful?

Sadie's lungs expanded. He could feel her drawing in a deep breath. "Oh, yes! It was wonderful."

His heart skipped a beat. He could almost feel it expand in his chest, as if the weight of the world had suddenly been lifted.

"Mmm." And then she looped her arms around his neck and tugged his face down to plant a kiss on his lips. "The best."

He grinned. He laughed. He couldn't help it. "You think that was good?" he said gruffly. "I'll show you good."

"Now?" Sadie squeaked.

"In a few minutes. How about that?" He rolled off her and drew her against him, marveling at how right she felt in his arms, against his side, as if she belonged there.

"I think I could stand it again in a few minutes," Sadie said after a moment's consideration.

"Good." He settled a hand in her hair. Turned his head to kiss her brow. Could barely believe this was happening. Was he going to wake up and have it all be a dream?

But the night passed…with more lovemaking. Lots of love-making. Spence was determined to show Sadie every kind he could think of. And it wasn't a dream. He was exhausted at dawn. Eyes bloodshot. Body drained. Brain dead.

He didn't care. Sadie agreed it was good. Very very good indeed.

They missed breakfast.

Well, not all of it. But everyone else had finished and was sitting around the lounge drinking cups of tea and coffee when they came in together, looking flushed and distracted and as if they'd spent the night in the honeymoon *bure* doing exactly what honeymooners were expected to do.

And they had.

And they were flushed and distracted because they'd spent the most amazing night together—all of it sleepless—and at dawn they had gone out for a swim.

Spence had suggested it.

"You want to *swim?*" Sadie had stared at him in disbelief. "I'll drown. I feel boneless."

"C'mon." Spence had tugged her hand to pull her up. "It'll be wonderful. You'll see."

He was right. It had been magical. The cool morning air, the water almost warm when they plunged in. They'd romped and played and kissed—and loved.

And then, floating there in the water watching the sun rise out of the ocean, it had become even more wonderful because she'd been floating back against Spence's chest, his arms encircling her, his breath soft against her ear.

Then, once the sky had changed from navy to a stunning mixture of violets and reds and oranges, and finally to the pale yellow and bright blue of morning, they had left the beach and come back to their treehouse *bure*, where they had showered together in the waterfall where Spence had watched her the day before.

Had that been only yesterday? Not even a full twenty-four hours? How was it possible that things had changed so much?

Sadie didn't know. She only knew the joy they had today. And that she felt a little stiff and sore, as if she'd used muscles she was unaccustomed to using. Imagine that, she thought, unable to keep the silly happy grin on her face.

Spence looked equally pleased, though his eyes were decidedly bloodshot and he hadn't shaved because Sadie had decided she liked his stubbly jaw.

She'd urged him not to shave. "Unless you think Mr. Isogawa will object," she'd said, aware that there were other priorities.

"You're more important than Isogawa," Spence had said, rubbing his whiskers lightly against her cheek.

And Sadie couldn't help feeling more important as they came into the lounge, with Spence's arm looped over her shoulders.

One look at them and Sadie was sure everyone knew what they had been doing. She was far too pleased to care. And even when Mr. Isogawa asked politely if they had slept well, she hadn't been able to stop grinning.

"We had a good night," she said. It was the truth, after all, even if they hadn't slept.

"I'll bet you did," Leonie said enviously.

Richard didn't notice, but Marion jumped in and said diplomatically, "It's a wonderful place. John and I enjoyed it, too. Not too hot. Not too cold. Peaceful. And all those lovely gentle waves."

Had she seen them? Sadie wondered, knowing her face was even redder. But Marion didn't give her a knowing grin or wink. Bless her heart.

Cathy beckoned them toward a table with two empty chairs. "Come sit and enjoy your breakfast. It's marvelous. Fresh fruit. Eggs. French toast. Whatever your heart desires, really. We ate too much. Marion and I were just talking about going for a walk while they're all in meetings. Want to come with us?" Her gaze included both Sadie and Leonie.

"Not me," Leonie said promptly. "I'm going to have a massage," she said with a knowing smile. "With Jale."

Jale, the young man who had taken them to their *bure* yesterday, was a definite hunk. And obviously he had more talents than carrying luggage.

Sadie shot a quick glance at Richard to see if she could gauge his reaction to Leonie's plan. But Richard didn't even seem to have heard. He was talking to John, not paying attention to his wife at all.

"I'd love to," Sadie said to Marion and Cathy, "but this isn't just a honeymoon for me. It's work, too. I have to be at the meetings."

Spence hadn't said so, but the truth was, she wanted to go to the meetings.

She wanted to be wherever Spence was, to watch him in action. She wanted to spend the whole day just looking at him, marveling at the fact that finally, after so long, he was really hers and that finally they both knew it.

They hadn't spoken much last night. When the barriers had finally come down it had been too startling, too new, too overwhelming. There had been words, but not many. There would be time later for them.

She had said, "I love you," though.

She'd dared that much, and had held her breath after she'd said it, fearing he would laugh.

He hadn't. He had groaned and kissed her with a desperation that told her he loved her, too. And she had been willing to settle for that. She believed he loved her even if he couldn't yet say it.

But he'd surprised her by pulling back and looking deeply into her eyes and saying, "I love you, too."

She'd blinked, amazed, then exultant. She was confident now that he was the soul mate she had always thought he would be.

Spencer Tyack had always been a guarded man, who charmed others easily, who had many friends—but who loved only a few.

He loved her. He'd said so. And she had no doubt that he would demonstrate that fact again as soon as they had some privacy.

And in the meantime she could watch him. She could take notes as needed, and when they weren't needed she could mentally undress him and rehearse all the things they would do when they were alone.

The very thought made her smile again.

"Newlyweds," Marion chided her, laughing at her dopey smile. "Stop your daydreaming and order your breakfast. You're making me envious, you are."

Sadie felt herself blushing again. But hastily she sat down and one of the waitresses instantly appeared with a menu.

"If you don't see what you want," the waitress told her, smiling, "we will find it for you."

It was hard to imagine anything she might want that was not on the menu. It was as extensive and amazing as Cathy had claimed. And Sadie saw far too many things she wanted because suddenly she was starving.

Finally she settled on a glass of juice, a muffin, an omelet and a cup of tea, though she could probably have eaten a lumberjack-size meal, she'd expended so many calories during the night. But she didn't want everyone to think Spence had married a glutton. She needed to behave properly and with dignity, moderation and decorum—as long as she could be a complete wanton in bed!

A giggle bubbled up.

Cathy and Marion looked at her, shook their heads, still smiling as they sighed. Leonie looked from Sadie to Spence and back again, then turned her head to look daggers at Richard who still didn't notice.

Sadie felt sorry for her and wished she could help, especially since it was due to Leonie's attempt to seduce Spence that she owed her own current happiness. Poor Leonie.

"Ah, I see you are happy this morning." The soft, precisely accented English made Sadie look up to see Mrs. Isogawa standing next to her table.

"I'm very happy," Sadie assured her. "I think this is the most wonderful place on earth!"

"Good place," Mrs. Isogawa agreed. "Happy place. Meet my husband here."

"You did? Here?"

"Yes, yes." Then she glanced over and said something to her husband in Japanese.

"It's true," he agreed. "She was with some friends on a holiday. I was working here. Designing these buildings. Except I couldn't take my eyes off her. I found a way to get introduced to her." His smile widened. "And the rest is, as you say, history."

Sadie was enchanted. It really was a magical place.

"Every year our family comes, too. They will be here later this week. Our sons and daughter and grandchildren. Maybe," he said, "you will come in the future and bring your family, too."

Sadie could get misty and starry-eyed just thinking about it. She glanced over at Spence, but he was listening to something Steve Walker was saying.

"You do not need to come to the meetings today," Mr. Isogawa told her. "If you wish to enjoy the island, my assistant can take notes and give them to you."

"I'd like to come," Sadie replied. "It is my job. But I really want to. I don't usually get to see Spence in this part of his work."

Mr. Isogawa nodded. "Very well. Enjoy your breakfast. We meet in an hour."

Sadie did enjoy her breakfast. And Spence, who was sitting with Richard and Steve, appeared to enjoy his. He was back in business mode, deep in conversation with both of them, barely touching his food as he listened.

But every now and then he glanced up and looked her way. Their gazes would connect and a corner of Spence's mouth would lift.

And Sadie—remembering last night and thinking of all the nights to come—felt joy fill her heart again.

The guys had been on him the minute he and Sadie had reached the dining area, Richard with a sheaf of papers, Steve and John with a host of questions.

If he'd been worried that they would wonder what he was up to all night, he needn't have bothered. This morning they were all too absorbed in things they wanted to talk about regarding Nanumi.

Nanumi. *Remember*, Sadie had said it meant. And now Spence felt he had a right to do just that. The instant he had borne her back onto the bed and wrapped her in his arms, he'd had the sense that he'd been here before. All the kaleidoscopic bits of memory—sounds, shapes, touches, feelings—that he'd made himself blot out, came tumbling back. And as he'd made love with Sadie last night, he had felt as if he were assembling pieces of a puzzle he'd put together before. He heard echoes of words he'd heard before and feelings he already knew.

It was fresh—and yet it was oddly familiar, too.

Mostly it was completely right.

In their lovemaking Spence recognized a feeling he'd never experienced before that single night four years ago— a feeling he hadn't felt since. He had lost it without even realizing he'd had it—in Sadie's arms he found again the feeling of being welcome, of finally, after a lifetime of searching, finding the place where he belonged.

With Sadie.

The notion still had the power to stun him when he thought about it too long. It was like staring into the sun. Brilliant but impossible. And yet—

Sadie loved him.

She'd said so. Fervently. Eagerly. Even desperately, or so it appeared.

Pretty much like he loved her.

He'd even told her. And that had stunned him, too. Spence could never remember having said the words to anyone in his entire life. But with Sadie, the words had come out unbidden.

She had said them first, and maybe he'd been responding to that.

But he didn't think so. He thought he really loved her—and had for a very long time.

That surprised him, too. Of course he had always liked Sadie, even as a knobby-kneed, gap-toothed five-year-old, when she'd tagged after him and Danny all those years ago. As he watched her grow up, he'd admired her determination, her intelligence, her talents.

He'd certainly appreciated her help when she'd first come to work for him. They'd had a great time. He'd missed her desperately while she was away at college in California—because she had been such an asset to his business, he'd thought then. And for that reason, he assured himself, he had done whatever he'd needed to do to make sure she'd come back afterward.

It was the truth.

But not the whole truth.

Spence understood that now. For years he understood there had been more to his relationship with Sadie Morrissey than he'd been willing to admit. Clear back when she'd been in high school, there had been those early twinges of sexual attraction, that awareness of her curves and mile-long legs, of the feminine attributes that changed her from the knobby-kneed, gap-toothed kid to a delectable, appealing young woman.

A young woman far too good for him. And if his own good sense hadn't prevented him from acting on his feelings, Danny's fierce "Leave her alone. You've got nothing to offer her," took care of any inclinations he'd had. At least until the trauma of Emily's defection had jolted him so badly that his instincts had taken over.

Then he'd dared ask a question buried so deep he hadn't dared to even think it. He'd done what his heart had desired. He'd married Sadie.

And ruined it all again the next day.

But he hadn't been able to ruin it forever. Quite by accident he'd been given a second chance. And he was glad. More than glad. Over the moon.

Last night Sadie had made him feel alive, whole. She'd made him feel like no one had ever made him feel in his life.

She'd made him feel loved—something Spence had always recognized more by experience of its absence than its presence in his life.

Other people loved. Other families. Not his.

But none of it mattered now because Sadie loved him. She'd shown him that love last night. All night. And this morning while he was supposed to be paying attention to Richard and Steve, he kept glancing over at Sadie during breakfast. And she glanced back, grinning all over her face.

Spence grinned, too, because never in his life had he felt like this.

He was the same Spencer Tyack he had always been. The same wrong-side-of-the-tracks son of down-and-out parents who had spent his life scrabbling to try to become someone—and had.

But frankly he felt reborn. Alive. Nothing he had earned or achieved or become came close to describing the gift Sadie had given him with her love.

"…listening to a word I've said?" Richard Carstairs's rough voice penetrated the blissful fog that clouded Spence's brain.

Spence dragged his attention back briefly from far more interesting contemplations. "What? Yes, of course I'm listening."

But he couldn't seem to focus on anyone but Sadie. She'd finished her breakfast. Where had she gone?

His gaze didn't stop moving until he found her out on the deck, the breeze lifting her hair, the late-morning sunlight kissing her cheeks. They looked redder than usual. Probably his fault. Whisker burn had been the last thing on his mind last night. And this morning she hadn't wanted him to shave.

"I like it," she'd said, rubbing her palm over his cheek. "Very sexy." He was glad she liked it.

"—build some stables as well," Richard said. "Don't you agree?"

"Mmm."

"Let the man eat his breakfast," Steve said gruffly. "He'll listen to you soon enough."

Richard grumbled, but put his sheaf of papers away, then looked around absently. "Where's Leonie?"

"Don't know." Don't care, Spence thought. But feeling generous—and in fact feeling as if he owed Leonie something for having inadvertently prompted him to bring Sadie along, he said to Richard, "You ought to find her. See if she's having a good time. Go for a swim with her."

"A swim?" Richard looked aghast.

"It's what Isogawa wanted us to have this week for," Spence

reminded him with the zeal of the converted. "Remembering what's important. Reconnecting with family."

Richard shook his head. "Leonie's my wife, not my family."

Spence didn't see the difference, but he was no expert. "Just a thought," he said mildly.

Richard grunted and went back to his papers.

Sadie spent the two hours before lunch and two hours after attending the meetings, taking copious notes—and Spence-watching. And if it was possible to find more reasons to love the man she'd married four years ago, Sadie did it that afternoon.

It had been a long time since she'd seen Spence at work other than in the office in Butte working one-on-one with her. But today she saw him working with people, listening to ideas, visualizing, synthesizing, concretizing. He took a group of men with diverse agendas and individual concerns and brought them to a group agreement.

It wasn't all settled yet, of course. The deal wasn't done. But he had connected with Mr. Isogawa. The respect between them was clear. And his rapport with the others was also there. When Richard seemed about to go off on a tangent, Spence tactfully and speedily redirected his focus. When John got bogged down in the details, Spence took him back to the big picture. He had a way with words and a way with people that gave them confidence and helped them zero in on the program.

"You were spectacular," she told him after when the meeting broke up for the afternoon.

He grinned, all boyish enthusiasm. "You're prejudiced," he told her.

"But that doesn't mean I'm wrong." And then, because she dared now show her feelings, she raised up on tiptoe and kissed him.

He kissed her back, a warm, possessive kiss. And when all

the men gave them a round of applause and a couple of cheers, he slung an arm around her shoulder and said, "If you'll excuse us, gentlemen, my wife and I have things to discuss."

They "discussed" for the rest of the afternoon. They made love in their bed and under the waterfall in their private outdoor spa. It was far more wickedly wonderful and erotic than Sadie had ever dared imagine.

Spence left her, boneless and replete, then had to get dressed to meet Richard and Mr. Isogawa to look at the place where Richard had suggested they might want to put in some stables.

"You don't mind?" he said.

"Of course not. It's what you're here for."

He bent over her on the bed and kissed her with lazy thoroughness. "Want to go for a swim tonight?"

"A swim?" She grinned.

"And all that that entails."

"Love to. Love you," she said, and smiled as she watched him stuff his feet into his flip-flops and head out the door.

Sadie took another shower after he left. Then she dressed and went for a walk on the beach.

Leonie was standing near a group of beach chairs, talking with Jale. He was smiling while she batted her lashes at him and ran a hand down his arm. When she saw Sadie, she waved him off, and, looking almost relieved, he hurried away.

"Just arranging another massage," Leonie explained as Sadie came up. "He's very good. Sure you don't want one?"

Sadie wasn't sure how much to read into the "very good" but she did know the answer to the question. "No, thanks."

Leonie sat down on a beach towel and stretched her legs out, wiggling her toes. "I suppose you don't need anyone else with his hands on you." She flicked Sadie a sideways glance.

"Besides Spence, you mean? No."

"He's obviously nuts about you."

A day ago Sadie wouldn't have believed it. Now she said, "The feeling is mutual."

"I can tell." There was a grudging envy in Leonie's tone.

Sadie let it go. "Are you enjoying yourself?" she asked.

"What do you think?"

Oops. Wrong question.

"I know how much you wanted to come and—" Sadie began to back pedal.

"Did Spence tell you about Barcelona?"

Sadie's gaze jerked over to meet the other woman's. The color was high in Leonie's cheeks, but she didn't look away. Nor did Sadie. At least they weren't going to have to pretend it hadn't happened. She nodded. "Yes."

"Figures." Leonie gave a bitter half laugh. "When I saw you with him yesterday morning at the airport in Nadi, when he said you were married, I thought maybe he was pretending—to avoid me, you know? To make sure Richard didn't find out and ruin the deal." She shook her head. "How's that for egocentric?"

Sadie hoped the question was rhetorical.

"Spence and I have actually been together for a long time," she said. "We just thought we shouldn't make an issue of it. You know, during work."

"I understand." Leonie grimaced. "Lucky you. I envy you. Oh, not about Spence." She paused. "Well, to be honest, yes, about Spence. He's dynamite. But it's more that he actually pays attention to you."

Unlike Richard.

Sadie understood. From what she'd seen, Richard barely seemed to register that his wife was there.

"Was that why you went to, um, Spence's...in Barcelona?" she asked, not quite finding the words to say it. "The reason for the massages? And Jale?"

Leonie nodded grimly. "I keep hoping Richard will wake up!"

"By making him jealous?"

"Why not? I want him to notice me… Remember that I'm his wife. How else can I wake him up?"

"Tell him?" It was more a question than a suggestion. God knew Sadie was the last person who should be giving advice about how to improve a marriage.

"Tell him I want a baby?"

"A baby?" Sadie stared at Leonie. "Do you?"

The leap from "notice me" to "want a baby" was substantial.

"I do, yes. I know Richard already has grown children. I know he thinks he's finished with all that. But I'm not! I love him. I want a child with him. A family. Don't you?"

"Yes, of course we do." Sadie didn't have to think an instant about that. She'd been dreaming about a family with Spence since she'd been old enough to know how babies were made. She already had names picked out for their children, though she supposed she'd allow him some input.

"But I didn't realize you did. Doesn't Richard?"

"We haven't discussed it," Leonie admitted. Then she got a mulish expression on her face. "How could we? He barely acts like I'm alive. It's weird, you know. He was all over me before we got married. I got complete attention. Once he had the ring on my finger, he went right back to work. Marrying me was like doing a deal. The thrill of the hunt. Once he got me, he wasn't interested anymore."

"Maybe you should tell him how you feel. Maybe he thinks you don't want kids."

"Maybe he's never even considered it!"

"You'll never know until you try."

"I guess I just hoped he'd realize…"

"Read your mind?" Sadie smiled.

Leonie shrugged. "Something like that."

"Trust me," Sadie said with feeling. "Speaking from experience. It doesn't work. You have to say the words."

Leonie sighed, then picked up a fistful of sand and let it trickle out through her fingers. Then she tipped her head to the side and looked at Sadie. "You are so lucky," she murmured. "Do you have any idea how lucky?"

And Sadie, thinking back over the past four years in limbo and the last night in Spence's arms, dug her toes into the warm sand and felt the kiss of the sun on her face and could only nod and smile.

"Yes," she said softly. "Yes, I do."

CHAPTER NINE

"I TALKED to Leonie this afternoon." Sadie was lying on her side in bed, tracing a line down the center of Spence's bare chest, then following it with her lips.

"Mmm." It was an acknowledgment that he heard her, but his attention was clearly elsewhere. He shifted as her mouth moved lower, then held still, sucking in his breath.

"You're very tense," Sadie murmured, teasing his navel with her tongue, then moving lower still.

"Not tense," Spence muttered. "Wrung out."

"But obviously not unwilling to continue." Sadie grinned and kept on tracing, touching, teasing.

They had gone back to their room after dinner, a memorable meal, succulent pork and locally grown vegetables cooked in a *lovo*, or Fijian earth oven. But while almost everyone else had taken Mr. Isogawa up on his offer of drinks in the bar afterward, Spence had said he and Sadie needed to go over some papers.

"Go over some papers?" Sadie had said doubtfully,

Spence had waited until they were out of earshot. Then he'd grinned. "We'll put them under the bed."

She didn't know if they were under there or not. She and Spence had been in the bed—except when they'd been in the waterfall shower—for most of the rest of the evening.

Their lovemaking had been by turns heated and passionate,

then leisurely and frolicksome. It was everything Sadie could ever have wanted it to be. It spoke of the closeness, the trust and the intimacy that she and Spence had achieved.

And in the joy of their love, she remembered Leonie's unhappy face.

"You were right," she said now, looking up between kisses. "She did intend to seduce you."

Spence jerked halfway up, weight resting on his elbows. "She told you that?" He looked appalled.

Sadie moved her shoulders. "She did, actually. She thinks you're gorgeous," she added with a grin. "But it was really more about Richard. She was trying to make him jealous. He didn't notice, apparently."

"And thank God for that," Spence said dryly. "Or this whole thing would have fallen through. It's too bad, though, if she really does care," he reflected. "Richard tends to get pretty single-minded at times." He settled back down, the fingers of one hand playing in Sadie's hair, making her scalp tingle.

She bent her head and continued her exploratory kissing. "At one time, apparently, he was single-minded about pursuing her. Like she was some sort of trophy. And then when he got her, he forgot her." She nipped his belly.

Spence's fingers clenched in her curls. "She's not exactly destitute. She's getting something out of the marriage," he pointed out. "World travel. A fantastic house. Three fantastic houses, for that matter. One in Florida, one in England, one in Costa Rica. She wouldn't be cavorting around Fiji now if it weren't for Richard."

"I don't think it's Fiji Leonie cares about. Or the fantastic houses. It's her marriage. It's Richard. She loves him."

"She's got a damn funny way of showing it, then. Why doesn't she just say so?"

"That's what I told her." Sadie eased her way down and let

her fingers walk along his thighs, first one and then the other, then dipping between them and making him squirm.

"Asking for trouble," Spence muttered.

"No. A baby," Sadie said, kissing him exactly where she'd been aiming for all along.

Spence jerked. *"What?"*

"Leonie," Sadie said, breathing on him, tasting him, making him gasp, "wants a baby."

Spence was strangling. "Forget babies! I don't care what Leonie wants! I want you!" Hastily he sheathed himself to protect her, then hauled her up to straddle him and thrust to meet her—to make them one once more.

And Sadie met him eagerly, delighting in the way they moved together, rocked together, loved together. Shattered together.

"I love you," she breathed as she collapsed on top of him. Her head rested on his chest. His heart thundered in her ear. She turned her face to press a kiss there, then she lifted her head and smiled tenderly up at him. "Sometime soon maybe we'll have a baby, too."

He didn't respond. He just lay there with his fingers threaded through her hair, relishing its silken softness. He turned his head and pressed a kiss against her cheek. "I love you, too," he whispered and wrapped his arms around her, holding her close while she dozed. He still wanted her and it wasn't that long before his body was ready again to love her.

He ran his hands down her back, began to kiss her.

She squirmed against him, as eager as he was to love again.

He smiled. "I think," Spence whispered against her ear, "that life is plenty full enough as it is."

"Richard thought he was hearing things," Leonie reported Friday morning.

They were on the beach while the men were tidying up the last details of the Nanumi agreement.

Sadie had wondered since their conversation earlier in the week, but she hadn't wanted to ask. And nothing in Leonie's demeanor before today had given her any reason to hope. But this morning the other woman's eyes were wide and there was a light in them that Sadie had never seen before.

"You told him?"

"Well, I had to get his attention first. I tried talking, but he kept right on working away on his damned laptop. So after three tries, I finally grabbed it and threatened to stomp it into oblivion if he didn't listen."

Now it was Sadie who was wide-eyed. "You didn't!"

"Well, I didn't stomp it, but I could have," Leonie admitted. "I may not be trying to seduce Spence anymore, but I still believe in dramatic gestures. I just had to find one that got his attention. That did."

Sadie was impressed. "I'll bet. So what did he say?"

"He was surprised. Stunned, really. I guess we never did talk enough before we got married. It was very rush-rush. I told you, he acted like he had to win me. And he did. But he thought I'd married him for his money, and that was all. The idiot didn't realize I really loved him!" Leonie shook her head and made a sound that was somewhere between a laugh and a sob.

Sadie was amazed. "And now he does?"

"He's…working on it. I think I gave him something to think about."

Sadie just bet she had. "And the baby? What did he think about that?"

"He couldn't believe I meant it. He thought he was too old. That *I* would think he was too old. I told him he wasn't the one who'd be pregnant! And then he wondered what his kids would think. I said, 'Ask them,' and that surprised him, too."

"That you would offer to let them voice an opinion?"

"I suppose. I think he thinks they won't approve. I think he thinks they don't approve of his marrying me. But that's not their decision. It's his, though they could certainly have told him if they wanted to. And they won't make this decision, either. But why shouldn't he ask if he wants to know how they feel?"

It seemed like eminently good sense to Sadie. And she said so.

Leonie smiled. "I hope so. We'll see. He's told me a hundred times what a big step it is. He says I should take a good look at the Isogawas' grandchildren tomorrow and see if I really want all that hassle. But he's not saying no. He's actually interested. Tempted, I think. Mostly, though, he knows I really love him now. And—" she threw her arms around Sadie and gave her a crushing hug "—we owe it all to you!"

"She says she owes it all to me," Sadie reported, grinning.

"Huh? Who owes what?" Spence was distracted, she could tell. He'd been eager to wrap her in his arms as soon as he'd found her on the beach. And he'd spirited her away from Leonie without a backward glance. Something was on his mind.

"I said, Leonie and Richard are talking to each other," she repeated patiently while they walked up to their *bure*. "He's actually listening to her. They're communicating! They might have a baby! And she says she owes it all to me." She was sure Spence would appreciate the irony of it.

But he just shook his head. "The woman's nuts."

Well, he'd had a hard day. While Sadie had only attended the morning meetings, he'd been tied up all afternoon hammering out the last of the details so that the new resort consortium was now a done deal. So he could be forgiven not caring one way or another about Leonie's family issues.

"You must be relieved that it's over," Sadie said as they climbed the steps up to the treehouse porch. Once there she reached up to knead the taut muscles of his shoulders and back.

Spence sighed. "Yeah." He let her hands work their magic for a few moments, then straightened. "I was thinking we ought to go home."

"Home?" Sadie's hands stilled.

"We can't stay here forever. It's paradise, yes. But the work's done."

"But the week isn't. Mr. Isogawa expects us to be here. Besides, tomorrow's family day." And she'd been looking forward to that.

Spence shrugged. "Isogawa's family."

"And we want to meet them. They come back every year— all of them—Mr. and Mrs. Isogawa, their kids and grandkids. It's what Nanumi is all about. It's what we've worked on all week."

Spence's jaw tightened briefly. But then he shrugged. "Fine. If you want to stay, we'll stay." He walked into the room and fell on the bed face down. His eyes shut.

Sadie sat down next to him and began rubbing his back again. "All the adrenaline's gone, isn't it?"

He rolled over and grabbed her, pulling her down on top of him. "Don't you believe it!"

He was still sound asleep when she awoke the next morning.

And no wonder, Sadie thought. He'd kept them up most of the night. He had loved her eagerly, urgently, almost desperately, in a way that reminded her of their wedding night four years ago.

But it wasn't like that, Sadie was sure, because there was no forgetting what had happened between them here.

It was nearly eight. She'd promised to meet the Isogawas and their family for breakfast at nine. That gave her time for a lei-surely shower—provided Spence didn't join her—before she had to be there. She wouldn't have minded at all if he had joined her. But she knew he was exhausted.

She looked at him now, her heart full to bursting at the love she felt for this man. She reached out and brushed a hand lightly over his tousled hair. He didn't stir. She leaned down and kissed his stubbled cheek. He sighed and smiled slightly, but he didn't wake.

She took her shower, then dried her hair and combed it, taking more care than she had all week so she would be presentable for meeting the Isogawa family. When she left at five minutes to nine, Spence still hadn't moved.

The sound of children's laughter woke him. Startled him.

For a moment Spence didn't know where he was. Then he opened his eyes and remembered. Family day.

Talk about a foreign experience.

He lay there considering the best way to avoid the whole thing, when there was a knock on the *bure* door. He frowned because in the entire week, no one had come knocking. Everyone had respected his and Sadie's privacy. But maybe Sadie had sent a messenger to see if he was ever getting up.

He pulled on a pair of shorts and opened the door, blinked when he didn't see anyone, then realized the knocker barely came up to his chest.

Two girls and three boys were standing there, hopping and jigging from one foot to the other.

"We've never seen a tree house this big. You live here?" The tallest boy asked him, eyes wide. He sounded like a Kiwi and looked like Steve, so Spence had a pretty good idea who he was.

"This week I do," he replied, as they craned their necks and peered past him into the room. Their eagerness reminded him of his own youthful curiosity. "Want to have a look around?"

Did they? He was practically trampled in the rush to explore. They were fascinated by the way the *bure* was built around the branches, that one of them was so big that it could be used as a "window seat." They were delighted with the private waterfall.

"Can we go in it?" the redheaded girl asked.

He shrugged. "Be my guests." And as they danced and

hopped and skittered through it, laughing all the while, Spence laughed, too. He told them his name and found out theirs. The biggest boy, Geoff, and the littlest, Justin, belonged to Steve and Cathy. The middle one was Keefe Ten Eyk. The redheaded girl was his sister, Katie, and the other was Mai, the Isogawas' granddaughter. She didn't speak English but the language barrier wasn't slowing them down any.

"This is amaaaazing," Keefe said. "I could live here my whole life!"

"Which is soon to end," came a voice from the door. And a very stern Marion appeared. "You know better than to bother the guests."

"We asked," Katie said. "Politely."

All the rest of the kids nodded in agreement.

"He said be his guest," Justin piped up. "Didn't you?" He looked at Spence for confirmation.

"Absolutely," Spence agreed.

"They didn't wake you?" Marion was still looking worried. "Sadie said you were exhausted, that you needed your sleep."

"I was awake. I was just coming down for a swim."

Justin grabbed one of his hands, and Mai shyly took the other. "C'mon, then."

"Leave Mr. Tyack alone," Marion said. "Out now. All of you. And say thank you for his kindness at letting you interrupt his life."

"They didn't. They were fine." And Spence took the hands of the kids who had dropped his and led them out the door and down the steps. "Hit the beach." He swung their hands up, and when he let go they all took off running, yelling whooping— even Mai who couldn't possibly have understood.

Marion lingered beside him. "Crazy children. They think they've been turned loose on Swiss Family Robinson's island. Thank you. I'm sorry they bothered you."

"It's all right," Spence said again. "They're fine."

"Glad you feel that way," Marion said, then patted him on the arm. When he raised a quizzical brow, she turned and nodded toward the group coming down from the lodge.

The group included both the elder Isogawas, a younger couple Spence presumed were their children, with two more grandchildren much smaller than Mai.

A little boy just learning to walk was holding on to Richard on one side and Leonie on the other while he took staggering steps toward the beach and Richard and Leonie laughed and made encouraging noises.

The other child was nestled in Sadie's arms.

"She's in her element now," Marion said, watching Sadie with a smile on her face.

And Spence, watching, had to agree.

He'd always known she'd doted on Edward, Martha and Theo's little boy. It was a woman thing, he figured, because every time Martha brought him in, Sadie scooped the little boy up and danced him around the office, blew kisses on his belly, made him laugh and told him nursery rhymes.

"She'll be a good mother," Marion assured him.

"Yeah." She would.

Sadie had enjoyed all the other days—and of course she'd loved the nights—but family day was the best.

She got to play with the Isogawas' grandchildren. She got to watch Spence playing with the bigger kids. She got to imagine what it would be like when they had their own children someday, even though she knew she shocked everyone when Leonie had asked her how many children she wanted and she said, "Eight."

"Ha!" John Ten Eyk had laughed.

And Marion had shuddered and said, "Rather you than me!'

"Sadie could handle them," Cathy said firmly.

But the look on Spence's face was so appalled she'd hastened to reassure him. "I don't really want eight," she said quickly. "I know how much work kids are now. So I think maybe three or four would be wonderful. Even one or two. Whatever we get, I guess. And if we don't get any we can adopt."

Something was wrong. Sadie could tell.

When the kids went to eat dinner with their parents, she and Spence ate with Richard and Leonie, who suddenly were acting more like newlyweds than she and Spence were. Leonie was bubbling with enthusiasm as they talked about the Isogawas' grandchildren.

Far from putting her off having children, the day had whetted her appetite. And Richard didn't seem to be averse to the idea.

"My kids—my *old* kids," he corrected himself, "will just have to get used to it if I have another one. It's not like they're teenagers embarrassed by everything Dad does."

"Of course not," Sadie said. "Tony Hunt, one of the artists in Spence's art co-op became a father again in his fifties three years ago. His son is his grandson's best friend. Right?" She looked at Spence.

"Yeah." He shoved a delicious piece of *lovo*-cooked pork around on his plate. He didn't say anything else.

Sadie studied him in silence during the meal. He had got more sun today than the other days. There had been no meetings, just fun and games on the beach. Maybe he'd got too much sun. Maybe he didn't feel well.

"I think," she said when she finished her own meal, "that I'd like to call it a night. I've got a lot of packing to do before our flight leaves in the morning. Do you want to come?" she asked her husband. "Or do you want to stay and visit some more?"

He shoved back his chair and stood. "I'll come."

They said goodbye to the Carstairs. Richard shook hands heartily. Leonie hugged both her and Spence hard and whispered, "You guys are the best. We have a baby, we'll name it after one of you."

Sadie laughed. "I think you should discuss that with Richard first."

They wished everyone else goodbye, too. Their plane was leaving early in the morning. The Carstairs were staying another week for some determined "together time." And both New Zealand couples had a later flight back to Nadi and then home.

The Isogawas bowed then hugged Sadie, probably because she hugged them first. "I know it's probably not at all the proper thing to do," she told them. "But this has been the most wonderful week of my life. So thank you. Thank you!"

"Thank *you* for everything, too," Mr. Isogawa said. "You are part of Nanumi now. You will come back." And then he bowed and shook Spence's hand. "It is not goodbye. It is a new beginning for all of us. I thank you. I look forward to seeing you soon on Nanumi."

Spence bowed and shook hands, too. He said thank you as well, his voice quiet and grave. He bowed to Mrs. Isogawa. He said good night to everyone else and then he walked out into the star-washed night with Sadie.

He held her arm so that she didn't stumble as they walked down the plankway. He didn't speak. Neither did she. She was drinking in the beauty, savoring the memories, knowing she would take them out and replay them in her mind over and over again.

Spence opened the door to their *bure* and held it for her. She stepped past him inside, then turned and wrapped him tight in her arms. For a second he stiffened. But then his arms came hard around her and he just hung on.

"It was wonderful," Sadie said. "It *is* wonderful."

He gave her a little squeeze and rested his cheek against her hair. He just stood there. Didn't let go. Until Sadie finally loosed her arms and took half a step away to look up into his eyes.

"What's wrong?"

"Nothing." He swallowed. "I'm fine. I—" He stopped, took a breath, then started again. He looked pale now and there were lines of strain around his mouth. "What you said about kids…"

Sadie laughed. "I was kidding! Don't worry. We won't have eight."

"No, we won't."

"But however many we have, I want them all to look like you."

"No."

"Yes. I've had a thing for you forever. For my whole life. And I can't imagine anything more wonderful that lots of dark-haired little rascals just like you."

Spence shook his head. "No. I can't."

"What?" Sadie stared at him, stunned. "Can't what?"

"Won't," he corrected. "Have kids. I don't want any kids at all."

CHAPTER TEN

"I DON'T want kids." He repeated the words again. "I won't have any."

And Sadie could see by the way he paced and by the ferocity with which he cracked his knuckles that, unlike her, he wasn't joking.

"Well, we might not have any," she said, taken aback by both the sentiment and the ferocity.

"But then you want to adopt!"

"What's wrong with adoption?"

"Nothing. Nothing at all!" Another knuckle crack. "It's great. Fine. Terrific. For someone else. No kids, Sadie. I can't do it."

"But—"

"I can't. I won't be responsible for giving a kid the kind of rotten childhood I had!"

"Oh, for heaven's sake. Is that what you're worried about? It won't be that kind of childhood!"

"How do you know?"

"I just know," she said stubbornly. "How can you even think that?"

"Because I lived it, damn it. It's hell—and it's what I know. I can't do it. I won't! No kids. I made up my mind years ago."

"Spence—"

He folded his arms across his chest. "No."

She wanted to argue. She wanted to pound on his thick skull and tell him to stop being an idiot.

But there was no arguing with Spence when he got bull-headed like this. What made him a great developer was his ability to be flexible, to see options where others saw only one outcome.

But he wasn't seeing any other options now. He saw only one—the life he'd had.

"Spence," she began, softening her voice, gentling, trying to get past the wall he'd built. But he shook his head.

"That's the way it's going to be, Sadie. No kids. Period."

Stubborn jackass. Mule-headed fool. She could go through a whole barnyard of obstinacy if he kept this up.

"You can visit all the kids you want. I'll never stop you."

"Oh, thank you very much." Her voice was sharper now. Gentleness wasn't going to begin to penetrate the steel he'd wrapped around his heart. "How very nice of you."

"I know you like kids and—"

"*You* like kids! That wasn't you out there today, playing with them? Jumping around in the water with them? Letting Justin climb all over you?"

"Of course I like them. But that doesn't mean I intend to raise them!"

"You can't just unilaterally lay down edicts like that."

"Of course I can. I just did."

"Spence—"

"No. And I'm not going to change my mind. Sorry. If it mattered so much, you should have asked. Emily knew. Dena knew. They were fine with it."

"Well, I'm not. And you never told me."

"I'm telling you now." Their gazes met, dueled.

"Not good enough."

He shook his head. "Sorry. That's the way it is." And

abruptly he turned away. He strode over to the closet and began packing, stuffing things in his suitcase, keeping his back to her. His movements were jerky, angry. There was none of the fluid ease she usually associated with the way Spence moved. Nothing he'd said since they'd come into the room was what she would have associated with Spence, either.

It wasn't like Spence to be dogmatic. He knew what he wanted, and he went after it.

But he'd always wanted her to argue. And he'd always listened.

"Spence," she tried again. "You need to be logical about this. You need to think clearly before you make hard-and-fast pronouncements like that."

He turned, leveling his gaze on her. "I have thought, damn it. What the hell do you think I spent my life doing?"

"I—"

"No, it's you who are going to have to be logical, who are going to have to think clearly and make a decision. Because if you want kids, Sadie—one kid or eight kids or 153 kids—you don't want to be married to me! You want a divorce."

She stared, openmouthed. Stunned.

Divorce? He was talking divorce? Again? After the most beautiful week of their lives?

"Divorce," he repeated, in case she hadn't heard him the first time he'd dropped the word like a granite boulder into the silence of the room. "Think about it."

Then he banged down the lid of his suitcase and stalked into the bathroom. The door shut. The shower turned on.

No waterfall shower together tonight, then. No eager lovemaking. No steamy passion.

Well, there had been passion. But it hadn't been steamy. It had been angry. Passionate anger. Irrational anger. Irrational thoughts.

Because of some fear of giving their children the same sort

of childhood he'd had. No chance of that! It didn't make sense. He had to realize that. Had to.

But she didn't think he did. Sadie sat down on the bed, feeling cold and sick as the realization that he really believed that sank in.

Don't overreact, she cautioned herself. *That's what he's doing. Calm down. Take it easy.*

So she took a deep steadying breath and made herself get up and start to pack. Taking things out of drawers and off hangers was mechanical and mindless, but somehow calming. And packing the various clothes she'd worn during the week made her recall the occasions when she'd worn them. Good times all. And even better times when they had come back to the *bure* and Spence had taken them off her. To make love to her. To share his body, heart and soul with her.

But he'd never shared this.

How could he not want children?

He was so good with them. And they had loved him.

They'd clambered all over him today. And Spence had instinctively known how to treat each of them. He'd roughhoused with Justin and Keefe, had listened intently to Geoff's opinions, had charmed Katie and had no doubt made a lifelong devotee out of Mai by picking her for his team when they'd played ball.

How could he not want to have the chance to do that for children of his own?

She didn't know. Didn't understand. All she could think was that he would come to his senses. He had to come to his senses.

Had to.

He'd known she would be shocked. He'd known she wouldn't be happy. And he knew that marrying her without having told her wasn't fair.

Of course, the fact that he thought he'd immediately

divorced her was somewhat of an excuse! He stood under the shower, letting steaming hot water pour over his head and down his body and tried to think.

It wasn't a big secret. He had told Emily, just as he'd told Sadie he had. Not that it had mattered, when she hadn't even bothered to show up for their wedding. There might have been significant things on which they differed—and there must have been, since she hadn't turned up—but his "no kids" edict hadn't been one of them.

He had been clear on the "no kids" count with Dena, too.

She'd been relieved to hear it. A consummate career woman with, as she put it, "not a single maternal bone in her body," Dena had broken off a relationship to Bahamian investor Carson Sawyer when he decided he wanted a family. She knew she didn't.

So she had been delighted when Spence had said he had no interest in one either. "I knew it," she'd said. "I knew we were right for each other."

But then Sadie had intervened. When she'd shown up at the courthouse with the news that she was still his wife, she'd thrown everybody's plans out of whack.

She'd also given him the most beautiful joyous week he'd ever known.

He couldn't forget that. Never wanted to.

But he couldn't lead her on, either. He couldn't pretend to want a future he had no intention of pursuing. He supposed he should have told her the day they'd been making love and she'd told him about Leonie wanting a baby.

But how?

Was he supposed to say, "Stop driving me madly insane with what you're doing for a minute so I can tell you I don't want children?" And then what? Tell her to go ahead and wring him out? Because that's exactly what she'd been doing.

And after, when she'd said she hoped they would have a baby someday, too, he couldn't bring himself to spoil the moment.

So, all right, he was a selfish bastard. An emotional coward. But at least he was honest. She had to give him that.

He shut off the shower and stood still in the stall, shivering. Cold clear through.

He didn't want to hurt her. He hated to hurt her. He loved her, damn it. But he'd had to tell her. He couldn't let her go on dreaming about some brood of children they were going to have.

She'd get over it. She was an adult, after all.

What if they couldn't have had children? Lots of couples couldn't. Would she hate him then? Would she love him less?

No. Not and still be Sadie. He knew it. He believed in the power of her love to the depths of his being.

She just needed time to adjust. To understand. He needed to give her time. Space. He needed to show her that he loved her—and then she would.

There were different kinds of silence. Sadie knew that. But she'd never experienced it so vividly as that night.

Spence came out of the shower, a *sula* wrapped around his waist, his chest still damp, his hair in wet spikes. He looked at her, his expression unreadable, then he turned away to stow his leather dopp kit in his suitcase. He didn't say a word.

Neither did Sadie.

She didn't know what to say. Everything that occurred to her would, she imagined, make matters worse. She knew Spence—or thought she did—well enough to know that backing him into a corner wasn't going to get him to change his mind. And pretending to give in to his demand wasn't going to help, either. She could hardly just smile and blithely say, "No problem."

It was a problem. That was the truth.

"Shall I set the alarm clock?" The question was very polite. Very civil. Very remote.

"Probably a good idea," she answered in a like tone. "We wouldn't want to miss the plane."

"Since we're going to be the only ones on it, I imagine they'll wait." He didn't smile.

They'd have laughed about that yesterday. Today she just nodded. "Do what you want, then."

He opened his mouth, as if he were going to tell her what he wanted. Or tell her something, at least. But he must have thought better of it because he closed his mouth again. His lips pressed into a thin hard line. He didn't speak.

He set the alarm and lay down on the bed, eyes hooded but watching her.

Another night she would have gone straight to him. She would have crawled onto the bed beside him and he would have wrapped her in his arms and started them down the path to bliss. Tonight, as he folded his arms under his head and watched her, she couldn't do it.

"I'll take a shower, then," she said tonelessly. And, plucking her nightgown off the hook, she disappeared into the bathroom just as he had. She shut the door.

She would have loved one last shower in the waterfall outside. She would have loved to have shared it with Spence. But there was no easiness between them now. No sense of togetherness. No "us" any longer.

And while she knew, if she did shower out there, that he would be watching her, she didn't feel like being on display. She wanted a shower in privacy, where if she cried—no, make that *when* she cried—Spence would never know.

Her eyes were so bloodshot when she came out, though, that if he'd been able to see her, he certainly would have known.

But when she returned, the overhead light had been turned

off. He had left on one dim light next to her side of the bed. He was still there, but lying on his side—turned away from hers.

Was he awake? She didn't know.

He didn't say a word.

In the silence Sadie shut out the light, then slid into bed beside him. It felt like Kansas again. Maybe Texas.

No. More like Alaska. Big and wide. And cold.

Her throat ached from crying. Not because she couldn't have her way. But because he'd cut off all dialogue. He'd made a unilateral decision based solely on memories she couldn't share. And then he'd retreated behind the wall of a childhood she couldn't change.

She sucked in a sharp breath and pressed her fist against her mouth to keep from making noise. But he heard it and rolled over at once.

"Don't cry, for God's sake!" His voice was as harsh and pained as her heart.

"I'll cry if I want to, you ass," she retorted, and did exactly that.

"Oh, hell." He reached for her then, hauling her into his arms, holding her, kissing her. "It'll be all right," he promised. "Shh. I'm sorry."

She hiccupped and tried to stop. But the feel of his arms around her, of his care and his concern undid her. It was so stupid. *He* was so stupid! How could he deny this part of himself to children he could love?

"Don't," he whispered urgently. "Sadie. Please. Stop." He kissed her then, in desperation, no doubt. How else could a guy shut up a crying woman? The kiss was urgent, hungry. In it was so much of everything she loved about Spence, she couldn't help but respond.

She kissed him back, wrapped herself around him, as desperate for him as he was for her. Their coupling was silent but for ragged gasps and breathing. It was fierce, demanding.

But in the end, instead of fulfilled and complete as he rolled off her and lay there staring silently at the ceiling, mostly she felt empty and lost.

She smiled the next morning. She talked to him. Yes, there was still a certain reserve there, a little strain, maybe a hint of dullness in her eyes. He didn't blame her. He knew she was upset. But it was early days yet.

She would get used to it.

He just needed to be patient.

Their trip back to Butte was long and exhausting but uneventful. Sadie slept as she had on the way out—and he watched her as he had done then.

He loved her now, couldn't get enough of looking at her. When she shifted in her seat and her shirttails parted to expose some pale-blue lace, he smiled. He knew all about Sadie's underwear now. It was wonderful.

But she was more wonderful. He was blessed.

"So, how'd it go?" Martha had enough discretion to wait until they'd been home overnight before turning up in Sadie's office the next morning, eyes wide and curious. "Ah, I see a ring!"

She grabbed Sadie's hand, exclaiming over her rings. "They're perfect. They're you!"

And Sadie nodded. She even managed a smile. Outwardly she could do that. It was inside she was hurting.

"You look tanned and beautiful and exhausted," Martha decided. "I hope the exhaustion is from not enough sleep." She eyed Sadie speculatively. "So, inquiring friends want to know. Did you…?" She waggled her eyebrows.

Sadie nodded, but didn't meet her gaze.

Martha peered at her more closely. "Don't tell me he's that bad in bed?" She sounded appalled.

"No!" Sadie went crimson. Couldn't help it. "He was—it was—wonderful."

"Yeah. I can tell how thrilled you are." Martha's tone was dry.

"It's just…there are…there *is*…a problem."

"Shall I kill him? Or just injure him?"

Sadie shook her head. It was so good to have a friend like Martha, who always took her side, no matter what. She smiled again. "Probably not kill him. Eddie needs his mother, and you wouldn't do him much good if they locked you up."

"Okay. Tell me what to do and I'll do it."

"I don't think there's anything you can do," Sadie said. She wondered if she dared take Martha into her confidence, then decided that she had to. Maybe Martha would think Spence was right. Maybe she was the one who was being foolish. Not him.

So she told Martha what had happened. "It was a wonderful week. A perfect week," she finished. "I love him. And I know he loves me. But we can't talk about this. He *won't* talk about it. Am I crazy? Am I wrong?"

Slowly, adamantly, Martha shook her head. "You're not wrong," she said. "He would be a wonderful father. Why does he think he wouldn't be?"

"I think because his father wasn't. His parents were…pretty dismal. He doesn't want the same for his kids."

"Oh, like that would happen." Martha rolled her eyes.

"I know that. You know that. Try convincing Spence of that."

"I can't," Martha said. "But you're not wrong. If you want this to work, you're going to have to."

Easier said than done, of course, once they were home and real life intervened. Spence was on the phone all the time. He was faxing and calling and sending messages on the computer. He flung himself back into work with a vengeance. And he never once mentioned the "no kids" issue.

Sadie almost began to think she'd dreamed it. But she only had to see him around Edward to know that she hadn't.

Martha brought her son into work often. She always had, especially when Theo was away sailing, which, as it was his job, happened regularly. Whenever Edward came, Sadie had always played with him. Tickled him. Played peek-a-boo with him and, now that he could fling a ball, played ball with him.

Edward was her pal. When Theo was home, Sadie even watched him so Martha and Theo could have an evening out now and then.

"You want Eddie some night?" Martha asked her. "Theo's not home. But I could always use some time to work. At least you'd have a natural lead-in."

Sadie remembered counseling Leonie just to talk to Richard. But when the shoe was on her own foot—and Spence was pretending that everything was fine—it didn't seem so easy. It was like the marriage elephant all over again. Only now it was the kid elephant in the room that neither of them could talk about.

"Yes, let me have Eddie," she said.

The evening with Eddie was a great success. He loved Sadie. Sadie loved him. He toddled over to Spence and grabbed him around the knees. "Da," he said.

"Not me," Spence said. But he didn't turn the little boy away. He picked him up and read him a story. Then the three of them ate macaroni and cheese for supper. They had jello cubes for dessert. Eddie even ate part of a jar of peas because Sadie convinced Spence to eat some, too.

"I'll bet Theo doesn't eat mushed peas," he complained. But he ate them. And seeing him do so, Eddie did, too.

Watching them together, Sadie dared to hope.

When Martha came and got him at ten, Eddie was asleep on their bed—next to Spence. Sadie went in to pick the little boy up and stood looking at the two of them, Eddie's small fingers wrapped around Spence's big thumb.

And he didn't want children?

How could he say that?

Martha took her sleeping son out of Sadie's arms and crossed her fingers. "Here's hoping," she said. "Good luck."

"Thanks," Sadie said. And after Martha went, she said to herself out loud, "just talk to him."

"We need to talk," she said baldly the next morning.

Maybe it wasn't the best time, but he was leaving for two weeks in a matter of hours, heading out for the Bahamas to see Dena and Tom Wilson, then going on to Naples to have a look at a project there. He was coming back via Ireland because he had a notion about buying some cottages near Cork for a retirement village. He had a lot of irons in his fire.

He didn't ignore her. He was attentive at home. He was the Spence she remembered at work. But the new elephant—the "child elephant" was always in the room. And she couldn't let him leave without talking about it.

"Talk? About what?" He was still keying in something on his handheld computer, but when she didn't speak, he finally glanced up.

Sadie took a breath. "Kids."

His features grew still. He didn't say anything for a long moment, as if waiting for her to continue. When she didn't, he said almost casually, "What about them?" and to underline his lack of interest, he went back to messing with the tiny computer.

Remembering Leonie, Sadie reached out and snatched it out of his hand. He looked at her then, astonished at her behavior. "I said I want to talk," she repeated.

His jaw set. "Talk, then."

"You can't just make a pronouncement in the middle of a marriage that you don't want kids."

"I can," he said. "I did. And don't start on me about telling you beforehand. You know it was impossible."

"Well, it's not impossible to rethink. To change your mind."

"I don't want to change my mind."

"Can't Edward change your mind?"

He frowned. "What's Edward got to do with it?"

"You loved him. You played with him. You ate peas for him. You fell asleep with him!"

"So?"

"So, why do you want to deprive children of a father like that? We'd be good parents, Spence!"

"You would."

"So would you! I know it!"

He didn't answer, just sat there, a human Mount Rushmore, except for the tension making a muscle tick in his jaw. They stared at each other, gazes dueling, grappling in silence. Finally he flicked off the computer without even looking at it, tucked it into his shirt pocket and stood up.

"I love you, Sadie," he said, his tone even, steady, flat. "And I think you love me—"

"I do love you, damn it!"

"Then try to understand that I'm not going to change my mind. My parents—"

"Oh, stop hiding behind your parents!"

His whole body jerked. "What did you say?"

"You heard me! You drag them out every time you don't let yourself do something. Yes, they left a lot to be desired. They were a couple of unhappy, sorry, miserable people. And if you give in to their influence, they win."

"They never won anything!"

"If you believe what they told you, they've won your mind," Sadie argued, knowing she was saying too much, cutting too deep, but unable to stop herself. "They own it. They own you!"

"The hell they do!" He was furious now. His face was scarlet. The veins in his neck stood out in sharp relief. "They never thought I could do anything. They always believed I was just like them!"

"And you believe it, too. I love you, Spence. And I believe you love me. The sad thing is, I don't believe you love yourself."

There was no sound in the room, in the house, in all of Montana, it seemed, after that. The world stopped. Sadie knew she had spoken the unforgivable truth. Spence's face simply closed up.

She didn't know how long they stood there—the silence beating between them—until finally Spence said, "I'll be gone two weeks. If you change your mind, I'll see you when I get back. If not, I suggest you leave and file for divorce."

"He told you to get a divorce?" Martha was apoplectic. If it were possible for a human being to carom off walls, Martha might have done it. She sat down in Sadie's office. She bounced up again. She paced. She banged doors. She hit window sashes. "What kind of idiot is he?"

"A stubborn one," Sadie said flatly. She felt dead inside. Gutted. She was alive but simply going through the motions. Had been since Spence had walked out the door yesterday afternoon.

"Maybe he'll be the one who comes to his senses, who changes his mind," Martha said when she finally settled down.

Sadie shook her head. "He won't change his mind."

Martha turned and looked at her closely. "Will you?"

"Will I what? Change my mind? I can't." Sadie knew that much. She'd lain awake all night thinking about it. "It's like when you left Theo in New York and came back to Montana even though he said he'd marry you. It was for the wrong reason. If I stayed with Spence now, it would be for the wrong reason. It would be because I didn't believe in him. And I do."

"So what are you going to do? Divorce him?" Martha went pale as she said the word.

"Maybe. We'll see. But I'm not going to live like this."

It was the longest two weeks of his life.

Spence, who ordinarily lived for the fast lane of travel, new faces and new places, was desperate to get home to his wife. Not that he'd said so. He'd only talked to her once—from the Bahamas.

It had been a stilted conversation. Polite. Distant. But he couldn't hang up without asking, "So, are you leaving me?" He was glad his voice hadn't betrayed any of his fear.

"I don't know yet," she'd said.

He'd sent text messages and e-mails and faxes after that, just like he had the first week that he'd known about their marriage, because he didn't want to argue. And he didn't want to hear what she had to say. She'd already said too damn much.

He tried not to think about it. She hadn't meant it. She'd just been angry. He was sure she missed him as much as he was missing her. And even though he'd liked what he found in Ireland, he could hardly wait to get home.

He even managed to catch an earlier flight out of Newark, via Minneapolis to Butte. Then, as it was still only three in the afternoon, he drove straight to the office to surprise her.

She wasn't there.

Grace Tredinnick was sitting at the computer, adjusting her glasses, then moving her head back and forth.

Spence skidded to a halt in the doorway. "What are you doing here?"

"Well, hello to you, sonny," Grace said, peering at him over the top of her spectacles. "Didn't expect you until morning."

"I got an early flight. Where's Sadie?" He looked around, up and down the hall, but he didn't see her.

"Sadie's gone."

"Gone home?"

Grace shook her head. "Gone away. That's why I'm here."

Spence felt as if all the blood drained right out of his head. Gone? Sadie? His stomach lurched. He felt suddenly hot and clammy, then cold as a Montana winter.

"Where?" His voice, even to his own ears, sounded like an old man's. "Where is she?"

"Texas. Austin, Texas. Took a job down there."

Texas? Who the hell did she know in Texas? Who cared who she knew? Why had she gone?

She loved him! She wasn't supposed to leave him!

"Left a letter and some stuff for you on your desk," Grace said.

But she'd barely got the words out before he had pushed past her into his office. There was an envelope on the desk, and next to it a small box.

Spence kicked the door shut, then sank down into his desk chair and picked up the envelope. She had written his name in her inimitable neat script on the front. He would know her writing anywhere.

Slowly he slit open the envelope and took out a single sheet of paper. More neat script. He felt a hard aching lump in his throat.

The letter said exactly what he didn't want to read—that she had taken him at his word, that she had gone. She had accepted a job working for Mateus Gonzales—starting up an office for him in Texas. It was all very simple. She never reproached him. She just said she was doing what he had suggested.

He opened the box. In it there were three rings—the two he'd given her on the airplane, the jade and Celtic gold that were so clearly her, and the one he thought he'd lost—his great-grandfather's heavy hand-carved ring.

He held them in his hand, rubbed his thumb over them, felt the smooth jade, the intricate filigree, the soft warmth of the pipestone. He rubbed them stroked them, turned them over and over, round and round. His throat ached, his eyes stung. His cheeks were already damp when his thumbnail caught on the edge of the inlay where the heart was broken.

It would get easier. Sadie knew that it would. Her new job was interesting. Mateus was easy to work with. He divided his time between Sao Paulo and Rio and Austin. So, frequently, like when she'd worked with Spence, she was left to do things on her own.

He never minded what she did. He was more laid-back than Spence. He worked hard, but he actually stopped to breathe now and then. He also believed in that wonderful Latin custom, the siesta, so while Sadie worked, in theory, longer hours, she was really just out of her apartment more. That was good because in the middle of the day she could get out and see parts of Austin, get used to the city, find new things to do and places to go.

It also meant she had less time to feel sorry for herself.

She knew she had done the right thing by leaving. She truly did love Spence enough to know that she couldn't live with him if it meant agreeing with his parents' definition of who he was. There was so much more inside him. So much love that he had given to her and that he could give to their children, if only he learned to spare some for himself.

He believed in himself at work. How could he not do the same at home? With her? He could. Sadie knew he could.

But it got harder and harder to stick it out on the moral high ground when days turned into weeks and weeks turned into a month and then two—and Spence never came.

She'd been sure he would. He would read her letter and understand. He would come after her and take her home again. She certainly hadn't made a secret of where she was.

She stayed in touch with Martha. She talked on the phone

with Grace. Once she'd even talked to him when he'd answered Grace's office phone.

"Sadie?" He almost choked on her name when she'd asked for Grace.

She had already done her choking when she'd heard his gruff, "Tyack Enterprises," seconds before.

"Hello, Spence," she said coolly. "How are you?"

"I'm...good. Doing fine." His cadence quickened. "Just off to Ireland again. The project there is taking off. It's going to be—" He stopped. "Never mind. I'm sure you're not interested. You've probably got a lot of equally interesting stuff going on down there."

"Quite a few things," she said airily. "Lots of excitement. We went to Rio last month. Mateus keeps me busy."

"I'm sure. Right. Here's Grace," he said abruptly, and the next thing she knew she had been handed over to the older woman.

It was the only time she'd talked to him. But it disturbed her dreams for the rest of the week. And she was only getting her equilibrium back when Mateus breezed into the office one morning and said, "Congratulate me. I'm engaged."

As he had been clearly smitten with a young *carioca* woman called Cristina when he and Sadie had been in Rio, it was not a big surprise.

"That's wonderful," Sadie said. "I'm so happy for you."

And of course she was. But it made her go home and weep for the love she'd lost. She hadn't filed for a divorce yet, but she expected any day to be served papers by Spence. There was no reason why he shouldn't. She'd left him. He could get the divorce and marry Dena now, exactly the way he'd wanted.

"Has he said anything about divorce?" she asked Martha the next time they talked. She'd told Martha about Mateus's engagement, and half expected to hear that Spence was contemplating the same.

"You think he'd tell me?" Martha said. "He doesn't talk to any of us. Not much. Oh, maybe he chats with Grace. Mostly he's gone."

Working? Sadie wondered. Or lining up a new wife?

She tormented herself with thoughts like that on a regular basis. She wished she could get past it. Get past *him*. But sometimes it felt as if she'd been born loving Spencer Tyack, and digging him out of her life—and her heart—was going to be a rest-of-her-lifetime project.

She told herself for the hundredth time this week to get started on it as she carried her week's dirty clothes down to the apartment complex laundry room. She took great pleasure in grabbing each piece of clothing and stuffing it unceremoniously into the washing machine, then adding the soap and dumping in the bleach. She needed bleach for her brain she thought. Something to get rid of Spence.

A shadow fell across her as she was putting in her quarters. "Sorry," she said without turning around, "I've taken the last one. You can have the washer after me."

"I don't want the washer. I want you."

At the sounds of that gruff, dear, familiar voice, she spun around, slinging quarters everywhere. *"Spence!"*

She wanted to run to him, grab him, hang on and never let him go. But he made no move toward her. He stood in the doorway, his thumbs hooked in his belt loops, looking like a gunfighter. His throat worked. He wet his lips, then let out a shaky breath.

"If you'll have me…and my children," he said. He didn't smile, but there was a light—a fire—in his eyes as they met hers.

"Oh, Spence!" She flew at him then, practically knocking him flat. And she knew the joy of his arms coming around her, crushing her to him, hanging on to her as if she were the only thing keeping him from drowning.

"Oh, God, Sadie, I missed you!" He said the words against her mouth, punctuated them with kisses, then buried his face into the curve of her neck, his arms still clutching her as if he'd never let her go.

That was all right with Sadie. She had lived too long for this moment, had dreamed of it too many times. And had, for a long time now been afraid it would never come.

"Excuse me?" A voice behind Spence sounded tentative. A tall black woman with beautifully beaded hair was looking bemusedly at them. "I just need to get to the dryer, please."

They stumbled apart, but Spence hung on to Sadie's hand as they stepped out of the way. "Come on," she said, "come upstairs."

Ordinarily she stayed and read a book while she did her laundry. Not today. She hauled Spence after her up the steps. The apartment was boring, nondescript, lonely. Not today.

"Why?" she asked him when she had him inside the door and their arms were around each other again. "After all these months, why now? What happened?"

"Mateus got engaged."

"What?" Sadie's jaw dropped. She couldn't believe her ears. "Mateus? What does Mateus have to do with it?"

"I…I thought you…and he…" Spence shook his head. "You left me. You went to him. He's…a catch. He probably wouldn't mind having a dozen kids." He shrugged. "I couldn't stand in your way."

Sadie was speechless. Mateus? She and Mateus? If it hadn't been so painful, it might have been funny. "No," she said at last. "We've never—"

"I didn't know. I wasn't fair to you, Sadie. I know that. And you're right. You would be a good mother."

"If we couldn't have kids, Spence, I could live without them." She already knew that. It would hurt. But she would survive. If she had him, she would always survive.

"If we don't, we can adopt some," he said.

"You changed your mind." It wasn't a question. She didn't need to ask the question. She could see the answer—the transformation—in his eyes. In the way he looked at her. In the way he smiled.

He loosed his grip on her and held up a hand for her to see. Next to the rose gold of the wedding band he still wore—the wedding band she'd given him—was the pipestone ring she'd returned.

"Grandpa changed my mind," he said. "And Richard Carstairs."

Sadie gaped. She pulled him over to her lumpy secondhand sofa and pulled him down on it, holding his hand, looking at the ring, running her finger over the inlaid heart. "It isn't broken anymore."

He shook his head. "I fixed it. Got a new piece. It's whole now." He didn't say the words, but she heard them anyway: *whole...like me.*

"The ring brought back a lot of memories. More good than bad," he said quickly. "My granddad was the one good part of my childhood. When I had it, when I started wearing it again, I started remembering him. He used to tell me not to listen to them—my parents. He used to say they tried to hurt me because they were hurting inside. He said they were sad and he wished he could do something to change who they were but he couldn't. 'They have to find it in themselves,' he said. 'It's inside you,' he used to tell me. 'You can be who you want to be.' I always thought he meant about business. I never thought beyond it. Not to my life, to the people I love. Now I realize it's about us, too."

He lifted her hand to his lips and kissed them lightly. "I got a call from Richard a few weeks ago. He and Leonie are having a baby."

Sadie didn't know whether to laugh or cry. "That's wonderful."

"It is." And he sounded like he meant it. "He said thanks, by the way. He said you woke them up, made them talk to each other, made him think about decisions he'd already made without even consulting his wife. Made him realize he'd made them because he was scared. A lot like me," Spence told her.

"I didn't want to be like my parents. Mostly I didn't want to not be the man I wanted to be, that you believed I could be. I was terrified. Still am." He smiled shakily. "But I figure Grandpa might be right, that if I work at it and take the risk, I can be the man I want to be—your husband, the father of your children, the man you love and who will love you—for the rest of our lives."

She was crying then, and hugging him, kissing him, wiping away tears that she thought were hers but might have been his. "I love you so much," she whispered, her voice breaking. "I thought I'd lost you. I thought you'd never come."

"I came as soon as I thought I had a chance. Do I?" His eyes searched hers.

"Oh, yes," Sadie answered. "Oh, my love, yes!"

It was the best Christmas Spence had ever had.

The snow was flying. The temperature was far below zero. The winds were howling out of the north, and the scene was as far as one could imagine from their Fijian honeymoon. It was a long way from Austin, too, where five months ago he had gone to bring her home.

But it was the best place in the world to be this morning, lying on the sofa with Sadie wrapped in his arms, looking at the Christmas tree—the first one they'd shared—which they had decorated together with ornaments they'd made to symbolize places they'd been, people they'd known.

Sadie had made a tiny papier-mâché house that looked like Spence's Copper King mansion. He'd carved a little birch canoe. They'd gone to Ireland and brought back a shamrock and to Cornwall and brought back a flag of St. Piran. Mateus had sent them a miniature map of Texas and, of course, one of Brazil. They had a plaster of paris circle of Edward's tiny hand, and a Statue of Liberty to recall their New York courthouse experience, and half a dozen others, including an exquisitely detailed copy of their Nanumi treehouse *bure* which Mrs. Isogawa had made for them.

"It's lovely, isn't it?" she said, snuggling close and leaning up to kiss his stubbled jaw.

"Perfect," Spence agreed. "Couldn't be better." Life couldn't be better as far as he was concerned.

"No, not quite perfect," Sadie said. "That one Grace made is out of place."

"What one?"

"There. Behind the *bure*. I can't think how it got there. Could you move it? Then it will be perfect."

"It's fine. Don't fuss." He kissed her.

"But it would be better…" She looked at him hopefully and grinned.

Sighing, he got up off the sofa and padded across the rug to the tree. "Which ornament Grace made?" Grace made a lot of god-awful ornaments. Knitted things like tiny antimacassars and dangly things that were supposed to be stars but looked more like Martian antennae.

"Behind the *bure*. See it?"

He plucked out another of Grace's knitted efforts. "This?" But when he got a closer look, he realized it wasn't an ornament. "Why does Grace knit booties for Christmas ornaments?"

"She doesn't," Sadie said, smiling. "She knits them for babies."

Spence stared. He swallowed. He looked at Sadie, dazed, disbelieving, and yet… "Is she—I mean, *are you*—sure?"

Sadie nodded, still smiling.

He felt oddly breathless. "Are you…all right?" He looked worried, nervous.

"I'm fine. Are you?" She was still smiling, but there was a hint of apprehension in her tone.

Was he? Spence thought about it. He thought about the burden, the stress, the responsibility, the potential for disaster, the sleepless nights and all the times his child would cry and he would not understand.

And then he thought about sharing a child with Sadie—about the honor and joy of being allowed to be a part of someone else's life—and a slow delighted smile spread across his face.

He crossed the room and wrapped his arms around his wife and kissed her. "Thanks to you, Sadie my love, I've never been better in my life."

MY TALL DARK
GREEK BOSS

BY
ANNA CLEARY

As a child, **Anna Cleary** loved reading so much that during the midnight hours she was forced to read with a torch under the bedcovers, to lull the suspicions of her sleep-obsessed parents. From an early age she dreamed of writing her own books. She saw herself in a stone cottage by the sea, wearing a velvet smoking jacket and sipping sherry, like Somerset Maugham.

In real life she became a school teacher, where her greatest pleasure was teaching children to write beautiful stories.

A little while ago, she and one of her friends made a pact to each write the first chapter of a romance novel in their holidays. From writing her very first line Anna was hooked, and she gave up teaching to become a full-time writer. She now lives in Queensland with a deeply sensitive and intelligent cat. She prefers champagne to sherry, and loves music, books, four-legged people, trees, movies and restaurants.

For Jenny

PROLOGUE

SAMOS STILAKOS leaned his tall frame against the bar. Displeasure darkened his stern, handsome face. Why, he wondered, had he allowed himself to be persuaded into attending the Sirius Bank's Annual Masked Ball? He was a financier, not some show-business scout. And where the hell was this woman who was supposed to be his hostess?

Nothing they showed him now could save them, anyway, he thought, strafing the throng of colourful characters with his dark gaze. Least of all a staff function at a beach hotel.

As often at celebrations, the urge came over him to stride from the room, head for the airport and fly. Somewhere. *Any*where. Some deserted isle, or a snow-capped mountain in Peru, where the only music was the rush of wind. Anywhere free from this noise.

He glowered at the ballroom's lavish decorations. For a bank about to plunge straight to the bottom of Sydney Harbour, no expense had been spared. Under the glitter of the chandeliers, the Sirius staff were switched into party mode, and seethed with an excitement bordering on delirium.

Exactly what his ex-wife would have loved, Sam

brooded, watching a scarlet-cloaked Romeo cavorting with a laughing, shrieking woman on the dance floor. His sensuous mouth hardened.

A pity they weren't tuned into the reality facing their bank.

An adventurous Catwoman swayed out of the mêlée and reached up to put her hands on his shoulders. 'Dance, gorgeous?' Through the slits in her mask her eyes gleamed with allure.

Sexy, he had to admit, but did the bank's directors really think he'd succumb to such a ploy? 'I don't dance,' he said, politely removing her clinging hands. She murmured something about Greek gods *any time* before she undulated her way back into the party crowd, but Sam didn't catch it.

He wondered if that had been the purpose of the courtesy suite they'd pressed on him. Was this woman they'd told him to expect intended as a sweetener? It wouldn't be the first time he'd been offered such an enticement.

They should have done their homework, he grimaced. If he did decide to rescue the ailing bank, they'd learn.

In the Stilakos Organisation ethics were everything.

'Sorry. Sorry about that, Mr Stilakos.' Stephen Fletcher, Sirius's portly Senior HR Executive, was unconvincingly attired as a gangster. 'I don't know what can be keeping Ellie.' He flashed Sam a quick, nervous grin. 'Are you enjoying the party?'

Sam stared incredulously at the rotund executive. 'Is this how you usually do business at Sirius? You invite potential investors to your staff parties?'

Fletcher gazed up at him with an earnest intensity. 'No, no. Not at all. Only you. We wanted you to see for yourself… We wanted you to *understand* the Sirius Staff Policy. At Sirius we want our team to *work*.' He thumped the bar to make the word stick. 'That, we firmly believe, means giving our folk ample opportunity to *play*.'

Sam's mouth twisted with sudden humour. 'Seriously? You thought this—' he swept one lean, bronzed hand towards the exuberant throng of assorted harem girls and Ned Kellys '—this would convince me to bail out your bank?'

'Well, not me alone. It was someone else who suggested showing you the *human face* of the Sirius Bank.' Fletcher's fist connected emphatically with the bar. 'She thought that your seeing the *actual people* involved—' thump, thump '—in a *personal* sense… The wonderful men and women whose livelihoods are *on the line*—' For an alarming second his hyperactive fist came close to seizing Sam's lapel. 'If you could only key into the real issues of *sincere human beings*, and try to *forget* the bottom line…'

Sam listened in thunderstruck amazement. No wonder the Sirius Bank was in trouble. What bank tried to operate with this folksy creed?

He lifted his brows in amusement. 'And whose was the great brain who thought I might be overwhelmed by the personal charms of your workforce?'

Fletcher saw unexpected warmth lightening the forbidding expression of the bank's rich suitor, as if the sun had been there all the time and was about to break through. For the first time since he'd met Samos Stilakos, he knew a ray of hope.

'Ellie,' he replied eagerly. 'Ellie O'Dea. Your hostess. She's one of my staff. You'll like her, I'm sure. Charming.

Charming girl. And a real looker, too. You won't be disappointed, I asssure you. She's been briefed and she's all prepared for you. She must be here by now. Ellie's not usually late— Hang on!'

He stood on tiptoe to scan the milling crowd, trying to pick Ellie out from among the fancifully garbed women, then turned and collided with black ice in Sam Stilakos's eyes. He felt the very breath freeze in his lungs.

Stilakos looked down at him from his considerable height, the essence of polished courtesy, though his smile chilled Fletcher to the core. 'I appreciate your assistance.' The clipped precision of his deep, cool voice injected an icy sliver between Fletcher's ribs. 'Fletcher, wasn't it? I've seen all I need. Don't let me keep you from your celebration.'

Fletcher shook his head in consternation. 'But—but I hoped I could introduce you—' With the cold realisation of defeat he met Samos Stilakos's unforgiving gaze. He hovered for a moment, then, his shoulders slumped, edged away.

Sam watched him go, then turned to survey the ball, disillusion in his heart.

Once the challenge of the Sirius Bank would have appealed to him. Its sad market performance and falling profits made it as attractive a proposition for the Stilakos Organisation as he could remember. He could buy it for a song, give it a drastic structural shake-up, and, with an exhilarating measure of risk, take it straight to the top of the tree. If its indulgent staff culture didn't hold it back. And if—

Face it. If he weren't so *bored*.

Lately his zest for winning against the odds seemed to have blunted. What he needed, he mused, was one damned good reason to buy the bank beyond making money.

A voluptuous Cleopatra spotted him and started an unsteady progress towards him. Not tonight, sweetheart, Sam thought grimly. What he wanted, what he needed...

An indefinable longing surged through him, reminding him of the nights of his youth. Nights when there'd been magic in the air, and mystery in a woman's face. Where had it all gone? All at once the noise, heat and activity reached an unbearable pitch. He loosened his tie and looked about for the nearest exit.

In the hall beyond the ballroom heavy curtains beckoned. He shoved some unsecured balloons aside, and threaded his way through the throng. If he could just get away from the relentless carnival atmosphere...

Thank God the doors weren't locked. He stepped out into the soft dark, onto a long balcony, and was met with a wave of fresh, salty air. The door closed behind him, and instantly the hullabaloo was cut.

It took him a moment to adjust. Still early in the season, the night was cool, but the promise of summer carried on the breeze like a woman's perfume.

He strolled over to the rail. Across the street from the hotel was the beach walk, and beyond it the vast, black heaving space of the sea. A gentle susurration spoke caressingly to him of the surf, curling itself up on the dark beach below the sea wall.

Flexing the muscles in his powerful arms and shoulders, he breathed in deeply, as if to inhale some energising essence from the brilliant night sky. He watched the moon's flickering progress under a few wispy clouds, then started as a small sound alerted him to a presence.

Something. Or someone.

He stiffened, every muscle on the alert, and searched

the dim balcony. In the furthest corner he thought he could make out a figure. He strained his eyes against the dark. The moon chose that moment to peep through, and something took shape that resembled a human form.

'Hello?' he said, taking a few steps that way.

At the sound of his voice the figure stilled, as though frozen to the wall. Intrigued, he began to walk towards the mysterious presence. Who would be lurking outside in the dark at this hour, unless they were up to no good?

'Whoever you are,' he said firmly, 'you'd better come forward and introduce yourself.'

The form moved, and at once he recognised it as being female. 'Don't come any closer,' a feminine voice said sharply.

He stopped in his tracks. 'Why not?'

There was a moment of silence, then she said in a strangled voice, 'Because you're invading my personal space. Now back off.'

He grinned to himself. 'Oh, come on. You can't claim an entire public balcony as your personal space.' Curiosity aroused, he strained his eyes to make her out. There was something strangely unearthly about the woman's pale form, like a wraith seen through a mist.

At that moment the moon burst from behind a cloud, drenching the balcony in its silvery glow. The breath caught in his throat, halting him to the spot.

She was an ethereal vision, gowned in shimmering white. An angel. A moon nymph. Beneath some glittery ornament, her long hair fell almost to her waist, and her face was strangely shadowed. A sensation of unreality, almost of magic, swept through him, as if he'd stepped into some childhood fairy tale.

'There's no need to come any closer,' she flung at him, a repressive note in her voice. 'I'm not in the mood for a chat, so you might as well stay right where you are.'

Sam laughed, his blood quickening. 'I'm not much of a one for small talk, myself.'

He felt rather than saw the glare from her shadowed eyes, and as he moved closer realised that of course she was wearing a mask.

'Now let me see…' He smiled as he took in the full extent of her slender, moonlit form, deliciously outlined in clinging satin. She held her hands folded at her breast, while on the ground beside her feet a couple of large, silver-trimmed wings reposed limply against the wall. 'What are you? An angel?' he enquired, smiling, then, recognising her crown, 'Ah, of course. You must be the Fairy Queen. What's her name? Titania, isn't it?'

Trapped in her worst nightmare, Ellie O'Dea clung tightly to her frail bodice. As her big, masculine discoverer drew nearer, she racked her brains for a way to get rid of him without betraying her gown's fragile coverage of her vulnerable breasts.

'Well done,' she said. 'Anyway, it was great to meet you. My boyfriend will be back soon, so don't feel you have to wait.'

She held her breath. The mention of her boyfriend—just supposing she still had one and he hadn't dumped her in favour of Antarctica—might have worked, as for the moment the stranger remained where he was. He was tall, at least six-three, she guessed, *big*, and though in the dark his face was shadowy, its lean planes and angles, tipped by the moonlight, suggested flaring cheekbones and chiselled male beauty.

At twenty-nine, she knew enough of the score about gorgeous men. Too gorgeous, she thought, noting his brilliant dark eyes and the flash of his white teeth. Too spoilt. Lethal.

Sam drank her in from head to toe. She was nearly tall enough to reach his shoulder. He couldn't determine the exact colour of her bright waterfall of hair, but with its lustrous sheen every slight movement of her head was an invitation to touch.

His eyes had accustomed to the light now, and he could see her more clearly. It was as if the moon had picked up the shimmer in the dress and somehow transferred it to her white, pearlescent skin. The slinky, ankle-length satin seemed moulded to her, revealing with her movements the supple slenderness of her waist, sweetly rounded hips and long slim thighs. The dress's bodice was supported by a silver chain that hung from her neck. Though she kept her hands folded at her breasts, it was easy to guess at their ripe, tip-tilted lusciousness. He tried not to stare, but it was an effort to drag his eyes from her bare satin shoulders and the creamy swells just visible beneath her sheltering hands.

He was overwhelmed by such perfect female beauty; his blood stirred, and a huskiness deepened his voice. 'Isn't your boyfriend concerned about leaving you alone out here?'

She drew a sharp, quivering breath. 'But I'm not alone, am I? Though I would be if I could be. If you hadn't *insisted* on intruding on my privacy.'

'Oh. Oh, I am sorry,' he said at once, turning half away. He felt a twinge of guilt, almost as if he'd stumbled onto sacred ground. 'I'll go away.' As he turned his back he threw over his shoulder, 'Enjoy the night air.'

He took a few easy strides in the direction he'd come, but with every step away the vision lured him back with a siren's power.

'Look…Wait—just a moment, will you?'

At the sound of her sweet, low voice a pleasurable sensation he'd almost forgotten could exist shot through him. He paused, and half turned in her direction. With a casual hitch of his shoulder he said, 'Are you sure? I don't want to cause you trouble with your boyfriend.'

'Oh, don't worry about him,' she said hastily. 'He isn't… He won't cause any… Did you happen to see anyone in there dressed as Scarlett O'Hara?'

He sauntered back, as cool as if the thrill weren't gathering in his blood like a wave. 'I'm not sure I know what Scarlett O'Hara looks like.'

In an excited burst of realisation, he didn't believe the boyfriend was coming back. What man would leave this beauty out here to be accosted by strangers?

He longed to see her face, but the mask frustrated him. From what he could make out, her lips looked soft and kissable, curling up with an enticing sensitivity, as if they'd respond to the lightest tongue-flick. Her chin was delicate, with a piquancy he was sure would apply to the whole of her face.

'My moonlight fantasy,' he exclaimed with a low laugh. 'At last I've found you.'

Her eyes glittered at him through the mask, and his hand twitched with the desire to tear it away. He reached for it, but she backed away and, as though unable to free her hand from her bodice, used her elbow to gesture.

He frowned. 'Is there something wrong with your

dress?' He leaned forward, his eyes narrowed for a closer look, and she stepped sharply away from him.

With the purest amusement he realised that she was holding the bodice and chain together with her hand. 'Oh, no!' he said. 'Has there been an accident? I think I can see why you're in hiding.' Instinctive thoughts of seduction crept in to colour his voice, and he added softly, 'I do hope you're wearing something under that.'

There was a tense silence. It dawned on him at last that she was embarrassed.

She surveyed him from behind her mask with glittering eyes. 'Laugh by all means.' Her lips curved in a proud smile. 'I've no doubt this does seem very amusing to one of the *heartless* species.' Despite her brave front, some strong emotion caught at her voice, and he felt chastised.

'I'm sorry,' he said with velvet remorse. 'You're right. It's no laughing matter. But can't something be done to fix it? Some pins or something?'

She was silent for a moment, as though struggling with herself to trust his good intentions.

After a while she said stiffly, 'I tried that, but it's no good. The taffeta has started to fray now.' She eyed him through her mask for a second, then indicated one side of the bodice. 'This here is only hanging by a few threads. It was these stupid wings that did it. Whoever designed the costume—! They're far too heavy for the fabric. They were supposed to hook into the clasp at the neck, here, and here. Look…'

She half turned to give him a rear view. The dress was charmingly draped across her lower back, and as she twisted to indicate the mid-point where the wings had hooked and further damaged the fabric her hair swished a little aside to reveal an alluring glimpse of smooth white back.

His mouth dried. He imagined seeking out the ridge of her spine, tracing the bumps with his fingers, grazing all the little hollows with his lips, tasting her white satin flesh...

'We pinned this back seam as well as we could where the hook was, but it's still unravelling, and the halter chain has started to separate from the bodice.' She straightened to face him, sighing, 'It's only a matter of time before the whole thing falls apart.' After a moment she added, 'One of my girlfriends is going home to get some clothes for me.'

He supposed he deserved to have been called heartless. The woman was in an embarrassing situation, yet all his thoughts had been about caressing her. Kissing her.

The breeze picked up, teasing the hair on her neck. She gave a little shiver, and at once his imagination flew him to a parallel universe, one where he could take her with him across to that moonlit beach, lay her down beside him on the cool sand, and...

But she was cold. 'Here,' he said, and in a swift fluid movement slipped off his jacket and stepped close enough to wrap it around her shoulders.

'Oh!' She received it with a surprised jerk of her head, and the sweet summery scent of raspberries rose to his nostrils in an intoxicating cloud. 'Thanks,' she said in a soft, appealing voice that wound its way into his bloodstream like an aphrodisiac. 'Thank you very much. I really didn't expect— You're very kind.'

To his regret she drew the lapels together across her breasts, though she still held onto her bodice. The jacket swam on her feminine form, and his loins stirred at the sight.

He had to rescue her from this, he thought with urgency. Take her somewhere safe. And private. 'You can't stay out here all night,' he said. 'Why don't I take you home?'

Ellie heard the warmth in his deep voice and her sexual antennae zinged as from a high-voltage charge. This charming devil, with his smiling assurance and desire in his dark eyes, had more than rescue on his mind. As if she'd let herself be picked up! Although, in his shirt-sleeves, with the power of his lean, well-made frame clearly defined, he was frankly gorgeous. And he seemed civilised, sophisticated…

When was the last time a high-powered man like him had come her way? He was a far cry from a geography teacher with the mountaineering bug.

She could see no wedding ring, though that didn't make him eligible. Hadn't she learned the hard way? The world was full of heartbreakingly attractive men who had no intention of settling down and raising families. Why else were women forced to go it alone? But—there was kindness in him. He *had* sacrificed his jacket.

His dark, sensual gaze drew hers and heat shivered through her. Unable to keep her consciousness of the pinging vibrations from her voice while she argued the pros and cons with herself, she said, 'Charmaine—I mean, Scarlett—should be back soon.'

He lifted his eyebrows. 'How long have you been waiting?'

'An hour. Maybe two.' She smiled and gave a shrug to cover her growing sense of dilemma. 'It's not my night.'

'It's not over yet.' Through the dark lashes his eyes lit with a sinful gleam, and her insides plunged into chaos. 'Come, fantasy girl. I'll take you home.'

She hesitated. 'I shouldn't really go home. I'm supposed to be in there helping to co-ordinate the programme.' And meeting Samos someone, the old Greek tycoon who was the bank's last chance. 'Are you—are you with the bank?'

'No.' His dark eyes ran over her, and she felt her flesh thrill like the breeze whispering in her hair. 'Maybe you can find some clothes here. Are any of your friends staying in the hotel overnight?'

'No. That's only for the big cheeses so they don't have to drive home afterwards.'

His brows snapped together, as though he didn't approve of that, then he gave a shrug and stood thinking.

'I'd—I'd better give you back this.' With reluctance she started to take off the jacket, but he held up his hand.

'No, no. Keep it.' His sensuous mouth edged up at the corners in a smile. 'I have a suggestion. To save you waiting for Charmaine, what if I ask the hotel to find you something to wear? You can change in my room.' He held out his hand, persuasion in his voice, smiling seduction in his eyes. 'What do you think? All right?'

This was it, she thought, her heart skipping. Just because she'd given up falling in love didn't mean she had to become a nun. It was a long time since she'd been held in a man's arms. She fingered the jacket's luxurious fabric, and inhaled its faint scent of expensive, sophisticated *man*.

He angled away slightly, as if he might walk off and leave her, while she struggled to make up her mind to do something daring for once.

He cast her back a deep, gleaming glance beneath his lashes. It was quietly, intimately sexual, a look between adults. Man to woman, it stirred her to her feminine soul.

What mature, twenty-nine-year-old career woman in charge of her life would hesitate?

'All right,' she breathed.

She allowed him to usher her through the doors, conscious of every touch, his wrist brushing hers, his hand light on her back. And for once she was lucky. There was a lift waiting, and none of the stragglers spilling from the ballroom even glanced her way.

In the light of the lift he looked to be in his late thirties. Blue highlights danced off his pitch-black hair, and there was a sardonic lilt to his black eyebrows that gave him a devilish look. Below his cheekbones, a shadow underlay his bronzed cheeks and jaw. He was a Greek god made flesh. She met the naked sensuality in his midnight eyes, and her blood surged.

'Are you staying here long?' she said, trying to keep her voice from betraying her.

He shook his head. 'I suppose you'd say I'm a guest of your bank. I hadn't intended to use the suite, but as it happens…I now have a reason.' A smile illuminated his face and shimmered in his dark eyes. 'I'm Sam.' He held out his hand.

When her ravished insides had settled back into place, the name filtered through.

Sam. An unusual name for a Greek Australian. Then realisation hit her. Not *that* Sam! As in Samos Stilakos. But of course it had to be. How many rich Greeks would be visiting this hotel on this night of nights?

She put her hand into his strong, warm grip, and as their palms met skin cells all along her forearm shivered with electric pleasure. 'Lovely—lovely to meet you.'

He didn't try to keep hold of her hand, as some men

would have, though her flesh yearned for it. He just waited
for her to respond, his eyebrows raised. The lift stopped
and the doors opened before she could muster a reply.

Her brain whirred rapidly. Samos Stilakos's awesome
reputation had dominated gossip in the staff canteen for
the past six weeks—his daunting standards, his uncompromising stance on ethics. According to the grapevine,
he'd struck terror into the department heads. She felt an
extreme reluctance to tell him her name. He might end
up being the big boss of the entire bank.

In the corridor she gave a light, embarrassed laugh. 'I'd
rather not tell you my name, if you don't mind.'

He frowned a little, his eyes glinting.

With a pounding heart she realised he probably thought
she did this sort of thing all the time. Went to hotel rooms
with perfect strangers. But then, how often did *he* do it?
Quite often, judging by how smoothly this little operation
had gone. How would it go down for her future in the
bank, if she knew he seduced vulnerable employees?

For her job's sake she should leave now. Thrust the
jacket back at him, ignore the risks, and risk walking out
to the taxi rank. At least she'd have the mask.

She should. But she let him guide her down the hall to
Room 525, and, with her adrenaline flowing, watched his
smooth, olive-tanned fingers slide in the key.

The room was pleasantly furnished in the impersonal
style of hotel rooms. The counterpane on the king-sized
bed had been turned down, and lamps on either side cast
a soft apricot glow.

The door closed behind her and she turned to face
him. The room sprang alive with sexual possibilities.

He nodded to her, 'Make yourself comfortable.' He

strolled to the desk and picked up the phone, murmured a few words into it, then covered the receiver. 'How does a maid's uniform sound?' She nodded and he spoke again, appraising her, his black lashes half lowered over his dark, sensual gaze. 'About five-seven. Size ten. Thank you.'

He strolled back to her with an easy, hospitable smile. 'It will take a few minutes. Would you like a drink after your ordeal?' He made a lazy gesture towards the mini-bar.

'No. No, thanks.' She tried to sound casual, to match his relaxed demeanour, but her senses were in uproar.

He said abruptly, 'Would you feel better if I went away?'

He was giving her an option, she realised, relieved her instincts about his essential decency had been right. She raised her chin. 'No, don't. Don't go.' Despite her bravado her voice sounded croaky, as if it was about to dry up.

Samos Stilakos didn't look ill at ease, however. He pulled off his tie and tossed it to a chair, the shimmer back in his dark eyes. 'Won't you take off your mask?'

'I'd rather not,' she said with a careless smile, knowing how rude and ungrateful and insanely weird it sounded, after he'd so kindly rescued her. 'Not yet.'

He moved closer, his gaze warm and compelling, and said softly, 'But I think I'll feel uncomfortable kissing a woman without knowing her eyes and face.'

She closed her eyes. The blood was thundering in her ears. 'Who—who said anything about kissing?'

Almost lazily he reached out to curve his lean, smooth fingers under her chin, tilted up her face, and bent to brush her mouth with his.

At the first touch, excitement ignited in her blood. He drew away, leaving her breathless, fire dancing along her lips. He frowned down at her, a flame in the depths of his eyes, then drew her firmly against his hard body, and kissed her properly, while her breasts swelled and her lips parted.

With sensual artistry he took first her upper lip, then the lower lip between his, to tease and tantalise until her knees gave way. Then he captured both lips firmly, and slipped his tongue inside her mouth, inflaming the delicate tissues while her bones liquefied and she nearly swooned.

Wildfire rose in her blood.

It was nothing, nothing like she'd ever experienced. So tender, so wildly, thrillingly arousing. It was as if he knew how to kiss a woman as a woman dreamed of being kissed.

A raw sound came from her throat, and she thrust her soft curves into the lean angles of his muscular frame. Forgetting her fragile dress, she linked her arms around his neck and clutched at his hair, aware with excitement of his big, vibrant body's charged response to her. Eagerly she helped him push the jacket from her shoulders, and let it slide.

He deepened the sizzling intensity of the kiss. In some way liberated by the mask, she threw aside constraint, and, instead of her usual polite co-operation, matched him tongue for tongue, caress for caress, without inhibition.

She was hardly aware that the weak threads of her satin bodice had given way, removing one of the barriers between his iron-hard body and her sensitised skin. Grazed by the friction of his clothes and belt buckle, her bare nipples thrilled to the delicious contact.

She'd never experienced such instant desire. Hotly aroused, she felt one of his seductive hands close over her breast, while the other slid to her nape, trailed tinglingly over her scalp, then snaked through her hair to pluck at the string of her mask.

At once her survivor instinct clicked in. In a lightning reflex, her hands shot up to secure the mask, and she broke from him. 'No,' she panted hoarsely. 'Don't take it off.'

He stared back, fire in his eyes as they devoured her naked breasts. His voice was rough and gravelly. 'Why not? Why does it matter? Are you married?'

'No. I just don't want you to see my face.'

'Why not? I need to know who you are.' He gestured with his hands. 'Don't get me wrong. It's erotic making love to a mystery woman, in a kinky sort of way. I might even get a taste for it. But if you stay with me tonight…'

His voice thickened with the words, and she sensed how much he wanted it. Wanted *her*. Somehow, it strengthened her instinct to keep her face covered. She said in a low, firm voice, 'I won't stay unless I can leave the mask on.'

He stared at her. 'You're not serious.'

'I am serious. I am.'

Calculation glimmered in his eyes, as if he was recognising the real possibility of his moonlit fantasy slipping away from him, then his lashes lowered.

'Try to see it my way.' His deep voice was almost a purr. He held out his hands and advanced to back her gently against the wall, his long muscular thighs grazing hers, melting her with his devastating sexual power. 'I don't want to feel I'm taking advantage of you.' With one long, tanned finger he trailed fire down her throat to the valley between her breasts, fanning her sweet erotic craving, and she burned for him to go further.

'Love-making shouldn't be an impersonal thing,' he said persuasively. 'If I can't see into your eyes it feels— soulless. Can't you understand?'

He was so meltingly, mouth-wateringly sexy, so honourable, she wavered. But just as his mouth began to tease her ear, turning her veins to liquid fire, some cool little internal voice piped up to remind her that the last time she'd believed a man was honourable she'd given him two years of her life, and he'd left her without a word.

His lips blazed a scorching trail down her throat and she shuddered with pleasure. 'I do see, and I do want to stay,' she panted when she could speak, 'but only if you agree not to snatch the mask off. And not—not to ask me my name.'

'But how will I find you again if I don't know your name?'

Even in her state of arousal she knew the smooth words for a ploy. 'You won't want to.' Wry cynicism deepened her huskiness. 'And I won't want you to.'

He drew back, a frown in his eyes. 'But you want me. You can't deny it.'

'Yes, yes. I admit it.' She leaned back against the wall and sighed, and stretched her arms voluptuously over her head, unable to keep her hungry gaze from his shirt-opening with its dark, sultry promise of chest hair. 'I do want you,' she said with throaty conviction, imagining the salt taste of that bronzed, hair-roughened skin. 'But only tonight.'

He gave a sexy, disbelieving laugh. 'Isn't that my line?' Then his brows drew together and he stared at her in bemusement. She could see how used he was to women falling at his feet. He took a deep breath, reefed his hand through his black hair. 'Why do you say that? Why only tonight?'

An amused, sophisticated little smile played about his mouth, but she could tell he was piqued. She supposed with his assets it was natural. She could hardly explain that, since the end of her romantic dreams, her job security was of critical importance. She wasn't one of those women who could face down gossip about their sexual antics with the bosses. If he took over the bank and news of this got out, she'd have to leave, if he didn't sack her first.

She touched his hand. 'You're very attractive, but I don't want an affair. Affairs use a woman up. If I stay with you tonight it will only be this one time, and you'll have to agree not to take off my mask.'

He shook his head. 'If I see you again,' he said, his tone charming but insistent, 'I'll know you, with or without the mask. I'd know the shape of you and the way you hold your head. Your mouth…' His voice deepened. The flame smouldered in his dark eyes, and she was tempted, *how* she was tempted, to wrap herself around his hard body. 'And that red hair is—unforgettable.'

'It's strawberry,' she corrected huskily. But she could see his point. He might recognise her again. If she stayed with him, she had little choice but to appeal to his gentlemanly instincts not to blab about her all over the building. And she wanted to stay, she realised, with an upsurge of desire.

'All right.' She could almost see the flat nipples under his shirt, and wantonness dripped from her voice like honey. 'If I ever did meet you again, and you recognised me, you would have to promise that you'd never, ever refer to what happens between us this night. To anyone.'

He gave a sharp, disbelieving laugh. 'As if I would—' He took a couple of impatient strides away and flung out his arms. 'Why should I? I don't bargain, and I don't make promises to get a woman into my bed.' He paused, his shoulders tense, and said with a cool shrug, 'The only promise I can make to you, sweetheart, is the one of giving you pleasure. If that isn't enough, we'd better both forget it.' He smiled, but there was an edge to his voice, his dark eyes glinting, his face suddenly proud and unrelenting, like the uncompromising Samos Stilakos she'd heard so much about.

It made him even more wildly desirable, if possible, and when the rejection had sunk in her disappointment was potent, but she said with dignity, 'Then I'll leave.'

He looked incredulous, and was about to speak when there was a discreet knock.

He tucked in his shirt and went to open the door. After a few murmured words he came back with a package, and thrust it to her with a burning, sardonic look. 'Your dress.'

She accepted it, her hands trembling, and with a muttered 'thank you' took it into the bathroom.

The maid's uniform was a white zip-up dress. She dragged off the ruined costume and threw it in the bin. Goodbye fantasy woman, she grimaced as she zipped the uniform. It was tightish, and only covered her to mid-thigh. But at least it was decent.

She raised the mask for a glimpse of her face, and met a stranger in the mirror. Her mouth was swollen from kissing, her blue eyes heavy-lidded, languorous with unfulfilled passion. Like his beautiful, expressive eyes. If only…

Images of the pleasures she'd turned down rose to torment her. She'd never met anyone like him before, or experienced such chemistry. But it was too late now, she reflected regretfully. She'd insulted him, and now he could hardly wait to get rid of her. She braced herself, and, with the mask back in place, opened the door.

Samos Stilakos stood waiting, brooding tension in the set of his powerful shoulders, his thick black lashes downcast.

He looked ready to leave, his jacket slung over his shoulder. He'd rolled his sleeves back a little, and she could see the dusky hairs curling on his bronzed, sinewy forearms.

He looked up. His dark eyes riveted to her, intent and smoulderingly sexual.

Her blood started to boom in her ears with a heavy, sensual beat.

'Come here,' he said thickly.

The fierce fire in his eyes compelled her. She felt a burning, primeval urgency to run into his arms and press her lips to his throat, but some stronger part of her forced her to her resolve and clamped her feet to the floor. 'Only if you promise…'

She held her breath.

The deep voice, when it came, was harsh. 'I promise.'

She allowed herself to advance a step, desire torching through her like a fever. Dared she risk pushing him further? She breathed, 'And do you agree, even if we should meet again, never to refer to this night, or to anything that happens between us here?'

The silence simmered while his dark, molten eyes raked her from head to toe. Her yearning for him reached a torrid pitch. She imagined his hard, virile length thrusting and thrusting to fill her. The sublime, delicious pleasure…

His mouth quivered. 'I agree,' he said rawly, then threw away his jacket, and in one long stride covered the distance between them and pulled her into his arms.

CHAPTER ONE

FOUR months later, Ellie sat at her desk, settling into the precarious role as latest in a string of PAs to the most ruthless and exacting boss the Sirius Bank had ever known. It was twenty-six days since she'd landed the job, and how she'd done it she still wasn't sure. But there was one thing she was sure of.

Sam Stilakos had a very poor memory.

Or a seriously overcrowded sex-life. How else could he have forgotten the night that blazed in her memory like an inferno? Not that she wanted him to remember, she hastened to reflect. If he did she'd be out on her twenty-nine-year-old ear with her life's plan shot to pieces.

Even so, it was distinctly lowering for a woman to discover how completely forgettable she was.

For a while she'd wondered if he was just a very good actor, but she'd stopped thinking that now. Not once in the weeks of seeing him every day, working with him in the tense atmosphere of his office, meeting his deep, inscrutable gaze across the table at board meetings, melting to his dark chocolate voice on the intercom—and he buzzed her constantly for the most finicky reasons—had

he shown the merest flicker of recognition. Or flirtatious-
ness. Just scrupulous politeness.

No wonder his ex-wife had issues with him.

A crash from inside his office jolted Ellie from her
reverie. The wife's visit wasn't going well. At almost the
same moment she glanced around to see an elegantly
groomed older lady appear at the outer door. The woman
approached the desk, and, with the assured charm of her
years, introduced herself as Irene Stilakos.

Ellie concealed her intense fascination behind her
professional face. So this was Sam's mother. But she
wasn't Greek!

'He's had an unexpected visitor.' Ellie smiled up into
shrewd grey eyes, wondering if Irene had heard the crash.
'He shouldn't be long. Would you like a coffee while you
wait?' She indicated the plush armchairs in the small
lounge area by the window.

Irene Stilakos smiled a refusal, and selected a chair.
Behind her, Sydney glittered in the morning sun like a jewel,
but oblivious to the scene, she bypassed the pile of recent
glossies and picked up a copy of Sirius's annual report.

She looks friendly, Ellie thought, covertly searching for
a resemblance to Sam's stunning chiselled features and
imperious dark eyes. With her softly waved hair and lively,
pleasant face, you'd never believe she had a son so—

The door to Sam's inner office burst open. Ellie
jumped, and Sam's mother looked up as a shrill, impassioned voice rent the air. 'Anyone can make a mistake,
Sam! Haven't you ever heard the concept of forgiveness?'

There was a deep, curt response, then the pert rear
view of Natalie, television soap star and Sam's ex-wife,
appeared in the doorway, arms flailing. 'You know why

you're scared to come to my wedding, lover?' she screeched. 'Because you haven't been able to find another woman in four years. And do you know why that is, Sam? Do you know why? I'll tell you why. Because you can't replace *me*! And you never—ever—*will*.'

She slammed the door so hard Ellie's filing cabinet shuddered. Then midway in storming across the room she halted, muttering, to feverishly rifle her bag.

She wore impossibly high heels Ellie had no trouble in identifying as Jimmy Choos, and a minuscule leather dress with peep-holes that showed her fabulous all-over tan. A flick of her ragged blonde designer hair, with its fashionable black roots, revealed the obligatory tattoo on her shoulder.

She looked like trouble. *Sexy* trouble, exactly the sort men went mad for.

Unconsciously Ellie patted the smooth coil at her nape. No wonder she'd made no lasting impression. She'd considered going completely blonde herself when Sam had taken over as boss, but had gone the other way instead, choosing a deep, rich, camouflaging red. It seemed to have worked well. Too well, she sometimes thought.

She watched as Natalie pulled out a handful of tissues to dab at her professionally modelled nose. All at once the blonde's eye fell on Sam's mother, and she froze rigid.

Her fashionable pout grew puffier and more defensive. 'Well?'

Irene Stilakos started, and sat straighter in her chair. 'Oh,' she said hurriedly. 'Don't mind me, Natalie. I was just thinking you should be careful in those heels. You need to look after those bones in your lower spine. Think ahead, dear, to when you'll be bearing children.'

Natalie hissed in an outraged breath, then to Ellie's alarm she whipped around to her. 'And what are you staring at, Miss Mouse? Hoping you might have a chance with him? It's what you've been hanging out for, isn't it?'

Ellie felt her face flame scarlet. Her lips parted in stunned denial, but there was no silencing her accuser.

'Don't try to deny it.' Natalie's rather high-pitched voice vibrated with passion. 'I've heard you talk to him in that drooly-drooly voice. You're after him. You all are. Don't you think a woman knows?'

Ellie scrabbled for her professional poise and drew herself up, searingly conscious of Sam's *mother* sitting there. And Sam himself was very sharp of hearing. 'That may just be the way I talk,' she retorted as coolly as humanly possible, in her low, admittedly quite husky voice. 'I don't have the luxury of screaming or throwing things. And I have too much work to do to go after anyone.'

'Yeah, right.' Natalie's brittle laugh rang out in the quiet room. 'Just look at her, will you? It's written all over her face.' She shrugged and started for the exit. 'You're welcome to the cold-blooded brute, if you think you can measure up to him.' Her eyes filled up with tears. 'Try living with a perfectionist.' Out in the corridor she flung rawly over her shoulder, 'See what's it like to be dispensable.' With a despairing hair-flick she stalked off in the direction of the lifts.

Ellie gathered her shell-shocked self together to find Sam's mother piercing her with her penetrating grey gaze, intensified by the lenses of her glasses.

'It isn't true,' Ellie said quickly. 'I don't like him at all.' Then, recollecting who she was talking to, she rushed to add, 'I mean—he's very good-looking, and brilliant and

everything, but he's not at all my type. He's far too demanding, and arrogant, and bossy. Not that that's a bad
thing, of course, when he's the boss.' She made a weak
attempt at a laugh. 'Please don't be offended—'

Sam's mother gave her a worried smile, as if she
needed convincing.

'—but I actually prefer less high-powered men. You
know—friendlier.' Her recurring vision of herself
enfolded in Sam's strong arms, his stirringly sexy mouth,
his midnight satin eyes slumbrous with desire, swam into
her mind, but she forced herself to stay on course. 'I like
men who are more—accessible. Emotionally. Do you
know what I mean?'

This was, in fact, a bare-faced lie. She only ever fell
madly in love with inappropriate men who were totally
*in*accessible.

Sam's mother seemed to know it, because she frowned
at Ellie and gave her head a very slight shake. Ellie
thought she must have gone too far and had better back-
track, and lowered her voice confidentially. 'I don't mean
he isn't good to work for. He is, he's wonderful, and he
can be so-o-o charming to people who don't irritate him,
but in a personal, or—or *sexual* sense I could never find
him attractive at—'

She broke off. Sam's mother's gaze had shifted to a point
somewhere above and to the right of Ellie, and Ellie had a
horrible sinking feeling that someone was standing at Sam's
door. She glanced down and saw a pair of handmade leather
shoes, polished to a very high gloss, trouser legs of the finest
fabric, and knew immediately who.

Her dismayed gaze travelled the lean, powerful length
of Samos Stilakos, and connected with his intelligent

dark eyes, brimming with an expression she couldn't quite read. There was a sardonic quirk to his sensuous mouth, and his black eyebrows were drawn.

Her heart jarred to a halt.

'Come in,' he said, holding the door wide for Irene without taking his eyes from Ellie. Irene gave her a warm glance as she went past, and Sam said in deep, clipped tones, 'I'll talk to you later, Eleanor.'

He closed the door.

Ellie plunged into turmoil. How long had he been standing there? She covered her burning cheeks. There was no chance he hadn't heard some of it.

What if Irene told Sam of Natalie's accusation? Wasn't it only natural she would? She would. Of course she would. She'd be telling him even now.

Sam absently steered his mother through some scattered shards of antique vase and across the luxurious expanse of his office. While she settled herself on the deep red leather chesterfield, he wandered over to stare moodily at the view from his wall-sized window. Curious how a couple of smudgy little clouds could take the shine off Sydney Harbour. That bridge could look bloody grim.

'She seems like a lovely girl, Sam,' his mother commented, crossing her ankles.

Sam gave a shrug, but something like a skewer slid through his intestines. *Why* had she said she didn't like him? Could he have offended her in some way?

He scrolled back through their exchanges about work. Her mouth was often grave—intriguingly so, for a woman whose blue eyes could actually glitter at times with mischief—but she'd seemed happy enough, calm and competent. She'd coped with all the projects he'd thrust her into with cool efficiency, surprising him at times with her instinctive grasp of the big picture.

She was a little too inclined to try injecting her feminine viewpoint into his careful strategies for the bank's recovery, but he could easily keep that under control. In all other ways he still found her—pleasing.

He'd honoured his agreement with her, and would continue to do so, although it had been extracted under duress. Her total rejection of an affair was impressive. Although…what more tantalising challenge had ever been given a man?

Not that he condoned personal relationships in the workplace. Purists might argue that he shouldn't have placed her so close to him. It had been a business decision, no more, no less, to keep his eye on her. In fact, once or twice he had actually fantasised having a section of the wall removed so he could see her face.

That face. For an instant his eyes drifted shut. The curious breathless feeling he experienced whenever she entered the room came over him. It was amazing how, once a woman's face had been forbidden to a man, that face could become so infinitely more alluring and desirable than any other.

But… He knew the rules and there was no risk. That invisible line she'd drawn around herself was as definite as a castle moat, and in twenty-six days he'd never tried to cross it. Not once.

So if she was unhappy… He felt a skidding sensation inside his chest. Could it be something to do with *that night*?

His mother cut in on his thoughts. She was studying him with a thoughtful gaze, her head a little on one side. 'I don't think you should take the things she said personally, dear. She assured me she only meant it in the sexual sense.'

He gave a careless laugh. 'Is that what she said?' Nevertheless the skewer made a savage twist. Women *always* found him attractive in the sexual sense. If Eleanor O'Dea was the woman he thought she was, whom his instincts told him she must be, she had every reason to find him sexually attractive.

Unless…unless he was mistaken.

He thought back to the first time he'd laid eyes on her after he'd taken on the bank. Wasn't it the Christmas party—?

He frowned, recalling how once again he'd been taken aback by the scale of it. Mature men and women carousing, hugging each other in boozy camaraderie at the company's expense, some far-gone woman from Sales actually performing a dreamy, inebriated dance on a table-top. When he'd enquired as to who had been responsible for organising this latest orgiastic extravaganza, someone had pointed out Ellie.

The name.

His lungs had momentarily seized, for there she'd been, a tallish slender woman standing quietly in the middle of the scene of riotous debauchery, in the thick of it, but in some strange way alone, as if she occupied her own small pool of serenity.

It was *her*, he was certain. Straight away he'd noticed her soft, curly lips. And her skin. How incredibly pure and satin-white he'd remembered it being, in contrast with her bright hair, and looked to be still under the revolving strobe light. But it was seeing her eyes for the first time that had affected him most. Luminous, sapphire eyes, with long curled lashes, sparkling at the antics of her colleagues like some laughing female devil's.

She'd been wearing very high heels and some brown thing—or was it beige?—with what looked like a strange glitch in its neckline. As he recalled, it had been quite shapeless. In fact most of the things she wore failed to make the most of her shape. The moonlit shape that haunted him.

His frown deepened. He hadn't been able to take his eyes off her, but when she'd glanced across at him, unbelievably those lovely eyes had looked straight through him.

It had shaken him. Could he have been mistaken?

His mother hastened to soothe him. 'It's not that she doesn't like you for yourself, dear, I'm sure. I think she's exactly what you need out there.' She gazed earnestly at him and added, her eyes as innocent as the dawn, 'Natalie didn't like her one bit.'

Natalie. A grenade lodged in his vitals, but he didn't move a muscle. 'Didn't she?' he said without expression. 'When did Natalie ever like another woman?'

'That's true,' Irene conceded, sending him a quick, searching glance. 'Natalie can be very threatened by the sort of woman she can't compete with.' She clasped her hands. 'That was what I wanted to talk to you about.'

Sam saw the anxiety in his mother's face, and shelved the mystery of his enigmatic PA. A woman who could so easily dismiss the most torrid sex he'd ever experienced was either an actress or a fool. And why a woman so lusciously endowed with feminine charms felt no need to display them to advantage was frustrating, but hardly important. As for her claiming not to *like* him— From what he could gather, Ellie O'Dea was one of the more popular staff members. She seemed to like everyone else, so why not him? As he recalled, she'd certainly liked him on that night.

'Sam?'

He snapped into focus. 'All right.' He dropped into the chair facing her. 'Go on, then.' Resignedly, he raised a hand to motion her on. 'Let's hear it—the wedding.'

Irene sat on the sofa's edge, the better to make her pitch. Her son's face was patient, but wary, his dark eyes watchful beneath their black lashes. She would have to tread carefully. After Natalie and the divorce she'd seen a tougher layer of cynicism added to his sophistication. His resemblance to his proud father ran deeper than his Greek colouring and hard male beauty. His handsome, urbane surface concealed a well of feelings that wouldn't easily be touched a second time.

'I'll be honest with you, Sam,' she began. 'I'm a little nervous about going to the wedding on my own. My being there is bound to upset Natalie, and she's such a volatile girl, who knows what might happen?' Her hand stole to her heart.

Sam noted the unconscious gesture with a frown.

'If your father were still alive—'

He leaned forward and took her lined hands in his strong, smooth ones. 'If Papa were alive he wouldn't let you go.' He made the effort to gentle his voice. 'You don't have to, you know. You could decline.'

'And then this horrible feud would go on! No, dear, whatever your father would have thought, I can't be cut off from my family for the rest of my life. For all his faults I miss my brother, and, although you'll never admit it to yourself, you must miss Michael. He's not only your cousin, he's still the closest friend you ever had.'

A blistering retort rose to Sam's lips but he suppressed it. Her frail heart wasn't up to the savage passions generated by the betrayal of his honour. It was clear enough what she was about to ask for. His attendance at his cousin's wedding.

To his ex-wife.

Smooth it all over, as though it had never happened. His fractured life patched together under a coat of gloss.

It had been a while, he mused, since he'd wanted to cut out both their hearts. Now he only wanted to wipe them from the universe, but he'd never mention it to Irene. She was a woman—essentially not even Greek. His father would have understood, if the strain of the dishonour hadn't killed him.

'I won't go to their wedding.' The intensity of the quiet words resonated in the silence for seconds.

His mother nodded. 'No one could blame you, Sam, but if you don't go, this myth Natalie's spreading around—that you can't get over her—will seem to be confirmed. Even my brother seems convinced you can't look at another woman.' She rolled her eyes. 'He wrote me such a sympathetic note, asking about your state of mind. "If Sam doesn't want to come we'll understand," he said. "Has poor Sam made any progress?" I have to admit, dear, I found it quite galling.'

Sam broke into a sardonic laugh. Though it was true he hadn't looked for a replacement. There'd been no woman in his life since the divorce. Perhaps lately his apartment had begun to seem quiet, tomb-like even, but one Natalie was enough for a lifetime. In the beginning he'd thought their differences would soon be ironed out, but they had only seemed to widen with time. There'd been no meeting of minds, no shared humour. The charmingly volatile young woman he'd married was too often a spoilt, destructive child. Too much of a child herself to be prepared for the responsibilities of parenthood.

His gut clenched at the memory of the unforgivable thing she'd done in the name of her career. Eventually she'd dragged his cousin into an affair, scandalised his family, and ended by splitting it in halves.

It occurred to him then, as he listened to his mother discussing the arrangements for Natalie's next wedding, that if he ever sought another woman she would be different. More subtle and elusive. The sort of woman who could inspire a man's imagination.

As it often had since the night of the masked ball, a vision surfaced in his mind. And the more he saw of Ellie O'Dea, the more he listened to her low, husky voice on the intercom—sometimes he called her just to make her talk—the more he was convinced that his first overwhelming instinct about her had been correct.

She was the fantasy woman. At least, he thought so. Since acquiring the bank, he'd examined several possible candidates, but it was amazing how many tallish, slim, red-haired women there were working in the building. Though none of the others had had her curious power of dislocating his lungs, he wanted to be absolutely sure. What he really needed was to see more of that fascinating arrangement of curves.

If only he could see her in different clothes, outside the office context. Perhaps he could arrange a conference, or a business dinner where she'd be obliged to wear something more revealing. Clinging, even. Satin.

And he was damned if he wouldn't break down that

barrier of reserve. The very idea of her not finding him attractive was laughable. He could enjoy watching her eat those words. In fact, it wasn't too much of a stretch to say that she'd flung him the challenge all over again.

At the possibilities this conjured his red blood cells stirred to the music and sprang to the salute. Dammit, if he couldn't find a way to rediscover the awe-inspiring flexibility of that slim, willowy body his name wasn't Sam Stilakos!

But…

He drummed his fingers morosely on the chair arms. The promise. It always came back to that bloody promise. Whilever he was bound by that ridiculous verbal contract he could see no way forward. With her gloriously passionate nature so cunningly hidden beneath her demure office persona, she was as maddeningly distant from him as some mediaeval princess in an ivory tower. Unless she could somehow be encouraged to break the embargo herself…

His mother's voice, still on about weddings and grandchildren, finally filtered through. 'I don't know why you can't find a nice girl, Sam. It's a pity you're so choosy.'

He stirred himself to reach over to his desk for his diary. 'It is,' he agreed, flipping it open to the day's schedule.

'If you could only find some lovely girl to take, it would shut them all up. I'd love to wipe the smug grins off their faces.' She heaved a sigh. 'If only I had a daughter to go with. Some nice, sensible girl I could rely on. Don't you have anyone here you could ask?' Her eyes flitted over his face, and beyond him to the view. She clutched at her heart and said, a brave little quaver in her voice, 'I suppose I'll just have to go it alone, and hope I don't drop dead in a strange place.' Dejectedly, she dragged herself to her feet.

Sam got up with her and gave her a bracing hug. 'Don't worry. I'm sure they have medical facilities in Queensland.'

Despite her talent as an actress, he knew her anxiety was well-founded. Natalie could be a hellcat, and the wedding would be stressful, not a good situation for Irene's health. Wild horses wouldn't get him there, but if she had to go it was up to him to find a means to protect her. Perhaps, he mused, he could send someone to support her in his absence.

It would take some calm, sensible person. Someone with exceptional interpersonal skills. Preferably someone who could stand parties.

An inspiration seized him then that was so fantastically brilliant, such sheer, diabolical genius, he was nearly swept away. Someone—*someone*—who'd need the appropriate clothes.

Suddenly energised, he planted a kiss on his mother's soft cheek. 'Leave it with me,' he said, the old thrill rising in his veins like an elixir. 'I'll find someone to go with you.'

Ellie sat slumped in her chair. A month in the job and she was finished. She wouldn't even have lasted as long as Sasha, Sam's first PA when he'd taken over as CEO.

Her thoughts flew back to the staff Christmas party, delegated, as usual, to her. The festivities had been in full swing before Sam had finished meeting with Gary, the finance manager, and descended from his alpine heights on the fifty-fifth floor for a brief chilly drink with the staff.

She'd done her best for Gary, writing out in detail exactly what he had to say to Sam in defence of the functions budget. A pity she'd had to leave it to Gary to deliver himself.

She hadn't spotted Sam at the party straight away. She'd been far too busy negotiating with Gary to come in off the ledge, but when she *had* seen Sam she'd been rocked by the sheer physical impact of once more being in the same room as him.

In the living, breathing flesh, in a suit cut by a master's hand to celebrate his wide shoulders, narrow hips and long powerful limbs, he was even more stunning than she'd remembered, his brilliant dark eyes more stirring. But the sight of him surrounded by all the executives eager to defer to him had made her realise how inaccessible he was to the likes of her.

That was when she'd noticed Sasha, enticing him to dance. She'd been flirting with him, swishing her long burgundy hair around in an obvious attempt to captivate him.

He'd declined, but by the time Ellie had recovered from her frozen shock she'd done the only possible thing, and pretended not to know him.

Rumour had it that poor, besotted Sasha had later draped herself around Sam's neck in the corridor and attempted to seduce him. Whether or not it was true was unclear, but what *was* clear was that when the office had reopened after the Christmas break Sasha had gone. Transferred to one of the Brisbane branches, someone had said. They'd all shuddered.

After Sasha there'd been an astonishingly rapid series of PAs who hadn't lasted the first week of their probation. Occasional glimpses of them had been caught on the lower floors as Samos Stilakos strode through the departments on snap inspections. They had followed along two-steps behind, gazing at him in adoration like Sasha, or blatant lust like auburn-haired Vanessa, but as quickly as they had seemed to snaffle the job, they had disappeared.

Ellie wouldn't even have dreamed of drawing attention to herself by applying, if it hadn't been for a fateful encounter with the man himself.

It had been after the staff farewell to Prue in HR. Poor Prue, still a beauty at forty-seven, had sacrificed the possibility of motherhood in search of a long-term relationship, and had ended up missing out on both.

Ellie had gone to great lengths to make the party one of her best. Afterwards, she'd been directing the caterers' tidy-up in the dishevelled function room, when a sudden fall in the noise level had alerted her to the presence of The Boss.

Her heart had gone into a series of crazed spins as he'd paused at the entrance, all six-three of commanding masculinity, his hair so black it was nearly blue, dark, lean and sternly handsome in a well-cut navy suit, with a crisp blue shirt and purple silk tie.

Her midnight lover.

He'd cast an appraising eye over the suddenly frozen activity in the room, then strolled the entire length of it to her.

Her heart had nearly stopped. Had he recognised her?

Once more he'd captured her in his dark, mesmeric gaze. 'Ellie O'Dea, isn't it?'

Somehow, hearing her name wrapped for the first time in that deep chocolaty timbre transported her straight back to that sizzling hotel room. Or maybe it had been the faint, tantalising spiciness of his aftershave. Or the controlled self-possession of his sensual, severely sculpted mouth.

Whatever, the flame he'd ignited in her blood that night flared back to intoxicated life.

'Yes,' she admitted breathlessly, once she'd recalled it. 'It is. Eleanor.' Automatically she held out her hand. The instant he took it in his firm, warm grasp, ninety thousand volts of electricity thrilled in recognition along her arm.

Did he want to thank her for the party? Perhaps, as she'd so often fantasised, with just the hint of a twinkle in his eye?

But his deep dark eyes were merely as cool and searching as any boss's meeting a prospective employee for the first time. 'Are you ambitious, Eleanor?'

Eleanor. Now why on earth had she told him to call her that? No one had called her Eleanor since she was five. 'I am, yes,' she tried to respond with the poise appropriate to a twenty-nine-year-old career woman with supremely marketable skills. Although, to be honest, she was confused. She knew he'd promised not to refer to that night, but he could have at least smiled.

'A vacancy has arisen in Executive Management for a PA,' he said with impersonal calm. 'It will be gazetted in tomorrow's Staff Bulletin before it goes out on the net. You might consider applying for it.'

She stared at him. A *job*? she might have said if she weren't in shock, but by the time she recovered he'd already walked away, detachment in every brisk, autocratic stride. The reality slowly sank through.

He hadn't recognised her.

At home that evening she drew the tattered mask from the satin box where she kept it, along with the postcards Mark had sent from remote locations around the globe, and other romantic memorabilia. She tried it on, and studied herself in the mirror from every angle.

To be fair, it covered quite a lot of her face, and gave

her nose an entirely different shape. In her suit and with her hair severely pulled back, she supposed she bore little resemblance to the woman at the ball. But shouldn't there still be something—some indefinable thing that was unique to her?

She couldn't wait to get her hands on the bulletin, and was at work even earlier than usual next morning to comb her pigeon-hole. As she'd hoped, the PA advertised for was his. His latest—experienced Schanelle with her sleek coppery bob, and, it had been wildly rumoured, references from Donald Trump—hadn't survived the week.

Someone in HR must have recommended her. Looking on the bright side, it was exciting, even flattering, to be included in the selection list out of a thousand employees. Professional recognition was something. She'd certainly done enough study over the years to give her the academic qualifications. And, despite the risk of him eventually realising who she was and despatching her to the back of beyond, the salary was strongly tempting. It would bring the goal she'd set for herself into view as a distinct possibility.

And she knew better than to follow the example of her predecessors, who hadn't been able to resist advertising their wares to him.

But underneath she was disappointed. Maybe it was irrational, but she wanted him to have guessed who she was. She'd had a sneaking little hope that he had, in fact, recognised her, but was honouring the promise she'd extracted from him by pretending not to.

The job offer wrote off that hope, though. Samos Stilakos would never allow her to work near him if he knew who she was. Unless…unless she'd meant more to him on that tumultuous night than just another one-night stand. Unless the job was a means of getting to know her!

What a laugh. There she was again, backsliding into fruitless romanticism.

'It's like being chosen by Henry the Eighth,' Beth, her friend, said, wrinkling her brow. 'Are you sure you want to risk it? What if he does eventually recognise you? God knows where you might be transferred. And what are your chances of not falling in love with him? At the Staff Appreciation Breakfast I even saw Schanelle ogling him with her mouth open.'

Ellie wondered how she could have missed that. She'd probably been occupied with settling the blood-feud that had arisen between the hired chef and the wait staff.

'If I keep my professional distance I should be safe,' she argued. 'And there's no chance I could fall in love with a man so—*spoiled* by women he can't tell one from another.' Indignation nearly got the better of her. 'Anyway. I told you. I've given up falling in love.' She noted Beth's unconvinced frown. No doubt mentally leafing back through the notorious O'Dea files.

All right, so once or twice she'd had her heart broken and her dreams shattered. It had cost her a few sleepless nights to be thrown over in favour of an ice-field, she could now freely admit. But that was the old Ellie O'Dea. She was stronger now, and in charge of her own life. Her heart was still there, large as life, but she'd locked it in an armour-plated box and it would never betray her again. If it showed any signs of weakening to the charms of some smiling predator, she had only to think of Mark.

'I have to think what the salary would mean,' she told

Beth firmly. 'Samos Stilakos doesn't recognise me, it's a great job, and I need the money. End of story.'

Beth eyed Ellie's suit with the knowledgeable air securely married women used for their less fortunate friends. 'You could get some new clothes. Brand-new. Like from real shops. In fact, I think you'd have to, in that position.'

'Possibly,' Ellie allowed stiffly. 'But I'm thinking of more important things. I'm not getting any younger. With the salary hike I could reach my target a year earlier.'

'Oh,' Beth muttered. 'Right. Your target.' She straightened the flowers in the vase she kept on her desk, replenished at least twice daily by her adoring husband. 'Look, Ellie, you don't have to give up yet. You're not even thirty, for goodness' sake.'

'When should I give up? Thirty-two? Thirty-three? Or wait till thirty-six when my poor brave little ovary buckles under the strain?'

Beth knew her ovary saga, and what the doctors had warned. 'Don't waste too much time to have your children,' they'd told Ellie back in her late teens after the painful cyst had been removed. 'There's no predicting how long your egg production will continue.'

It wasn't just the damaging scar tissue that had been left behind. It was the distinct possibility that it could happen again, and ruin the other ovary's chances as well.

She hadn't thought twice about children until Isabella, her sister, had given birth to her first little girl. Ellie would never forget the day. It had been just one week after Mark had left her.

She could still see Isabella gazing radiantly at the newborn in her arms, while her awed sisters crowded around the hospital bed, exclaiming over the baby's tiny pink perfections. 'Every woman should have a daughter,' Isabella had crooned on high from her cloud.

Ellie had been stabbed then with such a sickening bolt of fear, she could still feel the pain of it. What if she'd left it too late already? What if she *never had a child*?

She had driven from the hospital with a growing certainty that she shouldn't waste any more time. Waiting and hoping for the next man to come along was a fool's game. Recent events had proven something she had long suspected. Though men might desire her, she was not a woman who could inspire a man to love her.

If she wanted a child, she'd have to go it alone. And she should do it while she still could, even if she had to break rules.

She knew Beth didn't approve. Thousands wouldn't. She could hardly bear to think of it herself when she tried to imagine herself actually going to an IVF clinic, and admitting to some professional that she was forced to resort to a clinical procedure.

It was all very well for happily married people who were secure in their egg supply. Beth thought she should rush down to David Jones and splurge her savings on a chic little suit. But Ellie had made sacrifices, and now her money had begun to mount up, especially since she'd let go the Kirribilli flat she'd shared with Mark, and moved further out of the city. Skipping lunch and forgoing drinks with friends after work had helped. She'd even given up the major vice that had driven Mark crazy of constantly buying new shoes with very high heels.

A quick costing from some infant catalogues had shown her just how expensive raising a child was likely to be, even without the childcare. Even if she was very frugal—and with Mark she'd learned to be *extremely* frugal—a safer car, as well as all the baby paraphernalia, would stretch her resources to the limit. The childcare would be the most difficult thing. It would all be much easier if she could bring the baby to work. Somehow, she would have to find a way to wangle that.

So, she reasoned, *plan*-wise, the advantages attached to becoming PA to Samos Stilakos far outweighed the risks.

She made practical preparations for the interview, determined to keep her reactions under control. If he gave her cool and impersonal, she'd give him super-efficient and remote. A man who couldn't remember her voice, or have any sense of her unique spiritual essence even after he'd slept with her, didn't deserve a drop of the Ellie O'Dea brand of personal warmth.

She rejected the idea of an expensive new suit, and chose a navy blue pinstripe her sister could no longer fit into. Tried and true, it looked dignified, even if the jacket was a little bulky on her and the skirt long. At least her last remaining pair of three-inch heels gave it some semblance of style. She rejected the sexy-camisole look for a crisp white shirt, loosely braided her hair into her nape, and was more than usually sparing with her perfume. If Samos Stilakos disliked secretaries who made their attraction to him obvious, she would give him nothing to complain of.

The interview got off to a disconcerting start. No other candidates waited with her in the outer office. After a lengthy wait, Caroline from HR—Caroline had waited too long and now had golden retrievers instead—emerged and gave her the nod.

With a pounding heart Ellie entered.

As tall, autocratic and darkly handsome as ever, Samos Stilakos was standing at his window, hands in his pockets, staring out. At the quiet sound of the door closing he turned, and her feet slowed to a halt. His dark eyes locked with hers across time and space, and she felt a dizzying whoosh, as though all the air were being sucked from the room.

The world held its breath, then Samos Stilakos moved, gesturing politely towards a chair with one lean, elegant hand, and she realised it was just that her lungs had forgotten to breathe.

The chair he'd indicated looked out on his Chief Executive view of the harbour. He chose the chair opposite, so the light fell on her face, while his was in shadow. He murmured a few crisp words of greeting, then for a long, drawn-out minute scrutinised her, his dark eyes cool and impenetrable.

She waited, her nervous pulse ticking along until the sound of it swelled to fill the room.

After an eternity he said very softly, 'You have a piquant chin, Eleanor.'

The blood rushed to her cheeks. 'Really?' she said, struggling not to be thrown by a weird personal comment that had no place in a job interview. 'I hadn't noticed.'

What had he meant by it? Was it a criticism, or a compliment? Could a chin even *be* piquant?

He flicked her an enigmatic glance, then opened her CV and got down to the task of rigorously grilling her. She managed to answer his questions coolly and pleasantly, and hardly noticed his lean hands leafing through her personnel file.

Only once did she feel herself begin to slip into the mad craving she could have for him if she let herself go.

It was during his line of questioning about her role on the Social Committee.

'I need my PA to be flexible, and not be afraid to show initiative,' he said in his deep, quiet voice. 'And you must realise, should you be successful in your application, that you won't have time to continue organising the staff parties.' He added drily, 'Of course, in the future there won't be so many to distract you.'

She gave a stiff nod. The stringent cuts to entertainment and the little luxuries of working life were sore points with the staff.

At that moment Samos Stilakos made a slight shift in position. She saw his trouser-leg ride up to expose a black sock. Beyond that black sock, her wanton imagination raced to envisage the hairy, muscular leg she knew resided inside the expensive fabric, and went on to roll out the whole, mouth-watering picture of bronzed, virile masculinity she remembered with such vivid power.

Without warning heat curled through her. Involuntarily her armpits and the palms of her hands moistened, and she felt her ears and other, more sensitive points grow hot.

'Are you finding it warm in here, Eleanor?' The deep polite voice cut through the steam of her flashback. 'Would you like some water?'

She met his cool enquiring glance and her flush deepened. 'No. No, thanks,' she said jerkily.

'Please,' he said, leaning forward, a dark gleam lighting his eyes, 'feel free to take off your jacket.'

She resisted that invitation, and somehow floundered the rest of the way through the interview, managing to keep all her clothes on, and to avoid any dangerous references to the masked ball.

She wasn't quite sure why, but a day later she had the job.

It was a tightrope, but not in the way Beth had predicted. Though Sam was always courteous and professional, a tension existed between them. When he was discussing projects with her, his deep, dark gaze intent on her face, sometimes she wondered if they were really talking about something else. Sometimes she felt his eyes dwelling on her face when he thought she wasn't aware.

At night she couldn't stop thinking about him, analysing everything that had happened between them during the day, even though she knew it was a dangerous weakness, and a path she mustn't travel.

And sometimes, right on the edge of sleep, at that moment when she had least control, she'd allow her mind to drift into wildly romantic fantasies, like the swooningly delicious one in which he'd acquired the bank solely because he'd fallen in love with her on the Night of Nights.

At work he smiled rarely, but when he did her insides were wrung. His deep, seductive voice swayed her concentration, and she had to fight to conceal her awareness of him behind a bland smile.

Though obviously she hadn't succeeded, she now realised with a sinking heart. And he would be sure to have heard by now what Natalie had accused her of. Alice Springs beckoned, possibly even New Zealand.

She bent to search her bottom desk-drawer for the photo of Mark camping in the Pyrenees. Even after fourteen months she hadn't been ruthless enough to throw it away. At least he'd come in handy for something, even if it was only camouflage.

She sat it upright on her desk just as Sam's office door opened and his mother came out. She bid Ellie a friendly farewell, although Ellie thought she could read sympathy in the older woman's eyes.

The advice she always gave to juniors in trouble with their bosses was to never apologise, only explain. And to justify, justify, justify. But how would she ever explain this without giving everything away?

With a growing sense of dread, she made an attempt to get on with doing some strategic tweaking of Sam's latest presentation for the board. There was nothing wrong with his basic ideas, just that they were heavily weighted towards the bank's profits. Usually time just flew when she was editing one of her boss's projects. Now it was the longest ten minutes in history before the intercom buzzed.

'Come in, will you, Eleanor?' the deep, cool voice said.

With trembling hands Ellie whipped out her compact and made a quick inspection. Paler even than usual, and not at all mouse-like, but outwardly under control, apart from her hands and the slight dilation of her pupils. Her neck suddenly felt very sensitive, but if Anne Boleyn could face it, so could she.

A little unsteadily she rose, corrected the slight left-wards list of her Country Chic suit jacket—bought brand-new from a last season's seconds shop in Chinatown—and, head high, entered the office.

CHAPTER TWO

Sᴀᴍ at work was nothing like the Sam in a hotel bedroom.

Usually when Ellie came in he would be at his desk, writing, or frowning at spreadsheets. He would look up and watch her approach with that brooding, inscrutable gaze, then return to his work, silently motioning her to be seated.

This time she saw with foreboding that he was upright, his lean hips resting negligently against the massive rosewood desk, arms folded, waiting. He looked taller, his powerful shoulders wider. From across the room she saw his eyelids half lowered over watchful eyes as unreadable as the night.

She waded across the rich crimson carpet to him, conscious that his deep gaze was measuring every centimetre of her progress. She came to a halt a few metres short, her heart thumping against her ribs.

The silence thundered with her disgrace, though even in her suspense she couldn't help noticing the outline of his long powerful thighs, highlighted as his posture tugged on the fabric of his trousers.

'Ah, Eleanor,' he said with sinister, velvet charm. 'Please sit down.' He swept one bronzed, lean hand to indicate her usual chair.

'Thank you,' she said, shaky but resolute, 'but I'd prefer to stand.'

His black eyebrows twitched up. His eyes lit with a disquieting gleam. He shrugged. 'As you wish.' He straightened, strolled a few paces to the right, swung round to shoot a look at her, then strolled a few paces back.

Searching for the words, she supposed. He should have been good at it by now, with all his experience.

His foot crunched on something, and he kicked it aside and came to a halt. Ellie shifted nervously as his gaze seared down her vulnerable throat, to the fragment of lace revealed by her disobedient jacket, down to her brave but slightly tatty heels.

Sam felt an overwhelming desire to reach out and unbutton that jacket, but he repressed it. He wished he had X-ray vision to see the curves under the demure clothes, but at least the skin of her throat was the satin-white he remembered. He noted the small, betraying pulse there with a quick surge of satisfaction. It wasn't just him. Miss Ellie O'Dea wasn't quite as cucumber-cool as she pretended.

He lanced her with a glance that held just the right degree of professional sternness. 'I may have mentioned during your interview, Eleanor, the need in your job for absolute discretion.'

His deep voice sliced through the silence as easily as a sword through a tender neck.

Ellie's lashes fluttered down. This was it. The chop.

'Of course. You did mention it.' She braced herself, and plunged bravely in with, 'Is there something you want to say to me, Mr Stilakos? Because if there is something I need to explain, I'm sure I can satisfy you.'

He gazed meditatively at her for long seconds, his eyes

narrowed, then said, 'I have no doubt of that, Eleanor. And, yes, there is something I want to say to you.' He strolled over to sit on the edge of his desk, and captured her eyes with his compelling glance. 'Until now things between us have been a little formal. I think you'll agree that the time has come for us to remove our masks.'

'Our—' The breath choked in Ellie's throat. 'What do you mean?'

The perceptive dark eyes scrutinising her face glinted. 'I think you know exactly what I mean.' Her blood had just started a panicked rush to her head when he added in measured tones, 'A personal assistant has to be just that. *Personal.* If we're to work as a team our relationship needs to be closer. That means us getting to know each other. Being open with each other. I'm sure you have issues with me I know nothing about.'

Relief he was only using *masks* as a figure of speech made her so giddy she was seized with a rush of generosity. 'No, no, I don't. Well, not that many.' The attentive tilt of his dark head made her conscious of her soft words seeming to crash around the walls. 'I dare say everyone has his or her own management style.'

He grimaced. 'Good — I *think*. I hardly dare to ask, but are there some suggestions you'd like to offer? To help me improve my—performance?'

His eyebrows made an ironic twitch and the sternness of his beautiful, sexy mouth relaxed. Instantly her imagination flew her back to that lamp-lit bed where he reclined, bronzed, naked and wickedly intent on giving her the ultimate in pleasure, and a tidal surge of warmth swelled her breasts inside her cut-price bra.

'No, no,' she said, shaking her head to crush any suggestion of sexual innuendo. 'Of course not. I'm sure your performance—I mean your performance as a *boss*—is very good.'

He smiled. It was a rare event and she wished he hadn't. His eyes crinkled at the corners and seemed to lengthen charmingly. It made him devastatingly like the Sam of the hotel bedroom.

'Of course I knew you meant my performance as a boss,' he said softly. 'What else would I have thought you meant?' A shadow of the smile lingered as he contemplated her with a shimmering, intent gaze.

The suspicion crept into her head that he knew very well who she was and was toying with her. She twisted her boneless hands behind her back. Was he tempting her to flirt?

He began to pace again, only this time, to her intense confusion, *around* her. He circled, inspecting her as if she were a slave girl in some biblical market-place.

He prowled behind her and paused, and she stared straight ahead, embarrassment warring with her overwhelming physical awareness of him. What was he looking at? Suddenly she remembered a little fault she'd forgotten to fix in the pleat at the back of her skirt, and felt herself grow hot. She whipped around to face him, concealing her discomfiture with a touch of hauteur. 'Was there something else?'

'Tell me, Eleanor,' he said. 'Are you finding your salary adequate?'

'My salary?'

She nearly gasped. Her feminine pride was stung, though she knew there were those who would say she deserved to feel some shame. She was earning more than she'd even dreamed, and could easily have bought a new suit. Her bank balance had received such a boost that her savings fund was becoming quite healthy, but, she'd reasoned, in extreme circumstances a woman was forced to take extreme measures to protect herself.

'It's more than adequate, thanks,' she admitted. 'It's generous.'

He stood looking thoughtful for a second, then strode across to the desk and picked up the phone.

He dialled, unnerving her with a keen, meaningful glance. 'There is something of a deeply personal nature I need to discuss with you, but this isn't the place for it. I'm taking you to lunch. Payroll?' he said into the phone, then covered the mouthpiece with his hand and said, 'You'd better warn the restaurant upstairs we want a quiet table. And cancel our appointments for the afternoon.' With a brisk nod he turned back to his call. 'Jenkins? What do we pay Eleanor O'Dea?'

He waved her away, but as she headed for the door she had the sensation that his eyes were burning through the back of her suit.

'No,' she heard him tell Jenkins. 'Yes. No. No. Take it up. Make it twenty-five per cent. Better still, thirty.'

Outside the office door, Ellie stood for a moment, her mind in a whirl.

Something—*everything*—had changed. It appeared she wasn't getting the sack.

But what personal thing did he want to discuss? Surely not the night of the masked ball?

She dialled the penthouse restaurant, then stood rapidly reviewing their conversation. She still had her job, which suggested he hadn't remembered her. Though some of the things he'd said...

And there had been a definite buzz in the atmosphere. Whether he'd intended it or not his behaviour had been seductive. Charming, even. Although, if she was to be honest with herself, she always felt that zing in the air when she was near him. The question was whether it was all generated by her.

It was highly unlikely he'd flirt with her. Still, did a sophisticated man like Samos Stilakos use the word *relationship* accidentally? Somehow she doubted it.

Although…although…

This was the man who'd transferred four assistants for falling in lust with him, *and* sacked his Advertising Manager for conducting staff performance appraisals in the Honeymoon Suite at the Crown Regis, one of Sydney's most salubrious hotels. He'd never risk starting an affair with his PA after setting his workforce such an uncompromising example.

And what was this about her salary? Unless she'd misinterpreted that phone call, he intended giving her a raise. She thought back to that unsettling moment when he'd been prowling around her, and nearly groaned aloud. Beth had been right. She should have upgraded her wardrobe. What if the deeply personal thing he wanted to discuss with her was her suit?

Though anxiety gnawed at her vitals, she still made an effort to concentrate on the booklet she was preparing to support Sam's strategy for bringing the department heads around. Should she, or shouldn't she, include that fascinating research she'd uncovered about childcare in the workplace? Surely it was a prime opportunity to inform them of what they truly needed to know.

Sam's door opened and he strode out with his firm, energetic step. 'Ready?' His glance shifted past her and he halted. His eyes narrowed, and he strolled over to her desk and picked up Mark's photo. 'Who's this?' He turned a veiled glance on her face. 'Your boyfriend?'

'No, no. He's—a friend.' She supposed Mark could still be called a friend, even after fourteen months without a word. Certainly he hadn't wanted to be called a husband, or the father of her children.

Sam held up the photo to examine under the light, tilted it this way and that. 'There's something about him,' he commented, frowning. 'Reminds me of someone. Yes, I know. The woodsman in that story—what's it called?' He clicked his fingers. '*Hansel and Gretel*—that's the one. Does he always keep that beard?'

'He's a mountain climber. An—adventurer.'

He'd made Mark sound so ridiculous she couldn't help feeling a bit defensive. Although why should she? Mark had never been into haut couture. Her yearning for beautiful, elegant clothes had been one of the contentious issues between them, and she'd long since learned to suppress it. But there was nothing so ridiculous about a checked flannelette shirt, was there? Millions of men wore them.

'He likes—a challenge.' She'd been going to say *wide open spaces*, but the truth of that could still hit a nerve.

'Ah.' He shot her an inscrutable dark glance. 'Don't we all,' he said softly, and gave the photo a careful wipe with his immaculate Armani sleeve, before placing it on the desk directly in front of her chair. He flashed her a wicked smile. 'There. Now you can see him clearly. Ready now?'

He curved his arm around her back to escort her to the lift.

The revolving restaurant on the top floor was packed

with the lunch-time crowd of executives and members of the public who wanted to enjoy spectacular views with their meals. She spotted several of Sirius's management staff, gossiping over their dry whites.

The news would be out in a flash, she thought, noting some curious heads turning their way as she made her entrance with Samos Stilakos. She could just hear them in the canteen—*Ellie is making it with the boss*. At least, though, with members of staff present he wasn't likely to spring any major surprises on her.

The *maître d'* swept all before him to lead them to a table in a discreet corner, magnificently set in white linen and crystal. 'Champagne, sir? Madam?' he said, after he'd seated them with a superb flourish of starched napery.

She was relieved when Sam said, his deep, quiet voice polite but commanding, 'Mineral water. This is a business meeting.'

Executives all over the restaurant hastened to conceal their wineglasses.

Sam gazed at her across the table, golden depths shimmering in his dark eyes, and her relief began to wane a little as her susceptible pulse picked up speed. 'Eleanor,' he said softly, ravishing her with a gleaming white smile. 'That's a Greek name. Did you know that?'

If only the smile didn't linger in his eyes like a caress. 'I thought it was French,' she answered, unable to prevent her own giddy smile from breaking out. 'You know, Eleanor of Aquitane and all that.'

'Eleanor of Aquitane was almost certainly of Greek descent,' he said. 'And I believe she also had strawberry hair.'

Strawberry. The word hit her like a thunderbolt and the smile was wiped from her face. If ever she'd needed proof of this man's pathetic memory here it was. Hadn't she provided him with a shining example of strawberry-blonde hair at the masked ball? On that occasion he'd displayed a passionate enthusiasm for plunging his hands into it, even burying his face in it. Having experienced it to the utmost, it was one colour he should have remembered.

It was glaringly apparent that to him all shades of red hair were the same. As no doubt all *women* looked the same.

'What is it?' His eyes lit with amusement and his thick black brows lifted. 'Have I said something?'

She concealed her chagrin behind the self-possessed demeanour she'd perfected for bosses over the years. 'I believe Eleanor of Aquitane was one-hundred-per-cent French,' she replied coolly. 'And my hair colour is usually described as Titian.'

His lean, handsome face betrayed no expression. 'Oh, is it? Titian. I must remember that.' He looked so solemn she had the strongest suspicion that for some reason he was pleased with himself, and trying not to show it. He motioned to her to open her menu, and perused his while she made a pretence of reading.

Food words danced meaninglessly in front of her eyes. Why were they discussing her personal attributes? Next he'd be bringing up her piquant chin. If she didn't know better, at any minute now she'd be expecting a sexy little après-lunch invitation down to the Crown Regis.

A nasty suspicion occurred to her. Perhaps he always seduced his PAs over lunch. Maybe that was why he then had to banish them to the ends of the earth.

She hated to believe it, but it fitted. Why hadn't she realised? For months the staff had speculated about those transfers. No one had had any doubt that the women had earned them with their unprofessional behaviour. But what if *he* had been the seducer? When he turned on his devilish charm he was impossible to resist, as she could testify only too well.

With growing disappointment she surveyed the handsome, inscrutable face absorbed in reading the menu. A serial sacker was one thing, but a serial womaniser quite another. For some reason she'd needed to believe in his integrity. What did it say about her, that she'd spent the night with someone like him?

'A lovely name,' he murmured. 'And yet—' He looked up to capture her gaze. 'You invite people to call you Ellie.'

She looked enquiringly at him over the top of her menu.

'Your friends.'

'Yes?'

'But not your boss.'

She was momentarily flustered. A smile warmed his dark eyes, crept into her veins and stole down her arteries like old cognac. She forced herself to keep on breathing as if it were an everyday experience for her to be teased by tall, dark, dangerous Greeks with beautiful, sexy mouths that curled up at the corners.

'I'd prefer it if you would drop the *Mr Stilakos* routine, and just call me Sam,' he added gently.

There was a pregnant silence while he waited for her to reply in kind. It was fortunate that just then a waiter materialised beside their table. She wasn't hungry, but she welcomed the lad as if he were her saviour, bathing him in her warmest smile. 'I'll have the salad, thanks,' she told him.

She was conscious of Sam leaning back in his chair, his long limbs idly disposed, his gaze flickering over her as he listened to the small exchange. When it was his turn he ordered the fish, and in a few brief words gave detailed instructions in exactly how it was to be prepared. After the waiter left, he moved his chair a little closer and said quietly, 'I'm wondering, Eleanor, if your friend will be able to spare you for a weekend, just over a month from now.'

A million unlikely scenarios raised their heads. 'Beth?' she said, taken off guard.

'Your friend. The *adventurer*.' Somehow he managed to invest the word with a subtle mockery.

'Oh, Mark?' She gave a small self-conscious laugh and mumbled, 'No, no. Well, he's not— He's not actually—' She folded her napkin carefully, folded it into smaller and smaller rectangles. She'd never intended to lie about Mark's presence in her life, only to divert suspicion. What if she had to produce him at some time? It would be so humiliating to be caught in a lie. Quickly she backed away from it. 'Why? What's happening?'

She felt his perceptive eyes home in on her nervous fingers, and forced them to stay still.

'So you'll be free?' There was a gleam in his eyes that suggested he hadn't been fooled by her little strategy.

Her heart lurched. Was he about to suggest a weekend rendezvous? For a wavering instant she allowed a shining mirage to float in her imagination—the two of them, making love in some decadent, luxurious hotel.

Despicable. Fatal. But such sweet poison. If the others hadn't resisted, how would she?

Breathlessly she replied, 'It depends what for.'

He hesitated. 'You met my mother this morning…'

She nodded, hypnotised by his mesmeric gaze.

'My mother has to go to a family wedding. Her heart isn't very strong and she finds she's nervous about having to go on her own. I wondered if I could impose on your good nature to ask if you would consider going with her?'

His *mother*! She nearly fell off the chair. This was nothing like she'd expected. Inviting her to a social function with his mother, his family—!

Her suspicions all fell in a heap. How could she have been so cynical? And foolish, suspecting him of seducing his PAs, even worrying about what he thought of her clothes when he'd probably never even noticed them. As for her fanciful dream of an afternoon of wild sex down at the Regis… She should have blushed with shame.

'Of course, I'll make sure you're handsomely reimbursed for your time and trouble.'

She pulled herself together. 'Why me?' she said. 'Why not you, or another family member, or a friend?'

He sat back. His lean, strong face hardened to become expressionless. 'It's a family affair. I don't know if you know anything about the Stilakos family—'

Only what everyone knew, that they owned a bank, half the media outlets in the country, and controlling interests in several trans-global corporations besides Sirius. She wasn't about to acknowledge what she knew of the personal stuff shooting along the office airways, and shook her head.

'It's my ex-wife, Natalie, who's getting married. You'll have met her this morning. She's marrying—another family member.' There'd been a hesitation, so slight as to be barely perceptible, but his dark eyes hardened to obsidian. 'On my mother's side.'

Ellie had a vague recollection of some scandal about Natalie a few years ago. While the star had been well known because of her television fame and wild-child reputation, at that time her husband's name had meant nothing to Ellie.

'As you might imagine, everyone in the family, all the *friends* of the family, are in some way involved with the bride and groom. You probably noticed this morning, Natalie can be temperamental…'

She gave a noncommittal shrug.

He laughed. 'Always the diplomat, Eleanor.'

A pleasant, unexpected glow irradiated her insides. Perhaps she should forgive him for forgetting her. After all, a man like him had serious things on his mind.

'Natalie can be— just a little volatile. Weddings are emotional affairs, and my mother is nervous of the possibilities. If she had some calm, sensible person with her, some neutral person, I think she might feel more confident.'

'You—haven't been invited ?' she hazarded.

His eyes darkened, and became so impenetrable she had the heart-gripping sensation she'd tripped a detonator wire set to blow her sky-high. For goodness' sake, why had she asked? Of course people didn't go to their ex's weddings.

'It's probably better you don't go,' she hastened to say. 'It would be sure to arouse painful memories.' His face remained tense, and she strove to lighten the tone with humour. 'I imagine the last thing anyone would want on their wedding day would be their ex turning up at the church. All their friends sitting on the edges of their pews… Everyone waiting for hell to break loose. I can see it all now—' she raised a solemn hand and intoned in a priestly voice '"—if any man here knows of any reason why this man should avoid marrying this woman…"'

To her relief his taut face relaxed and he broke into a laugh. 'It may surprise you to know I have been invited.

My ex-wife has infinite faith in my ability to keep my mouth shut. She begs me to come.' He added drily, 'That's what you were hearing this morning. Natalie persuading me.'

He smiled, but Ellie felt a little chill thrill down her spine. There were jagged depths beneath that brooding calm. She would hate to be the one who disturbed them.

'What do you think?' He scanned her face for a moment, then lowered his black lashes and said, 'This doesn't mean your job is on the line if you refuse, Eleanor. This is apart from your work. It's personal, and I'll understand and accept it immediately if you choose not to be involved.'

She'd been wrong. Absolutely wrong on all counts. The man wasn't a scoundrel in any way. He was a concerned, affectionate son willing to go out on a limb for his mother, even if it meant exposing his personal skeletons to a stranger. A mere employee!

The waiter arrived with the meals, and she took advantage of the distraction to think.

How she'd misjudged him. It was sobering to see how close she'd come to turning into a cynic in her old age. She looked up to meet his dark, velvet gaze and her heart warmed. What a relief to be able to think well of him. 'All right,' she said, smiling. 'I'll do it. If you're sure your mother will be comfortable with me.'

His eyes lit with satisfaction. 'Good.' He took up his knife and fork and added, 'I've phoned her and she thinks she will be. Now, eat up your salad. We'll need to see her and do some shopping. And we'll need to discuss the travel arrangements.'

Ellie raised her brows.

'Didn't I mention it? Natalie's parents live on the Gold

Coast. The wedding's at the Palazzo Versace. You'll be staying there.'

Ellie was dazzled. The Palazzo Versace was supposedly one of the glitziest resorts in the country. She tried to remember what she'd heard of it. Television ads she'd seen had left her with vague impressions of a glittering palace floating on a moonlit lagoon; beautiful languid people, lounging on luxurious chaises longues, sipping piña coladas. She could easily imagine Natalie there, but could Ellie O'Dea be one of those people?

'Great,' she said doubtfully.

'You might need to take your swimsuit,' he said, considering her over the rim of his glass. 'Just because it's a wedding doesn't mean you have to suffer the whole time. There're bound to be things you can do to pass the time while my mother catches up with her family—beaches, sailing, wind-surfing—you know the sort of thing...' He made a careless gesture with one lean, bronzed hand, then paused, contemplating her with an intent shimmering gaze.

'I'm not much of a one for beaches,' she confessed. 'I have to avoid too much sun.'

His eyes flickered to her throat. 'Ah, yes. I can see that. You are very fair, aren't you? So you never go to the beach?'

Ellie felt herself grow warm. This was too reminiscent of a conversation she'd had with him before in quite a different setting. Was it a coincidence that so many of the things he'd said to her since ten o'clock that morning in some way recalled the Night of Nights?

She gazed searchingly at him. 'Early mornings, or—or late afternoons are fine. I do like to swim. Sometimes I—' she waved her hand in a stiff gesture '—use the pool at the gym.'

'As I recall, there is quite a lovely pool at that resort. A spa, no less.'

'I'm not sure I can imagine myself at that sort of place.' She gave a small laugh.

'*I* can imagine it,' he said softly. A gleam lit his dark eyes. 'I can imagine it very well.' He looked silently at her for a long minute that grew longer and more deafening by the second as questions danced again in Ellie's brain. 'And there is always the night,' he murmured, still gazing at her.

She stared back at him in amazement. 'The night?' Her voice came out deeper than she expected; it sounded almost croaky. 'I don't think I'd feel safe on the beach at night.'

His eyebrows went up, then he laughed, a low, sexy laugh. 'Wouldn't you? But what if you were with someone?'

Her heart skipped a major beat while her lashes fluttered in shock. 'Who? You mean…someone I met at the wedding?'

His eyes chilled and his fork arrested in mid-air. 'I certainly didn't mean that.' He pinned her with a severe gaze. 'Try to remember this, Eleanor. You'll be there to keep my mother company, not for the sake of a hot weekend.' He must have seen her dismay because he added, his deep, smooth voice rich with charm, 'Though, of course, I know you aren't the type of person to ditch your responsibilities for a fling with some stranger.' He smiled at her, and turned his attention back to his meal while her head buzzed with indignant thoughts. *He* wasn't above a fling with a stranger. So why even mention it? Why, unless he was giving her some sort of signal?

She stared at her barely touched salad. All at once the uncertainty became too much. What sort of a pathetic coward was she to allow this cat-and-mouse game to continue?

If he sacked her, he sacked her.

'Look, Sam...' She took a deep breath and on a rush of bravado leaned forward and murmured in a voice just above a whisper, 'Are you—are you by any chance referring to the night of the masked ball?'

As soon as the words were out a blush the size of a tsunami swamped her. She clenched her entire body and held her breath.

Across the table Sam's bronzed hands stilled. She lifted her gaze and met his brilliant dark eyes. They were gleaming with a deeply unsettling intensity.

He spoke so quietly she had to strain to hear him above her madly thundering heartbeat. 'I'm not referring to it,' he said. 'I'm very carefully not. If you want me to discuss it, you'll have to release me from my promise, won't you, Eleanor?'

Relief washed through her. Impossibly, she felt the colour deepen in her cheeks. 'Oh. Well, of course, of course. I *do*... There's no point... I'm certainly not trying to...'

'Good. I'd hate to think we'd come this far for nothing.'

Her nerves jumped in shock. *We'd come this far...?* Towards...what?

Sam Stilakos laid down his knife and fork. When her glance fell on his hands she noticed that they weren't quite steady.

The waiter came with fresh water, creating such a welcome diversion she and Sam both hastened to chat warmly with him. After the boy had gone, Sam lounged back in his chair and said idly, 'So who is this boyfriend? What's-his-name—Tim?'

'Oh. You must be meaning—Mark.'

His thick black lashes screened his gaze while she

gathered herself to reply. She drained her glass and took her time refilling it from the carafe, then said with a careful lack of expression, 'Mark went to Antarctica.'

His brows lifted and he scanned her face. 'Antarctica! For a holiday—or…?'

She rearranged her salad. 'An expedition.'

His brows went up again. 'Ah. And do you—*when* do you—expect him back?'

She shrugged. 'Oh, some time,' with an airy wave of her hand. She didn't want to let on how long he'd been gone. And that he'd since been seen in Melbourne with a blonde whose idea of couture was to wear army boots with a denim skirt.

Samos Stilakos continued to study her face with a veiled gaze. After a long moment he remarked in a low, musing voice, 'Antarctica. That's a long way from here.'

CHAPTER THREE

'I THINK you've been in this car, Eleanor, haven't you?'

The lazy enquiry rocked Ellie on her heels just as she was about to get into Sam's Porsche. Of course she'd been in it. He'd driven her in it to Circular Quay, and kissed her long and lingeringly as the first rays of dawn had ignited Sydney Harbour in a sunburst of molten ecstasy. It had been the highlight of her life to date.

'Remind me again,' he said, flashing her a glance through his black lashes, 'which do you prefer? Roof open, or closed?'

Smiling, she indicated her hair. 'What do you think?'

He strode around to the driver's side and lowered his long frame into the seat next to hers. His hand moved to the gear stick, and she instinctively shifted her knees, although of course she knew he wouldn't have touched them. Not this time.

But it was far too reminiscent of the last time, when he'd driven her to the ferry terminal in the sweet haze of afterglow. Then, the city streets, the very air she'd breathed, had seemed intoxicating. It was intoxicating *now*, sitting beside him as he threaded a path through the traffic with breathtaking efficiency, his beautiful hands relaxed on the wheel.

No wonder Schanelle and the others had ogled him.

Scorchingly conscious of him in the confined space, she tried to restrain herself, but somehow her eyes were drawn to drink in his sexy mouth, so grave in repose. A suggestion of shadow on his firm, lean jaw evoked a stirring memory of his early-morning face, nuzzling a bristly imprint on her tender skin.

'Something wrong?' he said, turning his head suddenly and catching her.

'No, no,' she said, flushing a little. 'I was just—er—thinking about Schanelle.'

'Ah. Now there's a coincidence.'

Her heart plunged to the floor. Could she be going insane? Whatever had possessed her to remind him of poor Schanelle? But he made a sudden swift lane-change, executed a heart-stopping but brilliantly adroit U-turn in the face of oncoming traffic, and drew the car to a smooth standstill at the kerb.

She stared confusedly out, and saw they were parked in front of a boutique with elegant lettering across its large, black-framed windows. 'Oh, the *shop*.'

He cast her an amused glance. 'You know this shop, of course.'

'From the outside,' she admitted with a grin, surmising they were here so he could choose a wedding present for his ex-wife. 'I'll wait in the car.'

'No, you will not,' he asserted. He sprang out and strode around to open her door, forcing her out with a firm, expectant gaze.

She stood uncertainly on the pavement in front of the

entrance. How did he think she would be able to help? PAs with savings targets didn't shop in places like this.

'Come on.' He took her arm and manoeuvred her inside.

A severely smart shop assistant, with sleek blonde hair and emphatic eye-liner, registered his approach with an open mouth. Ellie wished a fly would buzz in, until she remembered her own first sighting and forgave her.

'We need things for a weekend wedding,' Sam told the woman, seemingly not put off by prolonged eye contact. 'Dresses, suits, shoes. Swimsuits. Size…' He turned a suave glance on Ellie. 'I'm guessing ten. Would that be right, Eleanor?'

Ellie dragged her eyes away from a shelf of fabulously high shoes with jewelled heels. 'What? *I* don't need anything.'

'Yes, you do,' he said. 'I can't plunge you into this without providing you with the necessary equipment. I've been through this kind of thing and I've learned the hard way about what's expected of women. You'll need dresses, shoes, handbags…' He began ticking a list off on his fingers. 'An outfit to be seen arriving in, casual things to lounge around in, things for daytime, evening, the church, and we mustn't forget the swimming.'

Ellie nearly tottered on her heels. She stared at him, then around at all the lovely creations poking from their racks. This attitude was absolutely the opposite of Mark's, who believed elegant clothes to be the trappings of empty vanity. It was religion with Mark that money should only be spent on functional items, like hiking boots and thermal underwear.

This was generosity on a scale she'd never encountered, but deep down she knew she couldn't accept it. She was a free and independent woman, and, whatever else Sam was, he was her boss.

She angled herself away from the interested stare of the saleswoman and mumbled, 'I have things I can wear.'

She felt the assistant's experienced eye assess her clumsy jacket and skirt, and tried to look cool and unconcerned, though she could feel her face turning pink.

'I know you do,' Sam said soothingly, 'but for this you'll need new things. Show us everything you've got,' he instructed the woman over Ellie's head.

Dollar signs danced in front of Ellie's eyes while the woman jumped to obey the command in his voice. Ellie watched helplessly as she reefed through the racks and pulled out hanger after hanger of gorgeous, to-die-for outfits, any of which would leave a massive hole in her savings.

'This is not the sort of thing I wear,' Ellie protested, waving away a purple suit with a short slim skirt. For the price on its label she could probably furnish a nursery and pay for five years of violin lessons.

Sam looked surprised. 'Isn't it? I think it'd look good on you. Try it on.'

She shook her head, 'This is very kind of you, but I don't *need* you to buy me anything, thanks.' She met his gaze steadily. 'I really can't accept this.'

Disconcerted, Sam stared at her, wondering if he was losing his grip. A delicate flush washed her flawless cheeks and disappeared into her hairline. There was a smile on her soft mouth, but her blue eyes were resolute. He felt a curious jolt, and was reminded of another time he'd come up against a brick wall with Ellie O'Dea. But surely none of the women he'd ever known would have refused clothes from this establishment.

He gestured to the saleswoman to turn her attention to other customers, and ushered Ellie to a quiet corner. It took him a moment to find the words. 'Let me explain, Eleanor.'

That deep, persuasive tone could melt steel, and Ellie braced herself for a major charm offensive, but the dark velvet eyes scanning hers were sincere.

'I don't wish to insult you,' he said carefully, 'but you don't know Natalie and her friends. You'll be competing in the most cutthroat market in the country. You'll need to wear something swish, or risk feeling uncomfortable. I can't just drop you in it. My mother would kill me.' He smiled and wrapped a reassuring arm around her, and every cell in her body surged. 'It isn't a big deal. Relax. I have to do this, believe it.'

The dark seductive resonance of his voice went straight to her head. Through the fabric of his suit she felt the heat of his large, lean body, and her blood went zinging on a dizzy dangerous course to her breasts and points south.

'You're—you're really very kind.' She quickly disengaged herself. Her ears felt as if they'd caught fire. She met the sensual awareness vibrant in his dark gaze, and knew he'd noticed her quick pull away, and understood the reason.

'Honestly, Sam,' she rushed to fill the awkward moment, 'this is too generous of you.' Her heart was racing, but she forced herself to keep her head. He was so persuasive. Beautiful things called to her from every direction, but to allow him to buy even one dress for her would be shameful, when she could very well buy something for herself. 'I don't need a whole new wardrobe just for one weekend. If I need a dress, I can buy it myself.' She made a small dismissive wave towards a shelf where shoes kept flashing in the corner of her eye like hot magnets. 'Or—or shoes, or whatever.'

His black brows knitted, and she could tell by the calculation in his gaze that he wasn't about to give in. 'Er…' He turned to glance around the shop in search of inspiration.

Suddenly he turned back to her, a gleam in his eyes. 'All right. Let's compromise. We don't want to offend these people, now, do we? You can't leave without at least trying something on. How about some of those shoes?'

Who was he, the devil? She glanced at them once, then averted her eyes. Somehow he'd homed straight in on her Achilles heel.

She shook her head and gave a small, reluctant laugh. 'You're very cunning.'

His eyes glinted. 'I *am* very cunning, and you'd do well to remember that, Eleanor. Go on. Try some.'

She looked over at the shoes. She could resist chocolate if she absolutely had to, for life-preserving reasons, but this was too much. She wasn't sure how it was a compromise, but with her blood churning like an excitable sea, she started with the shoes, and it wasn't long before two sales assistants were plying her with the clothes.

Obviously experienced with the ways of women in dress shops, Sam found an alcove with a pile of newspapers and dropped into a chair.

Ellie tried on the purple suit, and saw it accentuate her curves and turn her eyes to violet. The saleswoman brought her more suits, frothy skirts and evening dresses in rich colours with beads and sequins—jeans, swimsuits, even bikinis. Despite her initial reluctance, the fever for lovely things gripped her. There was a time for being frugal, she acknowledged to herself, and a high society wedding wasn't one of them. She had to accept that he knew what he was talking about. She did need at least one good dress. She would just have to make an adjustment to her IVF timeline.

Several times the woman dragged her to a large mirror outside the cubicle. Sam lounged across the room, buried in his newspaper, though once Ellie glanced towards him in the mirror and felt a small shock as she met his intent gaze.

'If madam would try these,' the saleswoman suggested, handing Ellie some extremely frivolous shoes with four-inch heels. She'd just finished zipping a short-sleeved dress, in a shade of pink so delicate it was nearly white. Cut to classic perfection, it moulded slinkily to her curves, emphasising the perky up-tilt of her breasts. The shade lent her pale skin a pearly glow, and her blue eyes sparkled like sea water. She examined herself in it with delight, feeling as if she could slither like a snake. She slid into the shoes, and her legs lengthened with the old fabulous miracle.

'I *love* this,' she admitted, twisting in the small cubicle to examine her derrière. 'It isn't too tight, is it?'

'No, no!' the woman cooed. 'It's made for you. Come outside and see.'

The saleswomen whisked her out to the big mirror and fluttered around her. One stood on tiptoes and tried to re-arrange her hair. 'How does it look out?'

She tried to explain that if it wasn't severely bound up it just fell straight, like a heavy curtain. She put her hands up to loosen it, knowing she was surrendering to more than letting her hair fall. For once she'd be breaking the embargo on her savings. But hadn't she been given a pay rise by the most generous boss a woman could ever...?

Her eyes slewed towards him in the mirror, and did a double take.

Far from being sprawled in his chair, he was sitting bolt upright, his big frame taut, his burning gaze riveted on her, as if on some vision. A thrill shocked through her at the concentrated wolfish expression of his lean, strong face. She felt his eyes sear her from head to toe, their electric message unmistakable.

Her mouth dried. Transfixed, she watched him drop the paper and rise to his feet.

'We'll take it,' he growled, striding purposefully across to her without shifting his gaze. 'And the shoes. Let me help you with that, Eleanor.'

The assistants fell back to give him space. He raised his hands to her hair, and she felt the sensual charge in his smooth fingers frisson in her skin as they coupled with hers to release the pins. Her nape, her scalp, the length of her spine tingled as his strong, lean fingers plunged into her hair. After a wild few moments in which her pulse roared through her veins like white-water rapids, he stood back to let the red silken mass fall free.

His hands gripped her shoulders and he held her to her reflection, a flame in his eyes. 'Look at you,' he said, gravel in his deep voice. 'You look perfect. Absolutely perfect.'

Her eyes glittered back at her from the mirror with a bluer intensity. His searing gaze locked with hers, their desire as seductive and compelling as it had been in that hotel room, and her breasts surged in a deep, responsive excitement. She felt a dizzy tide of unreality, as if she weren't in a shop with her boss, but with her lover in some private moment, on the verge of an explosive flare-up of passion.

But…he wasn't her lover. Not now and never again. Whatever images glowed in their memories were just that. Memories.

Restraining what felt like a natural compulsion to turn and embrace him, she lowered her lashes. 'I—I'd better take it off.' She made a move towards the fitting room.

'No,' he breathed. 'Leave it on.' His grip tightened for an instant before he released her. 'It's—ideal for where we're going next,' he said gruffly. A faint tinge of colour darkened his olive tan.

He swung abruptly away from her. She slipped back into the fitting room and took some deep, trembling breaths in an attempt to compose herself. One of the saleswomen came in to remove the labels from her dress, and took away the items she'd put on the possibles pile.

Ellie plunged into her bag for her hairbrush and did a quick tidy-up, her rapid heart thudding. She wasn't sure how she was going to face him when she came out. Something had happened between them, something irrevocable. Could they just pretend it hadn't?

She could hear the murmur of his deep voice in conversation with the saleswoman. 'We'll take them all,' she heard him say. 'And throw in all the matching shoes, et cetera.'

Though her poise was barely recovered, nonetheless her pride came roaring back.

'No! Wait.'

She burst from the fitting room, and hurried over to insert herself between Sam and the startled assistant. 'I'll take this dress and these shoes I'm wearing now,' she told the woman. She whipped her credit card from her purse, and pushed Sam's aside to lay hers on the counter. 'These are all I need,' she said with a firm glance at him, 'and *I* want to buy them. But thanks, anyway, for your most generous offer.' She smiled and added softly, 'I really do appreciate it.'

Something flickered in his intent dark gaze, and his brows knitted, but he must have seen the resolution in her face, because he stood back and allowed her to complete the transaction without argument. The assistant wrapped her work clothes and old shoes in tissue, and slipped them into stylish carrier bags.

She floated hazily beside him to the car in her chic little sexy dress and shoes, still in something of a turmoil. She'd expected a bigger fight over the matter of payment. Nonetheless, though she was still reeling at the price, it was a victory to have out-argued an autocrat who had an entire workforce quaking in its boots.

But there was the other thing. That moment in the shop.

He'd hardly spoken a word since, and, though he seemed as assured as ever, she had the feeling he was as burningly conscious of it as she was herself. It was hard to meet his eyes, but when she did they brimmed with satisfaction, and something more. Something very akin to the desire she'd seen in that mirror.

The trip in the car was surprisingly brief. She'd thought they were heading for the bridge, when, against all her expectations, he swung the Porsche into the driveway of a grand hotel. She craned her neck, trying to read the inscription over the portico. Wasn't this the—?

The doors were opened by uniformed valets. 'Welcome to the Crown Regis, Mr Stilakos.' And with a deep bow. 'Madam.'

CHAPTER FOUR

Sᴀᴍ ushered her into the marble lobby. The concierge, the porters—everyone greeted him by name.

'Wait here a moment,' he said, steering her towards a plush velvet sofa.

Ellie stood still, besieged by doubts. Hadn't he said he would take her to visit his mother? She watched him stride across to Reception, and lean over to murmur something to the receptionist, who picked up the phone, spoke briefly, then handed him something.

Ellie's pulse quickened. She thought she could guess what it was.

In a second he was back, his eyes glinting when they lighted on her like a wolf with his prey in sight. With a light touch on her arm he guided her to the lifts. This was the time to call a halt. But what mature, twenty-nine year old woman would refuse to allow the most thrilling lover she'd ever known to escort her to the Honeymoon Suite of Sydney's most salubrious hotel?

In the lift they stood slightly apart, watching the floor count on the display panel, Ellie's heart in a dilemma, rapids churning in her veins. What was she doing?

'She's expecting us,' he said as the floor count reached thirty-five.

'Who? Oh. Do you mean then—? Your mother is staying *here*?'

He glanced down at her, his devilish brows raised. 'Of course. Didn't I say? She always stays here when she comes up to town. Why else would we be here, Eleanor?'

The doors opened then, sparing her the impossibility of replying. Either she was a horribly confused woman, or her imagination had just taken her overboard. Or— Samos Stilakos was playing a game with her. A flirty, tantalising and very sexy game!

His mother opened her door to them and greeted them both warmly, although she regarded Ellie with faint surprise in her eyes.

'You've met Eleanor, Mother,' Sam said, with a glance at Ellie. 'I think she might be the person you're looking for.'

Ellie held out her hand. 'Hello, Mrs Stilakos.'

'Call me Irene,' the older woman said, taking her hand and looking her over with admiration. 'You look so nice. Is that how you were wearing your hair this morning?'

Ellie shook her head, conscious of Sam's eyes on her.

'Eleanor's hair was meant to flow free,' he stated.

She nearly gasped, wondering what Irene made of this, but the older woman merely beamed. 'And it does suit you. Come through, Eleanor.'

'*Ellie*, please.'

Sam's eyebrows twitched ironically at that, but he was silent as they followed his mother through to the suite's elegant sitting room. Irene showed them to winged chairs beside a large window, which overlooked the harbour and the Opera House. Other windows revealed different aspects of the city, sparkling in the afternoon haze. It might not have been the Honeymoon Suite, but it was certainly appealing.

Irene sat facing them on a crimson sofa. She'd changed from her chic morning suit to casual trousers and a dusty-pink top, and her hair was slightly flattened on one side, as if she'd recently woken from a midday snooze. With the light from the window on her face, Ellie could see lines of tiredness around her eyes and mouth.

'I'm so glad Sam had the brilliant idea of asking you, Ellie. Eleanor…' She tilted her head to one side. 'Is that a family name?'

Ellie could feel Sam's interested gaze on her face as she responded to Irene. 'My parents named us all after queens. One of my sisters is Cleopatra. There's an Isabella, and a Liz, of course, and I was called after Eleanor of Aquitane.'

'All very powerful women,' Irene nodded approvingly. 'Are your sisters married?'

Ellie found herself describing her family, including her father's work in the music department at Newcastle University, and her parents' rambling home on Lake Macquarie.

'Do all your sisters have children?'

Ellie nodded. 'Nearly all.'

'I bet you make a lovely auntie, Ellie.'

Ellie smiled. 'I do my best,' she admitted, although she didn't acknowledge her understanding of what this little fishing expedition was all about. Not with its unwary subject sitting right there in all his lazy drop-dead gorgeousness. She wondered if she would be like this with *her* sons? Always on the lookout for an eligible wife and mother for the grandchildren?

If she had sons, she thought with a small anxious pang. If there was an egg left by the time she could afford it!

Still, Irene's skills in helping her to relax, while extracting information from her about her family in the gentlest, least offensive way imaginable, were impressive.

There was so much one could learn from an older woman, she mused. Unless the older woman's son was sitting across from her, dripping with sexual charisma and soaking up every word.

'Mum! For God's sake,' he growled when Irene's curiosity threatened to go too far, and occasionally he rolled his eyes or exchanged an amused glance with Ellie, but she could feel his sharp intelligence weighing everything she said.

She had a slight respite when a knock came at the door, and Sam got up. A waiter wheeled in a table swathed in white linen, and set with Wedgwood china. Clever little warming drawers inserted underneath held a feast of toasted sandwiches, scones and a fluffy passionfruit sponge.

At Sam's insistence, Ellie accepted a toasted sandwich of baked ham and avocado. 'You don't know how long it will be before you get your dinner tonight, Eleanor,' he said. 'You'll need to keep your strength up.'

Tonight. She looked quickly at him. The dark eyes dwelling on her face were veiled, his sculpted mouth grave. She felt the heat rise in her cheeks. She took a small bite, but, delicious though it was, her appetite seemed to have deserted her.

Irene's bright gaze swung from one to the other of them, then she busied herself in pouring the tea. Ellie wondered how attuned the older woman was to picking up vibrations.

'I don't know how much Sam has told you about the wedding, Ellie,' she said. She inclined towards Ellie and confided, 'I'm afraid it might turn out to be quite dramatic.'

Sam's mouth curled wryly. 'Eleanor *has* met Natalie, Mum.'

'Well, I hope Ellie doesn't think I'm a coward.' Irene smiled at her. 'Milk?' She handed her a cup and saucer. 'Tea, Sam?' He waved a refusal, and she continued, 'I'm not really nervous. I love weddings, and I'm so looking forward to seeing my brother and his wife—the whole family! It's just that I like to have someone to talk to when I'm travelling.'

'Of course,' Ellie responded warmly. 'I understand exactly. No one likes travelling alone. Especially to weddings, where everything is about couples.'

Sam lounged back in his chair, his smooth, lean hands idle. Ellie could feel his dark gaze from beneath his sloopily lowered lashes scorching a pathway of sensual masculine interest from her Titian hair all the way down to her ankles.

Irene continued to give an excellent impersonation of a woman with energy to spare. 'That's true,' she agreed, her grey eyes sparkling behind her specs. 'And that's how you feel, don't you, dear?' she said earnestly to Sam, whose slumbrous gaze snapped into startled focus. 'A man without a woman is always twice as suspect at a wedding.'

Sam looked thunderstruck, but his mother ignored it, turning animatedly to Ellie. 'I knew you'd understand, Ellie. You and I'll get along perfectly.' She loaded a scone with cream. 'I'll let my brother know you're coming. And I'm sure you won't have any trouble with Natalie. She'll have so much on her mind she won't even notice you're there.'

'What?' Sam demanded, recovering. 'Why should Ellie—*Eleanor*—have trouble?'

Ellie's heart skipped an anxious beat for fear of what Irene might say, but she merely leaned over and patted her son's knee. 'No need to be alarmed, Sam. Ellie will be quite safe.' She gave Ellie a conspiratorial glance and said with a small, nervous laugh, 'If it comes to a showdown, Ellie and I can defend ourselves. We aren't scared, are we?'

'A showdown?' Sam's eyebrows shot up and he turned a sharp gaze from his mother to Ellie. 'What sort of a showdown? Why should anyone be scared?'

'Don't you worry at all, dear,' Irene said, her voice quavering a little. 'This is secret women's business. We don't need any men to protect us, do we, Ellie?'

Sam scoured their faces in such bemusement Ellie found it hard not to laugh.

As if in total innocence of the effect she was having on her son's peace of mind, Irene continued, 'Now, Ellie, you won't have to be stuck with me the whole time. I'll probably be gallivanting about with my relations for quite a lot of it.'

Sam shot his mother a quick frowning glance, but Irene went on, 'You're bound to meet up with someone your own age you can have fun with, isn't she, Sam? There's so much to do on the Coast.'

Ellie gave a noncommittal laugh. 'Either way is fine with me. I'm sure I'll find something to do if you're not around.'

She felt Sam's dark gaze searing a hole through her skull. His eyes were narrowed, and there was a sardonic little curve to his lips. 'What might you do, Eleanor? Planning on taking a good book?'

'Perhaps.' She gazed coolly back at him, refusing to let him mock her in front of his mother. 'Perhaps not.'

Irene glanced at each of them, and said brightly, 'Well, it won't worry you whatever Ellie does, will it, dear, because you won't be there.' She beamed at him and turned to Ellie. 'Michael—he's the groom—is a keen yachtsman, like Sam, and I believe some of his young friends from the yacht club are sailing up there in advance of the wedding. The Palazzo Versace has a marina, so you might have an opportunity to do some sailing.'

Sam frowned. 'Sailing would be a mistake for Eleanor,' he said, in cool, clipped tones, his gaze on Ellie's face. 'She can't afford to get sunburnt.'

'Nonsense, Sam,' Irene exclaimed. 'She doesn't have to be wearing a tiny little bikini like some of them do, but if she does want to there's always sunscreen. And I'm sure you'd look lovely in it,' she added with a warm glance at Ellie.

Ellie felt the blood rise in her cheeks as the vision of her bikini-clad self dangled in the air.

'The jury's still out on the efficacy of sunscreen,' Sam said, holding her pink face under the spotlight of his sensual dark gaze. 'Eleanor would be better to stay indoors.'

'Oh, well.' Irene shrugged. 'If she prefers to she can always stay in her room and order a massage from one of their health professionals. I've read that some of those fellows are artists with their hands. I think she'd find it very therapeutic.'

Uncontrollably, Ellie's gaze flew to Sam's. The image flooded her brain of his smooth, bronzed hands as she'd known them on that night. Massaging her wild, willing body, with such masterly expertise. Kneading and caressing her breasts to erotic ecstasy. Exploring her satin secrets, his beautiful sexy mouth rousing her to rapture.

'She wouldn't,' he said, his voice as smooth as silk. 'You wouldn't want some man coming to your room to rub you all over with essential oils, would you, Eleanor?'

Ellie was forced to lower her lashes. She felt an over-whelming rush of warmth to her breasts. 'I might,' she said, concealing her confusion behind an unfocused smile, her betraying voice overly husky. 'I'm not ruling anything out.' She felt his eyes on her hands, and saw they'd curled themselves up. Deliberately she made them unclench, and raised her gaze to his. His dark eyes were amused, but there was a hard sexual challenge in their depths that sent a fierce, responsive pang through her.

Irene gave a sigh of what sounded like contentment. She set down her cup and leaned her back against the sofa cushions. 'It's such a relief you're coming, Ellie. I had wanted Sam to come in the first place, but I think I'll have more fun with you. He never lets me have my head. I'll be able to try out the casino and the nightclubs, shop till I drop, do all the touristy things—'

Sam turned a thunderous gaze on his mother. 'I don't think so, Mum. You'll find it tiring enough just going to the wedding. Eleanor's job will be to keep you out of trouble.'

Irene looked solemn. 'I'll try to stay out of it, but you know how I am after champagne, dear. And knowing Jack and Rosemary, it'll be flowing from the moment we arrive.'

Ellie's lips twitched with the temptation to laugh, but she saw fatigue in Irene's face then, as if her store of energy for the day had suddenly been used up. Sam must have noticed it at the same time, because he got to his feet and ended the visit, with a peck on his mother's cheek and a quiet reminder to take her medication.

At the door Irene said, 'It's so kind of you to do this, Ellie. I hope Sam will be able to get along without you while you're away. But we won't be thinking about him, will we? We'll be too deeply immersed in the flesh pots of the Coast.'

Sam gave her an austere look and his lips thinned to a grim, straight line.

Ellie suppressed a laugh. She had to hand it to Irene. When it came to pressing buttons, she was a champ.

Sam was silent on the way down in the lift. He leaned against the wall, his hands in his pockets, his brooding dark gaze occasionally flicking to Ellie. When the doors opened on the ground floor the sound of a piano wafted their way. It was coming from the piano bar, set like an oasis in the vast lobby.

'I need a drink,' Sam said, taking her arm. 'This way, Ms O'Dea.'

The bar wasn't busy. The few customers chatting at nearby tables weren't audible above the notes dripping like honey from the fingers of the pianist. Ellie accepted the offer of a glass of red wine, and slid onto a bar-stool next to Sam's.

Her dress rode to mid-thigh, and she crossed her legs as the only possible safety measure. Sam swivelled his bar-stool round to face her, his dark-clad knee only centimetres from hers. 'You did very well then, Eleanor.' His gaze slid over her. 'My mother likes you.'

'I like her. She's funny.' She smiled at him, still cool, efficient Ms O'Dea on the surface, though her heart seemed to be in training for the Olympics.

'Funny, but deadly serious. She's a worry.'

She suffered one of those dangerous, weak melty moments she'd resolved to eliminate from her dealings with men. So he cared about his mother. Didn't they all?

She raised her wine to her lips. Sam continued to watch her while she took a tiny sip, his lashes half lowered. He murmured, 'Which queen was it whose skin was so transparent you could see the wine trickle down her throat?'

She met his shimmering dark gaze and felt her pulse hasten. 'Mary, Queen of Scots, I think. Though, you know, Sam, I suspect that story isn't true.'

'It might have been true, Eleanor,' he said gravely. 'If she was a Titian-haired beauty with skin like white satin.' He lapsed into a meditative silence while her head spun dizzily. Was this a compliment? Was he really saying that *she* was a…?

The wine radiated through her with a mellow warmth. It was so—pleasant being with him, not knowing what he might say next. She dangled on the edge of sweet suspense, waiting, in fact, *longing*, for him to make a move.

But he stared absently into his scotch. The bar's muted overhead light glanced off the chiselled planes and angles of his face from cheekbone to jaw. She had an overwhelming desire to touch his cheek and trace the lines with her fingers. Run her fingertips along that masculine mouth.

He held his glass loosely in his lean fingers, and gave the amber liquid an idle swirl, before connecting again with her eyes. 'It wouldn't be a good idea to let Mum do too much gallivanting, as she calls it.'

She nodded, uncrossing her legs. Funny how hard it was to keep four-inch heels on when perched on a barstool. Whichever way she disposed her legs, one of the shoes slipped halfway off to dangle, like some nightclub siren's. She wasn't intending to act seductively, but she couldn't help feeling it. It was the dress, and the look in his eyes whenever they lighted on her. She anchored one foot on the crossbar and let the other swing a little.

His heavy-lidded gaze scorched the length of her and back again. Her flesh rippled with fever, as if his lean, beautiful hands had actually touched her. Glances could burn, she mused, aware of that deep, sensual excitement she'd felt on the balcony at the masked ball. There could be the sensation of contact, even when people weren't touching.

His deep, dark voice seeped into her veins like an aphrodisiac. 'I'm depending on you to keep an eye on her.'

'Maybe you would be better to keep an eye on her yourself.'

He grimaced. 'No force on earth could get me to that wedding.' His gaze drifted to her mouth. 'All you have to do is to keep her from going overboard.'

'I'm sure she won't,' she rejoined, as steadily as possible for someone melting to the sexual pull of the most gorgeous man in Sydney. 'Irene doesn't strike me as someone who'd take unnecessary risks.'

His devil's eyebrows made a sardonic twitch. 'You don't know her. Once she gets with Aunt Rosemary there'll be no holding her.' He took a sip of his scotch. How could lashes so long and thick be so essentially masculine? 'It would be best if you could keep her in the suite.'

She roused herself from her voluptuous contemplation of him. 'In the suite!' she exclaimed. 'I'm going as her companion, not her gaoler.'

He put down his glass and leaned an arm along the bar, somehow enclosing her in a private little intimate enclave.

Her heart made an adrenaline leap. If body language was anything to go by, Samos Stilakos was feeling very open towards her.

'Try to see it my way, Eleanor.' His deep velvet voice swayed her senses into a giddy hypnotic state. 'If you insist on all this sailing and carousing on the beach with strange men at midnight, how much of a companion are you likely to be?'

She gasped, and waved her glass in protest. 'I'm not insisting on anything!' A few drops of wine sloshed over the rim onto her fingers.

He took the glass from her hand and set it on the bar. Before she could reach for a paper serviette, he produced a beautifully laundered handkerchief, took her hand in his firm, light grip, and wiped her fingers with patient thoroughness.

'There, now.' He continued to hold her hand, and she held her breath. Desire coursed through her, sweet and irresistible as nectar. A piercing sensual gleam lit Sam's dark gaze, and for an electrified instant she thought he was going to raise her fingers to his lips. He said softly, 'We don't want to spoil that amazing dress. Not when you have to do dinner in it.'

Her voice came out as a husky croak. 'Dinner? Who said anything about dinner?'

He laughed and his deep, dark eyes lit with delight, and something like triumph. What had she said that was so funny?

And what did he have to feel triumphant about? She hadn't actually agreed to go to dinner, although there was no reason why she shouldn't. She was wearing a sexy, elegant dress, she was with a sophisticated man who made her feel desirable and interesting, and all she had planned for the evening was a comparative survey of the donor options offered by the various IVF clinics around the city.

She slid off the bar-stool and accompanied him out to where the car waited. Outside, she was surprised to see the first glimmerings of dusk. Lights seemed to be coming on all over the city. Somehow, in that wine bar, she'd lost all track of time.

Once in the car he gave his jaw a thoughtful rub. 'Er—do you mind coming home with me and waiting while I change, Eleanor?'

She looked quickly at him, but his expression was innocent. Nothing like that of a man set on whisking his PA to the nearest secluded venue, so he could ravish her into total delirium.

'Of course not.' She smiled, with her usual calm acceptance of anything a boss could throw at her.

CHAPTER FIVE

APARTMENT towers of steel and glass were hardly Ellie's style, but she couldn't deny the heady magnificence of Sam's sensational views across the city to the horizon. If he'd wanted to train a high-powered telescope on Hornsby, he'd probably be able to see the front door of her flat.

He parked her in his living area—although she wasn't sure who could ever live in such clean, uncluttered surroundings—while he vanished through an archway. The all-white room she was in disappeared around a corner into the unknown. It was all soaring ceilings, white marble surfaces and spiral staircases. He'd lived here for three years, he'd told her casually. Which meant post-Natalie.

Not the home of a man who wanted children in his life, was her first thought.

She wandered out onto the terrace, thankful for its high balustrade. Vertigo wasn't her favourite sensation. There was an inviting pool and spa, with lights glowing in their blue-green depths. A man attending to the Babylonian-style hanging gardens around the pool nodded to her, before gathering his equipment and disappearing inside.

If a man had all this, she reflected, a Porsche Carrera and a bank, what did he have left to strive for?

Around her the city was a-glitter as dusk gave way to dark. Neon signs on neighbouring buildings pulsed with the same nervy rhythm the home territory of Samos Stilakos inspired in her heart.

However had she come to be in this place of all places? There was no way she should allow herself to succumb to another fling with him. Already she was struggling to maintain the barricades round her heart. She tried to remind herself of Mark's treachery, but found it hard to think of him here.

'It's too early in the evening for our balcony scene. You'd better come inside.'

The deep, mocking voice made her start. She turned and the breath seized in her throat. Sam stood at the terrace doors. He'd changed into casual trousers and a black, open-necked shirt. It deepened the velvet magnetism of his dark eyes and the olive tones in his skin, hung elegantly on his powerful frame, hinting at the muscled contours of his chest.

He looked relaxed and ready to play. Not the office Sam. The other one.

He strolled across to her. His hair was still damp from the shower, and he smelled of clean masculinity. He was her boss, she told herself giddily as an erotic mixture of tangy scents whooshed to her head.

Nothing was going to happen.

He reached out to touch her hair, further destabilising her. 'I can't wait to see you at the managers' meeting like this.' There was a glow in the depths of his dark eyes. 'I might have to make you do the presentation, so I can properly appreciate you from all angles.'

'Oh, but,' she replied, laughing, her pulse escalating,

'I can't just keep wearing this dress all the time. I've worn it today, and now tonight… It sounds as if you don't ever want me to take it off.'

He laughed wickedly and his arm snaked around her waist. 'Nothing could be further from the truth. Come inside and we'll talk about it.'

Inside the white room, a throaty female voice rendered a sexy old jazz ballad with a moody mellowness. Candles had been lit, adding warmth to the room, and some anti-pasto and champagne had been laid out on a buffet cabinet. If this wasn't a scene set for seduction, her wires were seriously in need of straightening.

Sam opened the wine with casual expertise. 'I told my housekeeper how much you've eaten today, and she's worried.'

'What?' She cast a quick glance about. 'You mean—you have a woman here, on the premises?' Her words conjured instant visions of a Hollywood-style maid in a frilled apron, stilettos and nothing else, and as soon as they were out she went scarlet. 'Oh! I'm sorry, Sam!' *Dying* with embarrassment. If only she could sink through at least twenty-seven floors. 'Truly! I didn't mean that as it sounded.'

He surveyed her, amusement in his gaze, and handed her a glass. 'I do have a woman. Not exactly on the premises, but close to the premises. She lives a couple of floors below with her husband. That was Martin. You might have seen him outside earlier. He doubles as my driver.'

'Oh. Of course.' She gave a foolish laugh. 'What else?' She sank down onto a white sofa with her wine, and nearly lost her balance as the deep, decadent cushioning dragged her down into its sumptuous embrace. She saw

Sam grin. What had happened to her legendary poise? Anyone would think she'd never been up in the stratosphere before with a sophisticated billionaire intent on having his way with her.

She laughed off her momentary disconcertion with graceful aplomb, but to be honest, faced with the old dilemma, her insides were churning. A massive risk was shaping up here. Her job, her plan, her foolish, stupid heart…

Looking too darkly sexy and nonchalant to be safe, Sam leaned against the buffet, sampling the occasional olive. He shot her a glance of lazy amusement. 'I'm sorry you find this room uncomfortable. If you like we can move somewhere else.' He tilted his dark head towards the archway.

What was through there? The master bedroom? 'No, no. It's not. It's—quite lovely here. Whatever makes you think I'm uncomfortable?'

'I've been studying your body language. I think I'm beginning to get the hang of it.'

A warning pang cut through her, but she saw the teasing light in his eyes and rose to the challenge, stretching her legs out in front of her and leaning back. 'You've got no chance,' she retorted with a careless laugh. 'I'm famous for my acting ability.'

'You're good, I admit that. *Yes, Mr Stilakos. No, Mr Stilakos*…as though we'd never been together.' He looked steadily at her and added softly, 'Never been lovers.'

Her heart made a wild leap and she quickly dropped her gaze, then, just as though his gleaming dark eyes weren't eating her up, and her pulse weren't madly racing, she said, 'What about you? You're very good yourself.' She put on a grim face and deepened her voice. 'So stern and dignified.'

His eyebrows twitched up in amusement. His gaze flickered to her legs, then met hers. 'Do you enjoy working?'

'Of course. I love it.'

'And you like the bank?'

She nodded.

'You've been there a long time,' he observed lazily. 'Have you ever considered exploring further afield?'

She shrugged. 'Not really. I've liked all the jobs I've had there.'

He picked up a small platter of the antipasto and strolled across to her with it. 'And you're very talented. Always cool, never ruffled. Always smiling and pleasant. Beautiful, efficient Ms O'Dea. But what goes on underneath?' He dropped down beside her and offered her the food. 'Who was the guy who taught you to play it safe?' His tone was casual, but no way was this a casual question, and his eyes pierced her with an alertness that threatened to penetrate her crucial internal fortifications. 'What do you think about when the lights go out, Eleanor?'

'Nothing.' She smiled and fluttered her lashes. 'You keep me working so hard, I just fall straight to sleep when the lights go out.' She accepted a caviare-laden cracker with the same calm smile, and forced herself to bite into it. But it was damnably hard to swallow. Her heart had started an uncomfortable pounding, and he was close. Far too close. This was hardly the seduction line she'd expected.

His long muscled leg was near enough to brush hers and light her up with fireworks. One part of her wanted it to happen, but another part wanted to run to the balcony and jump on the first passing jet to Hornsby. Was it fair for a boss to delve into the private personal heart of his PA?

Her aching cheeks needed a rest. She got off the sofa and strolled about, pretending to study the art works with interest, as conscious of the current between them as if it were tangible. In need of a breathing space, she stopped in front of a square of white canvas.

'What do you think?' he said, coming to stand next to her. The black hairs on his forearm lightly grazed her arm, with electric results. 'Inspiring? Uplifting?'

She put her head on one side as coolly as if her awareness of him weren't pulsing through her veins. The skin where his arm had brushed hers instantly craved it again, and she couldn't resist swaying imperceptibly closer for another touch. 'It's white,' she said, fleetingly closing her eyes to savour the brief tingling contact. 'Certainly a clean look.'

'Not empty and lifeless, like this place?'

'Don't you like it here?' She glanced wonderingly around at all the trappings of understated luxury that could only be available to the very, very rich, and risked turning to look at him.

His sensual dark gaze riveted her to the floor. 'I think I like it better this evening than I ever have before.' There was no easy smile with the words. His gorgeous, sexy mouth was as grave as if he were speaking from the heart.

With masterful ease he caught her in his arms. The dark desire in his eyes seared her like a flame. She'd play it cool this time, her wild thoughts flew. Hold back. Try not to expose herself as a weak, vulnerable fool.

But he held her head between his hands and kissed her, and her susceptible body surged to his remembered touch in rapturous welcome.

There was no playing it cool. At the first brush of his lips desire blazed in her blood like a bushfire. Just as he had the first time, he tasted her mouth with a tenderness so ravishing it turned her knees to water, and her breasts swelled in arousal as he slid his teeth across her lower lip with slow, sexy eroticism.

He pulled her hard into him and deepened the kiss, intensifying the intimacy by slipping his tongue inside and plundering her mouth with an artful teasing she was powerless to resist.

Helpless thrills quivered through her as his long fingers stroked the length of her spine and moulded her to his hard, vibrant body. She clung to him, her bones melting, a sweet urgency between her thighs, her breasts and straining nipples in delicious friction with his chest.

She kneaded his powerful shoulders and gave herself up to the voluptuous pleasure of his big, lean frame in contact with her soft curves. The taste and scent of him fuelled her potent memories of him, and fanned the flames of her secret longings.

He snatched the very air from her lungs. The kiss deepened to a molten pitch, her passion for more of him fighting with her need for oxygen. But he was in supreme control. In the very nick of time his sensual hands traversed her arms to her shoulders, and he ended it, breaking from her.

She swayed a little on her four-inch heels, light-headed for lack of oxygen, and he put a hand on her shoulder. 'Steady there,' he said with some amusement. But for all his cool, his deep voice sounded dark and gravelly, and through his dark lashes his eyes were black fire. 'That's how I remembered you tasting,' he said, exultation in his voice.

Knowing she was flushed and dishevelled, she angled away from him and made an effort to tidy her hair and smooth down her dress. 'How?' she said croakily, panting, shocked by the uncontrolled response he'd raised in her. With just a kiss!

'Sexy. Sweet. *Wild.*'

His eyes were smouldering, and her heart trembled at the intensity betrayed by his voice. Summoned by his mesmeric gaze, she felt overwhelmingly tempted to throw caution to the winds and melt back into his arms. Dimly her mind grappled with the awesome strength of the passion threatening to unleash itself in her. Had it always been there, or was it only when *he* touched her?

'I've thought of you so often since that night, dream girl,' he said thickly, reaching to twine a strand of her hair behind her ear. 'I've never met a woman like you.'

Dream girl! *Her?* But he was Samos Stilakos, and she was just... If he knew even the half of her ordinary old reality! No one had ever said anything so romantic to her, and, though he sounded sincere, how could he be believed? It was all happening too fast.

Unsure of how to respond, she backed a little away from him. 'Isn't it time for us to leave? For—for the restaurant?'

He blinked, but before he could make another move she excused herself as gracefully as she could, considering the strained breathlessness of her voice, swooped on her bag, and escaped to the guest bathroom.

Safe inside, she leaned back against the door and closed her eyes. *Dream girl.* The question had to be faced. Had he given her the job because she'd slept with him? And...because he wanted a repeat performance of that night? But he would have to remember her absolute rejection of an affair. He must.

Perhaps, though… An excitement there was no repressing uncoiled inside her. If there was a chance he was sincere, if that night was still as vivid to him as it was to her…

If he'd truly felt that deep connection, and craved *more*…

She hugged her arms tightly around her. There were reasons she mustn't succumb, she knew, but she needed time to recall them. Just a little time.

After a few moments of deep breathing, she recovered some semblance of sanity and came to a decision. If he did expect more she would have to remind him of her unshakeable stance on affairs, leave with stylish dignity and go straight home. Otherwise…well, otherwise, she'd just go with the flow and…go with the flow.

She washed and applied fresh make-up, and smeared her lips with moisturiser.

When she emerged Sam had slipped on a jacket, and held the car keys dangling from his lean fingers. The glance he gave her from beneath his dark brows was searching.

'Everything all right?' he enquired.

She smiled and arched her brows. 'Of course. Everything's fine.'

They didn't have far to drive to The Rocks. He parked the car in one of the small, private car parks converted from the old cellars of some adjoining buildings in the wharf area. As they climbed the stairs to the street he put a hand on her elbow to steady her, almost as a lover would, or a husband.

The restaurant he'd chosen was famous for its cuisine and glittering clientele. She made a covert survey of the room for famous faces, only to find numerous heads swivelling *their* way.

Their table was discreetly placed, perfect for a lover's tryst, or a quiet interrogation between boss and PA. 'Every man in this room envies me,' Sam murmured, with a gentle but possessive touch in the small of her back as the *maître d'* pulled out her chair.

She looked enquiringly at him, and her heart trembled at the warmth in his dark glance. 'Do you sweet-talk all your PAs so outrageously when you wine them and dine them?' she said, once they were settled and he'd ordered the wine.

Amusement glimmered in his eyes. 'I don't wine them and dine them.'

Questions clamoured in her brain. The evidence pointed another way. She needed to get things straight. Was she dining with him as a woman, or as his PA? 'But here you are,' she persevered, 'wining and dining *me*, sweet-talking me—'

'*Kissing* you.' His eyes darkened and he leaned forward, making her gasp as he traced her lower lip with a sensual fingertip. The bold desire in his eyes threatened to send her insides into meltdown all over again. 'How else am I to get to know you?'

Her heart bounded in her chest. Could she be hearing aright? Wasn't this the theme of her most extreme fantasy?

He sat back, a small frown creasing his brow. 'I know what's worrying you. It's tricky when office rules get tangled up with a genuine attraction. The important thing is not to let it get in the way.'

Her breath caught. 'The—the attraction?'

'No. The office.'

The words sank in. Samos Stilakos, worldly, sophisticated, gorgeous and elusive target for equally sophisticated, beautiful women, was spelling it out. To *her*.

'Do you believe in magic?' His warm, ardent gaze thrilled her. 'It might sound like a cliché, but what else can you call it when you meet someone—in the unlikeliest circumstances!—and instantly feel that rare connection?'

The breath caught in her throat. Hadn't this been her own instinct at their first encounter?

'What do you think?' he added, seduction in his dark eyes, in the smile playing on his sensuous mouth. 'Am I telling it like it is? Do you feel it too?'

Her lashes fluttered uncontrollably, much like her unsafe heart. Sweet talk had rarely been more convincing, or exciting. 'I think you're giving me the rush,' she said huskily, almost needing to cling to the table edge. 'I think you're making my head spin.'

'I hope so, Eleanor. I hope your head's spinning. You're not convincing me with that oh, so cool and collected act. Not when I know how hot the little siren is who's hiding behind that face.'

Visions rose in her mind of some of her unprecedented, adventurous acts of passion on the Night of Nights, and she couldn't prevent a fiery blush from rising up from her toes and infusing her entire body.

He grinned, as if the scorching scenes flashing through her mind were just as visible to him. Impossibly, she felt her blush deepen. In an attempt to cool her confusion she reached for her wine, took a much larger gulp than was wise and nearly choked.

Sam laughed and his lashes descended in satisfaction. 'Paydirt! Come on, then. I want to know everything about you. If you could have anything you wanted in the world, what would be your deepest, most fervent desire?'

She gazed at his lean, handsome face, smiling at her with such challenging warmth, and the truth resonated in her heart with a certainty that shook her to her soul.

Her chance to have a child, that was certain, but was that all? Didn't she want it the easy way? The old-fashioned, loving way? With someone she loved, who could love her?

Someone like…?

Her mind reared back from the unthinkable. Her lips parted, but no words came.

All her flippant protestations at Beth's warnings flashed before her now for the hollow bravado they had been. Who had she been kidding? She hadn't just taken the job for the money. She'd wanted to be close to him. How foolish and predictable. If she didn't fight it, the same old dreams would drive her to heartbreak now as inexorably as they had in the past. The next thing she knew, she'd be giving in to imagining floating down the aisle, visualising nights in the arms of her loving husband, dreaming of his beautiful, dark-eyed children…

'All right, let me guess,' he said. 'You'll never be happy until you're CEO of the bank. You want my job.' He spoke lightly, but all at once the question in his gaze was serious.

But if there was one certain thing her advanced years had taught her, it was how fast he'd vanish in a puff of smoke if she revealed the naked truth. So she deflected the query with an easy laugh. 'You're so right, Sam. How did you guess? And—and what would be your most fervent desire?'

His eyes veiled, and he lowered his black lashes. 'Ah…well…ordinary things. It's amazing how hard they are to come by, though, isn't it? You think you have them in your grasp, and then...' He shrugged and drained his glass.

What couldn't he come by easily? she wondered. A man as blessed as he'd been, with wealth, charm, genuine masculine beauty... Was he referring to Natalie?

'I often think now it would be good to live on an island,' he continued, 'without all the chaos, where life was simple.' He shrugged. 'There, that's probably my genes talking. My grandfather hailed from Samos, in the Aegean.' His eyes smiled into hers, and he reached across the table for her hand. 'I'll take you there one day, Eleanor, and show you.'

Such a beautiful promise. How many women had he made it to? But it enchanted her all the way down to her curled-up toes.

He told her other things, about his boyhood, his father, the mischief he and his cousin had got up to together. His words evoked a world of family life and good times, of beaches and bush picnics, far removed from the world he inhabited now. Despite her turmoil, she felt herself falling deeper under his spell. If only he wouldn't grin in that seriously weakening way. It was too easy to visualise the boy he must have been—the sweet, sexy, macho boy.

Perhaps she could risk one more time. Mightn't it be possible to have one more fling with him? One last fantastic night?

The waiter brought their meals, but she hardly noticed the food. She was too heavily in thrall to the most charming seducer in Sydney. But though he flattered her with his wicked words, there was sincerity in his gaze too, and warmth in his smile. His velvet eyes dwelled on her as if she were the most interesting and desirable woman in the world. She found herself telling him things about her life and her friends as if *he* were a friend. He flirted with her, mocked her and made her laugh, just as he had on that night.

All the time, though, it was clear where it was heading. The knowledge was in his every glance, in every brush of his fingers.

When they were offered the dessert menu, he said, 'Shall we stay here for dessert, or head somewhere else?' His mouth was grave, but the shimmer in his dark eyes was the colour of sin.

When had she ever resisted dessert?

CHAPTER SIX

Was he drunk, Sam wondered, or was it the summer night that made him want to leap and spin about in some crazy dance? Strolling the uneven streets beside Ellie O'Dea, he pretended to catch his shoe, and lingered back a step to drink in the radiance of her heavy fall of hair, the subtle sway of her taut little edible behind.

The image of her moonlit shape on the hotel balcony rushed back to him with its erotic power, and his blood stirred with the old enchantment. She cast him back an enquiring smile, a sparkle in her eyes as if she guessed his small subterfuge. He grinned and caught her up again. The chemistry was magic, he thought with escalating excitement, but still he sensed a tension in her, a restraint.

How did she manage to remain so elusive? He could gaze into those clear, smiling eyes till he drowned, but why did it feel as if she were still wearing her mask? Since the first, every step he took with her was a tread on eggshells. Any false move, and she might vanish into the night as easily as she'd slipped through his fingers on that fateful dawn.

They reached the entrance to the car park and he used his security key to unlock the street door. Despite their renovation, the fishy harbour smell still permeated the dank walls of the old cellars, and rose to greet him as they descended to the lower floor. The few other cars parked there earlier had departed, and only the Porsche remained. Their steps echoed in the empty place.

They reached the shadowy alcove where the car was parked, and stopped to face each other. In the sudden silence and isolation, Sam felt an urgency to break through the constraints. They'd been lovers once. They would be again. Why pretend?

He scanned her face and said, his voice catching with the force of his desire, 'Do you know how much I want you?'

In the shadowy light uncertainty swirled in her eyes as she searched his face. After a heartbeat's hesitation she said, 'No—yes. Perhaps.'

'Do you ever tell the truth?' In mock frustration, he wound a swathe of her hair around his hand, held it to his face and inhaled its honeyed scent. The intoxication of it, the memories it evoked, flooded him with lust, and he groaned. In his urgent need to pin her down he took her smooth, satin arms in his hands. 'You do know. We both know. Tell the truth. You haven't forgotten what it was like that night! You still want me!'

His passionate conviction swept Ellie along on a giddy, irresistible tide. With her pulse thundering in her ears, she confessed tremulously, 'No, Sam, I haven't forgotten. I want you.'

He held her a little closer. His deep voice, his dark eyes, were compelling. 'And we'll always be honest with each other. Lovers without lies. Do you agree?'

Lovers. On his tongue the word had such thrilling connotations she felt as if she'd been transported to some magic realm where everything was possible. Hope shivered down her spine.

'Hey.' Concern shone in his eyes. 'You're cold.' He slipped off his jacket and hung it around her shoulders.

The moment was so reminiscent of that first night, she was overwhelmed with the strongest sensation of *déjà vu*. He stood surveying her in it, his eyes growing more darkly intense and smoulderingly sexual, and her stomach coiled in excitement.

He pulled her against him and kissed her with hungry passion. His insistent lips demanded her equal response, and she surrendered to the sizzling assault and gave in, kissing him back with fervour as the ready fire ignited in her blood.

Her knees weakened, and she raised her arms around his neck, clutching at his thick black hair, heedless of the damp pungent smells of harbour and wet cement in the old converted cellar.

The element of risk in their dark corner reminded her of the forbidden flavour of their first embrace. She remembered how they'd urged each other on to greater and greater acts of abandonment, and it induced her to throw caution to the winds. She wanted him to do more than kiss her, and he seemed to know it.

He pushed her back against the car, his mouth on her throat and collar-bone, his lean, bronzed hands caressing her swollen breasts, seeking the taut nipples, inflaming them through her clothes.

He lowered his dark head, and through the light fabric took first one, then the other sensitive peak in his mouth to suck and tease. It brought her to such an intense pitch of wild, sweet pleasure that her desire roared through her like a firestorm and flamed between her thighs.

But their clothes were in the way. With feverish hands she tore at his shirt buttons and revealed his powerful, bronzed chest. Then, with hands and mouth, she explored the rippling satin skin with its whorls of black hair. She felt his flat nipples tauten under her tongue, relishing her power to send pleasure shuddering through his big, strong frame.

Panting, she stood back to enjoy the sight of him in disarray, his gorgeous chest gleaming from his open shirt, his breath tearing and catching like hers, his eyes dark and heavy-lidded in arousal.

She wanted more.

Instinctively, as though attuned to her hunger, he pushed up her dress and laid her thighs bare. 'Such charming thighs,' he murmured, his voice gravelled, eyes black as Lucifer's.

She waited, panting, for his next move. She felt as if she were on fire, her body a vessel of desire, his every light touch a match to the flame of her overheated flesh. He placed a caressing hand on her knee, then, with tantalising slowness, traced a wicked, purposeful finger up her leg, slipping it inside her inner thigh to tease the silken, sensitive skin there. With charged fingers he stroked closer, and ever deliciously closer, to the hot, urgent place concealed by her flimsy little panties.

She dug her fingers into his powerful shoulders, and held her breath, her heart's blood thundering in her ears, aching, aching for him to go the whole way. At the elastic's edge, his caressing hand paused for an electric, tingling instant, then, when suspense brought her nearly to breaking-point, crept on, to traverse the fabric across her vibrant mound. She clung to him, unbreathing, hypnotised by the dark magic of his touch.

He slipped his fingers underneath the fabric, and she quivered and gasped in delight. With sensual, knowing strokes he parted her sensitive folds while she leaned back against the car, half clinging to him in swooning ecstasy, on fire for him to find the pulsating pleasure spot at the centre. He made contact and she gave a small, wrenching cry. Tenderly, expertly he caressed her throbbing clitoris, then slipped a finger inside her slick, moist channel and stroked, rousing her with astonishing speed to a sweet, sobbing climax.

She sagged against him, supported in his arms, her face buried in his strong neck. He held her there for some heart-thundering moments, then tilted her back and brushed her face with quick little tender kisses. After a few seconds he let her go, and they contemplated each other in the pulsing silence.

Her heart thudded. Challenge gleamed in his fierily aroused eyes. Instinctively she understood the question. How far did she dare to go with him? In tacit response she ran her tongue-tip over her dry lips, then gasped with shock as in a quick, wicked movement he whipped down her pants.

His audacity exhilarated her. The element of danger pushed her passion and excitement to an even wilder pitch. Spurred to respond, she grasped his belt buckle and released it, and heard his sharp intake of breath as she slid her hand down to caress the promising virile bulge inside his trousers.

'Quickly, quickly,' she panted, and tried to help him to ease the zip down over his erection.

He gave a strangled laugh, and pushed her hands away to free himself unaided. With wide-eyed anticipation, she surveyed his impressive arousal, rock-hard and rampant.

He swept her onto his lap as he lowered himself onto the car's bonnet, and, with swift efficiency, positioned her so she was face to face with him.

She gave a sensual little wriggle, then levered herself to ease down on him, gasping with delight as his velvet hardness filled her. Then, holding her tight in his arms, his chest grazing her breasts, he rocked her, gazing into her eyes as he thrust repeatedly into her. In an escalating rhythm, he stroked her inner flesh, completely filling her sheath with such delicious, heavenly vigour, she could only cry out with each amazing plunge.

The sweetness and intensity of being held and gazed at and rocked with such thrilling intimacy rushed her up a wild, steep curve of gasping excitement, to an explosive, rippling climax.

After the last rapturous aftershock they stilled, gazes meshed in a primitive communion. At last the distant sound of voices from the street jolted them from their pleasure. Sam eased her onto her feet. Shakily, she scrambled to tidy her clothes, while he refastened his.

He stared at her, his breathing ragged as he surveyed her panting dishevelment. 'Let's go home,' he murmured, and opened the car door and ushered her inside.

He settled in beside her and bent to softly kiss her mouth. When he drew back she touched his face. She felt wrapped in a cocoon of blissful accord with him, knowing she was able to match his need for passion and excitement, as he matched hers.

'Not the place I would have chosen,' he murmured in his deep voice, his hand possessive on her thigh. 'We'll do better next time. Where do you live?'

'Hornsby.'

'Hornsby! My God,' he groaned, then fired the engine. After he nosed the car out into the street, he gave her an intense, glowing look. 'Has anyone ever told you what a beautiful and exciting, *sensual* woman you are?'

'You did,' she answered huskily. 'On the night of the masked ball.' He laughed a husky laugh, and, secure in the warmth of his admiration, she stayed enveloped in her dreamy, magical cocoon all the way to Hornsby.

It wasn't so far, now the night-time traffic had diminished a little. After a while her breathing calmed and she fell silent. The silence pulsed with the anticipation of more passion to come.

Sam occasionally glanced her way to make some observation, but she was barely aware of the Sydney nightscape. She was thinking about what would happen next. About making love with him again. In her bed.

Samos Stilakos. In her bedroom.

She made a mental review of the room, trying to visualise him in it. She hoped she'd made her bed. After the luxury of his sky-palace she wondered what he would think of rugs picked up cheap from the Taj Bazaar, and cushions embroidered by her mother's tapestry circle. It was hard to imagine him in her flat. She had the unpleasant realisation that it would declare, far more stridently than words ever could, the inequalities between the Boss and his PA.

What if one of her friends drove by and saw the Porsche? How would it look to them? The romantic cloud she was floating on lost a bit of height. A nasty little voice from her daily down-to-earth self piped up. What had he actually said to her that meant anything? Had she just allowed herself to be carried away?

'You'd better direct me from here,' he said in his deep, quiet voice.

She started, realising how close they were, and with a racing pulse gave him some directions that brought them into the entrance of her street. 'Along here, on the left.' She almost wished she could tell him to turn around and go in the opposite direction.

She swallowed. 'That's it there. The duplex.'

Her heart seized then as she was struck by the most horrible thought.

Hadn't she left all that stuff she'd downloaded about the IVF process on the kitchen table? *And* there were coloured brochures from the clinics.

She blenched at the thought of him seeing them. How much would it reveal about her? Her failure to find a partner in time. Her *desperation*…? A man with his razor-sharp intelligence would put two and two together and comprehend it all.

Perspiration broke out on her upper lip. She couldn't invite him in.

She dug her fingers into her palms. It would be too much to hope he'd had enough loving for one night. Even if he didn't want to make love again, he'd expect her to ask him in for coffee.

Her heart began to thump with the most ridiculous, erratic rhythm, and she uncurled her hands and surreptitiously put them to her cheeks. What had she done? She'd asked for this. She'd got herself into it, and now there was no graceful way out.

He drew up under the streetlamp in front of her gate and turned off the engine. The silence grew electric. She sat taut and still in her seat, tension gripping her throat.

He turned his head to examine her with a questioning gaze. She knew what he expected.

What she'd led him to expect.

He thought she would take him through her front door, lead him to her bedroom, take him into her bed. Or at least show him into her kitchen and sit him down at the table, with a coffee mug filled with instant.

He smiled and touched her cheek, his dark eyes warm. 'Is coffee on offer?'

Her eyelids lowered. How could she refuse? 'Of course.' She forced a smile.

His brows twitched curiously as he studied her face, but he sprang out and swiftly came around to open her door. She got out, and, with his arm around her, walked through the gate and up the path with him, every step a step closer to mortification, her brain teeming with desperate measures.

She would have to make him promise on his honour not to read anything. Or he'd have to promise not to go into the kitchen. But what if she'd left the literature on her bedside table? That was a real possibility. If she had, what were the chances he'd be able to avoid it?

There was only one solution.

No way, *no way* could she let him in, and she would have to find a compelling reason.

They arrived at her front door, and the security lamp switched itself on. She delved into her bag for the keys, but her shaking hands were ineffectual. After a hectic few moments, Sam took the bag from her hands, held it to his ear and gave it a shake. He plunged his hand in, and with a couple of deft movements produced the keys. 'Is this them?'

She nodded.

He handed them to her, murmuring, 'One of the few worthwhile things a man derives from a marriage. The ability to find a woman's keys.'

She slipped the key into the lock, then turned to face him, her back to the door. She cleared her throat. 'Look. About the coffee, Sam—' Her voice was embarrassingly strained.

He searched her face. 'You're out of coffee?' He smiled, desire smouldering in his eyes. 'What is it? You don't want to invite me in, is that it?'

She'd thought of a reason. Still, her heart pounded like a coward's to use it. 'I can't,' she said. 'Not—not tonight. Not like this.'

'Like what?'

She made an inarticulate gesture. 'Like—the way we are.'

His dark gaze scanned her face. 'How are we?'

'I like you very much, of course—'

He laughed, but his eyes were watchful. 'I'd hope so, after what just happened.'

She flushed, intensely conscious of her wanton compliance a bare half-hour before. 'Yes, yes, I know, but—' she steeled herself '—you're my boss.'

The silence missed a heavy beat. 'So?'

With trepidation she realised that a rejection now would go hard, but anything was better than risking him seeing those brochures. She took a deep breath, and asserted with only a slight tremor in her voice, 'I work for you. It's not exactly a free and open relationship, is it?'

Somewhere underneath her bravado her heart was still madly thumping. She studied him suspensefully, her hands clenched.

He shook his head and blinked in disbelief. 'Let me get this straight. You're bringing *this* down to office politics?'

The stunned question in his eyes, and the tone of his voice, made it sound as if he believed that what was happening between them was something very special and romantic. She was swayed with sudden doubt. There had been those moments, compelling moments, when she'd believed in his sincerity, those tiny glimpses into his real self.

Shame threatened her certainty. The word *betrayal* popped into her head.

'Oh, well,' she faltered confusedly, 'isn't it a matter of ethics?'

Samos Stilakos made a searing intake of breath. His eyebrows shot up and he stared at her. 'What? You're telling *me* about—?' He straightened up to his full height and reeled back a step, as if his very honour had suffered a mortal wound. His eyes turned to jet. For an instant his strong, handsome face was frozen in outrage.

Then he met her paralysed gaze and made a visible effort to recover his control.

Guilt began to flood through her, but after a few heart-stopping seconds he merely shook his head and shrugged. If he was enraged at such an insult, he summoned formidable restraint to conceal it.

Why did he have to be such a gentleman? It made her excuse all the weaker.

'So it's goodnight, then,' he said, back to being polite after the warmth and intimacy of the evening. He searched her face with a frown, then shrugged again and turned away from her, his eyes as chill and remote as the polar icecap.

She felt punished. It was as if the sun had gone out.

Irrationally then, she wished he could at least kiss her goodnight. 'I'm sorry, Sam,' she said nervously before he could walk down the path and leave her alone. 'No hard feelings. Won't you at least—shake hands?'

He turned. The glance he shot her from beneath his sardonic brows pierced her as if she were transparent, right through to her marshmallow spine. It was deeply discomfiting. 'Would this be about the *adventurer*, by any chance?' he said drily.

She gasped, momentarily struck speechless, and shook her head in utter, absolute rejection. 'Wh-what?' she stuttered. 'What are you talking about! No! As if *he*— As if *that*—' She took a deep breath. '*That* has nothing to do with *this*.' Anger made her unusually reckless, and she started to talk very rapidly, her words nearly falling over each other in her need to defend herself. 'If you must know I'm wondering about the others,' she blustered, with a defiant glare. 'You know Schanelle, Vanessa, Sasha…' She waved her hand about agitatedly to indicate the dozens, probably thousands of women he'd seduced and forgotten, but when she saw his expression her heart shuddered to a halt. 'Everyone knows what happened with them,' she squeezed out.

His eyes had turned as hard as stone, his mouth a grim, straight line. She felt more than a bit frightened. For once she'd really lost her cool.

He said in a clipped, level voice, 'Sasha left because her fiancé was transferred to Brisbane. Schanelle got a better job offer in the Prime Minister's department in Canberra. Vanessa lost her position because she'd falsified her qualifications and wasn't up to the job.'

'Oh.' There was no mistaking the authority of the

words. She sagged back against the door, aghast at the fool she'd made of herself. 'Oh. Oh, I'm sorry. I shouldn't have said— Sam…'

'Forget it,' he said coldly. 'You were right. *This* would be wrong. My mistake, Ms O'Dea. I apologise for harassing you.' He swung sharply on his heel and walked away.

She didn't watch him leave. She turned her face to the door. As her key turned in the lock she heard the gate click shut. It cut through her with a lonely, final sound.

She nearly fell into the hall, tripping over a pile of rubbish just inside the door. She kicked it aside and hit the light switch. Numbly, she stumbled to the kitchen.

A jumble of indigestible emotions seized her, so intense she could have screamed. She noticed the muddle of papers and booklets scattered across the table, and swiped them to the floor. Then she thought better of it, picked them up, tore them into frantic little pieces and thrust them into the bin.

This was the time for alcohol. But she never kept the stuff in her flat, and had to resort to warming milk in the microwave. She drank a few sips, then made for the shower, taking care not to look at herself in any mirror along the way.

She felt as if something huge and jagged had lodged in her chest. It wasn't until she emerged from the bathroom clean, scrubbed and pyjamaed, her hair in a pony-tail, prepared for a final check of the locks, that she noticed the rubbish in the hall.

It had been a pile of bags and boxes delivered by courier, no doubt neatly stacked inside by her kindly next-door neighbour, who must have used the emergency key she held. Now it was a dishevelled mess, boxes with their lids off, tissue-swathed fabrics spilling out, shoes she could never have afforded, skewed across the floor.

She recognised them all, of course. They were the other things she'd tried on today that she'd liked. They amounted to a fortune's worth. How could a man so concerned with the bank's bottom line be so generous?

Then with sudden anger she thought, how dared he do this? How dared he not accept her refusal? What sort of man could not take *no* for an answer?

Long into the restless night, as she tossed in her empty bed her brain churned with the answers. *Arrogant, domineering, controlling, underhanded, cunning...*

She kept remembering that humiliating moment when he'd looked at her as if he could see right through to her very soul. The sheer, infuriating gall of it.

What could a man like *him* know about a woman like *her*?

CHAPTER SEVEN

SAM groaned and rolled over.

A minute later he was on his feet, dragging on gym shoes, shorts and singlet. A brisk run through the dawn streets of the old city was often the most pleasant start to the day, but not this day. This day required a punishing routine in the basement gym, followed by a stiff workout in the pool.

By the time he'd showered and shaved, donned an impeccably laundered shirt and tied his silk tie, he'd worked out a sane approach. He'd tell her succinctly that any personal association between them was in the past. He'd make it clear he had a bank to run and would not tolerate the distractions of feminine behaviour. He'd offer her a transfer...

Though what if she took it up?

No. He doubted she would. Where would she find conditions to equal what she had?

But as for the *personal* front...

In the Sirius basement he used his pass-key for the lift. As the lift drew closer to his floor the recollection of her astounding behaviour grew sharper and more stinging. Ellie O'Dea would learn he was not a man desperate for

the company of beautiful women. The world was awash
with redheads more beautiful.

More honest. More open, more straightforward.

More receptive. More compliant.

More *grateful* to have been offered the opportunity of
enjoying an entire night with a virile and sensitive lover.
If she only knew the desperate lengths some women had
gone to to catch his eye. Actresses. *Models.*

Contrary to what he'd expected, and had carefully
primed himself for, she wasn't at her desk, and there was
no sign of her having arrived and gone off somewhere.

He frowned. Excellent. That gave him more time to
concentrate on the important matters of the day.
Although... She wouldn't have taken the day off,
would she? Or...

A paralysing thought struck him. What if she'd
decided against coming back at all?

Ellie woke late. She knew Sam would have been expecting her to be there before him, but after the heavy night
she found it impossible to hurry.

Her hair took ages to dry, it wouldn't twirl neatly into
its roll, and in the end, in desperation, she left it down. When
it came to dressing she remembered that her better business
suit was in Sam's car and the other at the cleaner's.

It was an emergency. She had her pride to consider. A
woman in her situation couldn't, just couldn't, face the man
again in nasty old clothes. There was only one thing for it.

On the way in to work she took a detour.

At David Jones it was early in the shoppers' day, and
there were few others to contend with. Knowing instinctively this was not a battle that could be won with inferior

weapons, she bypassed the floor of cheaper brands to head straight for the designer section.

Driven by the clock, she had to make her choice quickly. The first thing that called to her was a slim black dress. It was chic and feminine, with small cap sleeves in black embroidered tulle, and a price tag she'd have gasped at only a day earlier. With her rich red hair and white skin it looked stunning. She agonised over it for several uncertain minutes. No one had ever shown up at work in such a dress. She'd have to adjust her IVF timeline. Was a job worth so much sacrifice?

Yes! The answer rang in her head like a bell.

The saleswoman looked doubtful when Ellie said she'd prefer to keep it on and wear it to work, but she'd made her decision. It made a hole in her savings account, but she paid for it with barely a flinch.

It was only when she left the shop that she allowed herself to acknowledge the knot in her chest connected with Sam. Every step closer to the bank was an ordeal, but if she could just get past this one difficult day with him...

By the time she arrived the building was humming. People she passed stared and said, 'Ellie! *Amazing* dress,' and she smiled as though it were a normal day and everything was fine. Not that she was nervous. Not exactly. He would be as courteous as ever, she felt sure. That was the hard thing about him. He could be polite and freeze people to death, even when he wasn't sacking them.

It was past ten when she stepped out on her floor. Almost time for his coffee. She dropped her bag beside her desk, and hurried to put the milk she'd bought in the fridge.

Inside, at his executive rosewood desk, Sam heard the

sounds of arrival. He tensed, and glanced at his desk-clock with narrowed eyes.

Let her explain *this*.

He rose, adjusted belt and tie, and strolled to the door with the commanding, panther-like stride of Company Director and Chief Executive Officer.

She had her back to him, organising the espresso machine. Straight away he noticed she had her hair out again, hanging like a rich, silken waterfall. At the sound of the opening door she turned, and his insides were blown away.

Black. The dress was black. And above the lacy bodice the hint of her breasts glowed pearlescent white, like satin. And her legs. Her endless, endless legs. And surely her mouth was fuller and riper after last night's kissing? And her eyes, glittering like some— Dammit, he had to get a grip. Hadn't he learned? That glittering quality meant she was calculating something.

He said brusquely, 'You're late.'

Ellie heard the accusation in his tone and flushed. 'I know. I'm sorry. I was held up.' She saw his mouth thin, and hastened to placate him. 'I— Would you like some coffee?'

His expression froze. She realised the ghastliness of what she'd said and her heart plunged. For a horrified moment she hung there speechless, then pulled herself together to say faintly, 'Are you ready for—?'

He cut her off with a cool rejoinder. 'I've had coffee, thanks. Have you remembered the managers' meeting at ten-thirty?'

'Yes. Yes, of course.'

Damn. She'd forgotten it, but she still had ten minutes left in which to set up the boardroom. She'd already prepared illustrated take-home booklets for the managers, to support the presentation she'd helped Sam put together. At least she had no need to be ashamed of her work. She'd put a lot into it, and the booklet was a classy little production.

Sam strode away, and Ellie hurried to the boardroom. She placed the stack of booklets in a safe place for distribution at the end of the meeting, while she checked the audio-vis equipment, and set out the requisite stationery and mineral water on the oval table.

The managers began to trickle in, most of them greeting her with the easy familiarity of long acquaintance.

'What's this about a crèche in the building?'

With a jolt of alarm, Ellie saw that Trevor from Sales had spotted the booklets she'd prepared, and taken one to his place. 'Don't tell me we're doing an about-face and changing into a sensitive New Age bank,' he complained, idly flicking through it.

She was about to dive over and snatch it off him when Margot from Product Assessments, who still wore big eighties hair, leaned over to squint at it. 'Where'd you get this?' She perused the page, raising her Elizabeth Taylor eyebrows. 'Show me where it mentions the crèche.'

The manager on Trevor's left wanted to see as well, and in a short space of time several of them were loudly debating the pros and cons of having a childcare facility on the premises.

Ellie watched in apprehension, fearful of Sam arriving while they were talking about it. At any other time she'd have been delighted by their interest. She'd had a vague hope that, by including the research she'd gathered so the managers could take it away with them, the idea of a bank-funded nursery to support working mothers might grow, and have a trickle-up effect. It had been a momentary impulse to slip the page in. She'd half intended to slip it out again before the meeting, but yesterday's tumultuous events had completely wiped it from her mind.

The trouble was, Sam hadn't exactly approved her initiative. In fact, he wasn't aware of it.

'Well, it would have made all the difference to me in my day,' Margot told her colleagues. 'I could have kept coming to work. *I'd* have been the CEO by now. Instead, I had this dreadful struggle to keep going, and in the end it was easier to just stay at home with the twins and raise them poor. Good on you, Sam.'

Ellie looked around in alarm from where she was adjusting the screen. Sam had just walked in. Margot's rather penetrating voice immediately caught his attention, and to Ellie's horror he strolled over to her. He frowned and bent to look at the page they were all poring over. Ellie heard him say, 'A what? Where does it say that?'

With her heart in her throat, she watched Sam pick up the booklet. He leaned casually on a side table to scan it, then raised his eyes. From across the room his accusing gaze lasered to clash with hers. The enormity of what she'd done resounded in her head, and she felt the guilt rise to her cheeks in flaming neon. But pride wouldn't allow her to lower her eyes to a man who'd called her his dream girl and made frenzied love to her. Though blistered from head to toe, she held his gaze.

A cover story. For God's sake, why couldn't her fertile brain deliver? She was still racking her brains for one when her old ex-boss, Stephen Fletcher, swanned in.

'Hello all,' Fletcher said, dumping his briefcase,

somehow not noticing Sam at the other end of the room. Then, beaming and holding out his hands, 'Ellie, my love.' He made a big production of looking her over and whistling. 'Now, don't you look scrumptious?' He swung a portly arm around her and gave her a hug. 'Still running the bank? From the top now, eh?'

'*Fletcher.*'

The deep, brusque voice fractured the air like a whiplash. Fletcher started away from her as if he'd been shot, and conversations dribbled to a close. All heads turned.

Samos Stilakos had taken his power position at the front. In his elegant dark suit, his imposing height, powerful shoulders and strong masculine eyebrows emphasised his authority. 'If you wouldn't mind taking your hands off Ms O'Dea…' He spoke coolly, but his imperious eyes held dagger points. He pointed Fletcher to a vacant chair. 'Sit. Please.'

The *please* was an obvious afterthought.

Poor Fletcher's face crumpled. An embarrassed hush fell on the assembled group.

Sam nodded forbiddingly towards Ellie. 'Eleanor. The doors.'

She strolled to close them as casually as she could, sensing his gaze follow her every move from beneath his bristling brows. When she slipped into her own chair, she couldn't restrain herself from sending him a scathing glance for his treatment of her old boss.

Despite an icy look in return, Sam delivered his presentation in a relaxed style, like the professional he was. It went over well with the managers, who hadn't warmed to him when he'd first taken over the bank and cut so many of their perks. Now they applauded him, appreciating at last that they had a competent and dynamic leader at the helm.

He hardly looked her way, although a few times she had the definite sense he wanted to, but when he did flick her a glance his chiselled mouth was stern, his eyes coolly unreadable. He'd never looked more handsome. More smoulderingly sexy.

She kept her spine stiff, hyper-conscious of the things she'd said to him. Why should she feel so guilty? *He* should be guilty. It wasn't as if he'd said he loved her, was it? So why did she have to feel this huge, unswallowable lump in her chest?

What right did a man have to demand honesty from a woman anyway, just because he'd said a few romantic things?

He directed some occasional comments to her. They were smoothly polite, even considerate, on the surface. Only she could detect the biting under-edge. Once, when she reached for the water, several of the men sprang to assist her but Sam interrupted his talk to smoothly swoop on the carafe first. He poured her a glass and handed it to her with extreme courtesy, taking care not to touch her fingers.

Briefly their eyes clashed, his glinting, perhaps with some memory of a similar moment last night. Unless… Her unquiet blood stirred. Could he have been thinking of the car park? Was the potent scene still as raw in his senses as it was in hers—their greedy kisses, their avid lips and hands?

She fought the image off with a little shiver. It was ironic. The managers seemed more at ease with him than ever before, though that only made it worse. Before they broke up, to her horror someone felt confident enough to revive the discussion about the on-site crèche. Too clever not to recognise its value as an ice-breaker, Sam allowed the topic to continue, sitting seemingly relaxed, his lean, tanned hands lightly resting on the table.

Hands that had caressed her. Hands even now she wanted to reach out and touch.

The pros and cons of small babies in childcare were being robustly canvassed.

Sam listened to the debate with half an ear. His glance fell on *her*, a couple of simmering metres across from him, black lace at her breast, her long hair catching the light. She appeared to be listening attentively, but there was a rigidity in her posture. He grimaced. *Let* her be nervous. As though sensing his scrutiny, she angled her face away from him. The distinctive tilt of her head, the curve of her cheek, grabbed at something in his chest.

His jaw tightened. She was a mystery.

Ellie forced herself not to glance at him, though super-imposed on her brain was the recurring image of his stunned face at her front door. So she'd used a convenient lie. What else could she have done? Would he have enjoyed a heart-to-heart about her ovaries?

She made an effort to tune into the discussion. One of the firm's old dinosaurs was opposed to mothers working in any circumstances and had aroused a storm of debate.

'We need a younger woman's point of view,' Margot asserted, looking around. 'What do you think, Ellie? Could you imagine bringing your baby to work with you?'

Ellie's heart froze. All eyes turned on her, including Sam's. She had the sensation of her stomach dropping several storeys. This was the last thing—the *last* thing—she could discuss in his presence. In other circumstances she'd have loved to run this discussion, with these very same people, and knew she could do it well. But not in front of Sam. Not—for God's sake—after last night.

She avoided his eyes, in dread of seeing his lip curl, but still she felt his burning gaze sear her face like an oxy-acetylene torch. Oblivious to the undercurrents, the managers were fired up to persuade her to their points of view. Unknown to them, every word they said wounded her tender sensibility like napalm.

'Ellie won't want to work if she has a baby, will you, Ellie? She'll want to stay home and look after the kid properly, like any decent mother.'

'Rubbish, Gary,' Margot said testily. 'Women have the right to work. Ellie's a career girl through and through. She won't want to give it up for nappies and milky vomit. She'll go for having it all, won't you, Ellie? The job *and* the family.'

'Why can't her husband support her until the child goes to school?'

'He mightn't have a job. *She* might be the breadwinner.'

'It wouldn't work to bring a baby here,' someone growled. 'Too much distraction from the job. She'd be better off to put the kid in a nursery down the street.'

The arguments grew even more excruciating.

'But what if she wants to breast-feed?'

'Then she shouldn't have a baby unless she's in a position to do it.'

The discussion raged. All the way through it she could feel the weight of Sam's scrutiny burning a pathway into her quivering soul. Finally one of them stopped arguing long enough to notice her frozen silence. 'Look at poor Ellie. Here we are grilling her when she hasn't even begun to think of babies yet. Give the girl a break.'

The combined forces of all their eyes turned on her again.

Panic gripped her throat. She knew what they were all thinking. They were assessing her age, speculating about her love-life and her diminishing chances. Her ovaries were in the spotlight. In a moment some wit would mention the biological clock, and tell her to get a move on and find Mr Right.

It was the career girl's worst nightmare.

Normally, when public exposure or boss trouble threatened, she could summon a serene smile and handle it with aplomb. But right then she couldn't. For once she experienced performance failure. Her face felt stiff, and she knew her eyes were glassy.

She managed to push herself up on her high heels, and say with jerky dignity, 'If you'll all excuse me, there are some things I have to do.' With a bright, unfocused smile around at the assembly, she walked swiftly from the room, closed the door behind her and sprinted like an Olympic athlete for the Ladies.

After a few drastic minutes of hyperventilation—in lieu of a paper bag she had to bunch up a paper towel and pant into that—she dashed cold water on her face, and tried to pat it dry without disturbing her make-up. This was the worst day of her life so far, and she'd brought it all on herself. Her small effort to improve entitlements for the bank's workforce had blown up in her face.

She couldn't bear to imagine what Sam was thinking of her after she'd so seriously betrayed his trust. And how mortifying, how utterly humiliating, that he'd witnessed her crumble like that. How much had he guessed about her? Her soul screamed with embarrassment. She felt ready to burrow a hole in the tiles and bury herself there.

That a man, a sexual partner, a l—she shied from the L word—should see her in the light of a desperate spinster.

It took some heavy-duty slow, concentrated breathing to bring her pulse-rate back to a point approaching normal, so she could start to think.

She had to face it. She was definitely in the wrong over that booklet. The knowledge was unbearable, but how to right herself in his eyes? Her usual tactic of a sincere explanation with a lorryload of charm hardly seemed adequate this time. How would she justify *this*?

And after last night, the issue was so complicated. Shouldn't she apologise, just this once? Throw herself on his mercy, show him she had a conscience about insulting him and hurting his feelings? Crawl on her hands and knees to beg his forgiveness?

She left the sanctuary of the ladies' room with a half-formed plan of humbly admitting she was at fault, grovelling, and somehow appealing to his sense of fairness to leave the events of last night out of the equation.

As she approached the entrance to her office a burst of laughter reached her from the hall. With a jealous pang, she saw it was the group of managers, congregating in front of the lifts, exchanging what sounded like light-hearted banter with Sam. Judging by the approving glances they were giving him, rapport had been established. They were all basking in the sunshine of his smile. Even Fletcher looked to have been charmed into the fold.

She'd never felt so excluded in her life. She made the painful acknowledgement to herself that she'd do anything to have Sam smile at her like that again.

He caught sight of her and his face smoothed to become expressionless. 'Oh, there you are.' He detached himself from his worshippers and strode purposefully towards her. 'Come in here.' He opened his office door. 'We need to talk.'

She accompanied him tremulously, some weak part of her longing to abase herself, kiss his gorgeous bronzed feet and ankles and beg forgiveness, but another, stronger part knowing it was a mistake to ever acknowledge to a boss that he had the upper hand.

He halted in the middle of the room and confronted her, his lean, handsome face stern, his sensuous mouth compressed. He was quite close to her, as the crow flew, but somehow the small distance between them was sharply defined, like an unbridgeable chasm. Unfortunately, her body didn't understand what her mind knew, and surged with shameless longing for him to touch her.

'We need to get some things straight,' he said. 'Are you on the pill?'

She blenched. 'What?'

His sardonic brows lifted. 'Oh, it's the innocent maiden routine.'

She flinched as from a physical blow.

His dark eyes flickered over her in merciless condemnation as he said softly, 'Let me remind you, Eleanor, that you had unprotected sex last night. In a car park. I find it hard to believe that any woman, even a woman prone to screwing in such casual venues, wouldn't be alive to the risks.'

Her sensibilities felt savaged, but feminine honour demanded she defend herself. 'The possibilities of infection, do you mean?' she countered coldly. 'Yes, I am aware of it, and I intend to have a medical check at the first opportunity.'

A muscle tightened in his jaw and she knew she'd scored.

'I can take it, then, you are using a contraceptive?' His

eyes were unfriendly. 'Considering that little discussion you took it upon yourself to engineer, it seemed reasonable to assume when you exited like that…a panicked gazelle springs to mind…that you might be fearful of being pregnant.'

She gave him a cold smile. 'I'm not fearful. There's no need to concern yourself.'

It was true. Pregnancy was probably the only thing left in life she wasn't concerned about. It was only two months since she'd given up using the pill, and with her ovaries, the chances of her conceiving so soon, if ever, were infinitesimal. Possibly non-existent.

'I can assure you,' she added sweetly, '*you* have nothing to worry about.'

She could tell by Sam's wintry expression the insinuation hadn't been lost on him. Anger flared in his eyes, and for a moment she thought he might seize her.

Goaded, Sam felt his hands twitch. He read the flash of uncertainty in her blue eyes, and clenched them to his sides. Touching her was now forbidden. With frustration he surveyed her slender form in the slim dress, her long legs fragilely balanced on the precarious shoes.

Her skin had never looked so meltingly soft and delicate as it did against the black lace trim. That white swell of breast just visible at the bodice was fatally desirable, or *would* have been if… He felt rising wrath. Where did a woman learn to be so unpredictable, so stubbornly intent on twisting things her way, so *difficult*?

Dammit, he was a man and he was in charge.

'My only concern is for your health and well-being,' he snapped. 'I wanted to assure you that, should a messy situation occur, you would be taken care of.'

Ellie wondered who would do the care-taking. Would he go with her himself, or send his chauffeur, or his housekeeper? 'I can imagine,' she said with heavy irony.

His eyes flashed, and he said very quietly, '*I* can only imagine what sort of men you've been with in the past, Eleanor, that you have such a low regard for them.'

She wanted to cover her face to protect herself from the shaming insults raining down on her. Instead she turned away from him. 'Is that all you wanted to say?'

'That's only the beginning.' He strolled right around her to plant his big, powerful frame in front of her and force her to look at him. 'I'd like to remind you that you aren't in control of this bank. What's more, this is a *bank*, not a testing ground for women's social agendas. Whatever your bosses tolerated from you in the past, for the pleasure of looking at you every day, won't be tolerated in this office. *I* am in control here.'

She gasped at the insult, but this was so much more the kind of fight she could handle. Her adrenaline surged and, along with it, her courage. Courage to justify, justify, justify!

'Of course I know you're in charge,' she said in a shocked, wounded tone, and added with quick sincerity, 'I can explain what happened, Sam. I knew how keen you were to find an issue that would bring the managers on-side. The crèche idea seemed ideal, being so controversial to their old-fashioned ways of thinking, without personally threatening any of them, and just the sort of thing you would choose yourself. I had intended to run it by you yesterday, but with all that happened—' Her voice grew huskier as an involuntary flashback to the car park nearly melted her defiance. 'It—it—I'm afraid it completely slipped my mind.'

She flashed a glance at him, but there was no soften-ing in the severe lines of his chiselled, sexy mouth. She dropped her lashes and made a conciliatory gesture. 'Perhaps you're right. The idea might be just a bit too— *out* there for this bank.'

It was a subtle shot, and she could tell it registered by the way his eyes glinted. She followed it up with an ap-pealing gaze through her lashes. 'You did say you liked PAs to show initiative. I suppose I must have misunder-stood what that meant.'

His eyes chilled to ice. 'That is not the issue here.' He whisked the ball from her hands by stating with relentless accuracy, 'This is about a breach of trust, isn't it, Eleanor?'

The blood rushed to her face as if she'd been slapped.

'And there is the little matter of dress. Since when have you felt the need to come to work dressed like a tart?'

She gasped, but he went on inexorably. 'I may not know everything about fashion, but it's obvious to me that dress isn't appropriate for the workplace. It looks like something you should be wearing with a suspender belt and lace-topped stockings. Why aren't you wearing a suit?'

She said stiffly, 'My suit is in the Porsche.'

He paused. 'Oh. The Porsche.' For a moment the space between them simmered. She had visions of his hot hands on her thighs, her rapid panting breath, their urgent coupling in the pungent, salty air.

His eyes darkened and he turned abruptly away from her. 'It would be a mistake to try to capitalise on anything that happened between us out of working hours. I don't want a secretary who advertises her charms. I expect my PA to be a role-model of modesty and elegance to the re-mainder of the workforce.'

She bristled with indignation. Her beautiful dress *was* modest and elegant. She thought of the hole in her hard-won savings, what that meant now to her precious timeline, all the little deprivations ahead, the waiting, the sheer sacrifice, and rebellion boiled up in her. 'This,' she snapped, 'is an extremely expensive dress by a world-famous Australian designer. It's a work of art. It even has its own title.'

He turned to sweep her with a gaze of satiric amusement. 'Really. And what title would that be?'

Her blood pressure jumped a couple of notches, but she said coolly enough, 'It's called Flirty Noir.'

'Forgive me. A *French* tart.'

The insufferable mockery stung, but still she hung onto her temper. 'Other people like it.'

His eyes flared dangerously. '*Other* people. You mean Fletcher. And the rest of your fan club who couldn't keep their eyes off you. Ogling you at every chance they got. I'm sure they did like it. They don't have to work in close proximity to you.'

She felt a hot rush to her head that set her very scalp on fire. 'And that's what *you* want, isn't it?' she taunted in breathless anger. 'More proximity.'

He grabbed her and pushed her up against his desk. She felt a furious, excited thrill as he brought his mouth down on hers, and clung to him, relishing the ferocious hunger of his searing lips as her bones liquefied and passion instantly ignited her blood. She kissed him back, as fierce and fervent as he, her hands flying to undo his shirt buttons, his belt buckle, wriggling in frantic urgency to assist him to drag down her zip, unfasten her bra.

She positioned herself on the edge of the desk, her

knees parted for him, the breath coming in quick little pants as he pulled the dress from her shoulders and laid her straining breasts bare. For an intense, electric instant he stared down at her, lust in the black eyes feasting on her white nakedness. Drenched in desire, she quivered on the verge of the wild ride to rapture, her nipples taut and aching, fever between her thighs.

Through his open shirt, his broad bronzed chest with its smattering of black hairs tantalised her unbearably. In her impatience, she leaned forward and gave his nipple a long, languorous lick.

A shock roiled through his body. His hands tightened fiercely on her shoulders, then, with an almost superhuman effort, he thrust her from him and swerved away. She lost her balance and half fell backwards. He stood with his back to her, his hands bunched into fists, sinews straining in his powerful neck and shoulders.

'Dress yourself.' The words were as raw as if they'd been wrenched from him. Their disdain cut her to the quick.

A tidal wave of shame suffused her. She slid off the desk and reassembled her clothes with clumsy, trembling hands. How could her body have so betrayed her? How could she have shown herself so ready to surrender?

Sam fought for the strength to shut her from his consciousness, and waited for desire to subside. He struggled not to smell her fragrance, not to think of smooth breasts aching for a man's hands, of firm, slim thighs edged by black lace.

His father's stern, honest face flashed before him and he winced. Self-disgust rose in his throat like bile. He was no better than the series of greedy, lecherous executives who'd brought the bank close to ruin.

How had he, Samos Stilakos, come to this? When had a woman ever brought him so low?

He heard the door close, and felt overwhelmed by a guilty sensation of relief.

Shaky, disoriented, Ellie stood outside, her face in her hands, mind and body a painful, aching turmoil. She sat down at her desk and stared blindly at her keyboard. Despair would settle in soon enough, she thought. What man had ever treated her with such contempt?

She stayed outside until her hands stopped shaking, and the blood ceased pounding her temples, then forced herself to go in to face him.

He was helping himself to a drink from the water cooler, his clothes once more immaculate, every movement as controlled as if nothing had happened. He strolled to his desk, paper cup in hand, and flicked her a look. Just for an instant, she thought she caught uncertainty in his glittering black glance.

She lifted her chin, not wanting him to see how vulnerable she felt.

'This can't go on,' he rasped. 'It has to stop. I can't have this.'

'You don't have to worry.' Her own voice was equally emotionally charged. 'Because as of this moment, I quit.'

A muscle twitched in his lean cheek and he stood still, looking at her for a second with a fathomless gaze, then he coolly sat down. 'That might be the best solution all round.'

He picked up a pencil and twirled it idly between his lean fingers. It snapped. He straightened his cuffs, and, without looking at her again, pulled out his computer keyboard. 'You might as well clear out your desk.'

He became immersed in his screen.

Outside, she covered her face with her hands and succumbed to a major shaking fit. Her legs gave way and she plumped down on her chair. She opened and shut her desk drawers a few times, then reached for an empty copy-paper carton. She stacked some useless things into it, tipped them out and started again.

After a few minutes the door opened and Sam came out. He took a few strides past her desk, then stopped as if he'd remembered something. 'Your contract requires you to give a month's notice,' he said in a cold voice.

She kept her gaze lowered. 'I'm leaving now.'

'If you do that you'll lose your severance entitlements.'

'Think of the profit to your bank,' she suggested.

He was silent for a moment, then said in a dry, steady voice, 'You will still have to come back to pick up your reference.'

She kept her head down. 'I won't be needing one from you, thanks. I have wonderful references from my previous bosses.'

His feet paused in front of her desk, then he strode back inside and shut the door with a snap.

When she'd piled as much as she could carry into the carton, she stood up with it in her arms and hoisted her bag onto her shoulder. The door burst open and Sam came out.

'Eleanor.' He stood directly in front of her so she was forced to meet his eyes.

Coldly, proudly, she faced her adversary.

'If you—if you did find yourself in a difficult situation—a crisis, like a—an unplanned pregnancy, for example, what would you do?'

Despite her anger with him his eyes were serious, as if he was genuinely concerned, and confusion welled in her heart. Why did he have to remind her of how he'd been before he hated her? A multitude of the glib, savage things she could have said sprang to her tongue and died there. Whatever she was, she was a woman, and she had a heart.

With icy dignity she said, 'I would see it as a situation requiring a practical solution, and I would deal with it.'

The lines of his face tautened. 'How?' He added drily, 'Or can I guess?' With a grimace he half turned away. 'No, don't tell me.'

Her anger sparked back to life and she flung him a withering glance. 'Is it so obvious?' She slung her bag onto her shoulder and started for the exit. 'I'd find a job in a company that cares about its workforce and has an on-site crèche.'

He strode after her, grabbed her arm and pulled her about to face him. 'Understand this, darling,' he bit out through clenched teeth. 'No child of mine will ever be dragged up in a public facility.'

Darling. That caught her on the raw.

She arched her brows and flashed him a cruel smile. 'No child you know about, perhaps.'

CHAPTER EIGHT

ELLIE'S state of shock lasted until she got home. Once the front door was closed behind her she peeled off her dress, collapsed on her bed and gave way to the huge black hole that had opened in her chest.

Afterwards, trying not to visualise Sam's cold eyes, she hauled herself up, changed into jeans, washed her blotchy face and tied her hair behind with a ribbon. She threw herself into some therapeutic house-cleaning, until she felt in enough control of her emotions to phone Beth to tell her the catastrophic news. Shocked, Beth promised to come over after work for a full report.

She drifted to the computer and half-heartedly keyed into a job-search site, but it was too painful. It only reminded her of how much she loved working at the bank. Surely she was a permanent fixture there. Wasn't she famous throughout the departments? So many of her friends were there.

He was there.

She still couldn't believe she'd thrown it all away. She stared miserably at the pile of things in the hall, then knelt to repack them in preparation for sending back to the shop.

How had she come to make such a mess of things? She

tried to think it all through with clear-headed logic, but Sam's furious face swam constantly before her eyes.

She couldn't imagine not seeing him every day. From the day he'd summoned her to the interview she'd been riding on a high. She closed her eyes and let herself dwell on her loss. The emotional impact of their first meeting each morning. Those charged moments at staff meetings when their gazes met. His deep, smooth tones on the intercom.

How flat her life would be now without it all.

If only she hadn't been forced to reject him last night.

But surely, all wasn't lost. Of course this morning she'd lost her temper, they'd both been carried away, but couldn't the situation be retrieved? It was obvious the passion between them was a living thing. Surely that must work to her advantage. And with her experience of talking bosses round, how hard could it be to persuade him she was worth another chance? If she went to see him in the morning and admitted her fault, apologised as she should have done today, instead of scoring points…

If only, if only she could have another chance…

She had a daydream that he would leave work and come in search of her. He'd beg her to come back, he'd apologise for the cruel things he'd said. Instead of being cool, clever Ms O'Dea she'd show him how she truly felt underneath. When he took her in his arms and kissed her she would…

Later, Beth brought over some chocolate éclairs to commiserate, and they sat in her little courtyard garden at the back while Ellie poured out the events of the last twenty-four hours.

True to form, Beth put her finger straight on the point at which things had gone bad. 'Couldn't you have just whisked all that IVF information out of sight?' Her green

eyes were wide with incredulity. 'Stuffed it in a drawer
or something?'

'It was too much of a risk. He might have seen it. He's
very astute. He doesn't miss a thing. You don't know
what he's like. He's—' Her throat thickened and she
couldn't trust herself to go on.

Beth wanted to see the two dresses. 'They're both
gorgeous, but this, *this*. Oh-h,' she moaned softly, finger-
ing the black one. 'To *die* for. But it's far too good for
work.' She examined Ellie with a rueful gaze. 'You didn't
buy this just for the sake of your job, did you?'

Ellie shook her head without speaking, afraid of
bursting into tears.

Beth stayed until after dark, then helped her clear up the
coffee things, and left with sympathetic instructions to
phone if she needed to talk more. After waving her off, Ellie
was still standing at the front window, staring at the empty
street, when a car nosed into the kerb in front of her gate.

It was sleek, dark and expensive-looking. Her heart
gave a hopeful, joyous bound. She dashed to the bathroom to tidy her hair and met her anxious eyes in the
mirror, huge and shadowy in her white face, their colour
intensified by the deep blue of her tee shirt. When the bell
rang her knees suddenly felt watery, and she had to discipline herself to walk to the door calmly.

Sam stood there with a carrier bag dangling from one
hand. He was still in his office clothes and his lean face
was serious and controlled, his severely sculpted mouth
firm, black eyebrows slightly drawn. He looked the
epitome of a powerful businessman. He flicked a veiled
glance over her, taking in her jeans and shirt, then
fastened his sharp gaze to her face. He made the slight-

est movement towards her. For a wild, fluttering moment she thought he was going to kiss her, but instead he just handed her the bag.

'Your things.'

'Thanks.' Her voice came out strangely, as if she'd been in a cave for twenty years without speaking. 'I— Would you—?' She cleared her throat. 'Please. Come in.'

She opened the door wide. His eyes glinted, and she knew he was thinking of last night. After a second's hesitation, he followed her down the hall and into her sitting room. For a tense, silent moment he stood facing her. His eyes were dark and sexual, and she felt an overwhelming desire to lace her arms around his neck and press herself into his big, hard body, but pride forced her to control it.

He sat down on her red sofa without touching her, his feet planted authoritatively apart in their hand-stitched Italian shoes, his intelligent eyes alert. She sank onto a chair facing him.

He glanced around at her bookshelves and pictures, the occasional photos she kept of family and friends, then switched his gaze back to her. His eyes travelled down her throat to the neck of her top, and she was overwhelmingly conscious of her bed, just visible through the half-open door to her bedroom, a few short metres away across the hall.

He wouldn't have come if he didn't want her. The knowledge drummed in her blood and swelled her breasts, and she had to force her hands still, to stop from reaching out to touch him. This was the moment to make her pitch, or lose everything.

'I'm so glad you came, Sam,' she said huskily. 'There are things I need to say.'

'There are things *I* need to say.'

'First I want to apologise—'

He raised imperious eyebrows, and she was silenced.

'No. I want to apologise.' He frowned down at his linked hands and drew a deep breath. 'I want to acknowledge that you were right in those things you said last night. I strongly regret the entire evening. What happened, and the way—the *place* it happened.' His hands lifted, eloquent of distaste. 'I blame myself. And—today. I should not have—exploited my working relationship with you in that way. You were my PA, and I should not have given in to… It was all my fault.' He looked up at her then lowered his black lashes and said quietly, 'You made the right decision.'

A shock wave roiled through her. She felt her life's blood drain from her heart.

'By—by quitting, do you mean? You're saying—it's a good thing I did?'

His eyes held hers with daunting firmness of purpose. 'I've written you a reference.' He nodded towards the carrier bag. 'It's in there with your things. In view of your long service with the bank, you will certainly receive all your severance and holiday pays.'

She was so stunned she could barely speak, but she couldn't just leave it at that. She gave a small, disbelieving laugh and made a weak gesture of appeal. 'I—I had thought—wondered, if you might try to talk me into changing my mind.'

'I'd like to.' His eyes on her face were grave. 'You're an excellent PA and I'll miss your input. You have skills and ability far in advance of PA work. In fact, I believe you can do better.' He dropped his gaze, and added quietly in his dark chocolate voice, 'And after what's developed between us on a personal level, Eleanor, I think you'll agree we can't work together any more.'

Her heart lurched. There was a buzzing in her head, as if all her worst-case scenarios had ganged up to confront her at the same time. 'So you—you don't want me back at the bank tomorrow?'

He looked gravely at her. 'Understand, I'd love to have you back. But it's not good for the bank when the CEO looks forward to seeing one face every day.' His voice softened. 'There is another of the Stilakos companies on the lookout for an executive PA, with opportunities for advancement to management. The salary is very attractive, better than what you were earning...'

Shock had sandbagged her brain to dullness, but her pride still had a vestige of life. She said with a stiff gesture, 'I can find my own position, thank you.'

He was silent for a moment, his dark eyes veiled. He examined her face, then lowered his gaze. 'Of course, of course. I know you can. You'll do well. With your talents and experience...'

Her mouth twisted. 'My pretty face...'

A flush tinged the olive skin covering his cheekbones. 'I—' He checked and made a stilted gesture. 'I shouldn't have said that. That was unfair. You're much, much more than...' With a stern effort he straightened his posture and met her eyes firmly. 'I take full responsibility for everything that has happened.'

Pain and disappointment closed around her heart like a vice, and she looked down at her hands. 'Tell me. Is this—is this really because of the crèche thing?'

'No.' His voice thickened. 'It's because of the passion thing.'

She turned her eyes away to hide them from him. Irrational, weak as it may have seemed, she longed for him to take her in his arms and comfort her for the hurt and desolation he was causing her. 'So, I'm just another statistic, after all,' she managed to say lightly, though the stranglehold on her heart made her voice hoarse.

Despite the cruelty of it, some treacherous part of her brain acknowledged the truth of what he was saying. There was no turning back the clock to the time when they hadn't made love. Everything between them now, every word, every gesture, was imbued with her almost tangible memory of his strong arms, his mouth and hands on her skin. Even now, while he was chopping her insides into little pieces, she craved for him to touch her.

But true to her feminine spirit, on the outside, at least, she kept her spine taut and her chin up, and stood up to signal him it was time to leave.

He rose with reluctance, as if racking his brains for what else he might say to help her swallow the bitter hemlock.

She gathered all the pride at her disposal and faced him coldly. 'You should know the passion thing was only ever a temporary aberration. It no longer exists. Thank you for calling.'

He shook his head and made a move to touch her, but she raised her hands to ward him off. 'Don't,' she said fiercely.

His eyes blazed. 'I'm sure, when you've had time to think, Eleanor, you'll realise this is the best way. How long do you think it would be before other people began to realise we couldn't keep our hands off each other?' He gesticulated passionately. 'Today I came close to having you on my desk. How long before we're taking afternoons off, missing meetings, locking my door to keep other people out while we make love? Everything is noticed and discussed at the bank; you said so yourself. This is not what I want for *us*.' His brilliant black eyes glittered and his deep voice took on a sharp, stern edge. Light glanced from his proud cheekbones, his firm jaw. His Greek heritage had never been more clearly defined. 'I am not a man who conducts affairs in his office. And you are not the kind of woman to enjoy being gossiped about.' He looked like the severe, uncompromising Samos Stilakos who'd commanded the workforce's respect. *Her* respect.

'You're assuming an awful lot,' she said in a low, trembling voice. 'You're assuming I'd be a willing participant.'

Sensuality stirred the depths of the dark eyes fixed on her face. 'I am, yes,' he said softly. 'I am assuming that.'

The naked desire in his gaze pierced her and she weakened. Longing for him rose in her to war with her embattled pride. He was only a metre's distance from her. She could reach out to him, press her mouth to the strong bronzed column of his neck. He would seize her and the dark flame would flare and consume both of them. She felt the dangerous erotic surge, and knew if he touched her she would surrender to the blaze, even as he was destroying her.

But how easily a man discarded a woman, even one he desired. And what foolish arrogance had ever deluded her into dreaming she could have the upper hand with Samos Stilakos? The bitter realisations clamoured in her brain. Her breasts rose and fell with the intensity of her struggle, and with her voice hoarse and trembling, she said, 'Whatever it was that happened between us is over, Sam. Thank you for returning my things.'

His lean dark face was focused and intense, his eyes

ardent. 'It's not over. We have hardly begun. You're upset now, understandably, but when you cool down you'll see. We both know the passion between us. If I touch you... even now, if I touch you, if we...' He took her arms in his firm, warm hands. 'We're meant to be lovers. I want you with me every night.'

She cried, 'You must be joking.' She gave a violent twist and tore herself from his grasp. Angry tears sprang to her eyes. 'The bank has been like my second home all the years I've worked there. Do you think this is nothing to me, losing my job? My *life*? And can you seriously believe I would want to carry on as your—toy? Can you imagine that after today I would ever want to see you again?' She brushed back her hair with impatient, shaking hands. 'You can have no idea—*no idea!*—of how much I have put into my work there. Of how much—over—over the years—I have *done*—' Emotion took control of her voice and she was forced to stop to take a series of breaths.

She caught a fleeting, almost unrecognisable glimpse of herself in the hall mirror, her face dead white, her eyes glittering with blue fire, and turned from the unbearable sight.

Sam said, harsh bitterness in his deep voice, 'Oh, I assure you, I am well aware of the sacrifices some women are prepared to make for their careers.'

'Just—just look at what has happened here,' she carried on in her distress as if he hadn't spoken. 'How are you different from all those big-time executives who ran the bank into the ground? And *I*—I know I've been just as stupid as all those secretaries. How could I? How could I have allowed myself to—?' She dashed away a tear with the back of her hand. More tears choked her throat.

The lines of his lean strong face clenched. Fire blazed

in his eyes. He breathed harshly. 'What has happened between us has nothing to do with other people. It is unique to you and me. If you can't see that I am different from those men...I don't have woman after woman. I only want...'

He drew a long simmering breath. After a moment he said, his deep voice uneven despite his effort of control, 'We need to talk about this rationally. You need to grow used to the idea of changing your employment, then we can talk about the kind of relationship we want. It doesn't have to be difficult for you to find a new place. I want to help you.'

Such cynical promises, while all she'd striven to achieve lay in smoking ruins, swept away the last vestiges of her self-possession.

'Oh, please.' She wiped her brow with a trembling hand. 'You don't have to pretend this is anything but what it is. A sordid office affair you want out of. Don't worry. I want nothing more to do with you in my life.'

His handsome face tautened. He gave a cool shrug, then swung stiffly for the door.

At the front door he paused with his hand on the knob, his shoulders rigidly set, then turned to scan her face. 'You'll find another position without trouble, I promise.'

'I'm sure I can rely on that.'

He lowered his thick black lashes, but not before she saw his eyes flash. He said through gritted teeth, 'Believe it or not, I *do* honour promises if I can.'

Her glance fell on the boxes of vain, frivolous clothes still awaiting the courier, and she nudged them with the toe of her shoe. 'I hope you know I'm sending these things back to the shop.'

'Why? Keep them. I want you to have them.'

Her voice trembled. 'I'd rather not feel like some rich man's mistress.'

He tensed and paused on her doorstep, his eyes chill and stern, and said quietly, 'I hope any woman fortunate enough to be my mistress, Eleanor, would also be gracious enough to know how to accept a gift in the spirit in which it is given.'

He spun on his heel and walked away.

Out of her life.

CHAPTER NINE

TILL hell freezes over, Sam thought.

Still, he kept his cool. He opened his car door, slid into his seat, snapped on the seat belt, every movement measured. He inserted the key and fired the ignition, not a tremor in his fingers. With controlled precision he drove to the end of the street, slowed at the lights.

A tidal wave of black emotion rose up to engulf him. His hands clenched the wheel.

Women didn't reject him. Not twice. He winced. Not *once*. The lights turned green and he slammed his foot to the floor.

He would have her. He would have his fill of her and she would be grateful. She'd crawl to him for more. She'd be on her knees, sobbing for an affair with him.

He sped through a small local shopping precinct and screamed the car to a halt at a street-crossing. A lone female pedestrian, paralysed in the middle of the crossing, turned an outraged glare into his headlights.

He yanked at his tie and loosened his shirt collar. He had done the only possible thing. So why did he feel like such a bastard?

Of course she was upset. It was only natural. She'd lost

her job. If he was guilty of anything it was of having underestimated just how upset she would be. He thought back to the moment when she'd first opened the door to him, the joyous expectation in her sapphire eyes, and his heart twisted.

For a moment he longed to do anything, *anything* to wipe away the pain he'd caused her. Drive back there, give her the job, set it all straight, turn back the clock…

Bleak dismay swept through him at the vision of her once-tranquil face, twisted in outrage and despair.

How would he ever retrieve himself in her eyes?

CHAPTER TEN

IT WAS shattering to find how soon she could be forgotten by friends, people she'd worked with for years.

In the days following the crisis they phoned, dying to know what was behind her departure. Ellie sensed the avidness in some of the enquiries. People fishing for gossip, hoping to hear some juicy scandal about her and Sam. It was humiliating, but she put on a bright performance, and pretended to have decided on a change in career.

All too soon, though, the calls began to drop off.

With frightening speed her bank world started to recede, and she guessed the reverse would also be true. Even the most popular staff member could leave, with barely a ripple to disturb the daily functioning of the big machine.

Sam didn't recede. Not in her mind, at least. Night after night she agonised over her last scene with him, raw with pain that he'd put his personal honour and reputation ahead of her happiness and security.

She didn't care who was right. Or that she was the one who'd resigned, she was the one who'd insisted on bringing in ethics, and she had been an equal and willing sexual partner. What she needed was for him to suffer as she was suffering. And to care, and feel sorry. And to crawl on his knees to beg her forgiveness, while she ground him into the earth with her heel.

But he didn't contact her. He didn't call to see how she was, or to check if she had anything to tell him about work, or to enquire about meetings and appointments.

It was cruelly frustrating, because she wanted to punish him properly. Shout and scream at him, shake him and show him how it felt to be cut to ribbons. And she wanted him to give her her job back, and make the terrifying pain better, as though it had never happened.

As two weeks turned to three his implacable silence slammed home the finality of his goodbye, and her anger turned to herself. How could she have allowed herself to fall into the same old trap? Once again she'd been beguiled by a man's charm, only this time the consequences had wiped her out. She'd wasted her savings, and it had been her own fault. She'd had a goal, she'd made sacrifices for it, and she'd allowed herself to be tempted from it.

She'd never fallen in so deep. Her passion for him was like a madness.

She knew she had to fight it, but she was weak. At every turn the shock of her loss asserted itself. Like an addict deprived of the fatal poppy, the touch and feel and taste of him were on her hands and skin as if he were a part of her very fibre.

She tried to fight the constant longing, but couldn't stop willing the phone to ring, running to the window to check every car that drew up in the street. She checked her message bank a dozen times a day; even, in some shamefully low moments, considered texting him, begging him to forgive the terrible things she'd said to him.

But of course he wouldn't. A man like Samos Stilakos

would never forgive such a blow to his pride, and she steeled herself to the daunting necessity of rebuilding her life and starting afresh.

Her practical side fastened to the task of getting back on course.

With a mental gritting of teeth, she set her sights on her next job and travelled daily to the city on the round of job interviews. Too proud at first to use it, her reference from Sam, when she eventually relented, opened doors to her that would certainly have been otherwise closed, despite her qualifications.

Weeks after her last conversation with him, she was plunged into a dilemma when a friend from the bank phoned to invite her to a farewell lunch in her honour. Ironically, it had been given the nod of approval from the top.

What did it mean? Her first instinct was to avoid the torture, but her friends didn't deserve such cold treatment. Besides, she would already be in town that day for her second interview with a firm of management consultants. Going back to the place she'd loved would be hard, but how much harder would be the possibility of seeing Sam?

She couldn't quell the pathetic hope that he'd arranged it so he could see her. That should have warned her. Her struggle to put him out of her mind and heart was still too new to be safe. Although, she argued with herself, he might not be there. Why would he be, when she'd told him she never wanted to see him again in her life?

Though if he didn't, if he took her at her word and she missed seeing him, what new vistas of pain would open before her then?

The day was overcast. A storm gathered on the horizon, giving the sultry sky a bruised, brooding quality. After a rocky start, in which anxiety made her feel almost nauseous, she dressed as neatly as she could in her best suit and steeled herself for another Oscar-winning performance.

It must have gone over well with the consultants, for she was scarcely out of the building and into the street before they phoned her to tell her she had the job. That was cheering, at least. Of her friends at the bank only Beth knew the truth behind her departure, and at least now she could honestly tell people she had another job.

Still, as she braced herself to pass through the familiar glass doors into the bank's marble lobby, and smelled the familiar smells of floor polish and copy paper, regret for the world she'd loved welled in her heart.

Her hand hovered over the lift button for Sam's floor. But the certainty of seeing some new lovely queening it at her desk, melting to Sam's velvet tones on her intercom, was too cruel to contemplate. She bypassed it and rode straight to the top.

Determinedly working at his desk, Sam tried not to glance at his screen-clock. Nevertheless, in the corner of his eye the hour flashed, then another minute, and another.

What if she didn't come?

The black void that occupied his chest swelled and threatened to engulf the world. It was everywhere—his apartment. This desolate bank...

She'd been true to her word not to contact him. There'd been nothing for weeks. Just a phone call from the boutique to inform him of the return of his gifts. The finality of the rebuff had cut him to the quick. It had been another sign of his clumsiness with her. Everything he'd done, it seemed, had offended her sensibilities. Everything he'd said.

He needed to find the right words. What were the words?

He thought of Natalie, the women he'd known before his marriage, and their greedy passion for expensive fripperies. Things he thought he knew about women had been turned upside down.

The desk phone rang. His insides clenched, but he forced himself to reach for it coolly. 'Yes?'

The party in the restaurant was quite lavish for the new regime. They'd arranged a cake, and achieved a festive air with flowers and gifts. The first thing that struck Ellie's notice was Sam's absence. Her disappointment was cruel, but she concealed it before her friends, who welcomed her with hugs and cheerful enquiries about her new job.

Amazingly though, a few minutes of listening to their small exchanges about current events in the bank already made her feel like an outsider. They toasted her and made speeches, and she forced herself to pretend with all her heart that a career change was what she'd wanted most in the world.

Towards the end a slight hush fell, and people sat straighter in their chairs. Her insides lurched, and she looked up to see the tall, autocratic figure of Sam at the entrance. Her heart swelled with its bitter-sweet knowledge.

His dark eyes skimmed the assembly until they lighted on her. From across the room she saw his lean, strong face tense, then smooth to become expressionless.

He strolled over and greeted her with quiet courtesy.

She tried to respond normally, but her burning awareness of him dominated her every small action. Her heart thudded with stress and she could hardly meet his eyes, she was so conscious of the insulting things she'd said to him at their last meeting. But as always before his work-force, he remained cool and composed. The last time she'd seen him he'd been all steel and fire. Now he was back to steel and velvet. In his elegant suit and crisp white shirt, he'd never looked more handsome, more remote and inaccessible, more achingly desirable.

He'd written a speech, and stood to deliver it in an easy, friendly style, as if he'd often done this sort of thing, and knew exactly the right tone to take.

She listened to all the flattering things he said about her with downcast eyes and a smile to cover her wounds. He must have gone to great trouble to prepare the speech, because he'd unearthed amusing anecdotes about her from years past at the bank that her friends recognised and laughed at uproariously.

Despite her turbulent heart she laughed too. At the end she stood to receive the customary bank gift. As usual it was a watch, and this one had the quiet elegance that signalled expense. Someone had chosen it with care.

Sam held out his hand and she gave him hers. For a brief instant their palms met. At the familiar leap of her untrustworthy pulse she couldn't prevent the quick rush of emotion, and had to lower her gaze to hide the shimmer of tears. He bent to brush her cheek with his lips. The faint masculine roughness of his jaw grazed her skin in a potent reminder of pleasures lost.

She made a pretence of linking the watch around her wrist. Sam saw her difficulty with the clasp and helped her. Her skin surged to his quick, deft fingers and she had to discipline herself to meet his eyes. After the small applause had died down, she didn't trust herself to give a speech of her own, beyond thanking everyone for their thoughtfulness.

Mindful of not overstaying their permitted hour in the boss's presence, people began to make moves back to their work. When the last noisy group had gone, the restaurant staff swarmed in to clear the tables.

She gathered up her gifts and flowers. Unlike everyone else, Sam hadn't yet made the move to leave. She eyed him uncertainly, and he tilted his head to indicate an alcove by the window, out of the way of the waiters. After a second's hesitation she joined him.

The moment grew tense, and they both spoke at the same time. 'Have you—?'

'Do you—?'

They each gave a strained laugh, then Sam started again. 'There's something I need to ask you. Have you remembered your promise to accompany my mother to the wedding?'

'Oh! The wedding.' She had forgotten. With the events of the past weeks it had been pushed to the back of her mind. 'Are you sure you still want me to go? Wouldn't you rather find someone else?' She made a tremulous effort at a smile but her voice caught. 'Sever all undesirable connections?'

Something flickered in his dark eyes. 'There isn't anyone else. My mother is counting on you. She's—fixed now on having you with her.'

'I see. Oh, well, of course, then.' She shrugged in acquiescence. 'I did—I did promise.' She felt her insides knot then as she remembered the cutting things she'd said to him on her doorstep about his promises, and she flushed and turned from his perceptive gaze.

'Look, Sam. I'm sorry I said those things to you the last time we—talked. I was upset at the time… About my job, you understand. But I shouldn't have been so rude.'

'You have nothing to apologise for.'

There was a short, constrained silence. She became conscious of the muted sounds of rattling crockery and bustle from the restaurant kitchen.

He touched her cheek lightly with his knuckle. 'You will settle into your new firm and be happy, Eleanor. I'm sorry it had to be this way.' His voice deepened. 'I'm sorry you've been hurt. That I've—hurt you.'

She felt her throat thicken and said huskily, 'Nice watch. Who chose it?'

'Oh, er—' he made a vague gesture '—a—a man—a jeweller brought some trays up for me—'

'Could those be actual sapphires?'

His hands shot out and he took her arms in his strong grasp. 'This wasn't what you think it was. You know one of us had to leave.' His sardonic brows were drawn, his eyes fierce with concern.

Emotion swelled in her heart. Everything in her yearned to step into his arms and sink into his hard body, let him comfort her and kiss her. But she daredn't risk it.

'I do know.' With a sharp twist she disengaged herself. 'I even know why it had to be me. Don't concern yourself with it. I'm fine, my life is fine, I have a new job and I'll like it just as much as I did the last one.' She forced a smile. 'I couldn't feel more—positive about the future.'

She hoped he hadn't guessed what a lie that was. Her croaky old voice might have told him that all she had in her was pain. She could feel his frowning gaze scouring her face.

'Is that true? Have you really come to terms with everything?'

What did he want from her? Blood? Did he really want to know the anguish she'd suffered when he'd discarded her, the agonies of fear and hope the possibility of seeing him today had put her through?

She knew with sudden certainty she didn't want him to feel guilty. She was to blame as much as he. It was time to walk away with her head high, no hard feelings. It took a supreme effort, even after all her experience. As usual, her voice was the hardest to control.

'I don't deny it's been hard.' Bright, sincere smile, airy shrug, if a bit jerky. 'A change always is. But in the long run it'll do me good. One thing I realised coming here today was that I've been in the one place too long. You were right about that. I needed to climb to higher ground.' Her emotions threatened but she crushed them down. 'It was a—a shame it had to happen that way. But I'm a big girl, I know the score…I always did, and I have no regrets.'

The words seemed somehow to clang in the hushed atmosphere of the restaurant. 'You know the score,' he murmured in echo, with a frown. He glanced at his watch. 'Look, let's go somewhere where we can talk.'

He flicked open his mobile and made a couple of quick calls, then took her arm and ushered her out to the lift. On the drive to his apartment the silence was charged. She glanced at him a couple of times, but his expression was grim, his mouth unsmiling.

The apartment was bathed in a dim hush, in waiting for its master. Sam opened some blinds and windows to let in the sultry afternoon, then turned to her. 'Drink?'

She shook her head, but he poured one for himself, half raised it, then put it down again, and loosened his tie.

'Come this way. Please. Through here.'

She followed him uncertainly through the archway,

into a suite of rooms. He showed her to a sitting room, which opened into a light, spacious bedroom with furnishings that were essentially masculine, including an opulent bed. A glass ceiling dome above it gave a thrilling glimpse of stormy sky. Light glanced off mirrors and discreet touches of gilt filigree set in the wall panelling. It reminded her of some exotic sultan's palace.

He turned to face her, his lean, stern face taut and strained, his dark eyes intense. 'I had decided not to see you again,' he said abruptly.

Her heart pained, and she folded her arms over her breasts to protect herself from more wounds. Why put herself through this? 'Then why—?' She made an inarticulate gesture. Her voice came out in a dry croak. 'Why are we here?'

'You know why.' The words were wrenched from him, as if he'd had a bitter struggle with his pride, and lost. He strode across and his hands lifted as though to touch her, but he controlled them sharply and let them fall. 'Seeing you again… You know what I want. What we both want.' His deep voice was harsh.

The fire in his eyes fuelled the old yearning in her, and played on her weakness. In a confusion of emotion and resolve, she clenched her hands against her to prevent herself from throwing herself into his arms.

As though he read the conflict in her face, a flush darkened the taut, bronzed skin across his proud cheekbones, and he swung stiffly away from her, and continued his impassioned words, pacing about with a fierce, relentless dignity.

'I am—deeply remorseful to have hurt you.' He cast her a searing look from beneath his lashes. 'I'm not *al-*

together heartless. I admit I didn't understand how much working at the bank meant to you. I hoped you would see that another job, in another place, would make it easy for us to—' He made an abrupt, wordless gesture and with simmering restraint, 'From your long silence, Eleanor, I gathered that with you the job was everything.' His shoulders were rigidly set, his hands bunched into fists while he waited for her reply.

Passionate, truthful words of her love and longing for him rose to her tongue, but her courage to express them failed her. Even so, as if he'd read them in her face, triumph lit the ardent gaze, and he added very softly, 'But seeing you now, I just can't believe that.'

He moved swiftly to her, his chest just a centimetre from hers. Her resolve to resist him warred with his formidable sexual power. His deep, seductive voice pulled at her with its smouldering intensity. 'You have to acknowledge that at least now there are no more barriers between us. I'm not your employer. You're not my PA. Now, we're just a man and a woman.'

The words stirred her to her depths, but her battles of the past weeks were too fresh to be dismissed. 'Sam,' she said unsteadily, shaking her head, 'it's not so easy.'

The dark flame flared in his eyes. 'Yes, it is. Don't try to deny this.' He curved his fingers under her chin and tilted up her face. His voice thickened. 'This isn't the time for us to lie to each other to save face, sweetheart. Passion isn't something you can hide.'

The endearment touched that deep inner spring she was fighting so hard to quell. Desire unfurled in her belly, and she felt the immediate, swelling heat to her breasts. She gazed into the dark eyes glinting in his proud, strong face, his mouth twisted with emotion, and the irresistible force of her love overwhelmed her.

She kissed him, and, as though it was the spark to the bonfire, he crushed her to him, and took charge, possessing her lips with scorching authority. Her body blazed like a torch, and she threw every atom of herself into his embrace with willing abandonment.

With wild, panting urgency they tore at each other's clothes, their hands barely steady in their haste to remove the constricting barriers to skin on skin. For a second he stood naked before her, in all his bronzed, muscled magnificence, feasting on her nude body with his aroused black eyes. Then he lifted her in his arms as though she were weightless, and tossed her onto his bed. He came down beside her, triumph mingling with the fire in his dark, devouring gaze.

In the first ferocious urgency, they made hot, clumsy love, rushing to a shattering climax in almost unbelievable concert. Then, long into the afternoon, while the storm raged over Sydney, with sizzling deliberation, Sam slowed passion to an infinitely more languorous pace, relishing every curve and hollow of her nude body, teasing the sweet strawberry nipples, tasting the honeyed secrets beneath her soft tangle of curls. With fierce, erotic tenderness, he roused Ellie to the wildest fever-pitch she'd ever known, until she begged for him to take her.

When he judged the moment right, he plunged into her, burying his hard shaft in her to the hilt, and pleasured her with slow, sinuous strokes, increasing the tempo into a virile, athletic rhythm that transported her beyond the pinnacle of ecstasy.

Much later, past satiety and exhaustion, she lay beside him in the huge bed, her head resting on his ribs, gazing drowsily through the domed ceiling at the midnight sky. Her body felt supple and replete.

'Tomorrow…' His deep murmur sounded sonorous against her ear. 'We'll send the car over to pick up your things.'

Ellie tensed. 'What things?'

'Everything you need. Your clothes, your books. Your music.'

She lay still for a moment, tilted her head around to look at him, then stirred herself to sit up. She pushed aside the red mass of hair tumbling over her shoulders. 'Why would we do that?'

'So you can be comfortable.' He surveyed her white nakedness with slumbrous satisfaction, then bent his dark head to graze her bare shoulder with his lips. His mouth curved in a grin. 'I think you would miss your shoes.'

She caught her breath. 'But—I don't need them here. I live there.'

With studied casualness he said, 'I think it's better if you live here. Hornsby's too far.'

She felt stunned. For a few moments she let the dream dazzle her. Belonging to him. Sleeping in his arms every night. The intimacy of it. Everything she'd hardly dared to wish. Well, nearly everything. Pleasure, romance and…

'For—for how long does this invitation extend?' she said lightly.

His black lashes flickered down, and he hesitated. His dark eyes connected with hers for an unreadable instant, then slid away. 'Who knows?' He shrugged, and a warning pang shot through her. 'A week, a year. Until we've had our fill of each other.'

He kissed her, stroked her hair back behind her ear, and said gruffly, 'That might take a while.' He pulled her down beside him, and gathered her against his broad, warm chest. 'We'll work out the details in the morning.'

She closed her eyes, but her mind wouldn't stop spinning. He could be hers. For a while.

A week, or a year...

A year of heavenly delights.

But after the year—what?

She had to face it, be honest with herself. He'd already shown her how ruthless he could be. How long before she was back on the scrap heap, another precious year of her life wasted, left with an incurable heartbreak?

But it was tempting. Could she do it, live the glamorous life? She would have to put aside thoughts of a child for another year or so. Then a year or two to get over him and save up again. Although after that, at thirty-three or thereabouts...

She fell off her cloud with a crash. Thirty-three was too late. Already she was in the danger zone.

She worried and churned while the moon sank low in the sky, and the starlight grew faint, then extinguished altogether. At last, in the first grey light, she carefully disentangled herself from Sam's strong, warm limbs, and slipped from the bed.

A few minutes later, a small sound impinged on his consciousness, and Sam stirred himself from his dream to a vague sense of bliss. The smile swelled in his heart in sleepy recollection. Eleanor. He reached for her.

Nothing.

He half opened his eyes. Her place was still warm. His eyes drifted shut and he drowsed, waiting for her. After a hazy time he resurfaced, and forced himself to lift his head.

Blearily he scanned the room. The shadows were shrinking into the corners, but there was no sign of her. With a sudden foreboding in his bones he got up, pulled jeans from a drawer and dragged them on.

He found her in the living room. She was fully dressed in her suit and heels, handbag slung on her shoulder, her glorious hair tamed into a neat coil in the nape of her neck. She was leaning over a table, frowning at a sheet of paper, her pen poised while she considered. She started, and straightened up when he walked in. 'Oh,' she said, her eyes widening.

Her eyelashes gave a nervous flicker, and with a lurch Sam knew. He nodded towards the paper. 'For me?'

She looked pale and drawn, her blue eyes bruised and shadowy in the pale light. Her dismay at being caught was almost tangible. 'I didn't want to wake you.'

He kept his expression under control, though he could feel an unpleasant blood-beat in his temples. 'Isn't it…?' He forced his lungs on. 'Isn't it early to be going out?'

'I'm…' She hesitated, then said, in her low voice, 'I need to go home.'

A coldness began to seep through his insides. To stall her, he tried the only thing he knew: drew her to him, kissed her cheek and the corner of her mouth. Generous girl that she was, she complied, put her arms around his neck. He crushed her to him, felt her precious heartbeat against his chest, then as the inevitable desire rose between them felt her pull back. In the empty space in his arms he felt the desolate chill of goodbye.

'But you are coming back,' he said, still careful, in the face of defeat, not to pressure her.

Her gaze wavered over him, down to his bare feet, took in his jeans and chest. Her soft mouth, still red from his kisses, made a telling little tremor. He considered seducing her back into his bed, but there was a certain nervy resolution in her posture, as of a decision reached, and he had his pride.

She brushed his bristly cheek with a gentle hand. 'Sam, I love—love being with you. But I'm afraid I'm not really mistress material.'

Mistress material. A blade sliced through him, but he kept severe control.

Her face was working with distress. 'Last night was won-derful,' she said, regret in her warm, husky voice, blue eyes swirling with some dark tragedy. 'It would be gorgeous being here with you, but I—have goals of my own.'

'Goals.' It was difficult to smile. His heart was slamming so hard he could barely breathe, and a hoarse-ness entered his voice. He didn't want to sound as if he was begging, but it was necessary to point out the obvious. 'I have no intention of making your career suffer, Eleanor. I know how important it is to you. I can be of great help to you.'

She shook her head, her slim hands fluttering, as if what he'd said had somehow proven how hopeless he was.

'Look—' He felt himself flush to hear the note of des-peration in his voice. 'I should have made myself clear.' As happened on the rare occasions he felt powerless, his hands flew around like some old Greek's. 'I—I fully recognise how independent you are. We'll get the lawyers to draw up a contract to protect your interests. You won't be worse off financially, far from it.'

She covered her ears in a small, defensive gesture. 'Please, Sam.' The words came out almost as a strangled cry, and she turned her face away from him.

Humiliation flooded his soul like blood.

She started for the foyer. Dimly he knew he'd said all the wrong things, but what were the right ones? With women, a man never knew.

'I'll drive you,' he said quickly, catching up with her, thinking of the long drive there. Plenty of time to talk her round.

'No. No, please,' she said, stepping into the lift. 'I've phoned for a taxi.' She turned to face him. 'It's better this way.' That fragile pulse was beating in her throat. He stared, unbelieving, as tears filled her eyes. 'Goodbye, Sam.'

A crippling pain inhabited his being. For a crazed instant he teetered on the verge of spilling his guts. Pleading, like some love-struck teenager.

Instead, he controlled himself in time and stood back with the dignity of a man. His face felt stiff, and when the words came he knew they sounded cold and formal. 'I wish you well on your climb to the top, Eleanor.'

CHAPTER ELEVEN

How the rich lived.

There was no need to phone for a taxi. Irene said she would pick Ellie up on the way to the airport, and at the appointed time a limo drew up at her door. A uniformed chauffeur sprang out to help her with her bag, and she was ushered to join Irene in its plush interior like Princess Mary.

It was clear now why Irene had seemed vague about reservations. The Stilakos family didn't make reservations. They had their own private jet.

She might have enjoyed it all more if she hadn't felt like such an imposter. Irene had wanted her on the basis of her being connected to her son, and now the connection was broken. Should she explain, or did Irene know? she wondered, eyeing the bright-eyed older woman after they'd greeted each other with a warm hug.

It didn't take long for the sore point to come up. They were in the sky, with Sydney passing beneath them like a sequinned cloth.

'What will Sam do without you?' Irene said. A gleam of satisfaction lit the older woman's eyes every time they settled on her. 'It will do him so much good to miss you.'

Ellie felt the heat in her cheeks. The choking pain

threatened to burst through her chest. 'Well, no. Actually I don't work for Sam now. I've got another job.' The words sounded so suspect, even to her own ears, she wasn't surprised when Irene arched her brows and looked keenly at her through her specs.

'I felt I needed to extend myself,' she explained. 'It's time to set my goals in place and carve my path to the top. I'm a career girl, you know, Irene. Through and through.'

Irene looked doubtful, and Ellie felt a spurt of exasperation. What would it take to convince this old woman?

'Oh, sure I liked my job at the bank,' she went on breezily. 'I'd been there a long time. Personal connections are all very well, but, between you and me, nothing can measure up to the thrill of discovering what you're capable of in the world of big business and testing your abilities to the limit. That's the real adrenaline rush.' The scepticism in the shrewd grey eyes only increased, and she added firmly, 'I've joined a team of management consultants.'

Irene's musing, 'Oh-h-h. Is that right?' was unsettling. Ellie could practically see her well-exercised brain-cells ticking into calculation.

Lunch was served by a uniformed flight attendant, but Ellie couldn't eat a thing. People who'd ruined their own lives had no need of sustenance. They lived on their regrets. She hadn't even been able to raise a laugh at the postcard she'd received from Tierra del Fuego. 'On my way home to you, babe. Sorry the team was held up. Love, Mark.'

Love. Ironic that. It was a word he'd carefully avoided in the past. That blonde in Melbourne must have taught him a thing or two.

The sight of sea and long white sandy beaches should

have lifted her spirits. As the plane circled Coolangatta Airport before coming in to land, the famous strip of high-rises shimmered in the sun with the old promise of holidays and pleasure.

Funny how the idea of pleasure could be so depressing.

An elderly couple wearing expensive-looking casuals and anxious expressions stood waiting in the arrivals lounge. When she and Irene walked in, there was a moment of mutual hesitation, then the couple and Irene surged forward to fall on each other's necks with teary sobs. In a storm of questions and protestations and more hugs, all three of them talked so fast no one could possibly make sense of anything anyone else said.

After they'd mopped up, Irene introduced them to Ellie as her brother Jack, and his wife Rosemary, explaining they were the groom's parents. 'And this is Ellie,' Irene said with a warm look at Ellie, 'a friend of Sam's.'

Jack's and Rosemary's brows shot up and they looked Ellie over with surmise. Ellie fired a questioning frown at Irene and was met with an innocent smile. Was there the faintest tinge of smugness in that smile? Ellie wondered.

The flight crew appeared with their baggage, then handed it over to a waiting chauffeur. With a minimum of fuss they were soon in another limo, cutting a swathe through the Gold Coast traffic.

'How are the preparations coming?' Irene enquired.

The couple looked at each other and Jack rolled his eyes. Rosemary inclined her head. Scarcely moving her mouth, she said, 'They've been problems.' She gave Irene a speaking look. 'I think you can guess.'

'Ah.' Irene narrowed her eyes and nodded. 'Yes, I think I can.' She slanted Ellie a meaningful glance.

'Luckily our villa is away from all the goings-on.' Rosemary's lips thinned. 'I hope you two won't mind being in the thick of it. We're hosting the groom's dinner tonight at the Palazzo, so fingers crossed.'

The Palazzo Versace was as elegant as its brochures promised. The resort was lapped by the ocean Broadwater. From where Ellie stood in the white-and-gold marbled vestibule, her view across its green lagoon seemed faintly reminiscent of Venice, but a gleaming, sprucified Venice, a Venice that was still gracious, but re-assuringly solid.

Theirs was not the only limo to draw up to its charming entrance. As Ellie smoothed down her slim dress more cars arrived, disgorging more glittering guests. Some she recognised from the television world, while others bore the faintly bored, relaxed demeanour of the very rich.

A noisy group were in occupation of the bar at one end of the lobby. Ellie's experienced eye could tell they were already into party mode. They kept shouting with laughter, and welcoming every new arrival with theatrical embraces and much witty repartee.

While Irene dealt with Reception, Rosemary and Jack made beckoning motions to someone in the bar crowd. A slight, intense-looking man detached himself from the group he was with, and tried to snag the attention of a vivacious young woman in the throes of relating some story to her friends. She was telling her story with gusto, throwing her arms about and screaming with laughter.

Natalie Stilakos.

Who else would flaunt hectares of her naked midriff between a couple of scraps of floaty gauze to her fiancé's family?

The black-rooted blonde spun about, and as her glance homed in on her in-laws, past and future, the laughter died on her face, to be reconstituted into a nervous, unconvincing smirk. She clutched her fiancé's arm, and it seemed to Ellie that the couple braced themselves. They started across the foyer, Natalie clinging tight to her lover's arm.

Michael composed his rather sallow face into a smile, and greeted his aunt with a few stilted, though friendly, words and a quick kiss, and Natalie was forced to follow suit, though her lips made no actual skin contact.

'It's so nice to see you, Natalie,' Irene said warmly. 'Welcome again to the family, dear. I'm sure you'll make Michael a lovely wife.'

Natalie's smile faded. Her black eyes glowered through the heavy kohl smudging their rims. 'What's that supposed to mean?'

Rosemary and Jack made nervous shuffling movements and pretended to look out at the lagoon. Michael quickly took his fiancée's wrist and gave it a little shake. 'Chill, darling,' he said, winking and giving everyone a grin. 'Wedding nerves. It'll all be over soon.' Everyone joined in the false hearty laugh.

Rosemary quickly eased the moment on, announcing, to Ellie's intense chagrin, 'And this is Ellie, Sam's girlfriend.'

Ellie would have denied it but for a sudden steel clamp on her elbow. No wonder Sam had such a strong grip.

She managed a smile and accepted Michael's hand. He examined her with frank curiosity, then leaned forward to peck her cheek as if she were family. Still with her smile in place, she turned to Natalie. After an awkward second, the blonde stuck out a hand for a brief brushing of fingers, her eyes guarded. 'But aren't you Sam's receptionist?'

'Oh, no, no,' Irene intervened before Ellie had a chance to speak. 'Ellie's a management consultant.' She gave a fond laugh. 'Sam gets all the benefit of her advice at home.'

Ellie swivelled an outraged look at Irene, who bestowed such an affectionate beam on her it was all she could do not to gasp.

A porter stood patiently by waiting to escort them to the condominium owned by the Stilakos family. Rosemary and Jack made moves to leave, with an arrangement to meet later, and to Ellie's relief the group broke up. Michael called after Ellie with an invitation to come back down once she was settled. The glance the bride flung Ellie over her shoulder was puzzled.

The Principessa Suite was spacious and filled with light, its gleaming marble floors exquisitely tiled with a mosaic design. Broad balcony windows opened to views of the Broadwater. Ellie barely gave herself a chance to take in the fabulous Versace furnishings, before advancing on Sam's mother, who was narrowly inspecting the master suite.

'What are you up to, Irene?' Ellie's hands were on her hips. 'What's the idea of telling people I'm Sam's girlfriend?'

'Oh-h-h…' Irene shuddered '…wasn't it harrowing?' Kicking off her shoes, she flopped onto a sumptuous king-sized bed, draped in the rich deep colours of the Renaissance, and gave a throaty chuckle. 'Did you see Natalie's face?'

'I could hardly miss. Why did you do it?'

Irene sat back up, all wide-eyed innocence. '*I* didn't say you were his girlfriend. It was Rosemary who said that.' She gave her head a despairing shake at Rosemary's chronic hopelessness. 'Trust her to leap to conclusions.' With a sigh she sank back on the assortment of tasselled cushions and pillows adorning the bed.

Ellie checked her retort and drew a deep, calming breath. 'You could have corrected her impression, though, couldn't you? You didn't have to encourage it.'

Irene arranged herself more comfortably, and cast Ellie an amused glance. 'Oh, don't give me that stern face. I get enough of that from Sam. Why can't you go along with it for a couple of days? It will serve that little piece right for letting people think Sam can't get over her. ' She leaned up on a gold and purple embroidered cushion and her eyes glistened. 'It would be better if he was here with you, of course. Why don't I give him a call and tell him you've broken your ankle?'

Ellie shook her head in bemusement. 'What are you talking about? Sam wouldn't... Don't, please, for heaven's *sake*!' She flushed. Her feelings about Sam and the things that had happened between them were raw. Too raw to be used in some game. With difficulty she said, 'I don't think you realise, Irene, how—how painful and embarrassing this would be for me if Sam found out. He was my boss, you know.'

'But he isn't now, is he? *Is* he, Ellie? It's a whole new ball game.'

Ellie's body suddenly felt twitchy and in need of fast, furious exercise. She walked out into the sitting room and back again, her hands as restless as her feet.

'Anyway,' she said, ignoring Irene's sly riposte, 'why should Natalie care what Sam does? They're divorced, aren't they? She doesn't have any hold on Sam. She's marrying someone else, for goodness' sake. She and Sam are—over.' She stopped to gaze out at the Broadwater, but all she could see was what she couldn't stop seeing. Sam's dark eyes, aflame for *her*. She turned to Irene and said in a choked voice, 'Aren't they?'

Irene was watching her from her room with a shrewd little smile. 'Of course they are. They've been over practically since the first.'

'Really?'

Irene gave her a long look and heaved a sigh. 'Yes, yes, yes. The whole thing was a mistake. I doubt if he'd have stayed married to her for as long as he did if it hadn't been for the baby.'

Ellie's eyes sprang wide with shock. 'They have a child?'

Irene compressed her lips. 'No, but I'm pretty sure there was one. I can usually tell when a girl's in the family way.' Her eyes clouded and she shook her head. 'I'm afraid the baby didn't eventuate. Goodness knows what happened. Whatever it was, things went very wrong between them. Sam would never breathe a word about it, of course. Then five minutes after the wedding Natalie was flaunting her affair with Michael, and the marriage was doomed.' She sighed and patted her cushion. 'To give the girl her due, she's tried everything she could think of to persuade Sam and Michael to patch things up. If Sam would only get over it and come to the wedding…' She lay back and lapsed into gloomy thought.

Ellie stood very still and forced herself to say coolly, 'I suppose it would be hard for Sam to watch his wife marry someone else.'

'Oh…!' Irene roused herself to make a dismissive sweep of her hand. 'The spoilt hussy barely was his wife. But Sam's an old-fashioned Greek man at heart. He's too much like his father. If he believes his honour has been insulted he can be very proud.' She rolled her eyes. '*Men*. Who knows how the creatures think?' With another hefty sigh, she rolled back on her pillows and stared at the ornate baroque ceiling.

Ellie went to her own room, which was as richly furnished as Irene's. Mirrors and sparkling Italian mosaics reflected the watery light from the lagoon, but it was hard to appreciate it all when her heart knew only darkness.

Would rejecting a Greek man three times constitute an insult to his honour? she wondered. Of course it would. It would sting any man like fury. He'd never want to lay eyes on her again.

But there was no use giving in to this dreadful, tearing ache. Wishing she'd taken a chance. Tears swelled her throat. Hoping…*pretending* love had happened to her too, the way she had with Mark. It was ironic really, how she'd thought she'd come to terms with all this ages ago. But the same old conditions still seemed to apply. For Ellie O'Dea, no love at all was better than half-love. So even if she loved Sam enough for ten people…

'Ellie?'

She pulled herself together. Irene had resettled herself on a chaise longue in the sitting room and was riffling through her handbag. When she saw Ellie she pushed the bag aside and threw up her hands. 'Oh, all right. I give in. Tell them all the truth about you and Sam if you have to. I'm sorry if you were embarrassed. I suppose I hoped you might be a woman after my own heart.' She placed a be-ringed hand over her breast and gazed at Ellie, her grey eyes sparkling with reproach. 'I had the impression you might enjoy a little graceful subterfuge. It never occurred to me you might actually *be* a goody-two-shoes.'

Ellie gasped and let out a shocked laugh. 'Irene. You are the limit!'

The older woman grinned. 'I sincerely hope so. Now be a dear, will you, and phone for some tea? And ask them to send up a butler.'

'A butler?'

She elevated her brows. 'Well, dear, we need to unpack. Someone has to locate my pills.'

Remorse snapped Ellie from her gloom. What could she be thinking of, ticking off an old woman with a heart problem? 'Yes, yes, of course,' she said, moving across to pick up the phone. 'And why don't you have a little rest afterwards so you'll feel nice and fresh to meet Rosemary and Jack?'

'Good idea.' Irene's eyes twinkled. 'I think I might need to be fresh. What about you?'

Ellie shook her head. She was restless, and she wasn't especially hungry. No, Ellie O'Dea, for all her faults, was an action woman. It was time to brave the bride.

Once the butler was ensconced and Irene was settled with some delicious pastries from the Palazzo kitchen and a fat romance novel, Ellie slipped into her room to change.

The party had dispersed a little in the time she'd been away. People had drifted out to the lagoon terrace. Natalie was still near the bar, hunched in an armchair, scowling morosely into space. Michael was engaged in urgent conversation with an actressy-looking brunette who kept glaring around him at Natalie, in between bouts of furious hissing and ferocious gestures with her fist.

Not a good time, Ellie's antennae suggested.

She paused for a moment to decide where best to head, and a waiter materialised beside her. She ordered a squash and sauntered through the glass doors to the terrace. At once she was assailed with the holiday smells of swimming pools, sunscreen and salt sea air.

An umbrella table was vacant at the edge of the party set, and in no time a tall glass garnished with lemon was misting with condensation in front of her. She paid and smiled her thanks, then settled in to watch the human drama.

Across the lagoon on the beach side, people—couples mainly—lolled side by side on loungers, reading or dozing in casual intimacy. Occasionally they'd disturb themselves to apply lotion to each other's glistening bodies, or drink from each other's glasses. They'd murmur things into each other's ears, and writhe with sexy laughter at their private little secrets.

Other people romped with their children in the turquoise waters. Happy people. People with love in their lives.

A shadow blocked out the sun, and she looked up. Natalie hovered there, a couple of splotches on her pretty make-up job that looked suspiciously as if she'd been having a weep.

'Are you and Sam really together?' She remained standing for a second, then pulled over a chair and sat down. Like a genie, the waiter appeared from nowhere and she ordered a margarita.

'No,' Ellie admitted.

'Oh, right.' Natalie's gaze clouded. 'I thought Irene must have been winding me up. I lived with Sam long enough to know that much about him. He'd never sleep with his office girl, unless he's changed a whole lot. As soon as any of them showed they thought he was hot…'

She grimaced and made a slashing motion across her throat. 'You're his receptionist, aren't you?'

'I was his Personal Assistant.'

'Was!' Her dark eyes widened. 'You don't mean he got rid of you, too?'

The raw spot must have grown its first delicate protective layer, for Ellie found herself able to say quite calmly, 'Yes, I'm afraid he did.' She took a long, sustained sip of her squash.

The bottle-blonde studied her, unexpected sympathy infusing her smudgy gaze. 'Oh. Oh, that's a shame.' She ran a pensive finger around the rim of her glass. 'But you must be still in there with a chance, or why has Irene brought you?'

Ellie shrugged. 'Oh, well, this arrangement was made a while ago. You know…before…' She echoed Natalie's throat-cutting gesture.

Natalie nodded her understanding, resting her head in her hands and staring gloomily at the table-top while she toyed with a coaster. 'I was hoping there might still be a chance of him turning up,' she said casually. 'If you two *had* been together, I thought you might've been able to talk him into it. I know he has all these really old-fashioned *ideas*, and he never forgives a person for *anything*, but it would mean so much to Michael if he would just get over it and—move on.' She shook her ragged head and chewed her lip.

Ellie stirred her ice cubes with the straw, wondering how long it took the average man to get over a divorce. Four years should have been long enough, surely. When would Sam get over it? What was wrong with him?

Natalie had lapsed into a frowning reverie, and in an

effort to distract her Ellie hazarded, 'You aren't having a hen-party? You've already had it?'

She looked up, then her dark eyes shifted to evade Ellie's. 'Oh, look, who needs one? I can do without people who have to turn every little thing a person says or does into a major Cecil B De Mille production. What do I care? All I want is to marry the love of my life on that beach tomorrow and forget about the world. I don't need anyone to hold up my train.' She flung out her hands. 'It's a beach, for God's sake.'

Ellie wondered if the brunette in the bar had been a bridesmaid.

Natalie finished her drink and rose. She made a move to leave, then turned back and bent towards Ellie. 'You know,' she said abruptly, 'Sam is really an old-fashioned Greek man, at heart, like his dad. And like mine. He doesn't understand that a woman might want to have a *life*. He thinks a woman should be *this*, or should be *that*, but she can't be both. What he wants is someone who's happy to be a good little wife and mother.' She turned away again, lifting a casual hand in farewell. 'See you.'

Ellie smiled, though an amusing irony was crushing her heart. Maybe that *was* what he'd wanted. At least, that was what he'd wanted with Natalie. He wanted a whole different ball game with his ex-PA.

The blonde sashayed away. Just what was it that made some women so desirable as wives that men would fight over them and move heaven and earth to win them, while others could only ever aspire to being mistresses or live-in housekeepers?

Was it their clothes, their hair, their beauty? Their wit?

Their senses of humour? And if Irene had been right about the baby, what was the tragedy that had driven the newly-weds apart instead of drawing them closer? She could just imagine Sam with a baby.

Suddenly the smell of sunscreen and swimming pool was too festive for Ellie's mood. She dragged herself up and headed inside for the lifts. Why had she agreed to come to a wedding, of all things? Weddings were only enjoyable to people who'd successfully had one, or people who had every chance of pulling one off.

A lift arrived almost immediately. The doors slid open to reveal it chock-a-block with Irene, the butler and all her baggage.

'Oh, Ellie. Good, good,' she said, bustling out. 'I'm glad I've caught you.'

'What's happening?' Ellie said, surprised. 'Are we leaving?'

'No.' Irene explained that Rosemary and Jack simply wanted her to stay over in their villa so they could catch up properly. 'You come if you want to, Ellie.'

'I think I might stay here,' she said, sensing she would be an intruder in the family reunion. 'I'll see you all at the dinner.'

She noticed that Irene didn't try to insist. In fact, she looked quite excited, as if she had some elderly mischief up her sleeve.

Ellie followed the small entourage to the hotel entrance, and watched the butler and Jack's chauffeur bundle Irene and her belongings into the limo. She felt a twinge of misgiving. Wasn't she supposed to keep her eye on Irene?

A tinted window slid down in the rear and Irene put

her head out. 'Mind you have a good time, now,' she warned before she was swept away.

How? Ellie thought with a flat feeling. What was there for a single woman to do, alone at the Palazzo Versace?

CHAPTER TWELVE

THERE were changes in the Principessa. The bed in the master suite looked as if it had been stripped and remade with fresh linen, and Ellie's clothes had been hung there, her toiletries arrayed in the bathroom.

Someone—Irene's butler, she presumed—had been busy.

Should she indulge herself by wallowing in that enormous spa bath before it was time to change for dinner?

While the tub filled she undressed in the steamy atmosphere, then caught up her hair in a clip. Over the gushing water, she heard what could have been a knock. Probably another maid with towels. She turned off the taps and slipped on a luxurious Versace bathrobe. The knock came again, strong and unequivocal. Hang on, she frowned, tying the belt around her as she padded across the marble floors in her bare feet.

She opened the door and her heart jolted in shock and an immediate deep, wild joy there was no repressing. Sam stood there, tall, dark and solidly real, his dark eyes glinting in instant connection with hers.

His lean, powerful form was encased in close-fitting jeans and a black tee shirt that outlined the contours of his chest, and clung to his arms and shoulders. The sheer sexual impact of seeing his bare arms again, bronzed, muscular and so close, trapped the breath in her throat.

His brilliant dark gaze ran over her state of dishabille as though her robe were transparent. Overwhelmingly reminded of the hungry, panting creature he'd reduced her to in those sinewy arms with such ease only a couple of days before, she had to restrain herself from stepping into his embrace.

Then the painful knowledge of the wounds they'd inflicted on each other reasserted itself, and she drew back. The gulf between them loomed deeper than the Tasman.

'Am I allowed in?' There was a dark shadow of beard on his jaw and upper lip. The lines around his mouth were grim, and seemed more deeply etched.

She flushed. 'Of course. Please. Please do come in.' She fell back to allow him past, and her glance fell on the suitcase he was towing.

He parked it inside the door, strolled through into the sitting room and turned to appraise her. Their last goodbye hung heavy on the air, though his eyes were cool and steady.

Her hand strayed to her hair. She saw his glance and knew the nervous gesture had betrayed her. 'I—I wasn't expecting you.'

'I can see that. I'm sorry if I've arrived at an inconvenient time. I don't mean to upset you.' The quiet, dry tones of his voice wrung her insides.

'I'm not upset,' she retorted quickly.

He searched her face with a veiled gaze, then glanced about, through the open door to the bedroom where her undergarments were laid out on the bed. 'Are we alone here?'

She nodded. As though more layers of clothing could hide her vulnerable feelings, she wished fervently she had the underwear *on*. Her hand crept to draw the lapels of her robe together at the neck.

His sharp glance caught the movement, and her feeling of being at a disadvantage deepened. His brows edged up. 'Mind if I ask what you've done with my mother?'

She explained about Irene's departure, adding, 'I'm meeting them all a little later at the groom's dinner.'

The space between them throbbed with her aching awareness of her love for him. He was so straight and tall and handsome, so intelligent and honest and stirringly sexy. If he took her in his arms now…

Indecision flooded her heart. What if she changed her mind? He was here. Might there be a chance he'd come because he still wanted her? If she agreed to be with him on his terms, it would ease this cruel yearning, at least in the short term. The more she thought of it, the more it seemed obvious that he *was* here for her. Who else?

She swallowed. 'Are you—? Do you…? Have—have you come to see Irene?'

He met her eyes coolly. 'Why else but to pay my respects to the bride and groom?' There was no softening of his expression, and her small hope died.

He strolled over to pick up his suitcase, then paused. 'Would it embarrass you if we were to go to this thing together?'

Her heart gave a wild flutter. 'Oh. No. Not at all. Where—where are you staying?'

'I'll take a room in the hotel.'

Regret washed through her for the constraint between

them now. 'Oh, Sam. Is that really necessary? This *is* your apartment. There's plenty of room.'

He looked down, then raised his glinting gaze to her. A grim little smile twisted his mouth. 'It is necessary, believe me.' He strolled to the door with his athletic, long-limbed stride, and every one of his steps tore at her with their finality. He paused with his hand on the doorknob. 'I'll call for you. At seven?'

She nodded, unable to speak because of the tide of disappointment rising to engulf her. The door clicked shut behind him. Nothing could have stated more clearly the impossibility of reneging on a rejection delivered three times to a proud man.

It was too late to change her mind.

She hauled herself miserably back to the bathroom and sank into the bubbles. At least she would have this one last evening with him. She made the stern resolve to conquer her grief and savour every precious last moment of his company.

Her wardrobe hadn't offered much choice, so for the dinner she'd decided to resort to Flirty Noir. In truth, she'd gone off it since that last fateful day at work, remembering how Sam had criticised it as inappropriate. She had an anxious moment wondering if he would remember it, then persuaded herself he wouldn't. What man ever remembered what a woman wore?

Still, with the most desirable man in Australia as her date, it did feel like an occasion worth some trouble. She rose from the bubbles and towelled herself dry. Despite everything, she did feel the tiniest glow of anticipation. Perhaps Sam would thaw out as the evening progressed. Perhaps they could recover some sort of ease with each other.

When she had the dress on, it still had the old magic. Her breasts were as full and perky, their swell just as defined through the embroidered black tulle. It was pleasing, she thought, turning sideways in front of the mirror. Perhaps even a little cheering.

She applied her make-up with special care, and didn't spare the eye-shadow.

She heard Sam arrive, and called out to him to let himself in and help himself to a drink. When she'd brushed her hair into a gleaming river, she squirted a cloud of perfume into the air, walked through it, and on a deep, quivering breath opened the bedroom doors.

Faint masculine scents of soap and sandalwood reached her. Sam was seated on a sofa, one arm resting on his thigh in the classic masculine pose as he frowningly perused some papers. He looked elegant, in a black evening suit and open-necked white shirt. His blue-black hair was still damp, his lean, tanned jaw smooth-shaven. He was so darkly gorgeous her heart surged with longing.

At the sound of the doors he glanced up. His black eyes flared into riveted focus, then made a slow, scorchingly sensual sweep of her from head to toe. For a few thundering moments the tempestuous passions of her last day in his office were potently present.

All at once she felt breathless, overwhelmingly conscious of the simmering desire snapping the air between them like an electric arc. Desire, she recalled now with a sudden lurch, that had been tinged with disdain. She felt an agonised doubt about her appearance. Did he think she looked like a tart now? What if he was embarrassed by her before his entire family? Red-hot humiliation threatened to surface, and she said stiffly, 'Do I—does it look all right? Do you think it's—suitable?'

He rose to his feet. Something flickered in his dark, impenetrable gaze as he looked at her. 'It's perfect,' he said softly. 'You've never looked more beautiful.'

Such unexpected generosity after the jagged emotions of their last goodbye pierced her heart, and her throat thickened.

His brows drew together and he looked keenly at her, and held out his hand for hers. 'Come on, then. Let's go and surprise them.' She made a constrained movement, but their fingers didn't quite touch.

Though thronging with billionaires and celebrities, the dinner was an informal affair.

There was a reception area outside the silk-panelled ballroom where Jack and Rosemary greeted their guests. The large crowd of family and friends were being served drinks and hors d'oeuvres. Some of the guests had wandered inside, where tables had been set around a sumptuous buffet, laden with delicacies. A few of the younger people were already on the dance floor.

When Ellie walked in with Sam, the first person she spotted was his mother. Irene appeared to be in sparkling spirits. She was holding a glass and laughing about something with Jack, while next to them Rosemary stood, deep in conversation with a middle-aged Greek couple. Natalie's parents? Ellie wondered.

Rosemary glanced their way and her eyes slid back in a double take. She leaned over to Jack and murmured something out of the corner of her mouth. Jack's head snapped back, and his bristly grey eyebrows swooped up in astonishment. 'Sam!'

At least ninety heads turned, in varying degrees of surprise and curiosity. After an uncertain pause, in which urgent, meaningful glances were telegraphed from woman to woman across the room, Jack surged forward with his arms outstretched. '*Sam*, my boy.'

It was the signal.

'Sam.'

'*Sam!*'

People came from all corners to welcome Sam. Ellie stood back while he was embraced, exclaimed over and had his back warmly slapped by relatives and friends, past and present. After the initial excited flurry, Sam turned his dark, inscrutable gaze on her, and with every appearance of pride drew her forward.

To her horror Rosemary burbled, 'Oh, yes, Sam, dear. We mustn't forget your lovely new fiancée.'

Mortification shocked through Ellie in a crimson tide. As though oblivious of the bombshell, Sam continued introducing her with suave aplomb. How would she explain? It would look as though she'd told people they were engaged. How did a woman inform a man that his mother was a mischief-maker?

Her frantic inner turmoil of possible explanations was interrupted when she felt someone's gaze burning a hole through her skull. She turned her head. Irene stood to one side, her hands demurely folded, the picture of a sweet elderly lady, but her eyes were dancing, pure wickedness pouring from her every blood vessel. Ellie glared at her, and the old she-devil responded with a gleeful wink.

Natalie's parents had retreated, stiff-faced, into a corner, but Sam strolled to greet them with the smooth courtesy he was master of. Natalie's father rose to the occasion with a formal, dignified, very Greek embrace, while her mother murmured some wary, indecipherable words. Ellie was just exchanging greetings with them herself when Natalie bowled in from the ballroom, Michael in tow. She stopped short, shrieked, 'Sam!' then covered her mouth with her hand.

The entire room held its breath. Incredibly, Natalie pulled herself together, seized her fiancé's hand and walked across to them with queenly dignity.

Ellie had to hand it to her. That soap Natalie was contracted to was way beneath her capabilities. Her award-winning performance enabled the greetings on both sides to go smoothly, Sam shaking his cousin Michael's hand with cool civility, even if it was tight-lipped and a little stiff.

The families then seemed to heave a sigh of relief. People started moving into the dining room and seating themselves. Irene murmured a few words to her son and went to join the oldies, while Sam steered Ellie to a table where some of his well-heeled yachting cronies were ensconced with their wives and girlfriends.

Champagne was poured, but Ellie felt it best to keep a clear head. In her dangerously emotional state, who knew what she might do to disgrace herself? The crowd converged on the buffet, and she and Sam followed, and allowed their plates to be piled with lobster and exotic salads.

Natalie came up behind Ellie at the buffet and whispered, 'You lied.'

'No, I didn't,' Ellie murmured from the corner of her mouth. 'It's a mistake. Honestly.'

'Be careful,' the blonde warned.

'What was that about?' Sam asked, frowning, when Natalie had darted away and they were back in their seats.

'Oh.' Ellie blushed, weighing up how to broach the ex-cruciating subject. She met his questioning gaze, took a deep breath and plunged in. 'Er—she was enquiring about that vicious rumour. You know, the idea your aunt seems to have.' Sam's eyes sharpened on her face in just the way they used to when she was justifying something she'd done at work. 'I don't know how Rosemary came to think it. I'm so embarrassed, Sam. Honestly. I was mortified when I heard her say that.'

'Were you?' He studied her face with a narrow, medi-tative gaze.

She suffered the most frightful suspicion that Sam thought she'd done it on purpose to plant the suggestion in his head. 'Well, yes,' she said urgently, imploring him with her eyes to understand that *this* time she was speaking nothing but the unvarnished truth. 'I honestly was. I hope you don't think *I* had anything to do with it. It wasn't my doing. I've no idea where it came from, only Rosemary and Jack seemed to get the idea, and now everyone…'

Sam's thick black brows made an ominous merger. 'Is the idea *so* distasteful to you? Would you like me to make a public announcement?'

She stared at him in confusion. 'Well, no, no. It's not distasteful to *me*! I thought it would be to you.'

He sighed, and glanced irritably about at the other guests at their table. 'Look, haven't you had enough of all this yet? Can't we leave?'

They'd barely embarked on their meals. 'What, *now*?' She gave him an incredulous look, then around the brilliant room at all the people. If they left now her last evening with him would be over. He'd go off somewhere, she'd be all alone in her room… 'We can't leave yet,' she whispered.

Was he so desperate to escape? She'd been so thrilled to have him with her. Couldn't he put up with the party if she was with him? A lump rose in her throat. She stared blindly at her poor dismembered lobster for a while, then, in need of a sanctuary to compose herself, excused herself at the first opportunity and made for the bathroom.

Natalie was in there, nervily dragging quick heavy puffs from a cigarette. Judging by the density of the fumes it wasn't the first. The toxic smell made Ellie feel sick and she backed outside again and stood in the corridor, fanning herself with her hand and trying to fill her lungs with oxygen to dispel the clammy feeling.

The door opened and Natalie came out. For a woman about to walk down Paradise Beach with the love of her life, she looked strung out, her dark eyes stormy and intense.

'I don't know how you got him here,' she said urgently to Ellie, 'but thanks.'

'It wasn't me.' Ellie shrugged. 'I don't know what inspired him to come.'

Natalie looked sceptical. 'Oh, come off it, Ellie.' She glanced about and edged a little closer. 'See if you can get him to talk to Michael.' She grabbed Ellie's arm in a desperate appeal. *'Please.'* To Ellie's horror she burst into tears.

'Oh, God.' Ellie gave a swift look around, then put her arm around Natalie's heaving shoulders and bundled her back into the Ladies. 'Here.' She shoved her a handful of tissues, and patted her back until the storm subsided.

When Natalie had blown her nose and had more of a grip, Ellie went to the door and waved it back and forth to help the fumes diminish. Thank heavens the bathroom had a super-efficient exhaust system.

'Weddings are supposed to be stressful,' Ellie said sympathetically. 'Is there anything I can do to help?'

'It's all going wrong,' Natalie squawked in her high-pitched wail. *'Again.'*

The floodgates reopened. Ellie thoughtfully closed the door and clicked the lock.

The bride dabbed at her nose with a tissue. 'Jen was supposed to be the Matron of Honour and Mad was the bridesmaid. Mad's gone off in a huff, Jen's gone home sick and Michael and I have had a fight. And I thought it was bad the *first* time.'

She gave Ellie an anguished glance through her wet mascara, and Ellie felt a wave of compassion. 'We've got all these people coming from all over.' She made vague sweeping motions. 'Athens, Italy, LA.' She put her face in her hands and rocked back and forwards on her heels. 'It was m-meant to be so beautiful. Now there won't even be a wedding party. There'll hardly be a *wedding.*'

'Don't you have a cousin or someone who can stand in for the bridesmaid?'

'Too fat,' she wept. 'All too fat.' Her nose started to run and Ellie swiftly thrust her more tissues.

Ellie sighed, and sat down on the nearest toilet seat. 'Does it matter so much if your bridesmaid is a little overweight?'

'It's the dress,' Natalie replied when the flow had stemmed a little. 'Mad's really skinny. The theme is Pisces, because that's both mine and Michael's star sign, so it has to be tight.' She glanced earnestly at Ellie. 'You know, fish scales.' Her voice veered up into her upper register. 'And now Michael will think that's my fault too.'

'The fish scales?'

'That I can't even get anyone to be my bridesmaid.' The tears started again. 'That's how it'll *look*.'

'Unless you find someone,' Ellie suggested. 'What about Michael's family?'

'They hate me. They *all* hate me. They all blame me for Sam and Michael being enemies now and...' She buried her face in her hands and sobbed. After a minute she lifted her head. Her reddened eyes slewed over Ellie and brightened a little. 'You could probably wear it if it weren't for your bust. I could get someone to work on it.'

'Oh,' Ellie said, alarmed. 'I don't think so. I don't think Sam would—'

'Sam, Sam. Always *Sam*.' As if driven stark raving mad, Natalie grabbed a couple of fistfuls of her blonde hair and made savage wrenching motions. Ellie noticed, though, that she was quite careful not to cause it any lasting disruptions. 'As soon as Sam appears everyone forgets Michael even exists. It's just Sam, Sam, Sam. He ruined my first wedding, and now he's ruining this one.'

'But you wanted him to come,' Ellie pointed out gently.

She rolled her eyes. 'Are you insane? Do you ever listen? Not for *me*. For Michael. Please, Ellie, *tell* me, will you look at the dress?'

Ellie heaved a sigh and got up. 'All right. I'll look at it. But I'd have to try it on. You can show me later.' She added firmly, 'No promises, now.'

Natalie was so pathetically grateful, Ellie felt remorse for her reluctance. But fish scales? Did a woman want to be seen by the love of her life, for what was probably the last time ever, dressed as a fish? Inevitably, her eyes misted over. She had hoped they could leave each other at the end with dignity, at least.

Outside in the corridor she was surprised to see Michael, leaning against the wall with his arms folded across his chest, scowling. He looked up anxiously, and she smiled and reassured him that Natalie was just coming. The brief exchange was interrupted by Sam, who strode up to them wearing the stern, inscrutable expression that terrified people at the bank. He directed a cold glance at his cousin, then examined her closely and muttered, 'Are you all right?'

She looked curiously from him to Michael. 'Fine. I've just been talking to Natalie. I haven't been gone that long, have I?' She gave him a searching glance. 'Were you worried?'

'Why would I be worried, Eleanor?' He turned his back on his cousin, took her arm and smoothly hustled her away from the infected zone. 'I don't think you should allow yourself to get too friendly with people like that.'

'Oh, Sam. They aren't so bad. I know Natalie's your ex, and no one likes their ex, but…' She met his chilly glance and bit her lip. 'Sorry.'

In fact, an idea had occurred to her inside that toilet cubicle while Natalie was going through meltdown. For all her drama, there was something quite vulnerable and endearing about the shaggy-haired blonde. Was this why Sam had fallen in love with her? Why he'd wanted to *marry* her?

A horrifying possibility began to unfurl its poisonous tentacles. She'd shied away from imagining him with Natalie because it cut her like hot knives. But now she couldn't stop imagining it. What if he was still in love with her? Was this the answer?

She supposed bitterly that he needed a woman who could bring out his protective instincts. Underneath all that smooth, sophisticated intelligence, he was still just a macho male animal. A together woman like herself, renowned for her independence and efficiency, could never have filled the bill.

'What's wrong?' Sam halted her to scrutinise her face. 'You're looking a bit peaky. I've noticed you've hardly eaten anything yet. I think you should finish your dinner, then go back upstairs and lie down.'

'Oh, thanks.' She knew he was raw over her not agreeing to be his mistress, but did he have to be so unflattering? It was as though he couldn't wait now to unload her. She decided to put an end to her misery, and know the worst, once and for all. 'As a matter of fact,' she said casually, 'I was just thinking…I can see why you fell in love with Natalie.'

His brows shot up, then he gazed at her for a long time, a frown gathering in his brilliant black eyes. 'Who said I was in love with her?'

'Well, you're so angry with her.'

Her heart was pumping like a marathon runner's, but she forced herself to continue on lightly, though her hands were curled into tight balls. 'I thought it must be because it's so painful for you to see her marrying someone else.'

'I'm delighted to see her marrying someone else,' he bit out. 'Only not *that* bastard.'

'Oh. Good.'

He wasn't very convincing. She realised the ice she was on was wafer-thin, but, having gone this far, she drew another tentative breath and met his gaze squarely, hoping her desperation and panic didn't swirl in her eyes. 'But you did marry her, Sam. You must have loved her at one stage.'

He stared at her for seconds, his mouth grim, his eyes

glinting in speculation, then took her arm firmly and urged her towards their table. 'It's not Natalie I'm angry with, it's myself. This is not the time and place to discuss it. The sooner we finish our meals, the sooner we can escape.'

He held her chair for her and resumed his own. It was hard to think of eating when the full heart-shattering impact of her insignificance in Sam's scheme of things had only just dawned. Strangely, apart from Irene, who wasn't likely to admit it anyway, she seemed to be the only person in Sam's life who'd never considered, until this weekend, that he might still be in love with his ex. She recalled the first time she'd ever seen Natalie at the office, and the things the peroxide blonde had been screeching.

The signs had been there all along. How could she have missed them?

Thankfully the remains of her meal had been taken away, and she was able to get off lightly with some thin vegetable soup Sam found for her at the buffet. During the lull, a dauntingly groomed billionaire's wife across the table from them leaned forward and said, 'Excuse me, Eleanor…'

'Ellie, please.'

The woman smiled, then indicated Ellie's dress. 'Do you mind if I ask? Is your dress a Dinnigan?'

'Yes.'

'Not Flirty Noir, by any chance?'

She nodded, and the woman sighed, 'How I envy you.'

Even while trawling the depths of despair, there were a few pleasures left to a woman. Sam would probably have forgotten the foul aspersions he'd cast on her dress and her spirited defence of it. Nevertheless, she couldn't resist a subtle sideways glance at him to see if he'd heard.

Amazingly, his eyes meshed instantly with hers, brimming with amused comprehension.

Smiling, he set down his glass. 'Excuse me,' he said to their neighbours. 'I have to dance with my fiancée.'

His use of the word cut deep, but she didn't protest. She let him lead her to the dance floor and draw her into his arms. Other dancers were jerking about as single, separate entities, but Sam, being the old-fashioned guy he was, liked to hold a woman close. His long thighs brushed hers, and she inhaled the familiar, masculine scent of him and gave herself up to the impossible torture of being held against the man she loved.

As if to add to her bitter-sweet joy, the band eased into a poignant old love song. Sam steered her through the open doors onto a small circular terrace that had been designed to vaguely resemble a small Venetian temple, and was open to the starry sky. The warm, scented Queensland night, meant for lovers, tormented her senses unbearably.

'Alone at last,' Sam said with a shuddering sigh. His hand slipped under her hair and stroked down her spine, moulding her close to his big, hard body. 'Do you know what torture this is for me?' he murmured, brushing her temple with his jaw. 'Do you have any idea what a living hell I'm in tonight?'

Hot needles of pain lanced her heart. She closed her eyes. 'I think I do.'

There was a hoarseness in his voice, as if he spoke from the very depths of his being. 'Imagine, Eleanor… Imagine knowing you could have been happy with the one person you belong to, who should belong to you, but, like a fool, you ruined all your chances.'

Misery choked her throat. 'I *can* imagine.' The song spilling from the ballroom swelled into its plaintive refrain of tragedy and heartbreak.

His deep voice grew laboured and emotional. 'If you knew…what it means to me to—smell the fragrance of your hair, to feel your soft breasts against my chest…'

She looked up blindly at him. '*My* hair? But I thought you… You know… Natalie.'

'Natalie?' Sam stood stock-still and stared at her, gripping her shoulders. Then he said, very softly and distinctly, 'I married Natalie because she was pregnant. For no other reason. It was my mistake. Then two months after the wedding she was offered the part she longed for in that soap. She chose to get rid of our baby rather than lose her big break.' As he gazed at her his stern, sensuous mouth twisted. 'And most of it was my fault.'

Shock, and the rock-bottom despair so eloquently expressed in Sam's wry unemotional tone, welled in Ellie's heart to join all her own grief and pain and disappointment, and flooded through her in a huge rolling wave. The tears rushed to her eyes and spilled over before she could stop them.

'Don't, *don't*.' Sam's voice was suddenly strained and urgent. He folded her in his arms and pressed her tenderly to him as if she were some piece of rare fragile china, stroking her hair. She could feel the tense emotion racking his big lean body as he murmured passionate endearments. 'Please, please Ellie, my sweetheart. Don't cry.'

For a while she couldn't even speak to deny the charge, and she was grateful when he hustled her back through the hotel, past the glimmering lagoon and up to the Principessa.

The lamps were on, warming the sitting room with their glow. Ellie mopped abjectly at her eyes with a handful of tissues. 'I'm so sorry, Sam,' she said, turning away from him to spare him the ghastly sight. 'I can't imagine what got into me. I'm not usually a weeper. It must have been the—the lobster, or...' She caught sight of her face in a mirror and saw to her horror that her mascara had started to drip.

Sam turned her around to face him and wiped under her eyes with his handkerchief. Sighing, he said, 'I thought—*hoped*—you might be feeling sad about breaking my heart.'

She looked to see if he was joking, but his eyes were darkly serious, intent on her face, the lines around his chiselled mouth taut. She gasped and her wet eyelids fluttered in shock. 'Your—your *heart*, Sam.'

He said hoarsely, 'We both know I'm not good at saying the right words to you, Eleanor. God knows, I've made mistakes. But I have to try one more time to...to somehow *show* you...what's in my heart, what's been in my heart since the first time I saw you on that balcony.' He kept gesturing very emotionally. 'I know I-I've hurt you. I upset your life, plunging you into an affair like a selfish bloody fool. Expecting you to forgive me when...' His hand made a passionate reefing motion through his hair. 'I thought you seemed to—I *hoped* you felt the same way.' He half turned away and said wryly, 'But then I understood it was your career you loved. I felt...'

Her eyes started to swim. 'Oh, no, Sam. No.'

He was gazing at her with the most earnest, and fiercely tender expression in his gorgeous dark eyes. 'You see, my darling Eleanor...'

All at once she had the most thrilling sensation that, against all the odds, the grand and magical moment she'd dreamed of in her wildest fantasies might have arrived. She touched his lean, tanned hand, and, to encourage him, said, 'Ellie, please, Sam.'

His eyebrows lifted and he broke into a laugh. 'Thank God, at last. *Ellie*.'

On his tongue her name sounded so romantic, almost haunting in fact, it was music to her ears.

He took her hands in his firm, warm grip, and grew serious again. 'You need to understand something. It's taken me a while to realise all this myself.' He let go of her hands and gestured his remorse. 'Looking back now, I have to accept most of the responsibility for the disaster with Natalie. When she discovered she was pregnant, I was horrified, to say the least, but I gritted my teeth and pressured her into marriage.' His expression grew very grave. 'In our families, you know, we don't deny our children. I suppose I knew vaguely how serious she was about being an actress, but I was intolerant.' He evaded her eyes and stared down at the floor, shaking his head. 'And as you can imagine, we didn't get on from the start.' He glanced up at her, a wry smile lighting his dark eyes. '*You* should have been there. You could have poured your magic oil. Every day was World War Three.'

Ellie could well imagine it. Volatile Natalie, with an icy cool, controlled Sam. Not a marriage made in heaven.

'Then,' he continued with an apologetic grimace, 'I'm afraid I made it clear that I expected her to give up acting when the child was born, and for several years after. In that industry, as she was always insisting, the opportunities have to be seized when they arise. I suppose she felt trapped.' He sprang up and started to pace restlessly about the room. 'I can never, ever excuse what she did. But lately I can't help wondering if things would have been different if we hadn't married. She'd probably have been happy to be a single working mum, given the chance. But I didn't really give her the chance.' He halted his pacing and stood with his face averted from her, his breathing heavy and painful, his powerful shoulders rigid. With a tortured sideways glance at her he said, very quietly, 'I was gutted when I found out, Ellie. I hadn't realised how much I'd looked forward to it.' He lifted his hand in a sharp, constrained gesture. 'The child.'

A hot, fierce surge of compassion flooded Ellie's heart, and she jumped up from the sofa. 'Oh, Sam,' she said, rushing across to throw her arms around him. 'You did what you thought was right.'

He held her against his chest, then put her a little away from him to frown intently down at her. 'I did, of course, but do you see? When you came home with me that last night I so wanted you to stay, Ellie. But I was afraid that if I put pressure on *you* to—to change your direction so drastically when you love your life the way it is, you would run like the wind.' The rueful grimace he gave tore her heart. 'But then you did, anyway.'

'Oh.' She shook her head in dismayed remorse. 'But I thought… You know, you said you only wanted me for a week, or—or a year…' Her voice started to wobble with the memory of the devastation it had caused her, and Sam drew her back into his strong arms and dragged her against him.

'Shh, shh,' he said, stroking her hair and tenderly kissing her neck. 'Don't cry any more, my love.' Pressed with such passionate tenderness against his warm chest, she felt his deep voice resonate through her. 'I was such a fool. I was so afraid of losing you, I said all the wrong things.'

She drew back to smile at him through the mist. 'What was that you called me? Your *love*?'

'Well, you are my love!' He looked wonderingly at her, and his voice deepened with raw emotion. 'You must know I love you, Ellie. I fell in love with you on that very first night, and then like a fool I let you disappear. But I couldn't forget you. I was crazy to find you. For God's sake, I bought a bloody *bank* to find you! You're the love of my life!'

Fireworks and starbursts were exploding in her heart, but Sam held her from him, a sudden uncertainty dawning in his eyes. 'And you? Do *you*…?'

She said softly, 'I do, Sam. I do love you. I adore you.'

With his dark velvet eyes glowing, he said very solemnly, 'So then, Ellie O'Dea, will you marry me?'

She hesitated. Her heart began to quake with a suffocating fear that caught her entire body in a cold, vicious clench. In a voice toneless with dread she said, 'Sam, there is something I need to tell you.'

He frowned. The shining light in his eyes was doused.

'It's possible—' She braced herself with a deep trembling breath. A blush rose inside her and flooded her all the way to her roots, but for all her faults she had her own code of honour. She met Sam's anxious, uncertain gaze, and forced her chin and voice to stay steady. 'It's quite possible, Sam, that although I would *love* to have your children, it may be difficult for me to conceive. This being the case, you might want to reconsider the idea of marriage to me.'

He let out a long breath and his eyes lit with the most fervent relief. 'Oh, Ellie. My darling Ellie. As if that could make me not want to marry you.' He gazed tenderly at her, his eyes ablaze with concern. 'There are alternatives, you know. There're…clinics…adoption—' He waved his hands expressively and said very firmly, 'There are options. Let's talk about all that later. You still haven't answered my question.' He captured her hands again in his warm, sure grip. 'Well, my love? Will you?'

An exquisite joy filled her heart to overflowing. 'Yes, Sam. Oh, yes.'

CHAPTER THIRTEEN

BEDS at the Palazzo Versace were exceptionally springy and comfortable. Just supposing a person had time to sleep and was in need of a pillow, there were seven varieties to choose from, each softer and more cushioning than the last.

After her night of sheer heavenly bliss with the most tender and virile lover a woman could ever expect to know, Ellie faced the dawn feeling energised right through to her soul, with her every muscle supple and relaxed.

She felt dreamily ready to embrace the day and take charge of her commitments. The first was the little matter of Natalie's and Michael's disagreement.

When she informed Sam of Natalie's wedding being in doubt, his first response was to yawn. 'Oh, for God's sake. Seriously?'

'I'm afraid so,' she said, lounging beside him in the sumptuous bed, enjoying the warmth and support of his gorgeous bronzed chest. 'Poor Natalie. After everyone's gone to so much trouble. What a shame if, at the end of all this, she's still Natalie Stilakos.'

She slanted a glance up at him, and noted, with some satisfaction, horror dawning on his stubbly morning face.

'Bloody hell,' he exclaimed with heartfelt fervour. 'What's it all about, anyway?'

She snuggled up to him. 'Oh, I don't know. Something about Michael wanting someone to forgive him for something he's done in the past. He's all depressed about it. You know how these things can fester.'

There was a heavy impenetrable silence, then he bit out softly, 'Some things are unforgivable.'

'Yes.' She sighed. 'I know.'

After a small lapse he said, 'What do you know?'

'I agree with you. Some things can't be forgiven.'

He enquired with what sounded like difficulty, 'Are you referring to the way I hurt you—the things that happened about your job? Or the other things. The things I told you about with Natalie.'

She arched her brows and said airily, 'No, no, no. I was merely making the point that while *things* can't always be forgiven, people can. Especially when you're happy.'

He smiled down at her for a moment, and whispered, 'I'm happy.' Then the smile grew sinful and his eyes lascivious, and he planted a greedy kiss on her bare shoulder.

Eventually she was free to deal with Natalie and the dress, which turned out to be a magnificently beaded sheath, with a fish tail to the ground, shimmering with sequins in blue, silver and pinky mauve. She managed to squeeze into most of it, although, as Natalie had predicted, the bust was a little in need of letting out. Fortunately her parents could summon seamstresses from afar at will, and did so without hesitation.

While the fitting was going on, she happened to glance out of Natalie's window, and with a pleased little glow saw Sam, strolling towards a table beside the lagoon, deep in conversation with his cousin. Michael seemed to be doing lots of fast talking, while Sam had that stern, listening demeanour she'd experienced on a few occasions herself.

After the fitting, and satisfied she wouldn't look any worse than the average rainbow trout, she allowed Natalie to sweep her off to the Palazzo beauty parlour, where she was pampered, manicured, waxed, painted and perfumed like a sultan's courtesan. Inspired by the fish frock, she opted for a return to her pale strawberry hair, ensuring it was more on the blonde side this time than the pink. She submitted to it all with enjoyment, thinking with a deep, joyous excitement of the magic night to come.

All the magic nights. Sam would appreciate it as thoroughly as any sultan.

Natalie's wedding was a romantic, twilit event. A Persian carpet, scattered with frangipani and flanked by hundreds of lights, was laid on the sand for the wedding party. An enormous marquee spread with more exotic carpets and big soft cushions, was provided for the guests to lounge upon like Arabian potentates. Dozens of security guards had been employed to hold back the sea of media cameras.

The bride looked beautiful in a diamond-and-pearl encrusted dress, with a veil and train worth millions, that was reminiscent of hanging seaweed. Michael wore a long white embroidered shirt-frock affair over his trousers. Ellie couldn't see that it was very fishy, but it was dignified, at least.

Ellie did her part gravely, walking barefoot behind Natalie along the Persian, in her beautiful fish frock and mermaid's hair. Though most people's attention was on the bride and groom, whenever Ellie looked at Sam, he was smiling at her.

When it came time to kiss the bride, Sam strode over to swing Ellie off the ground and kiss her, then a beaming Irene dashed over to kiss and violently hug her as well. While the wedding barbecues and bonfires were lit, and people plunged into the party, Sam held Ellie's hand and walked with her along the beach. And while the festivities raged on into the night, Sam took her up to the Principessa and made passionate love with her till dawn.

'Is Ellie always this cool, calm and collected, Sam?' a friend queried the next day, when Ellie and Sam were lazing by the lagoon, wrapped in blissful contemplation of each other.

'Not always,' Sam said, pausing in taking a sip from Ellie's straw to gaze meditatively at her. ' I think I may have seen her get a little frayed around the edges, once or twice.'

Their smiling eyes met.

EPILOGUE

Samos, Greece.

Dear Beth,

So lovely to hear your fabulous news. I know you'll be thrilled to hear that Sam and I have some too, at long, long last! Our darling Lilli-pilli was born last Thursday, almost two years to the day of starting the programme. So far she looks to have all Sam's gorgeous colouring, although it's hard to say how her eyes will go. (Though Irene says she knows.) Right now they're as blue as sapphires, like the sea around this wondrous isle.

We won't be home till autumn, so we want you here with us soon to join the family celebrations. Tickets are on their way.

Love…Ellie

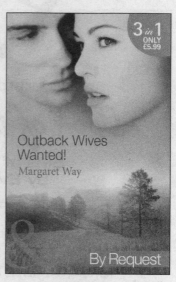